All
My
Mothers

JOANNA GLEN

THE BOROUGH PRESS

The Borough Press
An imprint of HarperCollins*Publishers* Ltd
1 London Bridge Street
London SE1 9GF

www.harpercollins.co.uk

HarperCollins*Publishers*
1st Floor, Watermarque Building, Ringsend Road
Dublin 4, Ireland

First published by HarperCollins*Publishers* 2021

1

A catalogue record for this book is available from the British Library

HB ISBN: 978-0-00-841058-2
TPB ISBN: 978-0-00-841059-9

This novel is entirely a work of fiction.
The names, characters and incidents portrayed in it are
the work of the author's imagination. Any resemblance to
actual persons, living or dead, events or localities is
entirely coincidental.

Set in Bell MT by Palimpsest Book Production Ltd,
Falkirk, Stirlingshire

Printed and Bound in the UK using 100% Renewable Electricity at
CPI Group (UK) Ltd

MIX
Paper from
responsible sources
FSC
www.fsc.org FSC™ C007454

This book is produced from independently certified FSC™ paper
to ensure responsible forest management.

For more information visit: www.harpercollins.co.uk/green

ALL MY MOTHERS

Joanna Glen read Spanish at the University of London, and lost her heart to Andalusia whilst studying at the Faculty of Arts in Córdoba. She went on to become a teacher of English and Spanish, and a school principal.

Joanna's debut novel, *The Other Half of Augusta Hope*, was shortlisted for the Costa First Novel Award and the Authors' Club Best First Novel Award. She and her husband live in Brighton.

Also by Joanna Glen

The Other Half of Augusta Hope

In memory of my beloved mother,
Jennifer Simmonds.

To Beth from Eva – March 2008

From the beginning, there were bumps under the rug where things had been swept, which meant I couldn't walk the way other people did.

Free and easy.

With a bounce in my step and my head held high.

That's the way I want you to walk, Beth.

I've swept nothing under the rug in this story.

Our story.

The story of you and me and your mother.

We're supposed to begin as the apple of our mother's eye.

But I was more the maggot in the apple.

Speaking of my mother's eyes, they were always darting about, as if she was following a fly, and not seeing me properly.

My father (who veered between London and his family's estate in Jerez de la Frontera) seemed to see me better. We liked to talk, he and I, and I often had the feeling that he was on the cusp of telling me something important and deciding against it.

Perhaps you'd like to hear about the little girl I was.

I was full of the most unbearable longing.

The Portuguese have a word for it: *saudade* – a yearning for a happiness that has passed, or perhaps never existed. My *saudade* was like travelling in a car on a dark road and seeing, for a second, a lit window, and then, very quickly, not seeing it.

I grew up in a smart part of London called Chelsea, like the football team, although I can't imagine that any of our neighbours were interested in football. They were interested in expensive cars and chauffeurs and the shape of their bay trees, which sat on highly polished steps around our private lawned square, in which there was a golden-rain tree, a row of cherry blossoms and beds of tall tulips in spring.

Our big posh house, at the corner of the square, was four storeys high, with a shiny black front door. My father's domain within the house was painted white with splashes of multicolour made by his modern Spanish paintings. It included the tiled hall, his study, packed with books from floor to ceiling, and the garden room, which led onto a courtyard.

When we first arrived in Chelsea from Spain, my father asked Rory the gardener to turn our courtyard into an Andalusian *patio*, sending him off on an aeroplane to Córdoba because the *patio*-gardeners of Córdoba are the best of anywhere in the world. (And, although he was wrong about most things, my father was right about this.)

On the ground floor there was a large kitchen, for which my father had bought black chairs with chrome-tubed legs that didn't meet my mother's approval. Next to the kitchen, there was a small apartment I never visited, where Mean Mary, our housekeeper-nanny, lived.

The rest of the house (except the roof terrace) was my mother's domain, and from the first floor to the fourth, it was rouge-pink, with ruched rose curtains and pink velvet sofas, my mother having rejected the teak and oatmeal fashionable in London circles at the time. There were thick carpets and fat cushions and triple-lined curtains, too heavy for my small hands to draw.

The school I went to was St Hilda's – a smart little private school, where smart little girls wore olive-green and grey uniforms.

I started there on 5 September 1979, the same day as Lord Mountbatten's funeral, which was taking place down the road at Westminster Abbey.

'The queen is extremely upset,' said my mother.

'Did she phone you?' said my father, not looking up from his enormous newspaper, which he held in his outstretched arms. The backs of his hands were covered in black hair. In fact, all of my father was covered in black hair. It burst out of his shirt collar and the tops of his socks, like those chimpanzees they used to dress up for tea adverts.

My mother stepped past him.

Her blond bob shimmered with Elnett hairspray.

She looked like my Barbie doll, which I never played with.

6

She took my hand, and I could feel her brittle fingernails against my skin.

In my palm, I felt the imprint of some softer hand.

A long time ago.

In some other place.

With some other feeling.

And here came the *saudade* longing, strong enough to break me in two.

Our hands fell apart as we walked, like they always did.

In the playground, you couldn't move for mothers' legs: tan-stockinged; bare and stubbly; fat as hams; or covered by enormous bell-bottom jeans.

Above me, the mothers gesticulated and shrieked.

One tiny girl was completely enveloped in her mother's lion-mane of hair, sobbing. Her mother was saying, 'I love you, darling,' over and over again, as if one of them was about to be taken off to be shot.

The girl's grey socks and polished brown shoes were spattered by tears.

One girl was making her baby sisters laugh by pulling funny faces and crossing her eyes. She was laughing her head off. So was her mother.

I loved this girl immediately.

I felt a kind of fizzing sparking feeling inside me right there in the playground as I wondered what it would be like to be her.

To be happy.

I moved a little closer to her.

I wondered what it would be like to laugh and laugh and laugh.

I loved her dark curly hair.

I loved the way one of her socks had fallen down to her ankle.

The girl stopped making funny faces and turned around.

'I'm called Bridget Blume,' she said. 'Shall we go in together?'

I followed Bridget into the classroom, anxiously.

There was a balloon for each of us, cut out of coloured card, blu-tacked to the wall, high up, underneath the Victorian cornicing.

Eva Martínez-Green, it said on my lime-green balloon.

31 January 1975, written underneath my name.

My birthday.

Always a strange nervy day, my mother's eyes darting about worse than ever, my father over-cheerful and all of us nauseous with sugar-icing.

I could read by the time I arrived at St Hilda's, Spanish and English: my father had started me off, and I'd kept going – there was nothing else to do. I had no brothers or sisters in my house to distract me. I asked my mother and father daily for a kitten. And daily they said no.

I was a bit disappointed that our teacher, Miss Feast, had chosen lime-green for my cardboard birthday balloon. I don't think lime-green is anyone's favourite colour, and it felt like a slight against me.

Miss Feast paused, opened a thin black hardback book and broke the silence with unfamiliar names, which would turn into girls, girls we would love and hate for seven years, who would run like ghosts through our memories.

'Lily Betts?'

'Yes, Miss Feast.'

With a little sob – she was still convulsing from the separation from her mother – like a newly dead fish.

'Bridget Blume?'

'Yes, Miss Feast.'

The happy girl from the playground, gorgeous as anything, all blue eyes, smiles and hope.

I smiled at her.

She smiled back.

Bridget Blume liked me.

My mother didn't exactly seem to dislike me, but she skirted around me as one might an unpredictable horse. My father quite liked me and, when he was home, he hung me upside down from my ankles (as some men do) or else he read me storybooks, which I preferred.

Onwards we went through the alphabet.

'Eva Martínez-Green?'

'Yes, Miss Feast. And also,' I started, in a very quiet voice, because there were eyes everywhere looking at me.

Miss Feast raised a dark eyebrow.

I stammered: 'I hope you don't mind me saying, Miss Feast. But it's Eva as in ever. Not Eva as in evil.'

Miss Feast smiled at me, and the mole above her lip quivered.

'I will remember that,' she said. 'Forever Eva.'

Forever Eva – a name made especially for me, by Miss Feast, the actual teacher!

The syllables seeped through my skin and circulated in my bloodstream, making me warm inside. Nobody else – at all at all at all – had been given a special name in the course of our first registration!

Oh, the untold joy!

'Are we ready to read?' sang Miss Feast.

'Yes we certainly are!' we sang back, as we'd been taught, as Miss Feast didn't like untidy words flying about on the classroom air.

She gathered us around her like a clutch of green chicks, and Bridget Blume wriggled over to me on her bottom and took my hand. My heart started racing. I looked down at our hands wrapped up in each other – my brown fingers and her white fingers. It was the nicest thing I'd ever seen, and the nicest feeling I'd ever had.

'*The Rainbow Rained Us!*' said Miss Feast.

We all listened, spellbound, as a small rabbit threw a stone at the rainbow from Noah's ark (Miss Feast turned the page) and the rainbow broke apart into hundreds of multicolour mothers who repopulated the earth with their children (Miss Feast turned the page) because the original families – along with every living thing except the ones on the ark – had all drowned in the flood, though this unfortunate fact wasn't mentioned.

Miss Feast let us pass the book around, and Bridget and I had to undo our hands. I remember running my finger, mesmerised, over the slightly textured splashes of gorgeous reds and blues and golds and greens, which were forming into mother-shapes, and I was shivering all over, and the *saudade* longing was making griping pains in my belly.

'Please pass the book on, Eva,' said Miss Feast.

The sound of my name made me blush.

'Aren't mothers wonderful?' said Miss Feast.

The other girls all nodded – *all nodded.*

The wonderfulness of mothers was not a subject for debate in our classroom, and this was a terrible moment because I knew for certain that my mother wasn't wonderful, and she was supposed to be.

(My poor mother, you're probably thinking, and that's right, but she'd made her bed – and now she had to lie in it. And she did love lying in bed.)

'Turn to the person next to you!' said Miss Feast in her sing-song voice. 'And tell her about your mummy! Anything you like!'

My heart was trying to leap out of my chest because I couldn't think of one thing to say. It was as if I didn't know my mother, as if I'd never got beyond the surface of her. My panic rose as things came pouring out of Bridget's mouth: her mother was an artist; she loved patchwork; and pinafores; and clompy boots; and telling the truth; and the sea; and making birds out of feathers; and cakes with butter icing; and on she went, smiling and sparkling, until Miss Feast blew her whistle and reopened the book. She held it outwards, so that we could see each different-coloured mother as she appeared on her own lusciously illustrated double page, with her happy, matching family.

There Blue Mother stood in a mesmerising cornucopia of blues, at the edge of the turquoise sea, laughing, the wind in her hair, surrounded by her blue family.

'Blue Mother is free and open and speaks from her heart.'

She sounded exactly like Bridget's mother – utterly perfect.

Miss Feast turned the page: Green Mother was serene and beautiful, barefoot in a glimmering field beside a mossy waterfall, her green daughters aloft in the grass.

'Green Mother is full of hope and healing.'

Miss Feast turned the page: Gold Mother, standing by her gate, a little sinister, seemed to be welcoming children into her perfect golden garden for a treasure hunt with prizes.

I didn't like her at all.

Grey Mother was soft-faced, wearing pince-nez glasses in a room full of rickety bookshelves, with a globe and an atlas.

Yes yes yes.

Pink Mother was sitting upright in a kind of fairy-tale bed, a bit like my mother and father's, a four-poster, with a roof and curtainy droops around it.

No no no.

'Pink Mother is delicate and feminine,' said Miss Feast, explaining that delicate meant *not strong*.

Oh no – a stab between the ribs! – Pink Mother looked weak and pathetic like *my mother*. I didn't know why she was always feeling faint, or anxious, or collapsing into bed as if she didn't have enough strength to be a normal human being.

(I think that sounds mean, but take it from me that a fragile mother is a scary thing for a child – it feels like your whole life is made of paper.)

Miss Feast was on to Purple Mother, who was dutiful and proper, her tidy purple children standing in a line. Definitely not. Red Mother was dangerous and wild, holding a flaming torch against the night sky. Far too frightening. Yellow Mother had rows of beehives and shelves of honey and was anxiously tying yellow ribbons to a tree to welcome a loved one home, perhaps a soldier son.

'Yellow Mother is busy and hard-working,' said Miss Feast.

And a bit tense, I thought.

My own mother was so tense that when you asked her questions, her entire body stiffened up. Something seemed to be wrong at the heart of her.

Miss Feast closed the book.

She said that each of us had been made by our own mother and father, and that's why we were all different shapes and sizes, and each of us just perfect for being ourselves. I wondered how mothers and fathers made children. I also wondered whether there was any chance that, in the process of the making, parent and child could somehow get separated, and a green could end up with a red, a blue with a pink.

Because – and this came like a punch in the stomach – my mother and I did not match. It was obvious. I'd somehow ended up with the wrong mother. This thought was both deeply shocking and deeply hopeful. It was a seed planted in the earth of me. It was the moment that my *quest* began. The quest to find out who I was and what my place was in the scheme of things.

When the alarm clock on Miss Feast's desk went off, we all nearly had a heart attack.

'It's dismissal time!' she said.

We had absolutely no idea what she was talking about.

It turned out that the school day was over – a day that had felt like a year on a new planet – and there was my mother, all pink like Pink Mother in the book, wearing a tight pencil skirt and a pink silk blouse with a too-big bow at the neck. The mothers next to her were wearing darker colours than she was, and she stood out like a pale pink ice lolly, a strawberry Mini-Milk.

Miss Feast adjusted my beret from behind me, and my body fizzed with the touch of her hand.

I wished my mother hadn't put on that big-bow blouse. I think she was trying to look nice for me. She loved clothes and she wanted me to love them too, so that I would look nice and we would understand each other.

But I was embarrassed by her.

I felt like crying at the sight of her.

Lily Betts started crying again because, although her mother was standing right in front of her, she wasn't allowed to talk to her.

'I know you're all dying to give your mothers a lovely hug,' said Miss Feast. 'But first we have to learn how to do dismissal properly.'

A bubble of panic started to rise up my throat at the thought that

14

my mother and I would be forced to hug each other in public. I swallowed it back down whole.

It wasn't only that I wanted my mother to be different. I think I wanted me to be different too. Or perhaps, from the beginning, I wanted *us* to be different.

What Bridget's father called our *alchemy*.

It was Bridget's father who told me later on, when I was eleven, that, scientifically speaking, the energy in the universe is not held in each particle, as scientists had originally supposed, but in the space between particles, that is, the energy in everything is in its relationship to everything else.

This, he'd concluded, was the case for people too.

By then, I had a special Quest Book in which I carefully recorded his insight, underlining *space between* – underlining being a significant part of my quest before I was old enough to do anything more proactive about my suspicions.

The space between my mother and me was approximately two metres as Miss Feast demonstrated the way to do dismissal properly at St Hilda's School.

I looked at her, and I felt no pull towards her.

We hadn't, as far as I knew, spent a day of our lives apart.

But I hadn't minded being away from her at all.

I'd even liked it.

She looked as if she was pulling in the muscles in her stomach and sticking out her little bosoms, well-padded in the bra she wore, which stood up by itself.

I remember wishing she didn't look so uncomfortable being herself. So awkward.

It made me feel awkward.

And that was our alchemy: awkwardness.

Bridget Blume's mother scooped up Bridget, laughing, kissing her cheek with a big smacky noise and throwing her over her shoulder. Such easy-breezy alchemy. She was wearing a patchwork pinafore and leather boots with thick soles, and she looked exactly like Blue Mother in the book, happy and free, with the wind in her hair against the blue sky.

The looseness of her, that's what I saw, and my mother's tightness.

That, and the way she and Bridget completely matched each other.

The *saudade* longing came over me like a wave as Bridget walked away into what I supposed must be her fairy-tale life, holding the edge of a double buggy containing two identical sisters with dark hair in ribbons.

Oh, sisters, how I longed for sisters.

I looked back at my own mother, who extended her thin arms stiffly towards me. When I tried walking into her, like Bridget had walked into her mother, I crashed into her tight stomach muscles, as if she was a wall. She put her hands on my shoulder blades, and left them there for a second or two.

I reversed out of her stiff arms, awkwardly, with my eyes smarting.

She said, 'How was your first day, darling?'

When she said darling, it always sounded funny, like she was trying it on but deciding against it.

I said, 'Fine, thank you.'

She said, 'Your father's in the taxi.'

(My parents used London taxis like a private chauffeur service, avoiding the inconvenience of walking along the pavement, taking the double-decker bus or parking their large car.)

When I got into the taxi, my father held my nose between his two fingers (like he often did), and when he let it go, I asked if he could please buy me my own copy of *The Rainbow Rained Us*, knowing he'd say yes because he loved books – and we stopped three minutes later at the bookshop. We read the book together that evening, and it was only then that I noticed the different-coloured fathers, lurking in the background of the pages, just as my father lurked in the background of my life, coming and going from Spain with a cylindrical leather holdall which had his initials stamped in gold, above the zipped pocket: JMM for José Manuel Martínez.

16

Miss Feast soon moved on from *The Rainbow Rained Us* to the life-changing saga of the baby photo.

'We have to bring in a baby photo tomorrow,' I said to my mother on the way home from school in the taxi, not knowing the impact that this would have on my quest, and indeed my whole life. 'There's a letter in my bag. Have we got one?'

A double-decker bus spewed fumes at us, and my mother closed the taxi window, making a strange little circle shape with her lips, like a cat's bottom.

My mother said, 'Your father's already tired of the school run.'

Which wasn't exactly answering my question.

The taxi meter went tick tick tick like the crocodile in *Peter Pan*.

As she hadn't answered, I wondered how I could rephrase the sentence for greater effect.

'*Miss Feast* says we have to bring in a baby photo tomorrow,' I said, and when I said Miss Feast, I blushed, as if she were forbidden fruit, my feelings for her secret and unmentionable.

Again, my mother didn't answer.

Then she did answer, but curtly.

'I don't have any baby photos of you here in London,' she said.

'You don't have any?' I said, feeling a cramping anxiety in my stomach.

She looked out of the window, away from me.

17

'Not here,' she said, drawing her hand over her sweaty upper lip.
Not here?

I wondered where on earth they might be.

The taxi stopped and started at the traffic lights.

When we got home, Mary had cooked macaroni cheese, which was
too creamy, and made me feel a bit sick, though I didn't say.

After I'd finished, I sat on the floor and read *The Rainbow Rained
Us* again.

'Wouldn't you like to read a different book?' said my mother.

I shook my head, and said, quite firmly, 'Have we got a baby photo
or not?'

She pursed her lips.

When my father came home, I ran into the hall, and he gathered me
in his arms – he smelled of citrus cologne and sherry. He tipped
me upside down and dangled me by my feet before turning me the
right way up and patting my shoulder. My mother rushed into his study
with him and slammed the door.

While my mother and father remained enclosed in the study, I
stared with my eyes half-closed at the paintings on the hall walls, the
orange circles on cobalt blue with stabs of buttery yellow, and they
turned into sun and sky and fields of sunflowers – another world,
appearing and disappearing.

My mother and father came out of the study, looking tense.

'Eva,' said my father. '*Esta foto es un poco problemática,*' this photo is
a little problematic.

We used to speak both languages at home, sometimes changing
mid-sentence.

I smiled determinedly at my father to stop myself crying – I really
badly needed a baby photo. Apart from anything else, it was *our first
ever homework*, and I didn't want to be told off.

'Come over here,' he said.

I walked towards him, watching my feet in their brown T-bar leather
sandals.

'Our albums – the ones with your baby photos in – were stolen from the beach house in Alvera,' he said authoritatively. (This was a key point, underlined years later in the Quest Book.)

'Stolen?' I said to my father, a bit shaken. 'From the beach house?'

'It must have happened when we were back in Jerez,' said my mother, staring into my father's eyes like she was trying to hypnotise him. 'Mustn't it?'

'Yes, yes, yes,' said my father.

'So a thief got in?' I said quietly.

My mother looked at my father, flushed and tense, and they both nodded.

'I thought thieves stole money,' I said, thinking of stories. 'And treasure.'

My father laughed, though it didn't seem to me a laughing matter.

'Do thieves steal *photo albums?*' I said.

'These ones did!' said my father, swapping (alarmingly) from singular thief to plural.

'So what will I take to school?' I said, trembling inside.

'You will take a photo of your mother,' said my father, smiling tensely. 'Nobody will know.'

My mother, looking doubtful, handed me a photograph of her as a rather fat and very pale baby, with no hair on her head.

'They'll know that's not me,' I said, looking down at my not-pale knees. 'We don't match.'

My mother was sweating; my father was laughing rather awkwardly, hahaha.

'Well, you can have a photo of me then!' he said, giving me a nudge in the arm.

'But you're a boy, Papá,' I said stiffly.

'Babies all look the same,' said my father.

They both went back inside the study, and when they came out, my mother was holding a photo of my father, in a silver frame, sitting up in an old-fashioned pram with a thick pelt of black hair.

'You look like a boy,' I said to my father, stammering slightly.

'That's only because you know,' said my mother, her bottom lip trembling.

She said she was feeling so anxious that she was going to bed, even though it was only seven o'clock in the evening.

Mary took me to my mother's curtainy bed to say good night, and she was all propped up like Pink Mother in *The Rainbow Rained Us*.

'Why did the thieves want my baby photos?' I said to her.

She didn't answer, so I asked her again.

'I don't want to talk about it,' she said in a small voice, letting her head flop to the right, as if she had no bones.

You're like a dog with a bone, she used to say to me, making no attempt to hide her exasperation. I asked Bridget if I was like a dog with a bone, and she said I was more like a beautiful bay-coloured pony, brown with long black hair and knobbly knees, rather shy.

She said bay ponies were her favourite, and she asked me what animal she was like, and I said a koala bear because they were (still are) my favourite animals.

'Except you're not at all sleepy,' I told her.

She said koalas weren't actually bears but marsupials, which carry their babies in a pouch for six months, and she stuffed a small koala from the class toy box into the enormous green knickers we were obliged to wear over white knickers called liners.

Our music teacher, Mrs Snell, said, 'Bridget Blume, what have you got inside your knickers?'

And Bridget said, 'Oh, Mrs Snell! What a question!'

Miss Feast put all the baby photos up on the display board, and it felt completely obvious that my old-fashioned photo with the faded frame-marks wasn't me, and I still remember the empty shaky feeling I had inside me all through that day, as if I was falling out of myself into nothing.

Also – this hit me even harder – all the other photos had a mother in them, a mother holding her baby. I desperately wanted a mother to be holding me, with her soft lips against my scalp, like Bridget's mother.

The other girls matched me quite easily with my father's black hair in the photo, although Lily Betts said, not unkindly, 'You look a bit like a boy.'

'No she does *not*,' said Bridget furiously, even though, obviously, I did.

Miss Feast asked us to say a bit about our life and our family, and, when it came to my turn, I had to concentrate very hard to find the courage to speak, with the other girls' eyes looking at me.

Nothing came out of my mouth when I opened it, so Miss Feast had to nudge me along.

'Do you have any brothers and sisters, Eva?' said Miss Feast.

'No,' I whispered, feeling shuddery inside.

'Or perhaps you've got a pet?'

'No,' I whispered.

Miss Feast moved on to Laura Stephenson.

But in the middle of Laura's turn, I blurted out, 'My father's Spanish, and I was born in Spain.'

Bridget put her thumb up at me, which meant well done, because she knew I didn't like speaking aloud. She knew a lot more about me by now and, gratifyingly, she still liked me.

Miss Feast, however, pointed to her right ear lobe, which was a sort of telling-off, and I knew that she hated me now that I hadn't had *listening ears*, now that I'd interrupted Laura Stephenson whose father was a well-known journalist.

How desperately I wanted Miss Feast to love me.

At break-time, Bridget said to me, 'You were a really nice baby, Eva. Probably the nicest of everyone in class.'

'Thank you,' I said, with a feeling inside me like drinking hot ginger. 'So were you.'

This was my first ever friendship, and it would change my life, for good, for wonderful, for terrible, but I didn't know that yet.

Bridget and I got on the seesaw, sending me shooting up into the air. It soon became clear that there was no way of getting me down without her getting off, which she did a bit too quickly, slamming my bottom (rather painfully) into the tarmac.

'I think the roundabout might be better for us,' said Bridget, taking my hand and making me feel like bursting with joy.

The Populars were on the roundabout, Sophia Carr cross-legged in the centre, the others orbiting her like planets around the sun. Bridget and I knew our place: we wandered about the edge of the playground, lifting up stones and looking for woodlice.

The woodlice girls, that was us – the lowest possible caste in the class! But I loved the nervous lifting of the stone, the *will-there-won't-there* moment, the sight of the woodlice squirming around and the way they rolled up into little balls, which Bridget then threw at the Populars when they weren't looking.

'Will that give them a headache?' I said anxiously (always anxious, you see, even about woodlice).

'No,' said Bridget. 'They can't feel a thing.'

I didn't stop to wonder how she knew this without being a woodlouse.

I believed her without thinking.

Because I loved her.

Already.

When Miss Feast gave my mother back my photo at dismissal time, she said, 'I love those old-fashioned prams.'

I blushed. My mother also blushed lobster-red, stuck out her little padded bosoms and made the cat's bottom with her mouth, but no words came out. I wished she wouldn't make that shape with her mouth, and I wondered if Miss Feast thought we had some sort of genetic blushing disorder in our family.

'What kind of pram did I really have?' I said to my mother in the taxi.

'Oh,' she said, biting her lip. 'Just a normal blue one. You know, navy blue.'

'Did I like being in my pram?' I said.

'Oh,' she said again. 'Yes, I think so.'

'You think so?'

'It's hard to tell,' she said. 'Isn't it? Babies don't speak.'

'So what's the earliest photo you've got of me?' I said to my mother when we got home.

She produced a pocket album.

I held my breath.

'Do you remember the beach house in Alvera?' she said.

'I don't know,' I said, feeling wobbly with excitement that we were actually going to talk about my life before now, my *Spanish life*, which no one ever mentioned but which made me feel exotic and special, even though I couldn't quite remember it.

Here were ten photos from *the beach house in Alvera* which seemed to have been taken on the same day – me under a palm tree; me by the swimming pool; me eating *calamares* from a large white plate, scowling.

I grabbed the album.

'Was I born at the beach house?'

My mother didn't answer.

'Questions, questions!' she said crossly, and I didn't feel I could ask again.

I stared at the photos very carefully, noting my scared eyes, and I asked my mother if I could please have the album and keep it in my bedroom. She said no.

My mother's hands were shaking.

They had eczema on them.

'Did I know anyone at the beach house?' I said to my mother. 'Any children?'

'Your cousins from Jerez visited one weekend,' she said.

I looked for them inside my mind.

Nothing.

I must tell Miss Feast I have cousins, I thought.

I turned the pages of the album, backwards and forwards.

The beach house had a blue gate with a pool, and two hundred palm trees planted by my father for my mother, and a plate of small squid with tiny cooked curled-up legs. And maybe I did remember it a bit, the way you remember dreams.

'How old was I there?' I said.

'Three and a half,' she said, fast as anything. 'It was June 1978.'

'Three and a half,' I said slowly.

'Three and a half,' she said quickly.

'You really like making everything match,' I said, in a slightly disapproving voice.

With my lilac dress, I was wearing a lilac bolero cardigan, lilac shoes and a lilac ribbon – as if I might be displayed in a shop window.

'You were my best present ever to your mother!' my father used to say, looking rather pleased with himself.

This made me think of cellophane wrap and gift ribbons, and when I lay awake in bed at night, I wondered if I was a strange mail-order child who'd arrived in Spain, three and a half years old, chosen by my father, a package, which my mother had unwrapped, like a doll, for dressing up. She did love to dress me up.

Perhaps I wasn't even properly alive.

I checked my heart.

It was beating.

I crept along the dark landing, took the nail scissors from the bathroom cabinet and tried cutting my skin.

It bled.

I stared at the birthmark on my right thigh.

Perhaps I came from an alien race with birthmarks on their thighs.

'Can I have this mark taken away?' I said.

'No, you can't,' said my mother. 'It's absolutely enormous.'

'But perfectly shaped like *the Iberian Peninsula*,' said my father, explaining that this meant the land mass of Spain and Portugal.

Eva from Iberia – it had the ring of a fierce female warrior, but I didn't feel much like a warrior, lying in bed in the dark, running my fingers anxiously across the raised edges of my birthmark, wondering why on earth thieves would steal anyone's baby photos, and then wondering if the thieves were lies, and the stolen albums were lies, and in fact, something more terrible than I could imagine had happened to me.

My father was at home less and less, which made my mother more and more anxious.

The house seemed darker without him.

Not only metaphorically, but because my mother had an obsession with closing all the triple-lined curtains while it was still light outside (which my father didn't allow when he was at home).

I remember lying in the dark, thinking that nobody cared properly about me.

Except Bridget.

And my father quite a bit (when he was here).

And Miss Feast (possibly). Miss Feast, with her long black plait, her tiny heart earrings and the mole above her lip. Miss Feast, who very quickly became Mrs Tomkins, though we never called her that. Almost immediately after changing her name, she was (to my mother's alarm and consternation) pregnant. Like Mary in the school nativity play – a pretty girl called Julia in Class 6, with a pillow up her dress, ready to give birth to Jesus.

Bridget and I dreamt of being Mary when we got to Class 6.

For now, we decided to make do with playing *nativity* in the play-ground using the rocking horse as the donkey.

To my surprise, Bridget got on all fours mooing like a cow to allow Baby Jesus to come out of her bottom.

'Do all babies come out of their mothers' bottoms?' I asked.

'Yes, and there's this big jellyfish thing that comes out with them,' she said authoritatively. 'Called the *percenta*.'

Wow!

I'd come out of my mother's bottom with a big jellyfish thing.

The more you found out about life, the weirder it seemed.

I was filling up with questions every day.

'Why was God a baby?' I asked Miss Feast when she was on break duty. 'Babies aren't any use to anyone.'

'Everyone starts off as a baby,' said Miss Feast.

'Are you absolutely sure?' I said, thinking that this might turn out to be a significant quest conversation. 'Every single person on the whole earth?'

She nodded.

'Also,' I said, 'was Mary Jesus's real mother?'

'Yes,' she said.

'And was Joseph Jesus's real father or was God Jesus's real father?'

'They both were.'

'Can a baby have two fathers or two mothers?'

'Not normal babies.'

'Might I have been a not-normal baby?' I said, thinking that this was hopeful, that there might be a second mother lurking about somewhere, maybe a lovely blue or green one.

She hesitated.

'This is very important, Miss Feast,' I said.

'So many questions, Eva Martínez-Green!' she said, bringing the conversation to an abrupt close and ringing the bell.

When I got home, I kept staring at my mother, trying to picture her on all fours mooing like a cow while I came out of her bottom.

It was very hard to believe that this had happened.

'Did I come out of your bottom?' I asked her in the end, concluding that it was the only failsafe way of finding out.

'Who told you that?' she started, before turning very pink, wiping her upper lip with a tissue and saying that these were not things anybody spoke about, and could I please not speak about them either.

If I hadn't come out of her bottom, whose bottom had I come out of?

These questions were blasted clean out of my mind when Miss Feast cheerfully announced: 'I will have to leave you all soon to go off and have my baby.'

Yes, cheerfully.

Did the poor woman know what was involved?

'When will you come back to us?' I whispered to Miss Feast.

'I'm not coming back,' she said. 'Mr Tomkins and I are moving to Ireland.'

You're not coming back to St Hilda's, I thought, never in your whole life?

'I'll think of you all,' she said.

I sat very still.

She'd think of us all – what was the point of that?

What about Forever Eva?

The woman hadn't even lasted the full year.

It was no sooner hello Miss Dixon and hello Class 1 than it was goodbye Miss Dixon because her mother had cancer.

Rumours swirled through the school that Miss Dixon had caught cancer from her mother, and now we were most probably all going to get infected too and die a mass death, slumped over each other under our desks, fighting for breath.

I'd spent my entire life worrying about my beginning, but I now started to worry about my end, and whether it might come far too soon, right there in the classroom – the classroom into which Miss Cracey, the headteacher, burst crossly to explain that cancer was not catching, so she didn't want any nonsense spoken about it, or any histrionics. Cancer happens, she said, when abnormal cells grow and spread very fast. Normal cells, she went on, know how to grow and divide, and they also know how to stop and die. But the abnormal cells don't know any of this, she said. They go on and on growing and dividing, and sometimes cause little traffic jams, or pile-ups, called tumours, which can be removed by surgeons.

'I thought people died of cancer,' said Annabel to Miss Cracey, bravely, as people didn't as a rule speak to her.

The class fell silent.

Miss Cracey swept her head right to left, like the grey parrot in the pet shop in Fulham.

'Of course not everyone dies,' she said tightly. 'The surgeons are very clever these days.'

Nobody spoke.

'I don't want to hear another thing about it,' said Miss Cracey. 'We have ten chicken eggs being delivered to your classroom on Monday. And if there's any more nonsense from you, they will go to Class 2 instead.'

Nobody moved.

'This is the end of the matter,' she said firmly. 'Do you hear me?'

Yes, we heard her.

That's what ears do, and even if you put your hands over them, as I did when my mother had arguments with my father, they still went on hearing.

'Not everyone dies,' that's what Miss Cracey said.

We were learning subtraction, using ten beach pebbles per table.

'Not everyone,' I said to Bridget, 'means nearly everyone,' and I took away nine pebbles, one at a time, putting them solemnly in the shadows under my desk.

'All the pebbles die except one,' I said.

We stared at the one alive pebble.

'Let's ask our parents about cancer tonight,' said Bridget. 'I'm sure it's not as bad as it sounds.'

I nodded and said yes yes, acting like we had those kinds of big conversations all the time in our house, oh we never stopped talking about life and death and terminal diseases.

In the taxi home with my mother, I sat silently imagining cancer like a bird of prey, up above us with its wings stretched out, deciding who to pounce on. And it came to me that up in the sky, behind the clouds, there were probably lots of other horrible beasts we didn't yet know about, all of them monstrous, with wings and hungry beaks, looking for prey.

The next day, Bridget reported that her doctor-dad had confirmed that cancer was indeed a serious illness.

But, good news:

'He says that there are treatments, which sometimes work.'

Well, good-ish news.

'What are treatments?'

'Medicine.'

'Like Disprin?' I said, trying to think of the names of medicines in my mother's bathroom cabinet. 'Or Prozac?'

'I suppose so,' said Bridget, looking a bit uncertain. 'And he said just because we know there are *wasps* about, it doesn't stop us going on a picnic.'

'I like that,' I said, repeating it in my head. 'I'll remember that.'

'"Enjoy the picnic," my dad said, "and if a wasp comes along, we'll swat it away together."'

It seemed to me – both then and as we moved into Class 2 with Miss Philips, in a whirl of seventh birthdays – that there were wasps everywhere: puzzles and uncertainties and unanswered questions, and during our visits to the King's Road library, I avoided the fiction shelves and took out books about God and heaven (and occasionally UFOs) because books never said back at you, 'Questions questions'.

Just before the autumn half-term, Miss Cracey announced that a woman called Sister Ruth was coming to visit us. Miss Cracey bigged her up like Sister Ruth was God himself, and said we could ask her any question at all, and she would know the answer. I could hardly wait.

Sister Ruth, when she arrived, had buck teeth, a pastry-coloured face and unusually large feet. She asked us if we ever thought about where we were before we were born and where we would go after we died, and not one person put up their hand. Nor did anyone ask her a single question about anything at all.

I went up to her on my way out of the classroom (as I still didn't like speaking aloud in front of the other girls) and I said, please, if she didn't mind, and if it was a suitable question, where *was I* before I was born, because I had no idea.

She gave me a bible and said the answer was in there.

By now, I was the best reader in the class, but it still looked like a very long and complicated answer.

I then asked her if it was true that all babies, without exception, came out of women's bottoms. She said this was indeed the case, and very quickly asked if I had another question about something else. I asked her where I might have been from when I was born until I was three and a half, where there seemed to be a long and alarming gap in my life.

She smiled very kindly, and said: 'In God's arms.'

'All that time?' I said. 'Wow!'

And she nodded.

I said, 'Could I have ended up with a mother who isn't my mother?'

She said, 'That question is too difficult for me. Perhaps you should ask God.'

Which was disappointing, in view of Miss Cracey's stellar build-up.

Sister Ruth took us on a very slow walk, and she told us to look around and notice everything, even flies and wasps and cracks in the pavement. As I walked along, solemnly and observantly, I remembered Bridget's dad saying: *If a wasp comes along, we'll swat it away*

33

together. And everything felt very OK in the world, like it didn't normally.

We all lay down and closed our eyes, and a big blob of peace fell on top of me.

'This is the sacrament of the present moment,' said Sister Ruth, and we paused, and the world seemed to stop and tremble, and her face lit up.

I wrote this in my diary and underlined it twice, with serious comments about the possibility that we had seen or at least sensed God's presence on the school lawn.

Then I said loudly into my empty bedroom, 'God, if I may please ask, have I ended up with the wrong mother?'

But, disappointingly, God didn't answer.

I asked him again, a bit louder.

Nothing.

Zilch.

Zero.

I leafed through the bible to see if I could find out where I was before I was born, but it was full of very small writing and very long words, so I gave up.

I wrote in my diary, *When I grow up, I want to be Sister Ruth.*

The next day, Bridget said, 'Sister Ruth was a weirdo.'

So I went home and crossed it out.

It was after Sister Ruth's visit that I started my Quest Book – subtitle, WHO AM I? – looking for some kind of a framework that might explain me. I wrote down important memories and underlined key phrases in thick black pen. Things like this:

Memory: my father calling me into his study and asking me to <u>choose a name for my mother</u> – Mum or Mummy or Mamá – and me saying I would call her Cherie, please, as he did.

Looking back, I wonder if I knew that this was a strange conversation, or that it was odd to call her Cherie unless you came from a very hip family like Laura Stephenson. Or, did I, a confused bilingual child, think Cherie was an alternative, mother-ish word?

These are things lost in the mists of memory.

I went back to *The Rainbow Rained Us* and noted key points in my Quest Book. I could now understand, with the aid of a dictionary, the section which dealt with the positive and negative aspects of each colour, but even the good things in the pink section – *delicate* and *sensitive* – seemed to me like bad things. And everything my mother did continued to seem pinker than pink.

From now on I shall think of her as <u>Pink Mother</u>, I wrote grandly, perhaps convincing myself that I was being clever and funny, but in fact making the distance between us even bigger in my mind.

Oh dear, Pink Mother is crying again, I'd think.

Oh dear, Pink Mother has taken to the chaise longue again.

It was as if I was trying to protect myself from the painful realisation that she didn't seem able to love me.

My father seemed to love me, sort of, or at least to find me diverting when he was in the right mood, which often came after a glass or two of his favourite fino sherry, when I took to asking him apparently casual questions relating to our family's past. I wrote any relevant answers he gave in my Quest Book.

He told me, for example, that Granny and Grandpa Green had chosen the name Cherie, which means darling, as she was their one and only darling, coming along, after ten years of waiting, when they thought they couldn't have children. This went straight into the Quest Book.

1 – Some married couples can't have children.

2 – Some have to wait ten years before they get them.

I felt sure these facts were relevant to the quest, but couldn't think exactly how.

I also wanted to ask my father if I might be, in any way, his darling, but I couldn't think how to bring it up, and anyway I wasn't sure if I wanted to know the answer.

'I met your mother when Granny and Grandpa Green brought her to Jerez on a wine-tasting holiday,' said my father, out of nowhere. 'I'd never met anyone called Cherie.'

Her name, spelled differently but pronounced the same, he went on, was the name for fortified wine – sherry – which was his favourite drink.

'Perhaps that's why I chose her!' he said.

I didn't bother to write that down because it was a stupid thing to say.

'Your Spanish grandfather's wine company,' said my father, 'makes sherry, and also red, white and rosé wine, and is the most famous in the whole of Spain. And now he's too old to run it, he's given it to me.'

Perhaps at the wine company, I mused in my Quest Book, there were fields of sunflowers and blue sky and orange sunshine like the paintings in the hall, and perhaps I was born there and put in a wine barrel, like Moses got put in a basket. Perhaps I floated down a river and Pink Mother pulled me out and kept me, like the Pharaoh's daughter kept Moses.

After my grandfather gave my father the wine company, he started to offload his Andalusian property portfolio as well, and my father would leave gorgeous photographs of glimmering white buildings on his desk, which I described at length in my Quest Book.

I tried asking Pink Mother some leading questions about my Spanish family, in particular my Spanish grandparents.

'Did they come to see me at the hospital when I was born?' I asked.

'I think they were too busy with the vineyards,' she said, taking hold of the corner of her cardigan.

'Were they picking grapes then?' I said.

She laughed.

'Not exactly,' she said, pulling at the tiny bobbles on her cuff with her long nails. 'Your grandmother was probably at church.'

'I thought you said she was busy with the vineyards?'

She changed the subject.

'When your father was a boy, your grandmother used to list his sins on a little blackboard and send him to confession.'

'What? With a priest in one of those wooden boxes?' I said.

'He never went,' she said. 'He used to put the blackboard in his pocket and go fishing instead. And his mother never knew!'

'That's lying,' I said.

'Oh, your father always loved to tell stories,' she said. 'And that hasn't changed!'

The truth was this: by the time my father was an adult, he'd made up so many stories about his own life, sometimes he couldn't remember which one he was living in.

My father also loved stories in books, and that was perfect because

English was my equal-favourite subject (alongside history, religious studies, and French, which Bridget was terrible at, and definitely not maths, which she liked best).

My father's favourite book was *Peter Pan* (of course it was, he never really wanted to grow up). And like Peter Pan, my father just said anything that came into his head.

Peter Pan was my favourite too (though I longed to grow up), and I knew it almost off by heart.

My father used to let me stand on the marble table on our roof terrace so he could point out the different landmarks of London, and we'd make up stories where Peter Pan jumped onto the hands of Big Ben and stopped time, or where the tick-tock crocodile swam up the Thames and ate Albert Bridge.

'If you think about it, Eva,' said my father, 'the Darling children were very boring before they met Peter Pan.'

'Yes, but in the end,' I said, 'though they liked being in Neverland, they were homesick.'

My father looked at me strangely.

'I think I feel sort of homesick too,' I said, thinking that this might be a way into an important quest conversation, and he stopped very still, like he never did.

'Homesick for what?' he said.

'I don't know,' I said, stammering. 'Something. Somewhere. Before.'

'But we're giving you a wonderful life here in London, your mother and I.'

I shut my eyes and breathed deeply.

'Can you explain what you mean, Eva?' he said.

I wished I'd never got started.

I opened my eyes.

'Come on!' said my father.

'I feel like . . .' I said, hesitating.

'You feel like what?' he said.

I opened my mouth to speak, and he opened his in time with mine.

'I feel like . . .' I said.

'Yes . . .' said my father, his mouth trying to urge my mouth into action.

'I feel like . . . when the thieves stole the albums, they stole a bit of me.'

I was hot all over, but at least I'd tried to find a way of saying what I felt inside.

I walked straight off the roof terrace, through the room with the wicker furniture in it and downstairs into my bedroom, where I couldn't stop myself exploding into sobs. I decided it was a very bad idea indeed to let my thoughts out into real life.

The next day, my father brought me a wallet of photos.

'This is your home in Jerez,' he said, coming into my bedroom, speaking very quickly and stopping to clear his throat. 'This is where you lived with your mother and me, and your Spanish grandpa, and some of your uncles and aunts and cousins. And hundreds of horses and fighting bulls. And fifty billion grapes!'

He laughed.

I had no idea why.

'When I was a baby?' I said.

He nodded.

'Until we came here?' I said.

He nodded.

'What about the beach house in Alvera?' I said.

'That was for holidays and long weekends.'

I spent a long time looking at my supposed home and my supposed life: the horses, the cows, the fighting bulls.

'You loved the horses best,' said my father firmly.

'Have you got a picture of me with the horses?' I said.

'Ah, this one was your favourite,' he said. 'Blanquita.'

'Have you got a picture of me with Blanquita?'

'I'm not sure I have.'

He moved to the photos of the vineyards.

'This is where you ran about,' said my father. 'Up and down!'

'I thought I was a baby,' I said.

'And here are the sherry *bodegas*, and look at all those wine barrels!'

I looked at the sherry *bodegas* and the wine barrels and not one thought came into my head.

Then I stared at the multiple photos of the many dark-eyed Spanish relatives sitting at the big shiny mahogany dining table, the inner courtyard with yellow stone walls and the long sandy driveway through the vineyards.

It was all very beautiful, but I wasn't there.

Not in a single one of my father's photos.

'Do you have any photos of *me* at the house in Jerez?' I asked Pink Mother.

She stiffened, and said she'd have a look.

'What actually happened in the first three and a half years of my life?' I asked, firmly, as I'd had enough of my questions never being answered.

'You're like a dog with a bone,' she said, backing away from me.

'You already mentioned that,' I said, trying to be a bit cocksure and funny like Bridget, even though I was feeling fragile underneath.

'Nothing happens when you're a baby,' she said, adjusting her silk scarf, which had horse stirrups printed on it, I had no idea why.

'Well, we must have done something,' I said.

She moved across the sitting room and sat down in one of the upright velvet armchairs.

'I've told you,' she said. 'We divided our time between the beach house in Alvera and our house in Jerez.'

'With the vineyards?'

I took a step towards her.

'Ghastly Jerez,' she said.

'Why was it ghastly?' I said.

She made a gesture with her hand, which seemed to be a way of flapping me away.

'What was I like as a baby?' I said, heart thumping.

'You were like all babies are,' she said, picking up a magazine.

So there was nothing memorable or special about me at all?

I felt horribly winded, and then, a second later, horribly frightened.

Because perhaps she didn't know what I was like when I was a baby.

'Bridget's twin sisters are going through the terrible twos!' I said, and I tried smiling at her, to see if she might smile back. 'Did I have the terrible twos?'

'You were quite normal,' she said, not smiling back.

Tears welled up inside my ducts.

She eventually found another of those pocket albums, this one with six photos of me – wearing a pistachio-green outfit, everything matching – at the house in Jerez, in the inner courtyard, which was totally bare except for a stone fountain with three stone basins on three levels in the centre and arched windows in all the yellow stone walls. The fountain had no water in it.

'How old am I there?' I said.

'Three and a half,' said Pink Mother briskly.

'Papá says I liked a horse called Blanquita,' I said. 'How old was I when I rode Blanquita?'

'You were three and a half,' she said.

'Was I always three and a half?' I said. 'My whole life?'

'Maybe you were younger,' she said, getting that red patchy rash under her pearl necklace.

'Why can't I remember Blanquita?' I said, and the tears tried to come up my tear ducts again and my sinuses ached. 'It feels like I would remember her.'

'Children don't remember things,' she said.

'Children do remember things,' I said to her, squeezing my eyes shut and forcing myself to drag my inside thoughts out. 'I have strange blurry memories. There's a huge table.'

'There was a big table in Jerez,' she said very fast, and when I opened my eyes, she was clutching her hands together and scratching at her eczema.

'But the one I remember is different,' I said, breathing deeply, needing to be brave. 'It's not like the dark shiny one in the photos of Jerez. It's a lighter colour, and there are lots of people round it, men I think, with beards, but I can't see their faces.'

'You have a huge family in Jerez,' she said, making the skin on the back of her hands bleed.

'And there are flowers,' I said, heart racing but making myself keep talking. 'Yes, flowers everywhere. Literally everywhere.'

A smell of hot rust caught in my throat.

'All houses have flowers,' said Pink Mother.

The courtyard in Jerez definitely didn't have flowers in the photos. I'd noticed this because I loved flowers from the beginning. I used to go into our *patio* in Chelsea before I left for school and tell the geraniums and hydrangeas how beautiful they were.

'It's not normal to talk to flowers,' Pink Mother would say repeatedly.

'Then please may I have a sister?' I'd reply. 'Or a kitten?'

When I told her I remembered the flowers from another life, she said, 'Stop talking nonsense.'

But I did remember them – red geranium petals and huge hydrangeas, bluey-mauve with pale green centres.

Those flowers weren't in Alvera, where there were two hundred palm trees and a blue gate. And they weren't in Jerez, where the courtyard was yellow and empty, and where, in the photos, I was always alone.

I wasn't alone any more – hurray!

I had Bridget by my side, and together we got through everything, even terrible Sports Day, where the Populars won medals, and Bridget and I walked around with stickers saying *Well Done* on our chests, which meant we'd come last.

But Bridget wasn't at my side during the dreaded school holidays.

I remember the awful last day of every term, especially the summer term, when it would be weeks without her – and it rained, and was cold, and my father said this bloody country doesn't have a summer, and days dragged on, with outings to see the grey parrot at the pet shop in Fulham, and damp boat trips along the river, and lying on my bed reading for hours.

My father and mother couldn't stop shouting at each other: she lay pinkly on the chaise longue crying and saying he'd never loved her. I put my hands over my ears but still heard.

One evening, I was reading about Islam in my library book on world religions: it started in Mecca and moved to Spain, and Muslims believed in angels, and prophets, like Adam and Abraham and Moses (who confusingly cropped up in the section on Jews and Christians too) and also Jesus (as in, *Away in a Manger*) who they called Isu.

It was all getting a bit bewildering, when I heard my father's footsteps on the landing.

I assumed that he was heading downstairs to his study, but he came in, looking agitated.

'I don't want you reading these kinds of books,' he said, because his mother had made him hate religion by writing his sins on the little blackboard.

Although I would normally have nodded and said OK, I didn't.

I stood up for myself like Bridget would have done.

I said, in a Bridget-confident voice, 'I'm looking for answers.'

'You won't find any answers in religion,' said my father. 'People made up religions to give themselves an excuse to hate each other.'

'Or because they need a story to help them make sense of their life,' I said. 'That's what Miss Philips said in religious studies.'

I thought my father was going to shout at me, but he smiled in a way that made me wonder if I was a little bit his darling.

'I wish there was just one religion,' I said. 'I'm getting a bit confused.'

'In the Middle Ages,' said my father, 'in the south of Spain, Islam, Christianity and Judaism lived together happily. For two hundred and fifty years. And, if God existed, that would have been what he wanted, don't you think?'

I noted the *if*, and I knew for sure that grown-ups didn't have all the answers.

'What are we?' I said to my father. 'Out of those three religions?'

My father looked at me.

'What are we indeed?' he said, without answering.

'Seriously?' I said. 'I think we're Christians, aren't we?'

'Your grandmother was more Catholic than the Virgin Mary,' he said.

'I thought the Virgin Mary was Jewish,' I said.

My father looked as if he'd never realised that.

My head was dancing with so many questions I couldn't think which one to start with, but my father didn't leave any space for questions that day, like he usually did.

He seemed in a great rush to tell me things.

He said, 'Just remember this – religion always starts well and ends badly.'

Then he said, 'Come to think of it, lots of things that start well end badly. Perhaps all things.'

I could see his jaw clenching under his skin as I said, 'What do you mean?'

He said, 'You'll see. It's just how life is. Write that down and see if I'm right.'

He sounded slightly mad, but I still wrote it down.

I said, 'Are you OK?'

He said, 'I'm sorry, Eva, I'm sorry.'

He fastened the middle button of his jacket and then unfastened it, and he said, 'I'm just not very good at being moored. Like Peter Pan.'

That's the line I remember most.

He opened the door, and I caught sight of two large brown leather suitcases on the landing, as well as his normal cylindrical travelling holdall with the gold initials JMM, and also a matching brown rucksack.

'You've got a lot of luggage,' I said, with my heart sinking into my belly.

He left my room without looking back and closed the door, and I heard his feet and his suitcases thump, thump, thumping down the stairs, not once but twice, and the front door slamming. I stood at the landing window and saw the pale sole of my father's left shoe disappearing into a black London taxi.

I wrote in my diary: *Papá has gone somewhere else*, with a sad face next to it, crying one fat tear.

Then I wrote: *With loads of luggage. I don't think he's coming back.*

I opened my Quest Book, and I wrote: <u>*Papá gone*</u>, and the date – *25 August 1982*.

I felt a horrible fluttering, as if a flock of birds were in my belly wanting to fly up my throat, and tears were pouring out of my eyes, and I wanted to chase him to the airport with the birds and beg him to come home to me.

I went downstairs, my belly aching so hard I almost had to bend in half.

I walked onto the *patio* feeling sick and shaky.

I gently touched the soft petals of the flowers, but they didn't comfort me like they normally did.

My hands were shaking.

Pink Mother was holding a glass of wine and speaking in a strange slurry voice, ordering Rory the gardener to smash up all the terracotta pots and rip out the geraniums and the fuchsias, the strawberry plants, the bougainvillaea, the hydrangeas, 'the whole damn lot!'

Everything felt precarious to me when she was like this, when she might suddenly shout or shriek or burst into tears.

'The whole damn lot!' she kept slurring at Rory, pointing at the plants.

'I'm afraid I couldn't do that, Mrs Martínez-Green,' said Rory, and he put his hand through his sandy hair. 'It would break my heart.'

'You will do it!' she shouted, with her lipstick a bit smudged, looking like a plaster puppet in a Punch and Judy show. 'Or you will be sacked!'

'I'm afraid I'll have to be sacked then,' said Rory, and he went and collected his box of gardening tools and his old green anorak from the tiny shed in the corner of the *patio*.

He turned and winked at me before he opened the side door, and I knew that I would never see him again, and that turned into a horrible fear that I would never see my father again either.

'The cheek of the man!' shrieked Pink Mother as Rory the gardener left.

'Cherie,' I said nervously, bravely. 'I don't want you to destroy Papá's special *patio* either.'

'Papá has destroyed my life!' she said, pouring herself another glass of wine. 'What is a *patio* compared to a life?'

And that's true, I suppose – what *is* a *patio* compared to a life?

But the *patio* seemed more tangible, and prettier.

Also, I realised, I didn't really understand her life, what mattered to her, what made her happy.

She drank a whole bottle of wine, one glass after another, but that didn't make her happy. No, instead, it made her pick up some clipping shears and take a swipe at one of the huge terracotta pots, which didn't break.

In bed that night, I couldn't stop thinking about her lunging at the pot, with her twisted smudgy face – it made me feel shaky inside. I consoled myself that she often had these strange outbursts, particularly in the evenings, and that by the next morning, she'd often changed back into a normal woman.

'I don't know what I was thinking,' she would perhaps say the next day. 'I was having one of my funny turns.'

After her failed battle with the clipping shears and the terracotta pot, she decided to destroy the flowers my father had loved by refusing to water them.

She couldn't hurt him, so she decided to hurt the flowers instead.

She locked the *patio* door and hid the key so that I couldn't water them either, but I talked to them through the window, and prayed for rain.

After my father left us, I read *Peter Pan* incessantly, trying to mimic my father's different voices for the different characters. I especially loved the part where Peter Pan held out his hand for a kiss, because he had no idea what it was, and Wendy gave him a thimble so as not to hurt his feelings. Now my father was gone, no one in my house ever kissed me.

But the long terrible summer holiday was coming to an end, and I jubilantly crossed off the last day on my chart.

Mary laid out my school uniform on my chair – and my soul sang.

It was term-time again – and Bridget!

And, joy of joys, I started going for tea at her house every Thursday. This was Mary's day off, and Pink Mother had a *weekly commitment*. I had no idea what this meant, but I wondered if it was similar to a monthly period, which Bridget had told me about.

Bridget's mother was (as I'd suspected) exactly like Blue Mother in *The Rainbow Rained Us*. I loved everything about her, especially the way she dried her crinkly blue scarf by twisting it around the banister of the stairs.

There seemed to be children everywhere at Bridget's house.

The little girl twins, Bessie and Bella, were hard to tell apart.

The big boy twins were not.

Boaz was very clever, and looked like a mole.

And Barnaby?

Oh, Barnaby!

I'll be saying much more about Barnaby Blume, who I allowed to loom over my life for far too many years.

The children called Mr and Mrs Blume D and M, and Mr and Mrs Blume even called each other D and M. Bridget's mother said that I could call her M if I wanted to, or Aunty M, like her nephews and nieces did. I did want to but I couldn't manage it. So I called her nothing.

At Bridget's house, there were beautiful wood-carved Bs nailed to the walls but, in her parents' bedroom, whose door was always open, there were the letters M and D on the wall above their huge double bed.

There were patterned throws over all the sofas and armchairs, which never tucked in properly, so you could see the velvet and brocade underneath poking out, and gorgeous Indian parasols propped in corners, and a great wire chandelier that Bridget's mother had made, with fake feather birds in it. There were massive paintings on every wall, and the sea roared and rolled and sprayed, and flocks of gulls made shapes against the clouds. Framed photos crowded onto every windowsill – of Bridget's parents' wedding day and great huddles of Blumes.

I noted in my Quest Book that we didn't have *photos like that in our house*.

In their big garden with weedy flowerbeds, Bridget taught me how to play. First, she taught me how to rotate a hula hoop around my hips. We did it one at a time, then two in together, and we became total pros. Then we went on to elastics.

If Pink Mother was late, Bridget and I would have a bath together in the Blumes' Victorian bathtub on legs, and we'd make up convoluted stories with a family of yellow rubber ducks and a pair of green frogs until the bathwater had turned cold, and I'd go home in a pair of Bridget's pyjamas, smelling like a Blume.

One Thursday evening, the yellow rubber ducks got married and had a yellow baby.

'Say goodbye to daddy,' I said in Father Duck's voice to the small yellow duck, looking up at Bridget, and then more loudly, 'I'm catching *a plane to Spain.*'

'A plane to Spain?' said Bridget, as I'd hoped.

'Yes,' I said. 'I'd been meaning to tell you. My father's gone back to Spain.'

'On holiday?' said Bridget.

'No,' I said. 'He's living there now.'

'He's living in Spain?' said Bridget, crumpling up her face.

'Yes,' I said.

'How long for?' said Bridget.

I shrugged my shoulders.

'Could it be forever?' said Bridget.

'Yes,' I said. 'I think so.'

'Is your mum OK?' said Bridget.

'My mum isn't really like a proper mother,' I said.

Bridget stared at me.

'It's because she's *pink,*' I said, trying to sound very matter-of-fact. 'She's too *delicate* to be a proper mother. Like in *The Rainbow Rained Us.*'

'Like in what?' said Bridget.

'You remember that book Miss Feast read us in Entrance Class?' I said, unable to believe that she'd forgotten.

Bridget frowned and looked slightly vague.

'Whereas your mother is blue,' I said. 'You must remember Blue Mother. She was the best one.'

'I remember her a bit,' said Bridget.

'I was thinking,' I said, 'maybe I could share your mother sometimes, because I like blue more than pink.'

Bridget said, 'I'm a bit cold. Are you?'

We got out of the bath, wrapped ourselves in towels and Bridget gave me a little smile.

'Yes, you can,' said Bridget.

'Can what?'

'Share her when you're here. We can share everything our whole lives if you like.'

'Oh, yes please,' I said, with no idea what this might mean. No idea at all.

Bridget hugged me, and her bare arms against my bare arms, a bit squeaky and damp from the bath, gave me a feeling I couldn't put into words. I dreamt of life being one eternal Thursday afternoon at the Blumes' – one infinite stretch of love and happiness and long baths and delicious cakes with butter icing and strange messy games you made up as you went along.

It was always a maximum of seven days until the next Thursday afternoon, and on long grey Sundays, only four days to go, school days which would race past – three, two, one, zero.

One Thursday, Barnaby asked us if we'd like to play prisons, and he hemmed us in under the snooker table with furniture for most of the afternoon.

'What did you play at Bridget's house?' said Pink Mother in the taxi.

'Prisons,' I said with great glee. 'Bridget's brother trapped us with furniture and swore at us.'

This caused her to phone Bridget's mother to say that if she wasn't able to provide higher levels of supervision, I wouldn't be able to go round to play any more.

My world turned dark.

I tried to think of ways to reverse the decision, suggesting that it was helpful for Bridget and me to work together on our joint project about animal adaptation because the Blumes had a whole library of useful books about camels.

My mother wasn't interested in camels.

She wanted to find fault in Bridget's mother, especially the clothes she wore, which made her look 'a terrible sight', she told Mary.

'The dear woman looks like a clown!' she said, smirking.

'Why do you call her dear then,' I asked, 'if all you want to do is criticise her?'

'You should have seen the trousers!' she said to Mary, laughing in that wolfy way she had.

The trousers in question were called harem pants, and Bridget's mother told me they were two thousand years old. Not her actual ones, though. The style. Turkish, Moorish, clearly more-ish to Bridget's mother: she had them in practically every colour.

Before we knew it, we were heading for nine years old, and it was time for advent calendars and the nativity play: a different long-haired girl put a pillow up her dress, and God abhorred not the virgin's womb again, and I prayed and prayed that my father would come home for Christmas.

I went to the Blumes' on Thursdays all through the autumn term because Pink Mother had relented, and on the last day of term, Bridget brought Barnaby's old light sabre into school for me as a Christmas present. I nearly died of joy. I sat in my father's study, pointing it at the street lamps and pretending to create light.

But look, there was Father Christmas getting out of a London taxi carrying a large sack of presents, walking with his feet splaying out a little, and, to my great surprise, climbing our shiny steps and ringing the doorbell.

'Don't answer!' shrieked Pink Mother. 'No one comes to my door unannounced!'

Father Christmas stepped over the black chain which bordered the flowerbed and tapped on the study window, and I hid behind my father's huge armchair, trembling with terror, and Father Christmas had a dark beard and dark skin and dark eyes – and Father Christmas was my father!

My prayers had worked and he'd come home!

Now we could all go back to normal, this Christmas and forever!
I rushed to the front door and opened it.

'Happy Christmas! Ho ho ho!' said my father, kissing my cheeks,
but not holding my nose between his fingers or dangling me upside
down – perhaps I'd got too big or too old, or maybe we didn't know
each other well enough for him to do those things any more.

'Let's put the presents here,' I said, gesturing towards the huge
tree in the hall, wrapped round and round with silver tinsel and
glistening with glittery baubles.

'*¿Por qué no los abres ahora?*' he said. Why don't you open them now.

'*Voy a esperar hasta Navidad,*' I said, trying out my Spanish
again. I'll wait until Christmas. The words juddered a little on my
tongue.

'But then I won't be here,' he said.

'Why?' I said. 'How long are you staying?'

'I've got a couple of hours,' he said. 'Then I'm flying back to Spain.'

I felt my heart drop into my bowel with a hurty thud.

The presents from my father were all books.

I tried to look grateful.

And normal.

I tried not to cry about the fact that his arrival was also a departure.

My father sat down in his leather Chesterfield armchair, and I sat
on his knee, and we started reading. When we finished the first book,
we started another. I made him read *Peter Pan*, and hearing all the
old funny voices made me feel wobbly as jelly.

Pink Mother came in, holding a camera. I didn't want her to waste
a single minute, so I looked at her impatiently.

'Can I take a photo of you two?' she said.

My father nodded.

She took three photos – flash flash flash.

'Can I get you a drink?' she said.

'No, thank you,' said my father. 'I'm about to leave for the airport.'

'Why didn't you tell me you were coming?' she said.

'I thought you wouldn't open the door,' he said. 'But I knew you couldn't refuse Father Christmas.'

'You're a manipulative bastard,' she said.

She walked out.

'How is she?' said my father.

'She's sad,' I said. 'And sometimes mad. And she's trying to kill all the flowers on the *patio*. To spite you.'

'How are you?' said my father.

I was just about to say a whole load of things when I decided not to bother.

'I'm fine,' I said, pushing all my feelings deep down, as usual.

'Good girl,' he said.

I'd noticed the teachers were all especially nice to me when Pink Mother went on her 'little breaks', which was very often through Class 4. Even Mrs Snell was nice, when she normally told us we were spoilt brats who had no idea what life was like in the real world, which was apparently over where she lived, in Croydon.

Bridget and I moved from fad to fad, and in Class 4, it was making whirlybirds out of paper, hooking the paper flaps over our fingers and trying them out on all the teachers: What's your favourite colour/animal/sweet/religion?

'Your favourite religion is whichever one you get,' said Miss Philips.

For some reason, I wrote this in my Quest Book.

Mary used to take me out into the square in the evenings when I'd finished my homework, and the neighbourhood cats would snake around my legs, and I'd close my eyes and feel hot kitten-skulls against my shins and dusty cat-tails blown up like bottle brushes *back somewhere before*. This went into the Quest Book too.

In the square, Mary would sit and read the magazines that came with the weekend newspapers. One of these had a special section where famous mothers discussed their relationship with their daughters, and famous daughters discussed their relationship with their mothers. I tore these out and kept them, and I still have them. I used to stare at the famous mothers and daughters hanging onto each other's arms and laughing into each other's eyes, and I would yearn for the special feeling I knew a real mother would give me.

Proper alchemy – warm and soft and telepathic: a wordless arm around my shoulders perhaps, or a hand squeezing messages through my palms, or a look between us that no one else could decipher.

Pink Mother came back home, but she hadn't changed one bit: she was strange and faraway in the evenings, and didn't get out of bed in the mornings, so Mary still took me to school, and picked me up, and came to my parents' evenings.

'Why doesn't your mum come?' said Sophia, standing staring at me with Annabel, Lily and Laura clustered around her, just as terrifying as they had been from the start.

'Is there something wrong with her?' said Annabel, staring.

'My mum says she's ill,' said Lily, staring.

'In the head,' said Laura.

They laughed their heads off.

There was no point telling the teachers.

The teachers thought they were all totally marvellous.

When they bullied Bridget for being fat, she used to sing, inside her head, *I will survive*, like Gloria Gaynor.

Bridget and I used to raid her parents' record collection and, using hairbrushes as microphones and badminton racquets as guitars, we'd don outlandish wigs and sparkly platform sandals from the dressing-up box, turn on the lights, open the curtains and stand in front of the glass doors, wiggling our bottoms at the dark garden and refusing, loudly, to crumble.

And we survived – oh-oh!

By the time I was in Class 5 and heading for double figures, we had a teacher called Mr Altman who was, shockingly, *a man*, a man who wore green velvet slippers with his initials on and a black cap on the back of his head fixed with girls' hair clips because, said Bridget, he was Jewish like the Blumes, although none of them wore velvet caps on the back of their heads (which was confusing).

He got us all to say what our religion was, and I said Catholic, and he said I would have a first communion and wear a pretty white dress like a bride, which I did not like the sound of at all.

Laura Stephenson said she was a secular humanist and we had no idea what she was on about.

I asked Mr Altman lots of questions about Judaism, and he said the main things were not to eat pork (like Muslims) and to be just and compassionate, and to go on waiting for a Messiah.

'Did the fact that Jesus was a baby put you off?' I asked him.

Hahaha, he said.

'My father thinks people made up religions as an excuse to hate each other,' I said.

Hahaha, he said, a bit more manically than the first time.

My father had never come back after he came back as Father Christmas.

I prayed and prayed for his return.

* * *

60

In the summer term, Pink Mother appeared in the hall one morning in her stirrupy scarf, with so much foundation on that it looked like her face wasn't her face.

She planted a lipsticky kiss on my forehead.

'Say goodbye to your mother,' said Mary.

'Goodbye,' I said, feeling that I dare not ask where she was going.

She turned and walked, very carefully, as if she was on a tight rope, through the door, and Mary followed her with the luggage.

When Mary came back inside, I plucked up the courage to ask where she was going, and she said to a lovely place, and I said what kind of lovely place, and she said a lovely place that will make her better.

I went into the downstairs loo, stared at the pink cat's bottom on my forehead in the mirror and rubbed it off with loo paper and water.

The next Saturday, a man arrived on the doorstep. Mary opened the door and he pushed a trolley into the hall. He started to box up my father's books, shoving them in, all messed up and back to front and upside down, with no idea that my father had arranged them in alphabetical order. As I watched, something fell out of a book. The man left the room with the trolley, and I picked up the *something* – a white sealed envelope – which I shoved into the chest-pocket of my denim pinafore. (Pink Mother had, despairingly, surrendered to my preference for baggy clothes without waistbands.)

The man took the modern paintings off the hall wall and swaddled them in bubble wrap.

The next thing I knew, Granny and Grandpa Green arrived.

Granny and Grandpa Green sometimes took us out to lunch at smart restaurants where they liked to complain about the food.

Grandpa Green was a kind of red-purple colour, and looked as if he might go off like a firework at any moment, and when Granny Green spoke, the wattle under her chin wobbled.

Mary made them both a cup of tea, and Grandpa Green told the man with the trolley to remove every single bottle of alcohol from the house.

The man started boxing up all the bottles of sherry and wine with my father's special horse label from Jerez, and I plucked up the courage to ask what exactly he was doing.

Granny Green said, 'Your father wants his things in Spain.'

Mary came in.

I said, 'Is my father never coming back?'

Nobody answered.

I said, 'Will I ever see him again?'

Grandpa Green said, 'That's a question that only your father can answer.'

I ran upstairs and grabbed my diary.

If he doesn't want me, I wrote, *I don't want him. And I shall never try to find him. Simple as that.*

Then Granny Green came in.

'We're going to be staying the night,' she said, rather surprisingly. 'Mary has to go on a special outing tomorrow, so we'll be looking after you.'

Granny Green was holding a jigsaw wrapped in cellophane, which she suggested that we should do together.

So we did.

It was a bit too hard for us but neither of us wanted to admit it.

The next morning, which was Sunday, Granny Green made me breakfast, and Mary walked through the kitchen wearing a navy blue dress
I hadn't seen before, with pink lipstick making her mouth look bigger
than it usually was.

Granny and Grandpa Green took me out to lunch and asked me
lots of detailed questions about the different lessons we did at school,
although their eyes glazed over when I answered.

Granny Green and I ploughed on with the puzzle in the afternoon.

Grandpa Green said, 'You're making heavy weather of this.'

He came over and stared at the puzzle for a while, and then he said,
'You've done all the easy bits,' and went and read his paper.

Mary didn't come home for supper.

I went to bed.

In the morning, Granny Green came into my room, opened the
curtains and told me that Mary was going to get married.

I burst out laughing.

I tried everything I could to stop.

Granny Green said, 'Stop that right away!'

I rushed into the bathroom, but the laughter didn't go away.

I sat on the floor and stuffed a towel in my mouth.

Mary called upstairs that it was time for breakfast, and hearing her
voice set me off again.

I went into the kitchen and told Mary the first joke I could think of, which enabled me to carry on laughing in little spurts as I ate my cereal. She looked at me strangely, but we kept going with our normal morning routines as if she wouldn't soon be prancing around in a bridal gown and sleeping in a double bed with a man.

At registration, I told Bridget that Mary was getting married, and she laughed so much she almost cried, which set me off again.

The laughter burst out of us again in a violent gush while we were singing 'Dear Lord and Father of Mankind' in morning assembly, and we had to write out the lines from the hymn one hundred times – 'Forgive our foolish ways: reclothe us in our rightful mind; in purer lives your service find'.

When I got home, Grandpa Green said Mary was owed lots of days off as she'd never taken a holiday, and this had *implications*, whatever they were.

He had some good news and some bad news to tell me.

'The bad news is that Mary will be leaving,' said Grandpa Green.

That was actually good news.

'And your mother may not be back by then,' said Grandpa Green.

'And we're going on a cruise for our Golden Wedding anniversary,' said Granny Green.

'But the good news . . .' said Grandpa Green.

If bad was good, could good be bad?

'. . . is that Mrs Blume has agreed that you can go and stay with Bridget until your mother comes home.'

This was the best news ever.

All my Christmases had come at once.

I started laughing again.

But for quite different reasons.

I never knew that laughter was so versatile.

I thought it was only for jokes.

I packed for Bridget's house with my heart full of joy.

While folding my denim pinafore, I felt a crumple of envelope, and remembered with a start the *something* that the man with the trolley had dropped, which had entirely slipped my mind because so many dramatic things had happened in such a short time.

I carefully unsealed the envelope and peered inside.

It was a photo.

Of a baby.

A baby who had black hair shaped like a swimming cap and pretty dark eyes.

I stared at the baby .

Stared and stared.

I started to feel something inside me, the same feeling I had when the first chick came out of the egg in Class 1, or when a goldfish flashed up to the surface of the school pond, or when I opened number 24 on my advent calendar.

Except this was a much bigger feeling.

I went into the bathroom and stared at my own face in the special magnifying mirror.

Then I held the photo next to my own face.

I looked at the skin on the baby's arms, and then I looked at the skin on my own arms.

I felt like it really, most probably, even definitely, could be, yes, yes, *me*.

I'd prayed for a baby photo, and God had sent one from heaven in a white envelope.

'Hello,' I said to the most-probably-even-definitely faded me, using the voice Bridget used for Bessie and Bella when they were little.

'Hello-o!'

I went back into my bedroom and stared at the photo under my desk light.

There were two quite old hands holding the baby who was probably, even definitely, me. The face of the person would have been in the photo, but it had been cut off with scissors. All you could see was a grey dress.

The grey person holding me had been beheaded.

Is the beheaded person my real mother? That's what came to me.

I started doing little shallow breaths.

I felt like I might throw up.

Either that, or burst with joy.

Real mothers didn't lie about in bed all day and not pick you up from school.

They didn't disappear without explaining why.

No, real mothers were made to mother you.

That's what their job was.

But why and how had I got separated from my real mother and ended up here in Chelsea with Pink Mother?

There were no photos of me before the age of three and a half.

Was that because Pink Mother didn't get me until I was three and a half?

Did she kidnap me?

Breathe, breathe, breathe.

The beheaded mother and I were in a *patio*, what looked like a proper courtyard from Córdoba, just like the Andalusian *patio* that Rory the gardener had made for us in Chelsea.

Why did my father make a replica patio?

Why did I love the *patio* so much?

The *patio* in the photo definitely wasn't the flowerless courtyard in Jerez with the yellow-ochre walls and the three-tiered fountain with no water in it, and it definitely wasn't the beach house with two hundred palm trees and a swimming pool.

No, this was a dream of a *patio*, with an old wagon wheel up against the wall, and every single white wall covered from top to bottom in brown terracotta pots, and pots lining the stone steps and placed around the edge of an old stone sink, all of them bursting with red geraniums and mauvey-blue hydrangeas with pale green centres – and two hot dusty cats asleep, left and right.

Cats!

Yes, there were cats!

Behind me and the beheaded woman, there was a tall whitey-cream statue of an angel.

I felt as if I was melting inside, and I might go on and on melting until I could be hung out on a branch like those Salvador Dalí clocks we'd been shown in art.

When I arrived on a rainy Sunday afternoon at the Blumes' with my suitcase on wheels, Bridget's mother took me to the corner of the kitchen and she let me sit on her lap in the big armchair.

'The others have all gone out with their dad,' she said. 'They won't be back until later.'

She wrapped her arms around me, and let me sink into the softness of her, and I felt sure that heaven must be full of bosoms exactly like hers. She held me tightly but she didn't say any words.

'What kind of place is my mother in?' I said, wondering if I should tell her that the woman she thought was my mother almost certainly wasn't.

'It's a cross between a hotel and a hospital, with special nurses who know how to help her get better,' she said. 'The sort of nurses who understand bodies and minds and feelings and how they all connect together.'

I burst out crying, though not about the hotel-hospital with special nurses, but because she'd kissed me on my head. That kiss brought all my feelings into the open, which was completely against my principles. And this was the longest, biggest, most tiring cry I'd ever had.

By the time I stopped, it was evening, and I was exhausted.

'We're so happy to have you here with us,' she said.

Gaspy sobs shook my body.

When Mr Blume and the five children got home, I wiped my eyes and slapped my cheeks.

Bridget raced across the kitchen and hugged me so tightly that my feet left the floor.

'Shall we pretend we're starting at boarding school?' she said. 'Like Malory Towers. And we've just arrived. Let's have a look round and find our dormitory. And our tuck boxes.'

We took a Tupperware box each and Bridget opened a kitchen cupboard and we started to put KitKats inside, and Quavers, and powdery strawberry bonbons and those fruit salad chews that pull your teeth out. I kept looking around nervously, expecting somebody to tell us not to do this. But nobody did.

Bridget's mother said, 'I hope you won't find us too bohemian, Eva! And I hope you'll cope with our funny old messy house.'

I opened my mouth, but no words came out.

We went up to Bridget's bedroom, and Bridget showed me my bed, which was covered in an old-fashioned eiderdown and masses of un-matching pillows.

Bridget and I moved the little table and pulled our beds together.

When it was bedtime, Bridget's mother rested the palm of her hand on each of our heads, saying, 'Peace and sleep and happy dreams!'

Liquid joy ran from her palm through my skin.

When she'd left the room, I said to Bridget, 'What's bohemian?'

'It's people who wear harem pants and shoes other people think are ugly,' said Bridget. 'And don't shave their armpits. You know, like my mother.'

I nodded, trying to look knowledgeable.

'Will you shave your armpits?' said Bridget.

This was a question that had never once crossed my mind.

'It's weird the places we get hair,' said Bridget. 'Isn't it?'

'Yes,' I stuttered, feeling very red in my face.

'Have you got any hairs down there yet?' said Bridget, pointing at her crotch.

I shook my head.

'Will you show me if you get one?' she said casually, as if showing people around inside your pants was a normal thing to do.

I didn't want to get our cohabitation off to a bad start, so I said yes in a way that sounded a bit like no.

'Let's make our code word *follicle*!' she said.

I burst out laughing.

I think it was nerves.

I remember limbering up, almost daily, to tell Bridget about *my secret photo*. I was planning to take it out, let her look at it, and then tell her my suspicions that I'd been kidnapped – but I couldn't make myself do it. It was so much easier keeping things inside.

Also, I wanted to find words that were big enough and important enough, because, I suppose, I knew how badly I needed a reaction that was big enough and important enough. Was it that, or was I just terrified of opening up to her? Or scared that she wouldn't believe that I was the baby in the photo? Or scared that I didn't totally believe it myself?

In addition to this massive thing I hadn't told Bridget, I also hadn't told her something else, and that was that I was madly in love with her older brother, Barnaby.

Barnaby was nearly thirteen. He was tall and broad with a mop of dark curls on his head and freckles on his nose and big strong arms which he let me fall into when we were playing the trust game. He wore a gold star, like two upside-down triangles, on a gold chain around his neck. (And we soon spotted that he was getting a load of dark hair in his armpits. This hair made me feel a bit funny. Not funny-haha, like I pretended to Bridget – funny-peculiar.)

I used to dream that one day all the other B children would have to go out for some reason, and Blue Mother would say that Barnaby and I could go into the playroom or the garden, just the two of us.

Just the two of us!

Like the song Pink Mother used to play in the rare evenings that she liked my father.

Anyway, once all the other children had gone out, in this daydream of mine, Barnaby and I would play the trust game, and I would fall into his arms, and instead of dumping me flat on the ground and going on to the next person, there wouldn't be a next person, so somehow we would swivel around, and I couldn't work out the exact physiological mechanics, but we would end up sitting on the sofa or the bench together, with my head in his lap, looking up into his dark eyes, with his gold star hanging over me, like a sign, and he would ask me if I would like to be his girlfriend because he had always been in love with me, ever since the moment he first met me.

This hadn't yet happened after my first week of living with the Blumes.

But Barnaby had said, 'You can call me Barny,' which made it very obvious where we were headed.

My crush on Barnaby practically knocked me over: it was the first blast of hormones, which came a bit early, like an unexpected summer day in March.

When actual summer came, Pink Mother still wasn't better, so Bridget's mother said I could go with them to Lyme Regis, and she took Bridget and me to Miss Selfridge and bought us both a pair of baggy denim dungarees – the nicest things I'd ever owned.

As we headed out of London, we ate sherbet dib dabs and sang along to Abba, and I felt the freest and happiest I'd ever felt in my life.

We stayed in a giant house with a dormitory bedroom. Sometimes when Barnaby was still asleep in the morning, I would look down from my top bunk, and see his gold star glinting under his undone pyjama top, and I'd think he was the most beautiful thing I'd ever seen.

The first two days, we went to Charmouth to find fossils, which was Barnaby's favourite thing on earth.

'What would you most like to find in the sand?' Bridget said to me when we were lying on the beach looking at the clouds. 'I mean, if you could find literally anything at all.'

I took a deep breath and said, 'A mother.'

'What do you mean? A mother?' said Bridget.

She sat up.

I sat up too.

We both talked with our eyes downwards, not looking at each other, fiddling in the sand with our fingers.

Come on, I thought, get started.

'Bridget,' I said. 'I'm not sure the person you think is my mother is my mother.'

'Whose mother do you think she is?' said Bridget.

Now that was a question I hadn't thought of, and it took me slightly off track.

'Maybe no one's,' I said, and that got me on to a possible explanation.

'Maybe,' I said, 'she couldn't have a baby . . .'

'Some women can't,' said Bridget in a dramatic tone of voice.

'So she stole me,' I said back in a dramatic tone of voice.

'Do you really think that?' said Bridget.

Then she nudged my upper arm, and said, 'Are you joking, Eva?'

I shook my head.

'I'm deadly serious,' I said, staring at her.

'Really honestly?'

I nodded.

'Well, why don't you think she's your mother?'

'She looks nothing like me,' I said.

'But don't you look like your father?' said Bridget. 'Kind of Spanishy.'

'Also,' I said. 'You might have thought the photo on Miss Feast's board was me, but it wasn't.'

I thought this was a bit of a showstopper.

'Photo on Miss Feast's board?' she said hazily.

Do happy people have less need to remember the details of their life, I wondered.

'In Entrance Class,' I said. 'We all had to bring in a baby photo.'

'Did we?' said Bridget.

'And I had to bring one of my *dad*,' I said.

'Did you?' said Bridget.

She was starting to annoy me now.

'Also, there are lots of other things,' I said. 'My mother can't seem to remember anything about me. What I was like as a baby. Whether I even liked my pram.'

'Liked your pram?' said Bridget.

'I haven't told you the main thing,' I said, now feeling a bit desperate. 'I have evidence that she isn't my mother. That she stole me from someone else. *Actual evidence.*'

Surely if I showed Bridget the photo of the woman with a cut-off head, and the baby who looked exactly like me (well if not exactly, then definitely quite a bit), she would see for herself what kind of a mystery I was wrapped up in.

But right at the moment that I was about to show her the photo in my pocket, I saw something gold glinting among the pebbles.

I reached down and I picked up a perfect gold-coloured ammonite.

'Look at that!' I said, placing it in the centre of my palm.

Bridget squealed and said, 'Quick! Let's go and show D!'

The dramatic revelatory moment – in all its bigness – had passed, and been surpassed by the tiny gold ammonite, which, I have to admit, was very cool.

Barnaby got all cosy and up close with me because he wanted to have a look at it.

I nearly collapsed.

I zipped the gold ammonite into my pocket with my photo (still unseen by anyone but me) as we headed off to a restaurant called Smugglers, decorated with dried-up starfish and fishing nets, where we over-ate deliciously and got home late.

The next day we went beachcombing on a different beach with our metal detectors, and we didn't find anything, and Bridget and I were never on our own long enough to go back to our conversation.

The next day we went beachcombing again. About five minutes after we arrived, Bridget uncovered a gold crucifix, and everyone got very excited even though it was just a normal modern one and not really worth anything.

I felt angrier and angrier with Bridget, and this was a horrible shock for me, as I thought I would only ever have nice warm thoughts about her. But the fact was this: she knew I had evidence that I'd been stolen when I was a baby, and she didn't care enough to want to see it or ask one single question about it.

I kept a bit of a distance from her, but she came over to me, and her hair was windswept, and her face was freckly and radiant, and she threw her arms around me and said, 'Forever Eva,' as she sometimes did. This was our code for the fact that we were going to be best friends forever.

Oh forever, you are the cruellest trickster of a word.

I didn't know then that time always runs out.

'You're my best-ever sister,' said Bridget, putting her arm around me, and all my angry thoughts started to dissolve in the glow of her love.

'Do you think everyone thinks we're sisters?' I said.

'Hardly!' she said, laughing. 'We're all white as snow.'

'Not the most original simile, Bridge!' I said, trying out a new abbreviated nickname at the same time as a new Blumey jokey tone, which sounded a bit weird on me.

Bridget wasn't offended at all.

'Give it a score,' she said.

'Really only about four out of ten,' I said, in my new teasing voice. 'Being generous.'

Bridget laughed her head off. I loved the way she laughed her head off, all loose and easy-breezy like her mother, and I tried to let go of all my pent-up anger.

I knew if I could be more Blumey, I'd be happier.

'Four out of ten is crap!' said Bridget.

We were both trying out mild swearwords – it made us feel fantastic.

'That's because the simile was crap,' I said.

And saying crap felt as wonderful as the wind blowing over the beach and the sound of Barnaby's voice and the depth of his dark eyes. I felt a curious whoosh inside my heart, which apparently was what you felt when you had sex, Bridget had told me, except not in your heart, but in your vagina.

This was the first I'd heard about this whoosh, and I couldn't really imagine it at all, though Bridget and I had started to talk about sex when we were alone, and it was beginning to feel like something we would want to do at some point. Possibly. I wasn't totally sure.

Barnaby shouted at us, so we stopped hoovering the beach and ran towards him.

He'd found an old-fashioned gold locket on a gold chain.

Mr Blume got a cloth out of his pocket and gave it to Barnaby, and Barnaby sat cross-legged and started to clean it.

'I think this is Victorian,' said Mr Blume, turning it over in his hand and giving it back to Barnaby. 'A little piece of history.'

My face lit up – a little piece of history – how cool!

'Real history?' I said.

'Yes, the owner of this locket was making history simply by being herself,' said Mr Blume.

'Wow!' I said.

These were the sort of amazing things Blumes said: big enormous things.

'It's the same for all of us,' said Mr Blume.

'Is it?' I said. 'I thought kings and queens made history. I've got one of those royal family tree posters with all the dates and everything.'

'No,' said Mr Blume. 'We all have our own family tree, and the branch we're on is the bit of history we're making . . .'

I felt strange.

I was on a branch making my bit of history.

I was going to ask Mr Blume if he was absolutely sure that everyone had a family tree, but Barnaby, to my astonishment said, 'Would you like to open the locket, Eva?'

Lightning flashed.

Thunder rolled.

Barnaby handed me the locket.

Our hands brushed each other's.

Whoosh!

Through my hands and up my arm.

'I love the way everyone has a story,' said Bridget's mother.

I must have a story, I thought.

But I don't know what it is.

I started to prise open the locket, and my fingers were shaking.

'Before you open it, let's guess what the photo is,' said Bridget's mother.

People guessed grandmothers, and babies, a handsome man with a dark moustache, a kitten, a pet rabbit.

Very carefully, I slid my fingernail between the two sides of the locket, and it started to open.

I held up the locket.

There was nothing in it.

Of course there wasn't.

I came from nothing, and I was nothing.

'You have it,' said Barnaby.

He tried to put it round my neck.

But the clasp was broken.

I held it in my sweating palm.

'Will you keep it forever?' said Bridget.

That word again!

I tried to nod in a very matter-of-fact way.

I felt like crying.

'Perhaps you'll put a photograph of your husband in it,' said Bessie.

My husband!

I'd never really imagined myself as someone who would have one of those.

The next morning, we got up in the dark and went to the beach to watch the sunrise.

Bridget's mother hitched up her dress and paddled in the sea.

My heart jolted.

Because she was – exactly – Blue Mother in *The Rainbow Rained Us*, at the edge of the sea, laughing, the wind in her hair and her blue children around her.

Us!

How I loved being *us* – and not me!

I think all only children dream of *us*.

I have a photo of all the Blumes in a long line with their arms around each other, and I still love everything about them: the balanced solidity of their bodies, the way they carry their weight evenly, their feet flat on the ground, ready for anything life might throw at them.

Life was about to throw something big.

We didn't know.

We thought we'd forever climb hills in the sunshine.

We set off with our rucksacks and at the top of the hill we stopped and laid out our rugs and started making our way through the Tupperware boxes of liver pâté sandwiches. Next came brownies, flapjacks, and meringues which were sticky in the middle – and we were allowed to have as many of these as we liked.

Blue Mother covered her head with her crinkly scarf to keep the sun off it, and Mr Blume added some ticks to his butterfly guide and muttered Latin words to himself.

Then Blue Mother took little pots of white chocolate mousse out of her rucksack.

Brownies, flapjacks, meringues *and* white chocolate mousses?

After we'd eaten our mousses, everyone lay down on the rugs and closed their eyes, but I went with Bridget (who I must have forgiven) to sit together on a grassy ledge, looking out at the sea.

Blue Mother came over and nestled between us, dangling her legs over the little drop, like us, and the sun danced on her earrings, which were shaped like swallows, and she put her cheesecloth arms around us, with her silver bangles clinking around her wrists.

'Aren't we lucky?' she said.

We both nodded.

I loved her so much I wanted to cry.

I wanted to tell her how grateful I was.

I wanted to tell her that at night I thanked God (whoever exactly God was) for giving her to me.

I didn't say any of these things, but I felt a piercing agony of happiness spread all over my body, down into my limbs, out to the tips of my fingers and toes.

Tiny boats floated like curled white feathers in the distance.

'I just couldn't be happier at this moment,' she said to us. 'Could you?'

Some days heaven touches earth.

And do we notice it at the time?

Or do we know it later – when heaven is snatched away?

Mr Blume was tidying up the picnic, making a rubbish bag.

He flapped away a wasp.

There's always a wasp.

However good the picnic.

When we got in the minibus to go home, I felt quite distraught. As if whatever I'd had for those two weeks I would never have again. I knew that, whatever it was, it was the nicest and most wonderful thing any person could have.

As we drove home, I kept thinking about Pink Mother.

Perhaps she might be better and I would have to go and live with her in Chelsea again.

Or perhaps she might have died.

A terrible thought jumped into my mind: the thought that I would be pleased.

I tried to get rid of this thought, but it jumped back up and wouldn't leave me alone.

Until Barnaby turned around and said to me, 'I never thought of this before, but if you took the *m* out of our surname, we would be blue, and you would be green!'

'And if you two got married,' said Bessie, 'you could be called the Blue-Greens!'

I could feel myself starting to sweat.

Everyone else laughed at the thought of Barnaby and me being called the Blue-Greens but I just tried to keep breathing.

'I want to be called Bella Blue!' said Bella, nudging Bessie.

'I want to be called Bessie Blue!' said Bessie.

Mr Blume chuckled as he drove, taking his left hand off the steering wheel to drink some water, so that he was driving with only his right, looking in the rear-view mirror to join in the conversation.

'Shall we change our name, D?' said Barnaby.

'We can if you like!' said Mr Blume, driving quickly and then slowly, like he always did. 'Why not?'

This *why not* was another reason I loved the Blumes so much.

It's so easy to say *why,* and so much better to say *why not.*

They did end up changing their name, but for a totally different reason, a reason that I can't bear to think about.

But anyhow.

We'll get there.

You can't change the truth of life, whether you're living it backwards or forwards.

On our journey home from Lyme Regis, a big white car, coming in the opposite direction, tried to overtake. I remember it heading towards us just as the car behind us pulled out.

Bridget's mother was in the passenger seat shrieking – and there was a strange fragment of a second when I knew that those overtaking cars were going to meet in the middle. Mr Blume's water sprayed everywhere as he manoeuvred into the side of the road with one hand. And the black overtaking-car crashed into the white overtaking-car, and then another car appeared from somewhere, and there was an almighty smash, and we all ended up facing in wrong directions.

'I hope no one died,' said Bridget's mother on our way home in the minibus-taxi, and I thought of those cars buckled up and scattered about, possibly with dead people inside them, dead people who had been alive seconds before. I wondered if cars should ever have been invented when they clearly weren't safe, and I saw, in a way I hadn't seen before, how close dying was to living.

I would see this again and again, as everyone does, and especially in eight years' time, the tragic summer of my A level results.

Why doesn't everyone get more worked up about the fact that we're all going to die, I wondered on the way home from Lyme Regis after the car accident. Adults didn't seem to mention death at all.

I now realise that the reason adults don't mention death is because they *are* worked up about it, not because they're not. It's not too small to mention – it's too big.

Now I'm an adult.

And death is too big for me.

When we arrived at the Blumes' house, Pink Mother didn't seem to have died. She'd sent us a letter wishing us a happy holiday. There was a mountain of post on the mat, which we all walked over, and which Mr Blume gathered up. He sat at the dining room table ripping envelopes open with a silver knife and scrunching them up and hurling them in the bin.

I stayed as close as I could to Bridget's mother because I was feeling wobbly from the car crash, and she stilled and steadied me, simply by existing, which is what happens with the right sort of mother.

I liked to breathe in the lavender smell of her skin and fiddle with her clinking bangles, and she'd often give my shoulder a quick squeeze, or my arm a stroke, or she'd run her fingers through my hair – and this would make me feel like silk blowing in a warm breeze.

But she didn't do any of those things on the day we got back from Lyme Regis.

She kept going in and out of the downstairs loo.

Mr Blume shouted, 'I heard from the Family Tree people!'

We all rushed into the dining room.

Except her.

The Family Tree people – these were the people who, if I asked, could possibly find my branch, and on my branch, presumably they could find the first three and a half years of my life.

'Where's M?' said Mr Blume.

I found her lying on the sofa with her arms wrapped around her chest.

It made me think of Pink Mother on the chaise longue.

She closed her eyes.

'Are you feeling ill?' I said, stroking the smooth skin of her upper arm.

'Don't look so worried,' she said.

'I don't like you lying down,' I said anxiously.

'I feel a bit funny,' she said. 'I think I'm just a bit car-sick. Or maybe it's delayed shock.'

'Mr Blume has heard from the Family Tree people!' I said. 'So why don't you get up?'

It was such a relief to see her standing up again, but I noticed that she looked extra-pale.

We went into the dining room together, with her arm around me.

'Look at that!' said Mr Blume. 'You and me, Eva!'

I couldn't think what he was about to say about him and me.

'All the way back in the Middle Ages . . .' he said.

'Yes?' said Bridget's mother, looking faraway (she never looked faraway, she was always right here, alert and attentive with alive sparkly eyes). 'What happened in the Middle Ages?'

'. . . my ancestors lived in Spain!' said Mr Blume. 'They were Sephardi Jews. In the city of Córdoba!'

'Córdoba!' I shouted.

The word rose and fell and shimmered.

'Is that where you're from?' said Barnaby.

'Yes!' I said. 'Or maybe. It could be there. Or Jerez. Or Alvera.'

I was stammering.

'It's just I lost the first three and a half years,' I said.

'Of what?'

'Of my life.'

Bridget rearranged her bedside table with all the things she'd brought back from our holiday, so I copied her, resting the gold ammonite and the gold locket on the base of my bedside lamp. Then we got into bed.

'Will your mother mind you having the crucifix by your bed?' I said to Bridget. 'When it's not your religion?'

She shook her head.

'I wish we knew what God meant,' I said. 'Like when you say horse. It doesn't matter where you are in the world, it's still got a mane and a tail.'

Bridget looked at me the way she did when I got too philosophical. But then, to my surprise, she took a deep breath and closed her eyes, and I could tell she was going to join in. It was obvious that Bridget had changed me in multiple ways, but this was one of the moments I realised I'd changed her a tiny bit too. I liked that thought.

'What do you think would be the ideal god?' said Bridget, putting her head on her pillow, her eyes still closed.

I lay thinking.

It was a difficult question.

I thought some more.

'Like a god-version of your mother,' I said. 'With her arms around us, at the top of the hill, looking out over the valley to the sea. That would be like a hundred times better than the old man pointing at Adam on the ceiling of the Sistine Chapel. You know, the one with his willy flopping on his thigh. Adam's, I mean.'

Although we normally found willies to be the funniest things on earth, Bridget didn't laugh, or say anything.

I stared at the ammonite, and I thought that maybe this was the moment.

I breathed deeply, and I said: 'I can't believe you don't want to ask me about the fact that I-was-almost-certainly-kidnapped-when-I-was-a-baby.'

It all came out in one breath.

Then I heard Bridget's heavy asleep-breathing.

She often fell asleep about one second after lying down.

I lay awake, with my heart racing, wondering if God was deliberately preventing me from showing Bridget the photo and also worrying about the way her mother had been lying on the sofa, with a faraway look in her pale face and her arms around her chest.

I wished and wished that we could be back in Lyme Regis with Barnaby's beautiful face beneath me and no worries buzzing in my head.

I lay worrying so long that I needed a wee.

I walked along the landing in the quiet dark house.

The door to Bridget's parents' bedroom was open, as it often was, and the light was on. When I got nearer, I could see Bridget's mother standing wearing her harem pants with no top on and Bridget's father kneading her large left breast with his right hand, like it was a lump of pastry.

Her other breast hung down: the pale pink circular areola looked like the sucker-things we put the tea-towels in. Breasts were so fascinating to me before I had proper ones of my own. (They still are a bit, their fruity variety: melons, mangoes, even curling-up ones like bananas. My own, more like plums.)

She kept saying, 'There, yes there!'

She was letting Mr Blume's hairy hands actually squeeze her melony breast, and she was saying, 'Not again.'

I thought I was going to throw up.

I stood very still and heard Mr Blume tell her that she was *invincible.*

I tiptoed back to the bedroom.

Bridget was fast asleep.

I switched on my torch and I looked around wondering if there was anything I could wee in because I was never ever – in my life – going out onto the landing again.

I opted for the pot with the droopy plant in, and I prayed Bridget wouldn't wake up while I was weeing. She didn't.

The next morning, I looked up invincible in the dictionary and was relieved to discover that Bridget's mother was *too powerful to be defeated or overcome.*

I didn't tell Bridget that her father had been squeezing her mother's breast.

Or that I'd wee'd in the pot plant.

In fact, I tried really hard to erase both images from my mind.

Bridget and I were now considered old enough and responsible enough to take our metal detectors and a picnic right over Battersea Bridge to where there was a stretch of grey beach at low tide. There, in a heady state of summer freedom, we found treasure and spotted birds (herons and greylag geese and cormorants) and ate ice creams sitting on the wall.

It was just Bridget and me, and long languid time, fluid and never-ending.

Until it ended, abruptly, when Bridget's mother sat down on the kitchen armchair and pulled me onto her lap.

'I've got some wonderful news for you,' she said. 'I'm going to whisper it inside your ear.'

I knew.

Before she'd whispered.

'Your mother's come home!'

The tears came bursting out of my eyes and falling into my mouth.

'It'll be lovely to see your house again,' she said, still holding me, and making my scalp tingle with her fingertips. 'All those familiar things you haven't thought about.'

'There's nothing familiar,' I said. 'It was emptied out for a re-design.'

'Well, that's exciting,' she said.

'I don't want to leave you,' I said.

'I think it's best for children to live with their mothers,' she said, sounding a bit doubtful. 'But some mothers find life easier than others.'

'Do you mean that my one doesn't find life easy?' I said, and as I said *my one*, I nearly told her that my alleged mother, in fact, wasn't my one. But I didn't.

She nodded, and said, 'It's not her fault, Eva. I know that's hard for you to understand.'

Then she said, 'You can come and see us anytime.'

Which I knew wasn't true because children have to do what their parents tell them.

I knew for sure that Pink Mother wouldn't let me go over Battersea Bridge for mudlarking and picnics any more, and the thought of those days being over hurt me inside my chest.

When I went to say goodbye to Mr Blume, he was in his study, where he kept playing the same piece of music again and again.

'You must really like this music,' I said.

'It's called *Quartet for the End of Time*,' he said. 'Messiaen composed it when he was a prisoner in a concentration camp in the Second World War. He'd found some old instruments and four people who could play them.'

'Did they actually have a concert?' I said. 'In a concentration camp?'

'Yes,' he said. 'The prisoners and the guards together. In the snow.'

'Didn't the music melt the guards' hearts?' I said.

'No,' he said. 'Human beings aren't as good as they imagine themselves to be.'

'We've learnt about concentration camps at school,' I said. 'And I felt really sick about all the Jews who died.'

Mr Blume nodded.

'Sometimes I wonder why God doesn't give up on humans,' I said.

Mr Blume stared out of the window at Bessie and Bella, who were having a space hopper race.

The Quartet for the End of Time went on playing – it was a bit stoppy-starty for my liking.

'I guess there are moments when we'd all like to climb out of time,' said Mr Blume.

'Like double maths!' I said, to try to cheer things up a bit, but he didn't answer.

'Anyway,' I said. 'I wanted to say thank you very much for having me.'

My eyes filled with tears, so I turned around and walked out.

Pink Mother was on the doorstep. She'd had a pageboy haircut, and she was wearing a tailored cream dress with roses growing up from the hemline, with a matching cream handbag and shoes, as if she was off to a garden party at Buckingham Palace.

'Come on in,' said Bridget's mother, attempting to embrace my not very embraceable mother.

She pushed me forward, and I crashed into Pink Mother, who lightly grazed my shoulder blades. When she sat down on the old sofa, amongst its piles of Indian cushions, she looked like a stiff kind of doll. She kept piling cushions behind her back to help her sit up straight, whereas nobody ever sat up straight on that sofa.

'Come and sit with your mother,' said Bridget's mother.

I nested inside a pile of cushions at the other end of the sofa from Pink Mother, who had too much make-up on.

'I can't thank you enough,' said Pink Mother.

'It's been a total pleasure,' said Bridget's mother. 'Your daughter is an absolute gem, and we all adore her.'

Pink Mother did a very strange smile.

I noticed that she'd sprayed her hair totally stiff so that it moved in one piece like a helmet.

I could hear Barnaby kicking his football against the wall at the end of the garden, and I thought, I never did call him Barny, and we never were left on our own so that he could hold me in his arms with his star hanging over me like a sign.

'Do you want to say goodbye to Barny?' said Bridget's mother, opening the glass doors.

I never ever want to say goodbye to Barny, I thought.

'Eva's going,' she shouted into the garden.

Barnaby turned around.

'Bye,' he said, just bye, and that was it, but then again, I thought, true love can make you a bit tongue-tied, especially when there are adults about.

Pink Mother took my black case on wheels and dragged it along the hall.

When Bridget came downstairs, she was crying, and seeing her cry made me cry too. I saw Pink Mother look up and down the whole of Bridget's body and I knew exactly what she was thinking.

'I'll miss you,' said Bridget.

'I'll see you at school – not tomorrow but the next day,' I said. 'Class 6!'

'This is for you,' said Bridget, and she handed me something wrapped in newspaper and fastened with one of her hair ties.

Pink Mother showed me around our house as if I was a visitor.

She felt, as I noted later in my Quest Book, like a stranger.

'Where did all these things come from?' I said in a not very kind voice. 'Have you been travelling around the world buying weird things? I thought you were ill.'

'I was ill,' said Pink Mother. 'As I think you know very well.'

'Well, who got us all this stuff then?'

'I employed a stylist called Lorraine,' she said.

'Quiche Lorraine?' I said.

'Don't be rude,' she said.

'Quiche Lorraine likes putting things in threes,' I said.

'Doesn't it all look lovely?' she said.

I took a smooth cream pebble from its arrangement of three, and I made a four on the other side of the cabinet, leaving a candle-stick and a wooden horse baring its teeth, and I fixed my eyes on Pink Mother.

She breathed in a strange way.

'Don't start,' she said, moving the pebble back to the candlestick and the angry wooden horse, and then laying her palm flat against her chest.

We stared at each other like we were two dogs in the park.

'Why don't you have any photos of your wedding?' I said, looking at all the empty un-Blumey windowsills. 'Did the thieves steal those too?'

She raised her hand to her cheek.

She blinked.

I'd hurt her.

More than I'd meant to.

I didn't know why at the time.

'Come downstairs and meet Jean,' she said.

Jean seemed to be our new housekeeper-nanny.

My mother sat down and fanned her face with a magazine.

Jean had a pale face, with beady eyes and a small nose, which she twitched like a rabbit when she felt her glasses slipping down. She was a little plump, and wore a white apron over a floral skirt.

She said, in a very calm, quiet voice, 'I made you your favourite: macaroni cheese.'

Pink Mother sat down at our new shiny table with a glass of water, and took small sips while I ate the macaroni cheese. I swallowed it in big creamy lumps looking at Jean's brown-and-grey hair, which was drawn into a low ponytail, reaching all the way to her bottom.

'It was a good thing for me that Beatrice Blume got ill,' said Pink Mother.

'What kind of ill?' I said, holding my breath, dreading the answer.

'Oh, I didn't know you didn't know,' said Pink Mother, blushing.

I could feel the macaroni sliding down my throat like snails as I thought of Mr Blume holding her breast in his hand.

'What I meant was that hearing she was ill gave me the impetus I needed to get better. So I could come and look after you.'

'Did Mr Blume ring you up then?' I said.

She nodded.

'Pineapple upside-down cake!' said Jean quietly.

'Is she going to die?' I said.

'She has breast cancer,' said Pink Mother.

I froze.

The great cancerous bird of prey had swooped down and chosen the person I loved most in the world. She was hanging like a blue ragdoll in the bird's beak.

I could see her with the wind in her hair at the edge of the sea, and I could feel her lavender arms around us as we looked out to the feather-yachts, and she would always and forever be beautiful Blue Mother, come to life and stepping out of the pages of *The Rainbow Rained Us*.

'Did you just say it was a good thing Bridget's mother got ill?' I said.

Pink Mother was blushing.

'Well, I didn't mean—'

I didn't wait to hear what she didn't mean.

I ran upstairs to my bedroom.

I got under my new cold shiny sheets and went down to the very end of the bed.

I started shaking all over my body.

It got darker and darker.

Pink Mother came up the stairs, and into my bedroom.

'Please will you come out of those sheets and say good night nicely?' I heard her say.

I didn't move.

She sat down on the bed.

I felt trapped and breathless under the tucked-in sheet.

'I told myself I was getting better for you,' she said. 'I tried so hard for you, Eva.'

I felt bad.

I still didn't move.

The door slammed.

When I was sure she'd gone, I slid up the bed.

I grabbed Bridget's present.

She'd written I LOVE YOU in different coloured pen all over the newspaper wrapping. I took off the hair elastic and, underneath the newspaper, there was a layer of tissue. I ripped apart the tissue and there was the gold crucifix she'd found on the beach.

There was also a card which Bridget had stuck stars onto.

Inside, she'd written: *It will be so empty in my bedroom tonight. You are the best friend I will ever have. I love you as big as the sea. (?/ 10)*

Although it was grammatically incorrect, I still decided to give her 9.5 for her simile because of the lovely warming effect it had on me.

I found a tiny piece of card also wrapped in tissue.

It said: Follicle.

Bridget had hairs!

I immediately pulled down my pants.

Nothing there.

I got up and looked at my armpits in the mirror.

Nothing there.

I put the gold crucifix on my new shiny bedside table, and I briefly prayed for the miraculous onset of puberty. Then I decided God probably didn't want to be bothered with that, so I kneeled down and put my hands together and said, 'If Blue Mother dies from this illness, you must make her come back to life like you did! Do you hear me, Jesus? Three days – like you – is the absolute maximum for her to be dead.'

How did God hear so many different voices all at once, I wondered.

He must have amazing ears, I thought.

And be very good at languages.

And also feel like he's losing his mind.

When I saw Bridget at school, it felt weird.

'Hello,' I said, in my bright new uniform.

'Hello,' she said, in her second-hand uniform, with the button missing on the dress.

When I thought about the note saying *follicle*, I couldn't think how to bring it up.

In fact, I couldn't think of anything at all to say to her.

Her mother had cancer – and she didn't know, and I did.

No words came out of my mouth.

'Did you get my card?' said Bridget.

I blushed.

'Really really?' I said.

'Really really,' she said. 'I showed my mum.'

'That's good,' I said.

'Was it nice to be back with your mum?' she said. 'Despite . . .'

'No, not really,' I said.

'Do you still think she isn't your mother?' she said. 'I never found the right moment to ask you.'

I was about to answer when the bell went.

Bridget and I didn't see each other much that afternoon because we were in different art and drama groups.

That evening, I remember taking my clothes off and examining my armpits and inside my pants right up close to the mirror. I didn't want Bridget to go racing ahead of me, when we'd agreed to do everything together at the same time in the same way forever. There were no hairs.

I sat at my desk staring at my homework list.

First, a presentation called 'A Memorable Moment from the Summer'.

I decided to phone Bridget to ask her whether we should discuss what we were planning to say, in case we both picked the same memorable moment. Really, I wanted to go back to the conversation about Pink Mother not being my mother, which we still hadn't had.

'What are you going to do for your memorable moment?' I said.

'Not last night but the night before,' Bridget answered.

I froze.

It was one of only two nights I hadn't been with her.

'Why? What happened?' I said. 'What was so good about it?'

'D made a campfire in the garden,' said Bridget. 'And we all went round and said the thing we loved most about M. And there was a shooting star. An actual shooting star. And D said don't forget this moment. Then he put up our big tent and we all slept in it together, like a family of mice.'

Before I could stop myself, I said, 'Did you have the campfire to celebrate that you'd got rid of me?'

'What do you mean?' said Bridget.

I turned flaming hot because, in a flash, I realised why D had made a campfire, why he'd made them say how wonderful their mother was, why they'd slept together in the tent.

'I'm sorry, Bridge,' I said.

'It was just the first thing I thought of when Mrs Williams said a memorable moment. Because D said don't forget this,' said Bridget.

'I'm really sorry,' I said. 'Forget I ever said it . . .'

Then there was a silence that went on a bit too long.

'What are you going to write about?' said Bridget.

'I'm not sure,' I said, stuttering.

The memory I wanted to choose was when Bridget and I were sitting on top of the hill and her mother put her arms around our shoulders. But I felt that wouldn't be right because, however much I wished she was, she wasn't my mother, and Bridget might find it odd that it had meant so much to me. Also, I couldn't bear to think about her right now.

'I could do something about metal-detecting,' I said, trying to sound casual.

'The others will think that's weird,' said Bridget.

'Or fossil-hunting,' I said.

'They'll think that's weird too.'

'So are you saying I mustn't mention either of them?'

'Sorry, Eva,' she said. 'M's calling me for supper.'

I wanted to rewind and start again.

I shoved my feelings deep inside me as usual, and I prepared a pathetic presentation about going on a picnic up a hill with some family friends.

When I finished, Mrs Williams said, 'Is that the end?'

One day Bridget wasn't at school, and when she came back, something had changed in her face.

I knew she knew, and I knew I mustn't let on that I knew too.

'Hello,' I said, wondering if we normally said hello in the morning or usually went straight into a conversation.

'Hello,' she said back.

'Are you OK?' I said.

'Yes.'

'Good.'

'Were you ill?' I said.

She didn't answer.

'We had a family emergency,' she said, like she'd been rehearsing.

I am part of your family, I thought, and I want to be part of any emergency you will ever have in the whole of your life.

'I can't talk about it,' she said in a very cold voice.

'OK,' I said, feeling like I might start crying.

'My mum's started painting again,' said Bridget.

'Why did she stop?' I said.

'She got too busy being a mother.'

'Isn't she still busy being a mother?' I said.

Bridget shrugged.

'She's going to do a painting for each one of us,' said Bridget.

I assumed that I wasn't part of *us* – no I wasn't, I knew I wasn't.
I breathed deeply and I gritted my teeth so that my jaw hurt.
'Also,' said Bridget, 'did you hear about the ducks?'
'What ducks?'
'There was this massive load of rubber bath ducks being transported
on a ship, and they all fell off . . .'
I nodded.
'And now they are floating all around the oceans.'
This was quite a random thing to say.
'I just love the thought of it,' said Bridget, with a funny little yelp
of laughter, which started and stopped very suddenly. 'They're going
to start landing on beaches in all different parts of the world.'
'Do you remember our bath-time duck stories?' I said.
'I wish it was then,' said Bridget.

Bridget said nothing at all about her mother's cancer.

For days.

For a whole week, then two weeks, then three.

Then, in the minibus, on the way to swimming, she said, 'My mother has Stage 4 breast cancer.'

I grabbed her hand.

I hoped there were 10 stages – I thought 10 was the round sort of number people normally used for things.

'There are medical advances all the time,' she said.

I tried to think what to say.

'Do you remember what D said about the wasp?' I said.

When I said D, it was as if she exploded.

The PE teacher said that Bridget and I didn't have to go to the swimming lesson, and we sat and cried together on a slatted bench in the changing rooms. Even though I hated crying, I couldn't stop myself.

'You don't have to be polite to me just because I have cancer,' Blue Mother said to me when I went round after school.

Then: 'You remember your mother got herself well again for you. Well, I'm going to do the same . . .'

For me?

'. . . for my lot,' she said.

Blue Mother, darling Blue Mother of the clinking bangles and the smooth skin, of the shoulder-squeezes and the tingly scalp-rubs, didn't get better. She got worse.

She lost her energy, and lay rag-dolled on the sofa, where we joined her, arranging ourselves into shapes which fitted into her, a litter of overgrown puppies, willing her to reinflate.

She didn't.

She listened to our stories, and took a deep breath to answer, to smile, to sparkle a second of brightness into her fading eyes.

We all felt like crying all the time when we were with her.

But we knew we mustn't.

She probably felt like crying too, knowing how much we needed her.

I say *we*.

But I was careful to remember it was really *they*.

I was careful to defer to them, to keep my distance on the sofa.

She, the most naturally brilliant mother, could no longer mother.

She could guarantee them nothing.

And, when you caught her off guard, you could see how much this hurt her.

She went in and out of hospital.

The chemotherapy ate her beautiful dark wavy hair.

She found it hard to breathe.

Bridget went to visit her in hospital and she literally froze when she saw her, so Mr Blume had to carry her out, her body stiff and seized up, and after that she refused to go back, not to the hospital or even the doctor's surgery to get her own verruca looked at. And she wouldn't talk about this, not even to me.

When Blue Mother came home from hospital, Mr Blume brought her bed into the sitting room.

'We must be big and hopeful,' she sometimes said, and she flexed her arm like Popeye, with a little giggle.

But her giggle was full of tears.

The cancer had broken through her membranes and made a huge lump under her armpit and in her lung.

When I saw her staring out of the garden doors, I could tell that she wasn't seeing the bald lawn or the cricket stumps. No, she was looking way beyond, to a mirage of the future, to her children's weddings, to her Blumey grandchildren.

Looking at her was painful.

I can't imagine how painful it was for Mr Blume.

And the children.

Because all the air was coming out of her, and her breathing was laboured, and she was shrinking, and she tried to hide herself under jewelled scarves because she didn't want to hurt us by being how she was.

Her eyes said I am sorry for looking like this.

For being like this.

I tried to think of ways to talk to Bridget.

'It must be so hard,' I said nervously.

'It's OK,' she said.

'Can I do anything?' I said.

'No, not really,' she said. 'She'll be better soon.'

Did she think that?

If so, I didn't want to contradict her.

Bridget didn't cry again with me after the day in the swimming pool changing rooms.

She started eating more than she'd ever eaten before in her life.

She was either very quiet or very loud, and this made me nervous, not knowing what to expect. She was like a fire alarm that might go off at any time. She forgot to give me a present on my eleventh birthday, and although I understood, it hurt me. Jean took me to the cinema, and out for pizza, and Pink Mother gave me a hard pink birthday cake, which I took into school in slices wrapped in rose napkins. Bridget ate the cake but still didn't give me a birthday present.

Mrs Williams did a Form Time on healthy eating as part of her excruciating puberty series, and we all tried not to look at Bridget.

My legs were getting so hairy that I was limbering up to ask my mother if I could shave them. When I did, a beautician appeared in the basement, unfolded a stretcher-cum-trolley and asked me to climb onto it, and she started slathering hot wax onto my legs and peeling it off, successfully ripping out every hair, one at a time, from its roots, but also relieving me of one layer of my own skin.

I lay back, panting, and she put cream on my legs and started rubbing it in.

In the middle of the rubbing, the phone rang.

Pink Mother picked it up outside the door.

'Oh dear,' she said. 'Oh dear.'

Gap.

'Yes, I will.'

Gap.

'I am so sorry,' she said.

She came in.

The woman stopped rubbing.

'Eva,' said Pink Mother, 'I am very sorry to tell you that Bridget's mother has died.'

I felt a massive wind blow through my body, and I had this strange feeling that all of me had been blown out of myself and was flying around the room like debris caught in a tornado.

I was an outline.

Drawn in pen.

Still lying on my stretcher-cum-trolley, with my desecrated outlined felt-tip legs.

I couldn't move.

I couldn't breathe.

I couldn't imagine a world in which Blue Mother didn't exist.

I couldn't imagine that people who were alive really did die.

It seemed impossible.

We prepare for everything, thinking carefully ahead as we put things in our suitcase for a holiday, for example.

But we cannot pack for death.

I leapt off the trolley and ran up the stairs, and up the other stairs, retching with pain.

I ran into my room, and I picked up the gold crucifix.

'Come back!' I cried, and shrieked, and begged on my knees. 'Resurrect like Jesus Christ!'

I bent over so that my forehead touched the carpet, and the carpet smelled horrible, and I was sitting on top of the hill with her blue cheesecloth arm around me. I beat the carpet with my fists.

'No no no no no!' I screamed.

'Come back!' I screamed.

'Don't leave me!' I screamed.

Then I ran out of breath and slumped against the bed.

'Two more days, God!' I whispered. 'I'm trusting you on this one!'

'One more day, God!' I whispered.

But Blue Mother didn't resurrect like Jesus Christ after three days, and I was destroyed.

Pink Mother didn't let me go to her funeral, so I stayed off school, curled in a ball under the sheets at the foot of my bed, like a woodlouse.

The next day, Mrs Williams leant the painting Bridget's mother had given her against the wall of our classroom because, apparently, this was what she wanted.

All the Populars gathered around Bridget, and didn't leave her alone all day.

I couldn't get anywhere near her.

I sat and stared at the painting – the churned-up sea on a windy day.

Bridget was still performing slightly hyperactively for the Populars.

I couldn't believe she didn't look sadder.

I couldn't believe that she didn't want me, and not them.

I stared at the painting, at the misty shore, right in the distance.

If you looked carefully, you could see a tiny yellow bath duck and a tiny green frog – like the ones we used for our bath-time stories – which were sitting all perky and bright on a gold nest.

'May I be excused?' I said.

I ran down the corridor and exploded with pain in the locked loo cubicle, retching and gasping and thinking that I loved her more than anyone, more than even her own children.

A few days after the funeral, there was a knock on the door.

'Don't open it!' shrieked Pink Mother. 'Let me check the camera!'

'It's Mr Blume,' I said, opening the door. 'I saw him through the window.'

Mr Blume's hair looked like he'd had an electric shock, and his shirt was crumpled and had come out of his trousers on one side. He was holding a big thin rectangle, almost as tall as him, wrapped in brown paper.

I wondered – could it be a picture for me?

No, stop it, I said to myself, don't hope, hoping is bad, it ends in tears.

Pink Mother stared at me, and went into the kitchen.

Mr Blume leant the long thin package against the hall wall and opened his arms.

I fell into them.

Then I tried to pull myself together, and took a step backwards.

'Come in here,' I said to him. 'This was my father's study.'

He leant the package against the wall again, and he sat down on the leather Chesterfield armchair.

He looked around him as if he'd never been in a room before.

'It must be awful for you,' I said. 'I know how much you loved her.'

I felt as if Blue Mother would have wanted me to be very open and honest about my feelings as she truly believed in openness and honesty, even if I found it hard. But perhaps I was a bit too open and honest, because tears started to gather at the corner of his eyes.

'It's awful for everyone,' he said, trying to be brave, picking up a gold shell ornament and stroking it.

'It's worse for you,' I said.

I remember him saying something about the special love between them, which was always there, from the moment they met right to the last moment of her life, and what a blessing that had been for him.

'Was it love at first sight?' I asked.

'Oh yes!' he said, and he tried to smile.

'What does that actually feel like?'

'It's like a chemical reaction!' he said.

I tried to smile back at him.

'The energy in the universe isn't held inside particles like scientists always thought,' said Mr Blume. 'It's held *between them.*'

I nodded.

'Love also has to be *between,*' he said. 'Do you see?'

He was smiling, though one tear was rolling down his cheek, and I told him that he looked like one of those days when it's sunny and rainy at the same time, and if he wasn't careful, he might accidentally make a rainbow. Then I felt like an idiot.

'Love and grief, joy and pain,' he said. 'They're very close together. Or perhaps sometimes they're not even different things.'

He asked me if I'd ever felt a piercing joy, a painful joy. And I remembered the day we went for a picnic, when Blue Mother was sitting between Bridget and me with her arms around us as we looked out to the huge sea, and the boats floating liked curled feathers.

I told him that in Lyme Regis I'd felt so happy it hurt.

Pink Mother came in.

She didn't mention Mr Blume's loss at all.

She simply said, 'Would you like a cup of tea?'

'Oh, thank you,' said Mr Blume.

'Milk and sugar?' she said.

And she went out.

'I brought you something, Eva,' said Mr Blume. 'It's something Aunty M painted for you.'

Pink Mother brought Mr Blume's tea in a cup whose handle was so small that he couldn't fit any of his fingers through it. She went out again.

'She painted one for me?' I stuttered.

'She really loved you very much,' he said. 'As if you were one of her own.'

I exploded.

I was drowning in my own tears.

I was part of her lot!

I had *a lot.*

'Why don't you open the parcel?' said Mr Blume.

He lay it flat on the floor, and I started to pull off the brown paper with my shaking hands.

It was a tall rectangular piece of metal.

And on it was a painting.

Of a girl.

Who was me.

With my actual face and long dark hair.

And she was also pretty, this girl.

She/I was sitting on a little wood-and-wicker chair, with a terracotta pot at her feet, with red geraniums in it, their petals dashed with dew or drops of rain.

The background of the painting was a grey-green colour, with about twelve terracotta pots on the wall, full of red and white geraniums.

'She was going to paint more pots,' said Mr Blume. 'All over the walls. You can see it's not finished. She ran out of strength. I never thought she would. You just can't imagine it will ever happen.'

'Did you like the painting?' said Bridget breezily the next day at school, acting weirdly fine, as she had consistently since her mother died.

Before I could answer, she headed to Mrs Williams' desk to hand in her homework.

'Are you OK with it?' I said when she came back to her desk.

'Why wouldn't I be?' she said, frowning.

'I thought maybe you wouldn't want me to have one,' I said. 'After all, I'm not her daughter.'

Bridget blushed, and the skin on her face trembled.

'By the way,' I said. 'Major follicle. It never seemed the right moment to say.'

Then it happened.

Bridget collapsed.

Tears seemed to be bursting not only through her eyes but through her skin.

Mrs Williams said we should go and have a walk together in the school grounds, and we could be as long as we liked. We walked across the grass, holding hands, and Bridget sobbed and shook, and I started crying too. We sat next to the pond where we liked to spot goldfish, and we put our arms around each other like my two koala bears that velcroed together, and I could feel the soft flesh she'd built up around her pain.

Bridget said, 'I'm so sorry but I didn't want you to have the painting!'

It was almost a relief to hear her say what I already knew.

'It was because you were so pretty in it,' she sobbed. 'And I'm not even in my one.'

'Oh no,' I said, because it was all I could manage. 'I'm so sorry.'

'It's not your fault,' she said. 'But all I got was a duck and a frog.'

'It's not her fault either,' I said, because I couldn't bear Bridget to be angry with her mother, now that she was dead and would be dead forever, which might mean Bridget would be angry with her forever, which would be too sad for me to bear.

As if she was reading my mind, Bridget said, 'I hate feeling angry with her. I've never felt angry with her before. And this is the worst possible moment.'

We fell into each other, so that we could feel each other's hearts beating, and we both knew that there was nothing we could say that would help, so we just let ourselves cry. After a while I said that I would never ever leave her or stop loving her, and that we would definitely go to whichever secondary school we both got into.

'There's one thing I'm dreading about going to secondary school,' said Bridget, between sobs. 'Do you think people will think of me as the fat girl?'

'You will always be beautiful to me,' I said.

'I miss her so much,' she said, and she tried to swallow her sobs. 'So much, Eva, that it actually hurts, you know, physically.'

I nodded.

'Sometimes I wake up in the morning and, for a millionth of a second, it feels like she's still alive.'

I held her hand and squeezed it, and when she could speak, Bridget said, 'It's just knowing I can never have another conversation with her.'

Now I couldn't breathe.

I wanted to tell her how much I missed Blue Mother too, but I knew it was her grief that mattered today. I also desperately wanted to tell her about the photo of the angel and the beheaded mother which I'd never managed to show her — but I knew it was her grief that mattered today.

'D looks so lost,' said Bridget, swallowing.

'He loved her so much,' I said. 'That should be a comfort.'

'It isn't,' said Bridget. 'If you have love and lose it, it's too terrible. It's not worth it.'

'Not having love is terrible too,' I said.

I wanted to say that you don't grieve in the same way for love you've never had, but it still feels like a punch in the stomach. I wanted to say that you don't get any sympathy cards for the love you've never had, however much it hurts.

'I don't think M would recognise D,' said Bridget, holding both my hands with both her hands. 'It's like he's a different person already.'

There *was* something different about Mr Blume.

He looked smaller.

As if Blue Mother had taken some of him with her.

I wrote a thank you card for the painting to Mr Blume because, once people are dead, you can't write to them. I also wrote a special letter to Bridget and a different one to each of the Blume children, thanking them for letting me be part of that last wonderful summer, the best summer of my life. I said I didn't know if I would ever feel that happy again.

Barnaby wrote back to say, on a piece of paper pulled out of a small spiral notebook, that this was what he felt too. And he also put xx at the end. I stared at the xx for minutes on end.

Whenever I was at a loose end, I stared at the xx.

And I was often at a loose end.

He wishes he could kiss you, I told myself.

It's all he thinks about.

Night and day.

Kissing you.

It's just there hasn't been the right time or place yet.

I kept his note with the ammonite and the locket, and I trembled every time I read it.

Bridget didn't get into Lewis College where I'd got a place, and where I'd always wanted to go because it was named after C. S. Lewis who created Narnia.

I kept quiet about this because I didn't want Bridget to feel bad, and we agreed to go to Sutton Court, where we'd both been accepted.

I can't remember how I got this past Pink Mother. She was probably going through one of her in-bed phases.

Bridget started her periods.

Her mother wasn't there.

Inside the bag of sanitary towels and tampons which her father produced for her was a stem of silk lilies and a note from Blue Mother, which said (I've got the actual one here in front of me):

Congratulations, Briddie! You're a woman now – and what a wonderful woman you will be! The bleeding is a bit of a pain, but the best thing about it is that it gives you the chance to be a mother. Being a mother to all of you was by far the best thing I ever did in the whole of my life. Much much better than being an artist. Although perhaps mothers are artists! You are far more beautiful than any painting I ever painted. I love you always. M xxxx.

When I read the note, the *saudade* longing came more strongly than I could remember, the longing to have been loved by a mother as Bridget had been loved by hers.

'When you read that note that her actual hand had written,' I said, holding back my tears as best I could, 'did it feel as if she was somehow still here?'

'No!' said Bridget, swallowing. 'It felt like she was on the other side of a massive wall, and there were no doors through it, and there would never ever be any doors in the whole of my life. Ever ever.'

I couldn't think of one thing to say.

Mothers are artists, I kept thinking, mothers are artists.

There must be something I can say about that.

But what I said to Bridget was, 'Are you using sanitary towels or tampons?'

'Towels,' said Bridget. 'I can't find my vagina.'

An envelope came in the post with the Blumes' address printed on the back.

On the front was what had always been my favourite of Blue Mother's sea paintings – the one with the choppy blue sea, and the bouncy clouds, and the sunlight caught on the sails of a yacht.

It wasn't my favourite any more.

Because up behind the clouds the cancer bird was lurking, ready to pounce.

I opened the card to see a printed message:

Please forgive us for not responding individually to all your lovely cards and flowers.
As we have lost our M, we have decided to lose our m.
We will no longer be called the Blume family, but the Blue family.
We're having our name officially changed in M's honour.
This was Barnaby's idea when we were all on our way home from Lyme Regis, our last moment of not knowing she was ill, our last wonderful summer together.
And blue we are, heartbroken at her loss.
We loved her more than life itself.
For M, blue didn't mean sad.
Blue was the happiest colour.

Her colour.
Elemental.
Like the sea.
And the sky.

Strange, yes, but then again, *why not?*

On the second to last day of term, Bridget came into school, looking as if she'd been crying all night.

'D's had to stop working,' she said. 'He couldn't concentrate.'

I put my arm around her.

'He's too sad to look after us,' she said. 'So we're moving.'

They couldn't be. They couldn't possibly leave the house on Turret Grove with the parasols and the Indian throws and the squishy sofas and the wire chandelier full of feathered birds.

I couldn't bear to ask her where they were moving to.

Maybe it wouldn't be Fulham or Chelsea. Maybe it would be miles away – like Chiswick or Notting Hill or Clapham – and I wouldn't be able to walk to her house any more.

'Also, I won't be going to Sutton Court in September,' said Bridget.

'But we've already been to the New Girls' Day,' I said. 'And also I turned down a place at Lewis College because we promised each other we'd go to the same—'

'We're moving to Israel,' said Bridget, 'where my grandparents live. It's D's favourite country, and just smelling the Israeli air is apparently going to make him feel better. And also the oranges over there are really juicy.'

I breathed deeply.

And she breathed deeply.

I felt dizzy and a bit nauseous.

It didn't seem possible.

It was a bad dream, and soon I'd wake up.

How could I live if Bridget wasn't by my side?

How could it be true that she would live thousands and thousands of miles away in a place I'd only read about in the bible, where people walked on water and came back from the dead and were shepherds?

'I just can't imagine not being able to look at your face every day,' I said. 'I love your face more than any face in the entire world.'

'I love yours,' said Bridget, and one tear came slowly down her cheek.

She wiped it away with the back of her hand.

I gritted my teeth and breathed deeply and tried to let the right words come, one by one, carefully, knowing that each one was very very important.

'I remember the first time you smiled at me,' I said. 'In the playground on the first day of school. And something happened inside me. For me, it was love at first sight. Your dad says love at first sight is like a chemical reaction. And that's how it was for me. Like a fizzing sparking feeling.'

Bridget couldn't speak.

But I hadn't finished.

'And the way you've always looked so happy to see me, every single morning,' I said, 'that has honestly changed my life. It's made me feel as if there must be something nice about me.'

'Actually,' said Bridget, sobbing. 'There are quite a few nice things.'

We held each other as tight as one human being can hold another, and then we came apart and stood looking at each other, and said how much we loved each other, and we were so there and so together that I couldn't imagine us ever being not there and not together, and

I realised that Bridget's blue eyes were the only eyes I'd ever allowed truly to see me because being seen is a scary thing. And I also realised that this was the kind of look a mother was supposed to give you. Every time she looked at you.

And now neither of us had a mother to do that any more.

A load of people were going to wave off Bridget's family from Heathrow Airport, wearing blue clothes and carrying blue balloons.

Pink Mother had agreed that Jean could take me in a taxi.

But the closer it came, the more I knew I couldn't do it.

Wave off my only friend, who was my whole true life.

Leaving me with my thin sliver of not-true life, which wasn't even halfway to being solved despite the reams of notes and underlinings in my Quest Book.

When I got out of bed that morning, I felt as if the floor was giving way.

I went back to bed: there was no way that I could go to the airport.

Jean didn't try to change my mind or jolly me along, because I think she knew the only way out of sad was through sad.

I lay listening to her smash the hoover into the stairs, and I imagined Bridget at the airport looking for me amongst all the blue people, and I cried so hard that I thought my heart would break into pieces and they would come sobbing up my throat.

And that would be a good thing, living without a heart.

Because who wants to live with one if having a heart makes you feel like this?

I'd learnt what everyone learns eventually: love hurts.

Pink Mother came in, and said quietly, 'I told you to make some other friends, Eva. I could see that it would end like this. And I didn't want this for you.'

In a burst of grief-fuelled courage, I took a deep breath and said, 'Out of interest, what *do* you want for me?'

She froze.

'What did you ever want for me?'

All the colour drained from her face.

'What is it, Cherie?' I said. 'My story?'

She closed the door.

I felt as if I was hyperventilating.

Why would this woman never talk to me?

It was true that these days, she didn't shout or shriek or cry like she used to because, if she started to get het up, Jean would soothe her with her soft, calm voice.

'You always said you wanted to go punting in Cambridge,' said Jean the day after Bridget left, softly and calmly. 'And I thought I'd take you.'

It was a relief to get out of the silent house, where Pink Mother had taken to her bed, refusing to see me.

Jean strapped an enormous bum-bag around the waistband of her flowery skirt, and we took the train, with a picnic and thermos flask, and we went punting in Cambridge, and it drizzled, and I put my cagoule on, and the views along the river were greyly beautiful, and I thought that I would like to go to Cambridge University one day, but Blue Mother was dead, Bridget had left me and I'd probably never see Barnaby again.

I was still stuck in a quiet lonely house, with no idea about what had happened to me in the first three and a half years of my life, or who I really was.

Once Bridget wasn't going to Sutton Court, I refused to go there either.

Pink Mother was still refusing to see me, and I'd started joking to myself that she was living inside the *trompe l'oeil* French garden she'd had painted onto the wall of the courtyard, no longer a gorgeous flowering Spanish *patio*. And perhaps my father was in there too – hahaha. Not so funny, really, for a grieving eleven-year-old to have no functioning parents.

I listened through the door to hear Jean quietly coaching and coaxing her out onto the landing, and once or twice she wafted ghost-like through the house in her dressing gown, and when I bumped into her, she tried to act as if everything was completely normal between us.

When I begged her to, Jean phoned the Registrar of Lewis College, and – hurray! – they still had a place. We went and bought the uniform together, and, oddly, Pink Mother made no comment.

The day before term started, a letter arrived from Bridget, which began, in huge scrawled letters: *WHERE WERE YOU?*

I folded the letter back into the envelope and put it on my bedside table.

That night, I got into bed, picked up the letter and put it down again.

I couldn't sleep.

I turned on the light and looked around the room. My heart was racing, and everything was losing its edges. The yellow trim on my new blazer was turning into wavy lines and dancing off the lapel, and I felt as if I was falling into nothing, like the day of the baby photo display at St Hilda's.

I woke at four o'clock in the morning, and I stared at my uniform lying stiff and new on the padded chest, and, to my relief, the yellow trim had found its way back to the blazer lapel.

I took out Bridget's letter, and read the next line.

I can't believe you didn't come to the airport.

I got out of bed and put the letter in my inside blazer pocket.

Around six o'clock in the morning, I put on my black pleated skirt and my black blazer with the yellow trim, and I knew how different my life would be if Bridget and I were meeting at the bus stop to go to Sutton Court together, and I thought, well, whatever you can't believe, I can't believe you went to Israel when we were supposed to be starting secondary school together. I hadn't realised you could feel angry with people who were suffering more than you were.

As I left my room in my stiff new uniform, Pink Mother appeared in her silk dressing gown, with all her hair scraped back in a towelling band. Her teeth looked bigger than usual, and she had a light coating of hair on her cheeks.

'Hope it all goes well,' she said nervously, double-knotting her belt.

'Thank you,' I said.

'I wonder if you'll talk to any boys,' she said, and she nudged me with her elbow.

It was most unlike her to do that, particularly when we were hardly speaking, and it turned me very stiff and serious.

'I imagine I will,' I said formally.

'Ooooh!' she said, nudging me again.

I couldn't imagine what was the matter with her.

'See you later!' I said, and ran downstairs.

I was fifteen minutes early at the bus stop for the school coach, as was a new Lewis College boy, my age. He was wearing wire-framed glasses and had a little patch of whiteheads on his chin.

We stood silently in the drizzle, and his glasses steamed up when we got on the bus.

When Mr Norris, our form tutor (one of a number of dizzying new Lewis College terms) came in, wearing mustard corduroy trousers, most of my form totally ignored him. This was not at all like St Hilda's, where we had to stop talking and stand up the second a teacher entered the room. It was strange seeing boys inside the classroom. They smelled different from girls – a bit like damp grass.

My loneliness made a noise inside me, like buzzing, and it flew me up to the classroom ceiling from where I watched myself having no friends, as well as being myself having no friends, as if I'd split in two.

At lunchtime, I went to the girls' loos and I locked myself in a cubicle and took Bridget's letter out of my inside blazer pocket.

I can't believe you didn't come to the airport. I thought maybe there'd been a traffic jam or something. But I knew you'd come. And I couldn't bear to leave without seeing you. We left it until the very last minute and then D said we had to go. I stood with my face against the glass. And you still didn't come.

I couldn't read any more.

I went to the library, picked out a book about personality types and hid behind a wall to read it. I did the quiz at the front. I was definitely an introvert. The world was, apparently, made for extroverts.

I went on creeping around the edges of school life until the first Spanish lesson.

The Spanish teacher was an Argentinian woman who reminded me of an eagle.

A boy called Henry Steele, who already looked as if he might be prime minister, made a joke about the way we beat the Argentinians in the Falklands War.

Señora García stared at him with her black eyes.

'People died,' she said.

The class froze.

She began to speak slowly in Spanish, drawing simultaneous sketches on the board to help the class understand. I hadn't heard Spanish for a while, and the *saudade* longing started to throb in my belly. I felt for my birthmark through my skirt and thought of my baby photo and the wagon wheel and the gorgeous flowery *patio*.

She made the class repeat, repeat, repeat.

Then she turned and asked if anyone spoke Spanish.

I slowly put up my hand.

Everybody was staring at me.

'*¿Dónde naciste?*' said Señora García – where was I born, the worst of all questions.

I froze.

I blushed.

'Jerez de la Frontera,' I said hesitantly, and then I nearly said, *or maybe Alvera, or Córdoba, I'm not sure*, but that would have made me sound like a total weirdo because who, by the age of eleven, doesn't know where they were born?

'We have a holiday home near there,' said golden Billy Orson, who was already one of the most popular boys in the class because he had a suntan and two older brothers, and knew the teachers' nicknames.

'*¿Dónde?*' said Señora García.

'Medina Sidonia,' said Billy Orson. 'But we're selling it and buying one in Crete.'

'*Una casa en Creta,*' said Señora García, drawing a house on the board.

Everyone repeated: '*Una casa.*'

Una casa, una casa, una casa.

I thought of my missing Spanish house whose walls were presumably just out of sight beyond the angel, no doubt glimmering and white like the photos my father used to leave on the desk in his study.

The bell went, and we all got up to leave.

'Are you Spanish?' said Billy Orson, smiling, with his hands in his pockets.

'Half,' I said, as we left the classroom.

'When are you going to be there next, you know, in Jerez?'

I said, 'I never go there.'

He said, 'Oh, where do you go?'

I said, 'I never go to Spain.'

He said, 'You're Spanish and you never go to Spain?'

I shook my head.

'You get tattoos in crisp packets in Spain,' he said, drawing up his sleeve to reveal a dolphin and a skull and a rose in a line on his skinny tanned forearm.

I stared at the tattoos and no words came out of my mouth.

'I'll bring you one in tomorrow if you like,' he said.

'Thank you,' I said.

(He did – a flamenco dancer who I tattooed with great joy onto my upper arm and who disintegrated bit by bit into little black specks in the bath.)

When I reopened Bridget's envelope to read the rest of the letter, she said she felt as if she was adrift in the world like the bath ducks who'd fallen off the container-ship.

'I will never love a friend like I love you,' she said.

I wrote back, asking if she remembered me telling her I had *evidence* that the person she thought was my mother wasn't, way back on Charmouth Beach. Since she never seemed to remember the detail of anything, I added, *Well, whether you do or you don't, the evidence is a photo, which I tried to show you twice. But the first time we found an ammonite, and the second time you fell asleep. So I'm wondering if God was saying I shouldn't mention it.*

In Bridget's next letter, she said that she didn't think showing a friend a photo was much to do with God, and anyway, since we'd basically lived together, I could have shown it to her any time, except now, when we were in different countries – so why didn't I? And could I describe the photo in words? Or get a photocopy? And, by the way, she was totally off God in a big way because he let her mother die. And did I think God was necessarily *he* because why couldn't *he* be *she*? And if *he*'d been *she*, *she* wouldn't have let her mother die.

I thought that maybe Bridget had gone a bit mad if she thought all hes were bad and all shes were good – had she already forgotten about Sophia Carr and the Populars?

It seemed a bit tiring to get into it all on the page, though, so I didn't bother.

In the school resources room, I made five illegal copies of the photo. But I couldn't make myself send one to Bridget – it felt too dangerous, sending my secret off in a thin paper envelope across the skies.

When she became very persistent, I tried to describe the photo with words: the stone angel and the wagon wheel and the headless woman in a grey dress.

'I bet you can't stop daydreaming about your real mother,' she wrote, surrounding the sentence with thought bubbles full of grey felt-tip hearts. 'Even if she doesn't have a head.'

Feeling a bit childish, I took out *The Rainbow Rained Us* and stared at Grey Mother: her grey topknot and glasses, her globe and her bookshelves, her face squinting with important thoughts, her twinkly eyes. I remembered the first time Miss Feast read us the book in Entrance Class, and the way Bridget came and sat close and held my hand.

I felt so alone without her.

Before going to bed, I would tiptoe upstairs, through the wicker furniture room, to the roof terrace, where I'd turn on the outside lights and climb onto the marble table.

I'd stand under the stars, and I'd call across the sky: 'Good night, Bridget!' And I could hear her answering, I really could. Because she was calling to me from the flat roof where they hung their washing, in Jerusalem.

In bed, I'd take out the photograph and look at my little baby mouth chewing away like babies do when they're teething, and at the grey arms holding me. I'd try to forget that when Peter Pan flew home to his mother, he found the window barred, and instead I remembered Wendy saying that a mother would always leave a window open for her children to fly back through.

I'd kiss the beheaded woman's hand in the photo and try to imagine her lovely motherly face. Though it's hard (even impossible) to make up a face from scratch. Try it.

When, in my first summer term at Lewis College, my year all went away to the big old country house owned by the school in France, Pink Mother had to come up with a passport for me. And inside my passport, my place of birth was not Jerez de la Frontera but Córdoba.

Córdoba!

I felt hot when I read it, and little darts of joy zoomed like fireworks inside my bloodstream.

I had a real, official place of birth!

A personal history!

Maybe even a family tree!

Everything was fitting together like pieces of a jigsaw puzzle.

Córdoba was the place I was born, as well as the place where the *patio*-gardeners were the best in the world.

It followed therefore that, if my baby photo was taken in the most beautiful *patio* you can possibly imagine, then my baby photo was surely taken in Córdoba.

I stared at my passport and my heart thumped in my chest.

I decided to start a new Quest Book immediately, with titles and sub-titles and a timeline, and a more serious and tidy secondary-school approach. I filled pages and pages with fevered scribbling, ending with the question: *Why was I born in Córdoba when we apparently lived in Jerez, or at the beach house in Alvera, down on the coast of Cádiz?*

I put my secret photo on my desk next to my open passport – *place of birth, Córdoba* – and I photographed the two of them together, matching and fitting and furthering my quest in the most dizzying of ways, and I begged Jean to get the film developed secretly, without telling Pink Mother.

I knew it was time to stop calling her Pink Mother, even in my head. I was twelve, and it was time to put childish things behind me.

With shaking hands, I stuck the seminal photo on the central double page of my new Quest Book, entitled, boldly, and without question marks, *My Birthplace*. Then I wrote to Bridget to tell her, in a rather adult and measured tone, that I'd definitely been born in Córdoba, but in her next letter, she didn't even mention it. She said that she didn't like being the Blue family. And she didn't like living with her grandparents. And she didn't like Israel.

I asked her if she'd made any new friends at school. She said that D was home-schooling them as a way of keeping himself busy, so there was no way of making friends, but the problem was that he kept bursting into tears and locking himself in his bedroom.

'Maybe you could meet some friends in your block of flats,' I wrote, hoping shamefully that she'd never find a friend as special as me.

'It's a bit tricky as I can't speak to them,' she wrote back.

I sat chewing my pen, trying to think of some new ideas.

I thought it would have been easier if she'd been younger and could invite other girls to play hoops or elastics, which didn't need much in the way of language. Whereas now we were over those things, but not yet ready for next things. These were the strange intersection years, caged in the middle of the adult-child Venn diagram, growing too big for it.

No helpful suggestions came into my head to enable Bridget to make more friends in Israel. Also, I had to finish the letter quickly and get it in the post before the coach left for our trip to France.

My mother told me not to do the climbing or the potholing, or I'd end up with scars on my knees.

Through Upper Third and Lower Fourth, Billy Orson and I became friends: we spoke in mashed-up Spanish together; we sat under a willow tree at breaktimes asking philosophical questions such as whether, if nobody ever saw you, you would exist; Billy imitated Freddy Mercury in Live Aid, using a tree branch as a microphone; we made up dances to Wham songs; and we ate Maltesers.

I wondered if he was the person I should show my photo to, and I kept a photocopy folded in my bra, just in case. But somehow the moment never seemed to come.

In the summer term, Billy said to me, with that stardust smile of his, 'My brother Michael fancies you – and he's in Lower Fifth.'

We laughed our heads off.

But when I went for the first time to the C. S. Lewis society, there was Michael Orson, sitting next to me, and it wasn't funny at all. It made me feel peculiar knowing on good authority that this older handsome boy actually fancied *me*. For the first time in my life, I couldn't concentrate on the castle at Cair Paravel.

On my third Wednesday at the C. S. Lewis Society, I realised that the Johnny who ran it was Johnny Orson, who was in Upper Sixth, and practically a man. Everyone called the three brothers the Awesomes instead of the Orsons.

Johnny and Michael went to almost every club in the school, but Billy said he didn't want to.

'I'm not a clone!' he said to me.

I took this to mean that he liked being different from his brothers, but I should have listened harder, and underneath.

Johnny and Michael Orson were tall and muscular whereas Billy was slight and handsome in a pretty, elfin way and if J. M. Barrie had wanted a male Tinkerbell, he would have done just fine. He flitted about the place, doing dance routines, mimicking the teachers and getting detentions for wearing a girl's hairband or missing PE.

'The C. S. Lewis Society sounds awful,' Billy said to me. 'And I'm lonely without you.'

I badly wanted to go to the C. S. Lewis Society, and I badly wanted Billy not to be lonely, but in the end I had to choose, and I still feel a bit ashamed that I chose the C. S. Lewis Society.

'I sat under the willow on my own,' said Billy.

'I bet you didn't,' I said. 'Everyone loves you.'

'Everyone finds me funny,' he said.

'Same thing,' I said.

'No, it isn't,' said Billy.

Which is true.

'Also,' he said. 'Everyone's not the same as someone.'

I kept going to the C. S. Lewis Society all through Lower Fourth, and I sat next to Michael Orson whenever I could as I wanted more of the peculiar feeling.

I started my periods the day after I turned thirteen, and the pain throbbed through me from my belly to my back, as if all my organs were being pulled out of my body through my vagina. The blood soaked through my sanitary towels, so that I had to double them up like bread rolls in my pants.

Billy said he wondered how thirteen-year-old boys would get on if blood started spurting into their boxer shorts every month. Plus backache. And weeping. I said I thought it might change the whole social dynamic, wipe the smiles off the boys' faces.

I didn't mention my terrible periods to my mother, like I didn't mention anything to her. I can't remember if I wrote and told Bridget, and nor can she. Jean handed me a lifetime's supply of sanitary towels and tampons in a huge Boots carrier bag, and she said that she recommended Nurofen.

That was it.

My preparation for womanhood.

Pain relief.

A boy called Guy Childers took over the leadership of the C. S. Lewis Society when I was in Upper Fourth, and by the time I was in Lower Fifth, fifteen years old, we'd exhausted most of C. S. Lewis's more popular books, and moved onto *A Grief Observed.*

C. S. Lewis's wife converted from Judaism to Christianity, showing that, contrary to Miss Philips' whirlybird answer, you could in fact swap religions. But even C. S. Lewis, who resurrected Aslan at the Stone Table, couldn't resurrect his wife when she died of cancer, so no wonder we'd had no luck with Blue Mother. C. S. Lewis had all the theological answers about suffering before he suffered, but now she'd died, he only had questions.

'The love of his life was dead. He couldn't ever have her back,' said Guy Childers.

Out of nowhere, I started crying.

This was both unexpected and excruciating, as I'd gone back to keeping my feelings well hidden inside since Bridget left.

'I'm so sorry,' I said. 'It made me think of someone I lost.'

Michael Orson – now in Lower Sixth and seventeen years old, golden-skinned, golden-haired and fancied by almost every girl in the school – came and put his arm around me, and I turned and found myself looking into his electric blue eyes.

That weekend, Michael and I went for a walk together in Battersea Park.

It felt very odd being alone in a park together wearing jeans, and I kept swivelling my head around to check nobody we knew was watching us. We walked about a foot away from each other and warmed up by talking about Billy.

He told me that his mother was worried about all Billy's detentions because *Orson boys didn't get detentions.* I said that we were the ones who'd asked him to moon-walk backwards into Spanish, so maybe we should have got the detention instead.

'It wasn't just that one,' said Michael. 'He's always in trouble.'

I should have said more, but I couldn't really keep my mind on the conversation as we'd moved closer together and the sides of our bodies had started crashing into each other as we walked.

Michael grabbed my hand, and this led to a stunned silence between us, which Michael broke by saying, 'Do you like pancakes?'

'Yes,' I said very quickly, somewhere between the pan and the cakes.

Then I blurted out: 'Billy's the best dancer I've ever seen.'

Michael said, 'What's that got to do with pancakes?'

I blushed.

He laughed.

I laughed.

He said, 'My mother won't let him do ballet.'

I said, 'Why not?'

He said, 'Obvious reasons.'

Then he said, 'I always fancied you, from the first day I saw you.'

I nearly fell over.

I wish I'd said that there were no obvious reasons at all why Billy shouldn't do ballet, but I was too carried away with being fancied.

Michael and I ate toffee pancakes on enormous plates at a little restaurant on the King's Road, and I became his girlfriend.

I was someone's girlfriend!

I remember walking home, wondering if people could tell.

I assumed that I was now ready for *next things*, and I also felt a bit sick – but that was almost definitely the toffee pancakes.

In my next letter, I told Bridget I was going out with Michael Orson, and she wrote back with a million questions.

She also said: 'I'll never get a boyfriend stuck inside this flat.'

As usual, I didn't know what to say.

I couldn't imagine her life, and I don't suppose she could imagine mine.

Michael and I went on dates, and he told me how much he respected his father's wealth, his mother's drive, his older brother Johnny's brain.

'What about Billy?' I said.

'It's almost like he's not an Orson,' he said.

'Surely he's allowed to be whoever he is,' I said.

'Let's move on to your family,' he said.

There was no way I was getting started on my family.

Instead, I showed him a photo of Bridget, and he said, 'She's very fat.'

(That should have worried me, but I wasn't sure what to expect of boyfriends.)

I started to tell him about Blue Mother, though I didn't call her Blue Mother to him because it would have sounded ridiculous out loud.

Michael said: 'Tell me about *your* mother.'

Help, I've no idea who she is, I thought, and she's probably a grey woman with no head, and she definitely isn't who you think she is.

'We're quite different,' I said. 'She's very fragile.'

I started asking him lots of questions about his parents in a slightly frantic way.

Michael Orson's father, Hugo, ran a hedge fund, which was nothing to do with gardens. During our relationship, Michael found a million ways to explain what a hedge fund was, but I never had the slightest clue what he was talking about.

Michael Orson's mother, Christine, had been a lawyer, and she gave up her career to look after her three boys in their mansion in Wimbledon.

Michael took me on lots of dates, and he said I was the best-looking girl in the school.

We started mooning around together at lunchtimes.

'I miss you so much,' said Billy.

'I can see you on Fridays,' I said, because Michael had team practice then.

'I'd prefer Mondays and Tuesdays and Thursdays as well,' said Billy. 'And Wednesdays, if you gave up the C. S. Lewis Society.'

'You're just being difficult,' I said. 'I'm offering to split my time.'

'I don't want to be an understudy,' said Billy. 'I used to be your first choice.'

'No one can help falling in love,' I said.

I feel a bit sick about that conversation now.

In fact, a lot sick.

In the summer term, Michael was made head boy.

'You're going out with the head boy!' said my mother.

'The head boy!' she said again, staring at me so intently she was making an exclamation mark between her eyebrows.

I honestly don't think I had ever seen her so happy.

When Michael first met her, he said, 'You're right. She's nothing like you at all.'

If my mother knew that Michael was coming to collect me, she would get herself properly dressed and made up, and she would waft into the hall, smelling of perfume, as if she was the one going on the date. She would lurk around, giggling at whatever Michael said.

If he hadn't been made head boy, would she have asked more questions?

If he hadn't been made head boy, would she have wondered what we were up to in the wicker furniture room next to the roof terrace, where we locked the door and started to take each other's clothes off?

She never once mentioned anything about sex or taking precautions.

I was fifteen and a half and maybe she thought I was too young.

'Shall we go all the way?' said Michael. 'Or are you not ready?'

'I'm not ready,' I said, because I knew I should wait a bit, but whether I was ready or not, my body was ready. Which sounds a bit like Descartes, who said that we were split in two, mind and body, and the body couldn't think.

My body definitely couldn't think – it was exploding.

Even during lessons, the feel of Michael would come back to me: the hardness of his thighs, the warmth of his breath on my neck.

Michael said that I should tell him when I was ready, he wouldn't ask again.

And instead of going all the way, we went all different ways.

Then we put our clothes back on, splashed our red faces and sat picking the Smarties off Jean's gingerbread men. When we took our tea tray back to the kitchen, Michael would sit discussing the beauty of the London skyline with Jean and my mother, and I would stare at him and not be able to imagine what we'd been doing just half an hour before.

On Michael's last day at school, he won loads of cups in assembly, and off he went on a six-week post-A level self-improvement project building schools in Mozambique.

I asked my mother if perhaps we could go on holiday to Spain. She started fanning her face with a magazine, saying, 'I'm never setting foot in that country again,' so I stayed in Chelsea, reading every book that had ever been written about the city of Córdoba, scouring London's libraries with an insatiable hunger to understand my own history, so that by the time I started in the sixth form, I was a genuine expert on Andalusia, but had still never been there.

I sat with my eyes shut dreaming about the orange trees which lined the streets, and the big old river, and the dark-eyed *gitano*s on the other side of the bank, dancing flamenco.

Michael called me every Sunday morning from a phone box to tell me about cisterns and trusses and porridge called *ncima*. We kept talking for up to an hour, as if giving up too early would be an admission of something we preferred to ignore – the fact that our conversations were quite boring. What I missed was the boyish smell of him, the feel of his arms around me, the taste of his mouth. Words weren't really what I was after.

'Love you,' he said, aiming to end with a flourish.

'Love you,' I said, because how wouldn't you?

I wondered if it meant something different if you kept the I in, like I used to with Bridget – she was the only person who'd ever said that to me.

When Michael came back, I ran out of reasons why I didn't want to meet his parents.

'Aren't you curious?' he said. 'To see what they're like?'

'Not really,' I said.

'I'd really like to meet your father,' said Michael.

'I don't suppose I'll ever see him again,' I said.

'You look just like him in those Father Christmas photos,' he said.

'What difference does it make?' I said coldly.

Michael took me in his arms and held me.

Like Bridget used to.

(But also not.)

Bridget said that if she wasn't going to have a relationship, the best she could hope for was living through mine.

The questions in her letters became more and more forensic.

Sometimes her letter was only a list of questions.

Why didn't I think that was strange?

'You must tell me about your life,' I said.

'I have no life,' she replied.

Hahaha, I thought, funny laughing Bridget.

'What do you do every day,' I asked her.

'Put on weight,' she replied.

Hahaha, I thought, hearing the words in her old voice, never wondering for a second if she might have a new one.

I didn't know that she was struggling to learn Hebrew, like she'd struggled to learn French at school.

That in Israel, with no mother, and no language, and no friends, her loud cheery voice had turned very quiet.

So quiet that even I couldn't hear her.

'Will you wear that white dress?' Michael said.

'Have your hair down, won't you?' Michael said.

'Wear proper shoes,' Michael said. 'Not flip-flops.'

When he came into the hall, my mother flitted about pinkly, laughing at his jokes and fiddling with the straps on her sundress.

'My mother is pretty full-on,' Michael said as we pulled into their massive gravel drive, with a fish pond in the middle, which Michael said had Koi carp in it.

I was wearing high-heeled sandals, bought by my mother. They were made of wood which didn't bend. And I'd put on the white dress. And kept my hair down. Which looking back seems oddly obedient.

Michael's mother came out.

She was wearing tight white jeans, and had very tanned skin, blow-dried blond hair and enormous gold earrings.

She stood next to the pond, and the front door was open, and you could see straight through the open glass doors of the garden room to a turquoise swimming pool beyond.

'Michael, show Eva the fish,' she said.

I said, 'Are the carp actually coy?' (which I thought was quite funny).

She said, 'It's spelt K-o-i, and they're just coloured variants of the Amur carp.'

Speaking is so risky, I thought.

'Oh, your skin,' she said to me. 'I'd pay good money for your skin. You look more Indian than Spanish, but you're gorgeous.'

(Did I? Was that worth noting in my Quest Book? I didn't think so.)

She nodded approvingly, as if I was a potential purchase, and I walked into the house like a dressage pony, with my wooden shoes clip-clopping along the path.

When I went into the house, Billy disappeared into the back garden.

I crept outside while Michael was in the loo.

Billy was playing ping-pong with himself, half of the table folded up like a wall.

'That's clever,' I said.

'What is?' said Billy.

146

'The table,' I said.

'Ideal for people without friends,' he said, and he laughed.

And I laughed too.

'I could play with you,' I said.

But Michael came into the garden, and I realised that I couldn't.

It was well known that Billy hadn't been encouraged to stay on for the sixth form. Rumours swirled that he'd been kicked out for fancying boys, but it was probably his poor grades. He was going to a boys' boarding school, Daunton Lodge in Dorset, and although I knew it would do him good to get out of the shadow of his brothers, it would be all jockstraps and testosterone, and not his thing in the least.

Michael's mother's phone seemed to ring every few minutes, and she answered very loudly: Christine Orson!

I saw a post-it note on the cover of her leather diary which said *Questions for Supper.*

Questions for Supper!

That is honestly true.

Out of the window, the table was laid next to the swimming pool under a rose pergola, with a white cloth and pots of lavender – all too perfect, like a film set.

Mr Orson rushed into the garden when he got home from hedging, freshly changed into a linen shirt, smelling of expensive aftershave, with fat feet in deck shoes. He kissed Christine's cheek and drank his large glass of wine with a big sigh of pleasure.

I stared at his stubby fingers, and his very clean nails.

'So, everybody,' said Michael's mother, 'what would you say is your guiding principle for life?'

(Oh my word – Questions for Supper.)

I started frantically trying to think what I might say, but I was entirely distracted by, actually, everything.

'You start,' Michael's mother said to Mr Orson.

'I'm going for success,' he said. 'What about you, darling?'

'Intentionality,' she said.

I'd never heard intentional made into a noun.

'That just gets you,' said Mr Orson appreciatively, in what sounded a slightly American accent.

He wasn't at all handsome.

Or, as it turned out, at all American.

'Michael?'

Michael was wearing a pale blue shirt and jeans, and he'd come home from Mozambique wearing lots of bands around his wrist. It was funny seeing him again after six weeks of absence. My eyes caught sight of his bumpy denim crotch, and I quickly turned away. I remembered what his penis looked like in my hand. How hot it was. And fragile.

'I wish you'd take those bands off your wrist,' said his mother.

'Michael?' said his father again.

'Knowing how to play the game,' said Michael. 'That's what guides me.'

The game? I thought. What game?

His father nodded, and said, 'You got it,' again sounding American.

'Billy?'

Billy said, 'Survival!'

Underneath his elfin smile, he wasn't smiling.

Everyone laughed, but surviving wasn't funny.

Not for Billy.

I wondered if Billy knew that I ripped his brother's clothes off in the wicker furniture room, if he knew that one minute I was a normal person, and the next, I was the Incredible Hulk, bursting out of myself. And then I thought, staring round the table, that this must be normal, it must happen to everybody else, even (weirdly) Michael's parents, even (maybe, a long time ago) my mother and father, but nobody ever talked about it.

This was certainly not the chosen topic for Questions for Supper.

'Eva?' said Michael's mother. 'What guides you?'

I could see that Michael was sweating a little, and I could see that his mother was judging me – not just me, everyone. Everything we said was being measured and graded into gold, silver, bronze – and fail.

Michael touched my thigh under the table, which didn't help.

'What guides me?' I said, using the trick that everybody knows because you are taught it in eleven-plus interview practice.

'Yes,' said Michael's mother, looking at me with an expression I couldn't read.

I looked into her eyes.

And I said, 'Longing.'

'Your mother's a very beautiful woman,' I said to Michael when we went for a walk the next Saturday evening.

'And my father is not a very beautiful man!' said Michael, smiling.

'I never said that.'

'My mother says that all men end up ugly, but not all men end up rich!' said Michael, killing himself laughing.

I didn't laugh.

'My mother found you enigmatic,' he said. 'Particularly when you said your guiding principle was longing.'

I smiled.

'What did you actually mean?' he said, and he stopped walking and sat down on a bench.

'What did you mean about playing the game?' I said, deflecting, because there was no way I could ever explain to a logical, realistic boy like Michael the longing that raged inside me, a feeling so strong that it was almost as if life was longing for itself, as if I lived permanently on the cusp of some colossal dawn.

'You just have to learn the technique,' he said, putting his feet up and leaning his back against the wooden armrest. 'Whether it's acing exams or getting into Cambridge. The whole of life is like that.'

The whole of life is a game?

No, the whole of life is a mystery and a puzzle, with no answers at the back, that's what I thought, but I wouldn't say. I was well-practised at not saying anything I felt inside. So I'm not at all sure, looking back, who Michael thought he was in love with.

Turning myself around to face him, I changed the subject.

'Are you excited about Cambridge?' I said.

We were sitting feet to feet, like mirror reflections of each other.

'Course I am,' he said, looking handsome.

'Wouldn't you rather be single at Cambridge?' I said, because the girls at school kept saying that boys were always unfaithful once they got to university.

'Course I wouldn't,' said Michael.

Sometimes, when I saw how much the other girls fancied him, I couldn't believe he'd chosen me, especially as I was two years below him and he'd been head boy.

In Bridget's last letter, she said I would definitely lose him if I didn't sleep with him before he started at Cambridge, and once I had, could I please describe the entire thing – *in detail.*

'I'm sixteen now,' I said to Michael. 'I think I'm ready to go all the way.'

Michael swivelled around and kissed me all around my neck, and led me back to his Mini which we'd left in the car park.

I hadn't exactly meant right this minute, but it was dark now, and his arms were around me, sending whooshes through my body, and I was hoping it would all go OK because sometimes a tampon seemed a bit of a squeeze.

Michael folded the seats down, and we collapsed on top of each other in a big flail-around of unbuttoning and breathing. At the start, I felt like I was watching myself through the car window, and then I forgot myself, and when it was over, quite quickly, I felt sore and stingy and odd. But Michael held me very tightly and said I was amazing, or it was amazing, or something was amazing, and that was a nice warm feeling.

Bridget wrote asking, 'Have you done it yet?'

I wrote back saying, 'Yes.'
But when I thought of describing it, I felt like crying.
She wrote back saying, 'You said you'd describe it to me.'
I wrote back saying, 'It's not very describable.'
And she didn't reply.

My father sent me four orange trees, from Papá, in typed print, with no further explanation, right after I lost my virginity. I don't remember feeling I'd lost anything, but it was hard to see what exactly I'd gained.

Whatever – the timing of the orange trees made me feel as if my father knew, which was horrible. Also, it was 25 August, the date he'd left us, but that was, I imagined, just another coincidence.

My mother took to her bed.

I made her echinacea tea.

With her eyes closed, she said, 'What did he say?'

'Nothing,' I said.

'Are you lying to me?' she said.

I shook my head, though she still had her eyes closed.

'Are you all right?' she said.

'Yes, thank you,' I said, picturing myself flailing about in Michael's Mini, wondering if she had the slightest idea about the reality of my life.

Jean asked next door's gardener to put the four orange trees on the *patio*, and I went and examined them, feeling the texture of their leaves and smelling their sweetness as if they would reveal some great secret about me.

'Your mother is not at all well,' said Jean.

She made a lot of phone calls.

Then Jean's mother died, and she had to go and be with her adult brother, Nigel, who couldn't live alone because of his Down's Syndrome.

'I'll be lost without you,' said my mother.

Jean gave her a shy shoulder squeeze.

'I hope you'll be OK, Eva,' said Jean, handing me an envelope and, most unexpectedly, kissing the top of my head, my first head-kiss since Blue Mother died.

'I'll try not to be too long,' said Jean. 'And you can always call your grandparents. And I also put my phone number on the card. You know, just in case.'

'I'm so sorry about your mother dying,' I said, still feeling a bit shocked by her head-kiss. 'And thanks, you know, for everything. Especially the gingerbread men. I'll miss them.'

I opened the envelope.

Jean opened the door.

I still have the card, and I'm looking at it now.

The blossom is swirling in the wind with a swarm of orange and yellow butterflies.

When I looked up, Jean was standing on the pavement.

I rushed down the slippery steps, and I hugged her. And she hugged me back. Tightly. She said that, on the worst days in her life, she would go for a walk and pray that she'd see something lovely. It might be a cat sitting in someone's window. Or a blossom tree. Or a baby in a bobble hat. She hoped that might help me, if I ever felt lonely.

It did help me.

It does help me.

That was when I realised that there was something lovely about Jean.

The minute she left, my mother plummeted.

She slept, almost all the time, in her rose-pink princess arbour, like Sleeping Beauty, waiting to be kissed awake. Which, eventually, and rather unexpectedly, she would be. We'll come to that.

For now, the house was silent as a tomb.

I don't know what I would have done without Michael Orson, and I'm not sure I ever told him that.

He was, honestly, all I had.

Since I'd failed to describe sex to Bridget, she hadn't written to me.

So I didn't write to her either.

When I spoke to my mother, she answered from far away.

Then she disappeared.

To the same place as before.

Home Place, it's called, accommodating, in en-suite bedrooms, the wealthy depressed and the wealthy addicted, hundreds of them, apparently.

Granny and Grandpa Green thought up all the reasons why they couldn't live at the house in Chelsea with me for longer than a couple of weeks.

I told Michael my grandparents were looking into different girls' boarding schools for me to start immediately. I was terrified: I'd always been slightly frightened of girls once Bridget wasn't there to protect me.

Oh, Bridget – I tried not to think about her.

My grandparents found a school called Hayworth Hall, in Exeter, which had places in the sixth form.

'Exeter!' said Michael, with a horrified expression. 'That's like five hours from Cambridge. And they'd never let you out to see me. And we'd never have any *time together.*'

I wondered if he was thinking, more specifically, that we'd never have any *sex together.* Once we'd done it once, Michael couldn't stop doing it. It was as if he was addicted to me.

I translated this as love, and was consoled, and also flattered, I suppose.

I knew this love was nothing like the Blumey love I'd once known, but they'd been gone five years, and this was the only kind I was being offered.

Michael said he'd speak to his mother, he was sure I could move into their spare room – after all, his parents would have no boys left at home, with Michael off to Cambridge and Billy to boarding school in Dorset.

He explained to his mother I needed somewhere to stay, temporarily, and confidently told me it should all be fine.

A few days later, he said again that it should all be fine.

I told him my grandparents were sending the deposit to Hayworth Hall at the weekend. He looked panic-stricken, and he said, 'I know my mother will come round! I'm her favourite!'

Then he said he'd clinched it. Coming round, clinching it – it didn't make me feel especially wanted. But I was used to that.

Also, still no letter from Bridget.

I waved the thought away.

If she wasn't going to write to me, I wasn't going to write to her.

If I didn't want to describe sex, I didn't have to.

I was of course avoiding her for a completely different reason.

If I wrote to her, I'd have to say how I was.

And I didn't want to find out.

'I told Mum she'd always wanted a daughter,' said Michael, looking rather pleased with himself.

And that was that.

I was moving into the guest wing, which had a large terrace, where the Portuguese gardener arranged my four orange trees. I smelled their sweet leaves and tried to imagine myself walking through the streets of Córdoba, where one day, when I was old enough, I would go. I felt alone and very small, as if I could see myself on the terrace from a satellite in space.

I went inside and lay on the enormous bed. I closed my eyes, and inside my eyelids, I saw Bridget spinning a hula hoop. But I didn't want to think about her. Or us. Or then. So I opened my eyes.

I put my ammonite (no longer gold, but sad and dull), my crucifix and my Victorian locket on my bedside table, and I folded Barnaby's note and Jean's blossom-and-butterflies card inside my diary.

I woke with a start in the night, feeling I was suffocating in the powerful smell of Christine Orson's lilies.

On my first morning at the Orsons' house, Mr Orson disappeared to the city; Michael went to buy books from his university reading list; Billy played tennis with a neighbour's son; and the cleaner sat on the sofa sewing name tapes onto all his clothes, even his boxer shorts.

I felt oddly visible inside the house, as if I was twice my actual size.

'How do I name his cricket box?' the cleaner asked Christine.

'Use this pen,' said Christine.

That was a terrible idea – what with sweat and pen and balls – but anyhow, and more importantly, Billy hated cricket, and this wouldn't go down well at a boys' boarding school.

I felt, suddenly, scared for him.

I went and read a book about the exiled Sephardi Jews of Córdoba under the pergola to take my mind off how horrible I was feeling, but I couldn't stop thinking about all the fun things Billy and I used to do together in our lunch breaks: the philosophising and the mashed-up Spanish and the dance we made up to 'Wake Me Up Before You Go-Go'.

I couldn't get the lyrics out of my mind, and round and round came the thought that perhaps it was true – I should have been with him instead.

I'd picked the wrong brother.

The wrong sort of relationship.

Perhaps it was better being a friend than a girlfriend at my age.

I could hear Christine Orson on the phone to her friends.

'Well, the school says it gives plenty of one-to-one attention . . .' I heard her say loudly.

And later, even more loudly, 'If we back it up with tutors in the holidays . . .'

And later, slightly less loudly, 'They had no idea how to deal with his ebullience at Lewis. With better handling, I'm sure he'll thrive. He's actually very bright . . .'

Billy came into the garden in his tennis whites, and he sat on the stone step by the pool, and his legs looked spindly and his face looked empty, and I felt a huge wave of love for him, so big it almost drowned me.

I walked over to him, and I said, 'I was thinking of that dance we made up to "Wake Me Up Before You Go-Go".'

He looked at me as if he didn't understand English.

I was going to say that I should have been with him instead, like the song, but what came out was: 'Are you nervous about boarding, Billy?'

'It'll be OK,' he said, and he got up and walked away from me on his twig-legs.

He walked away from me.

Like I'd walked away from him.

That's what came to me.

I'd done to him what my father did to me.

Also, I was staying in his house and he was being sent away.

Was there something I could have done that day?

Should I have refused to stay?

Would it have made any difference?

As Billy walked off, Johnny arrived with his ravishing Russian academic girlfriend, Antonina, who wore a white bikini and a gold waist chain. I sat there trying to imagine why anyone would wear a waist chain.

Every few minutes, Antonina took a mirror out of her bag and stared at herself, as if worried that she'd turned into somebody else since she'd last looked.

I moved my chair under the apple tree.

Billy was commandeered by his mother to help with lunch.

I wondered why Johnny didn't have to help with lunch.

Was Billy doing penance for his lack of academic ability?

Being the first Orson ever to get C grades at GCSE?

Billy brought salad bowls to the table under the pergola and he sat down with an expression so blank you felt that all his feelings had retreated deep down inside himself and might never again be found. Rather like mine.

Sometimes I couldn't work out what I felt about anything any more.

Except my secret photo and my passport – my heart still raced when I looked at those.

But the quest was somewhat stalled.

Michael rushed into the garden, sweating, slightly later than his mother had required, a point she laboured until he'd apologised for the trains being messed up.

'Punctuality matters,' she said. 'You'll find that at boarding school, Billy.'

'*Fucking* boarding school,' said Billy, getting up from the table, the sharp edges of his forbidden f-word making an enormous tear in Christine Orson's film set, as he made off across the lawn, slamming the back door behind him.

The rest of us, stunned into silence, ate with our cutlery clinking loudly against the china plates.

On the morning of his departure, Billy put on his tropical fish swimming shorts, held his nose and slid down the slide into the pool. I remember having a horrible premonition that there was no water in the pool and he was going to smash himself to pieces. But there was water in the pool, and he didn't.

He left for Daunton Lodge, looking thin and small, with wet hair. He was wearing a grey suit, with an eagle crest on the pocket of his jacket, and his gold complexion was grey too.

The next day, Johnny and Antonina went on holiday to South America, and a card arrived in the post for me.

Dear Eva
I hope all is well with you.
Please send my best to Michael and his parents.
I am being very well looked after.
Good luck in the sixth form.
With my love

Mummy

You are not Mummy, I thought, when I read it.

I went up to my bedroom and stared at the headless grey woman and the mass of geraniums all over the white stone walls.

I replied, *Dear Cherie*, saying I was pleased that she was being well looked after and everything was great at the Orsons'. She didn't try the Mummy thing again.

We wrote to each other once a week from then on – short stilted letters, like armour.

Michael's mother bought me a wardrobe of coordinating sixth-form clothes, skirts with waistbands (like my mother's) and tailored jackets.

Three weeks after term started, Michael and I set off to Cambridge in his mother's Mercedes, as Michael's stuff wouldn't fit in the Mini, and anyway his mother wanted to *style* his room.

We got back to quiet Fairmont House, and his mother took out a gold necklace she'd bought me with a gold M pendant, which she fastened at the back of my neck, so that I was always wearing Michael.

'Thank you very much,' I said to her.

'How was your day?' I'd ask.

'Oh, I was just sunbathing,' she'd say. 'We're having crab salad/risotto/sea bream for supper.'

'Thank you very much.'

I would do my homework under the pergola, while she sat drinking wine and phoning her friends to boast manically about her children. This, and tennis, was what they did together when I was at school – the boasting definitely more competitive than the tennis.

In the evenings, we'd swim lengths together.

Then we'd go into the poolside sauna.

She'd lie naked with her hair in a towel.

'Don't feel you need to keep your costume on,' she'd say.

But I did feel I needed to keep my costume on, thank you very much.

When I had my period, I told her I didn't want to swim.

'Why ever not?' she said. 'Don't tell me you're using towels.'

I didn't say I was using tampons and towels both together, and was considering putting a pillow inside my pants.

My period pains contracted through my bowel, pinched my ovaries, cut me in half. But I didn't want to talk to her about them. I couldn't face the thought of all her solutions.

'You could have that birthmark on your thigh removed, you know,' she said. 'I know just the man.'

'I like it,' I said. 'It's the same shape as the Iberian Peninsula!'

'It's a bit unsightly,' she said. 'What does Michael say?'

I didn't care what Michael said – it was my leg.

Whatever the pendant said.

And it *is* my leg.

I quite liked my leg, still do.

I was still *Eva from Iberia*, but the warrior in me had got hidden somewhere, and would certainly not be welcomed into the house by Michael's mother, whose principal anxiety that autumn was the fading of her tan.

She was furiously fake-tanning her legs in the pool changing room when she told me that a pupil had committed suicide at Billy's school.

'He hung himself,' she said.

I had no idea what to say.

'Billy was apparently best friends with him,' she said, vigorously rubbing her left breast. 'He was called Archie.'

'Are you going down to see him?' I said, mesmerised by the malleability of her breast.

She washed her hands with soap and a scrubbing brush.

Then she wrapped an enormous grey towel around herself.

'The priest is seeing all the boys,' she said, in an efficient voice. 'And he tells me Billy seems fine.'

'Do they know why the boy did it?'

'Personal problems,' she said.

Obviously, I thought, he's a person.

'Poor boy,' I said.

'Poor parents,' I said.

'I hope Billy's OK,' I said.

She shook her head, like a horse ridding itself of flies around its eyes, and she said cheerfully, 'Will you do my back?'

'I've never done this before,' I said.

'Just keep it even,' she said, flinging off her towel.

I started.

'I'm so pleased he's at a Catholic school,' she said.

I rubbed her back, frantically, up and down, hoping the tan would be OK and trying not to leave fingerprints on her buttocks.

'Everyone says the priest is being amazing,' she said. 'He's talked to them all individually.'

I washed my orange hands.

'Are you a Catholic?' I said, thinking how odd it was that Michael and I had never discussed religion when it was one of my favourite subjects.

'No,' she said. 'But you couldn't find a better way of living.'

'Maybe you should consider becoming one then,' I said, trying to be both logical and polite.

'For children, I mean,' she said, looking at her tanned self in the mirror. 'And young people.'

I wouldn't counter her logic.

'And schools,' she said. 'All the best schools are religious.'

I sat on the wooden bench and felt tense.

I tried to think of something to say.

'Did you enjoy being a lawyer?' I said, somewhat out of nowhere (Questions for Supper – I was getting the hang of them).

'I loved it,' she said.

'Why did you give it up?'

'Hugo felt there was only room for one big job in our marriage,' she said.

I opened my mouth to ask her if she regretted it.

But then I changed my mind and said nothing.

'I became CEO of our family!' she said, laughing. 'On a stonking salary!'

'How's it been?' I said.

'Well, let's see how the boys turn out,' she said. 'So far, so good. One Oxford, one Cambridge. Two gorgeous girlfriends.'

Poor poor Billy.

'Do you really think you can make people turn out how you want them to?' I said.

'I see it as a mother's job. To show her children the right way. To set them up for greatness!'

I couldn't think what to say.

'You have so much potential, Eva,' she said. 'And if you listen to me, I will make sure you succeed.'

'Thank you very much,' I said, taking a deep breath. 'I think I'll go inside now.'

It was a relief to be in my own room, away from her. Why did she make me so tense, I wondered, when I knew she was trying to help me. How ironic that all I'd wanted was maternal attention, and now I'd got it, I couldn't stand it.

You're never happy, I told myself, what's the matter with you?

When I went down for supper, she took a bag off the table and said, 'You need to read these books. It's vital to read around your subjects.'

'Thank you very much,' I said.

She was loving me in the only way she knew.

A buying-things and bossing-me-about kind of way.

Which is what love can be, I suppose, for lots of people.

Keeping people on a string, like a puppeteer.

But love is supposed to be a watering hole, where you come and go by choice, and leave refreshed. That's what I'm aiming for, anyhow.

Michael's mother bought me designer dresses and diamond earrings, which I wore to black-tie dinners in panelled halls in Cambridge with Michael. We went punting with his friends, and drank champagne, and I realised that I was no longer that same young girl, teary in her cagoule, drinking from Jean's thermos flask, on the Cam.

Who was I though, instead of that girl?

There were so many ways in which I didn't know who I was that it scared me to death.

I pushed that thought firmly into a special safe I'd made inside my brain, which locked on closure. On the door, it said UNWANTED THOUGHTS. There were quite a lot in there already.

On Wednesday afternoons in the sixth form we had Enrichment in the newly built lecture theatre and, in a particularly private school sort of endeavour, we were making our way through the entire history of the entire world.

This particular Wednesday afternoon, the deputy head introduced us to the speaker, Dr Lourdes Jameson, who had auburn hair with a wild, blown-about look, and big bosoms and a warm freckly face, and who was wearing boots with – look! – thick leather soles and – look again! – a gorgeous crinkly scarf.

Dr Lourdes James carried her weight evenly, feet flat on the ground like Bridget, like all of them – there they were, standing in a line by the sea in my mind.

As I sat staring at her, she started turning into Blue Mother.

She caught my eye.

I was all trussed up in my matchy-matchy clothes – a tidy cream collared blouse and my gold M pendant.

She would think I was a posh uptight girl at a posh uptight school.

And maybe I was.

Would Blue Mother even like me any more, I wondered.

Now that I wore tight skirts and belts pulled in at the waist.

Would Bridget still like me?

I couldn't bear to think about her.

It was over five years since we'd said goodbye, it came to me, with a blast of longing for what we'd had, for what I didn't have any more, for who I'd been then and wasn't now.

Someone patted my shoulder in the row behind to say my jacket had fallen off my chair. I put on my fitted tailored grey jacket that Michael's mother had bought me, and it felt horribly constricting.

I don't like myself – that's what I thought when Dr Jameson smiled at me.

'So, let's pick up the story from about 750,' she said.

I settled into the start of her talk, anticipation fizzing like sherbet dib dabs.

Abba and sherbet dib dabs on the way to Lyme Regis.

Bridget's sparkly blue eyes and wild curly hair.

'You hear the term medieval and what do you think?' said Dr Lourdes Jameson.

'Backward,' said the girl next to me.

'Smelly,' said some boy trying to be funny.

Dr Jameson's eyes twinkled at him.

I still didn't give answers out loud.

'We may need to think again,' she said, smiling as if she was holding in some great secret, which was about to burst out of her.

She paused, took a sip of water and removed her crinkly scarf.

Oh, Blue Mother's crinkly scarf around the banister!

'Where do you think you would find the most advanced culture in Europe at this time?'

I felt a gauze of colour across my cheeks.

I knew the answer.

This was my history.

I had a history.

Various know-it-all boys made suggestions, none of them right.

'The cosmopolitan and multi-religious culture of Spain,' she said.

One or two people looked at me.

'And the zenith was in the city of Córdoba.'

I grew taller in my seat – Eva from Iberia.

'Córdoba, at this time, was the most extraordinary place,' she said. 'A city of nine hundred public baths; tens of thousands of vibrant shops selling rich fabrics or Arab slippers or tapestries or prayer mats; hundreds or perhaps thousands of mosques; a total of seventy capacious libraries, and the caliphal library holding some four thousand volumes at a time when the largest library in the rest of Europe held four hundred!'

And taller.

'A young Muslim, probably in his late teens, called Abd al-Rahman abandoned his home in Damascus after his whole family, the ruling Umayyads, were murdered. He set off on horseback on an extraordinary journey . . .'

I pictured his route – alone on horseback, how thrilling – through Palestine, the Sinai, into Egypt, to Morocco.

'He crossed the narrow straits from Morocco and became the first ruler of Islamic Spain,' said Dr Jameson.

'Europe's never been Islamic,' said a boy at the back.

'Except that Spain was,' said the speaker. 'Far out on the Syrian steppe stood the mysterious walled city of Rusafa, where Abd al-Rahman's family had been murdered. He began to build a new Rusafa in Andalusia, in the south of Spain, filling it with things from his childhood, thousands of palm trees, a memory palace . . .'

A memory palace?

I thought: I have my very own memory palace in Córdoba too – a flower-draped *patio*, with a wagon wheel leaning against the wall and an ancient stone angel in the centre. I have a history. I am somebody. It's just I don't know exactly who. Not yet. But I will find out.

'As the first Emir of Córdoba, Abd al-Rahman responded to the *dhimmi* – a word for special protection – in a particularly generous way, protecting the two other peoples of the Book – the Jews and the Christians – as his brothers and sisters, and kindred spirits.'

I thought of my father saying, we all lived together for 250 years – Jews, Muslims, Christians.

My father!

Nearly ten years since I'd seen him.

I thought, I must get to Córdoba, somehow – it must be possible.

'And,' Dr Jameson continued, taking off her jacket to reveal a crumpled blue linen dress, 'perhaps Europe has never been as enlightened as it was for those glorious years of tolerance and coexistence in Córdoba, with the Muslims, the Jews and the Christians living alongside each other in what is now known as the *Convivencia*.'

What did my father say? Religion always starts well and ends badly. So many things that start well end badly.

'Any questions?' said Dr Jameson.

'What happened?' said a girl at the end of the row. 'How did the *Convivencia* come to an end?'

'It wasn't the Andalusians who started to fight each other,' said the speaker. 'It was Berber Muslims from North Africa who had a different application of the *dhimmi*. And it was the crusading Christians from Latin Christendom. They met on the plains of Spain at Las Navas de Tolosa in 1212. Ready to kill each other for God.'

She paused, and then said again: 'Ready to kill each other for God. Think about that. It happens in every era.'

'What about the Jews?' said someone, and I saw Mr Blume in his study playing the *Quartet for the End of Time*, which didn't stop the guards killing the prisoners at Stalag VIII-A.

'The Jews had prospered magnificently in old Andalusia,' she said. 'But when the Black Death came, they were blamed for it. It's strange how often the Jews get the blame, isn't it? People said that God was so angry about the intermingling of the three faiths that he sent down a plague. An edict expelling every Jew from Spain was signed on 31 March 1492 by the Catholic kings. And the Sephardi Jews, along with the Muslim Moors, who had all contributed so profoundly to Andalusia, were gone.'

Human beings really are a terrible idea, I thought.

When Michael came home from Cambridge for the summer, his mother said that she was perfectly happy for us to sleep together from now on, and she stared at us with a greedy look on her face. On Saturday evening, we had sex underneath the duvet, trying not to make any noises, and Michael wrapped the condom in practically a whole roll of loo paper like a miniature mummified baby.

Afterwards, weirdly, I thought of Bridget, how she never wrote to me any more, how much I'd like to see her, how much I'd like to be back in her bedroom, instead of Michael's, with our beds pulled together and the mountains of pillows and the old-fashioned eiderdowns.

On Monday morning, we had sex in Michael's en-suite shower in a wordless sort of frenzy, and I got shower gel in my eye. Then we did it again on the carpet. Michael made another mummified baby, and when we went downstairs, he asked his mother for more loo roll.

She said, 'You got through that quickly!'

I nearly died.

'What's happened to your eye?' Michael's mother asked me as she drove me to school. 'It looks very red.'

I made a strange gesture with my hand meaning nothing.

'You are using the right sort of contraception, aren't you?' she said when we stopped at the traffic lights.

'Oh, don't worry!' I said, blinking my red eye and wondering how she'd guessed it had something to do with sex, in which eyes weren't usually involved, as far as I knew.

'I'm happy to run through the options with you,' she said, sounding curiously energised about her son's contraceptive choices.

'No,' I said, looking out of the window. 'It's all fine.'

We drove along quietly, and while I blinked, she morphed effortlessly from contraception to my essay on Augustine, and how I needed to develop my argument in a slightly different way to gain full marks, she'd read the descriptors.

'So, History at Cambridge,' she said, once university discussions started at school. 'If you don't take a gap year, you and Michael will overlap for a year.'

I'd done quite enough overlapping with Michael.

I needed some space around me.

'Gap years are completely unnecessary,' she went on. 'There's plenty you can do during the holidays.'

In the holidays, I went out for a strained lunch with my mother, who was pale and faraway, trying a period of rest at Granny and Grandpa Green's. Then I went to Crete with Michael's family, staying in the villa the Orsons had bought, overlooking Mirabello Bay.

In the autumn term of Upper Sixth, Michael's mother and I were in the car on the way home from school when I took a deep breath and said, 'I'm not applying for Cambridge. I'm applying for Edinburgh.'

She stared ahead at the road, and so did I.

'That's too far from Michael,' she said.

'At Edinburgh, I can specialise in Medieval Córdoba – 750 until 1492.'

'Eva, that's ridiculously narrow,' she said. 'And Edinburgh is miles away.'

'But Professor Wells at Edinburgh is *the* expert on the *Convivencia*,' I said calmly.

'You're missing the point,' she said.

'What point?'

Was she actually bothered about my future or only my proximity to her son?

'It's not about your particular interest,' she said. 'Your degree's your passport to the next thing. You always need to have your eye on the next thing.'

Our eyes were firmly on the road.

'I don't know what my next thing is,' I said, choosing my words carefully, as we stopped at the lights. 'Nobody does. And if your eye is always on the next thing, you can never enjoy the current thing. I just want to lose myself in medieval Córdoba for three years.'

'You're being totally naïve,' she said.

'None of us knows what will happen next,' I said. 'You probably thought you'd be a top barrister. But in the end, you weren't.'

'I could easily have been.'

'Exactly, you could have been, but you weren't. And you wouldn't have known that.'

'I'm getting all of you where you want to go,' she said curtly. 'That's my *job*.'

No, it isn't, I remember thinking.

Mothering is a serious technical difficult job when children are small. I know this now very well. Then children grow up – and the job turns into a relationship. But, I realised, nobody had told her this. She didn't know that she'd been made redundant.

And, even though she was impossible in so many ways, that makes me sad now.

She'd given so much of herself to find her children's potential and, along the way, she'd lost her own.

In my bedroom, I took out my diary, and I read the note Barnaby Blue had written to me seven years earlier. I stared at the xx, and realised, to my surprise, that I still really wanted to kiss him, when I should only have been thinking about kissing Michael.

But aren't the un-kissed always going to be more exciting than the already-kissed, I wondered, and if that was the case, how did anyone ever risk getting married?

I read Barnaby's note, which I knew off by heart.

I feel so sad that some days I want to die too. But M taught us how to live. And maybe that was the point of last summer. So I'm going to try to live, and will you try too, Eva? I wonder who will end up in your locket!

I picked up my locket, thinking how badly I wanted to live again, the way I had with Bridget.

Michael's mother came in without asking.

'What's that?' she said, grabbing the locket.

'I found it on a beach in Dorset with my best friend,' I said, feeling my breaths shortening. 'When I was ten.'

The time that I was happy.

It seemed a long time ago, being happy.

Bridget still didn't write, so I didn't write either.

When Christine left, I took out the blossom-and-butterflies card with Jean's phone number inside it.

I dialled the number.

'Jean, it's Eva,' I said, and to my surprise, I felt a terrible welling in my chest, and couldn't speak for some seconds.

'Are you OK?' said Jean.

'How's Cherie?' I gasped. 'She doesn't really say anything in her letters to me.'

'I feel as if she's on the way up,' said Jean.

'Is she coming home then?'

'Not yet,' said Jean.

'I'm making decisions about university,' I said. 'I want to study Medieval Hispanic History, focusing on Córdoba, and neither Oxford or Cambridge offers a course like that.'

'I see,' said Jean. 'You must do what feels right.'

'Thank you,' I said. 'And do you think I might be able to go and live in Chelsea again at some point?'

'I need to work out what's going to happen to Nigel,' she said. 'Then I can come back.'

A big hiccup of tears surprised me from nowhere.

'Sorry,' I said.

'No, I'm sorry,' said Jean.

'And how are you and Nigel?' I said, trying to sound normal.

'It's strange without Mother,' she said, 'although she was a very difficult woman. All she wanted was a son. And after Nigel was born with Down's Syndrome, all her dreams were crushed. I suppose she was depressed.'

'I understand,' I said.

'Yes, I suppose you do,' she said. 'But the difference is that your mother loves you.'

'Does she?' I said. 'I didn't know that.'

There was a pause.

I felt it might be my moment.

'Jean,' I said. 'I need to ask you something.'

She didn't say anything.

'The thing is,' I said, 'I don't think Cherie is my mother, and I didn't know who to tell.'

There was another pause, and a sob gasped up my throat.

'Do you know if she is, Jean? It would really help if you could tell me.'

'Of course she is,' she said.

'But I look nothing like her.'

'You're the image of your father,' she said.

'Are you honestly sure?' I said, my voice trembling.

'Of course I'm sure,' she said, and I couldn't catch the tone of it, how sure her sureness was.

'She might not have told you the truth,' I said.

'She does tend to confide in me, Eva,' said Jean, quite convincingly. 'So you can put that thought right out of your head.'

She paused.

And said again, 'Right out of your head.'

'Also,' I said, 'sometimes I feel like I can't breathe. Do you think that's normal?'

Michael went crazy when I said I wasn't applying for Cambridge.

He said why wouldn't I want to go to the best university in the country.

He said he could stay on after his degree was finished, and we could live together. Or, if the Cambridge course wasn't right, I could go to university in London, and he could do an MBA at King's or UCL or LSE, or get a job. And we could be together every day and every night. (This sounded a bit exhausting: I didn't sleep very well when he was in the same bed as me.)

'Well, I'll think about applying for London,' I said.

To keep him quiet.

Did I ever love Michael?

That's what I'm wondering.

I remember sitting on the window seat watching him arrive from Cambridge, park the Mini and crunch over the gravel. I'd walk slowly down the stairs, and he'd hold out his long bronze arms, with his head slightly tilted.

I'd stop halfway down and say, 'Yes! And how can I help? Were you looking for something in particular?'

Something?

Objectifying my actual self!

What was I thinking?

'I certainly was,' he'd say, racing up the stairs and taking me in his arms.

Michael bought me a diamond necklace for Christmas, and his mother (alarmingly) bought me a matching diamond bracelet and a tiny oval-shaped photo of Michael exactly the right size for my locket, showing she'd been snooping about in my bedroom. I put the photo in the locket, clipped it shut, put it in my drawer, then opened the drawer, opened the locket and took the photo out.

Granny and Grandpa Green sent me a Christmas card (with a sizeable cheque) from the Maldives, explaining that my mother was back at Home Place, and that this was for the best.

That spring – it must have been April because the gardener had put my orange trees back on my terrace – I stopped sleeping.

Some nights I lay on the sunlounger, inhaling the heady scent of orange blossom and dreaming of Córdoba. I breathed, in and out, in and out, and I counted sheep and stars, and I tightened and relaxed every muscle in my body, but I still didn't sleep.

I felt sick and fearful and on edge.

I thought constantly about Bridget.

The way we'd lost each other.

The way Michael didn't fill the space she'd left.

The way I couldn't stand being at Fairmont House any more.

And then it came to me, with a jolt.

I'd never told Bridget I was here.

Here I was refusing to write to her like some vengeful arse, and perhaps there was a whole bundle of letters waiting for me on the mat in Chelsea.

I had to get back there.

Quickly.

Then I'd be able to sleep.

Feel normal again.

I spoke to my form tutor, Miss Hadley, and she smiled and said that a solution would be found, who should she phone?

I suggested she might phone Jean, because we absolutely couldn't disturb my mother, and my grandparents were unlikely to be especially helpful.

When Jean agreed that she would come back to Chelsea to be with me, Miss Hadley phoned Christine.

'Was she cross?' I said to Miss Hadley.

'I said how grateful you were to her,' said Miss Hadley. 'I also said it was very normal for pupils to feel the pressure of A levels, and it was very normal that you wanted to take your exams from home.'

'What did she say?' I said, trembling because, deep down, I was frightened of her, like I was frightened of my mother, but slightly more.

'She said she understood,' said Miss Hadley.

But when I got back to Fairmont House, I knew that she did not understand.

'I couldn't have done *more*,' she said icily.

'You couldn't,' I said, clutching my hands together to stop them shaking.

Granny and Grandpa Green came to collect me from Fairmont House, smelling faintly of Ambre Solaire.

'We're so grateful to you for having Eva,' Grandpa Green said to Christine Orson, who'd had a blow-dry in preparation for their arrival.

'It's been a total pleasure to help,' she said, glowing with her own goodness.

'This is for you,' said Grandpa Green once we got in the car, handing me a blue box.

Christine Orson gave up waving at us and went inside.

When I opened the box, it had a glass paperweight in it, engraved with the name of the cruise-ship they'd been on, and I strongly suspected they'd been given it for free.

'Thank you so much,' I said. 'It will be very useful.'

'Well, we thought with all the studying . . .' said Granny Green, her sentence trailing off nowhere as we set off.

Soon I was back on our tiled Chelsea porch, flanked by my leathery grandparents and their peeling noses.

'Your mother's hoping to join us sometime soon,' said Jean, letting out a big burst of paint-smell as she opened the door.

'Thank you,' I said to Jean, and I felt tears in my eyes seeing her flowery skirt and her kind face again.

I looked anxiously for a pile of letters with Bridget's writing on, but the hall shelf was empty.

Jean's brother, Nigel, came walking down the hall, wearing bright blue suede loafers. He looked, yes, rather dapper – and I hadn't expected him to. He threw his arms around me, and he smelled of sandalwood.

Jean said, 'Nigel's very affectionate! I hope you don't mind!'

Granny and Grandpa Green looked at Nigel as if he was an escaped zoo animal, and turned around and fled.

Nigel took a bottle of Prosecco and three glass flutes out amongst the bay trees, said 'Bottoms up' and nearly fell off his chair laughing.

We clinked and sipped.

'Jean,' I began. 'Were there any letters?'

'Letters?'

'For me?'

'I'll have a good look,' she said. 'The decorators have been in so perhaps . . .'

'It's quite urgent,' I said.

And because Jean was such a nice person, she didn't ask in what way the letters might be urgent. No, she simply opened every cupboard and drawer of the house, coming back, not with a bundle, but with one thin pale blue one.

One thin one with Bridget's writing on.

A fizz of anticipation.

'I've sent you three letters that you haven't answered,' she wrote flatly. 'I assume you're very caught up with Michael.'

Caught up?

Like in a net?

Was she right?

Also, how dare the decorators throw away my letters?

Blame the decorators.

So much easier than blaming myself.

Bridget said that she, Bessie and Bella were now living in a kibbutz, which was currently converting to the renewing kibbutz model, which she wrote about at length, and which I skimmed because it really wasn't interesting.

Wasn't interesting?

A bubble of pain rose up from my belly because Bridget surely would always be interesting to me, and if her life wasn't interesting to me, maybe my life wasn't interesting to her, so we were officially losing each other, may even have lost each other already, and that was a true tragedy. Because she was the person I loved most in the world and we were supposed to share everything our whole lives.

'Barny's back in England,' wrote Bridget. 'He's reading Archaeology at Durham.'

I'm ashamed to say that the power of Barnaby's name overshadowed my anxiety about Bridget, and I'm also ashamed to see the shallow inadequacy of my letter back to her, a letter I absolutely don't remember writing – oh the danger of the self-justifying memory – but which she kept and is in front of me, right now. It's clear I was rushing it off to make sure the message got to Barnaby.

Dear Bridget
I never got your letters – so sorry.
My mother is very ill (again) so had to move out quickly.
May not have sent my temporary address?

(May not? Such a lie. Weirdly, I don't say that I've been living with the Orsons, and I don't say anything about Michael, probably to leave the coast clear for Barnaby. Consciously or sub-consciously.)

Thanks for all the news.
Kibbutz living – amazing! Completely amazing!

(Is that honestly all I could manage? It was so obvious I hadn't read it properly.)

Head currently in A levels.

(Where were my verbs?)

Tell Barnaby to give me a call if he ever comes south. Or could meet halfway? Makes so much sense he's studying Archaeology!! Remember Charmouth beach?! The locket?!

(Far too many exclamation marks and surely not those double ?!s.)

So many happy memories!
Hugs from London xx

It was the sort of letter, thinking about it, that Christine Orson might have written.

Fast and exclamatory, with a cold trophy busyness about it – must dash, no time for full sentences.

But I was in the land of love again, and perhaps Jean's unshowy kindness and Nigel's hugs would warm me up.

The next day, Michael appeared wearing a linen jacket, looking handsome and agitated.

I felt guilty about how much I wanted to see Barnaby.

We stood a foot apart from each other, both of us with our hands in our pockets.

'Evs,' said Michael, taking his hands out of his pockets, but not knowing what to do with them. 'Why didn't you tell me you were leaving?'

'I don't know,' I said, but I did know, I knew he'd have tried to stop me.

'You mean the world to me,' he said. 'And obviously so does my mother.'

'Has she decided I might not be such a good proposition after all?' I said.

'She's just worried for both of us,' he said. 'Any mother would be.'

'Your mother has been very good to me,' I said, in a strange voice I didn't recognise.

I started crying.

Partly to make Michael feel sorry for me, instead of cross with me. If I'm honest.

I watched as Michael took a little packet out of his pocket, pulled off its sticky strip and neatly unfolded a tissue, one section at a time.

'She thinks the world of you,' he said, handing me the unfolded tissue. I knew she didn't.

I knew how hard it is to love people who don't love us.

Nigel appeared with Prosecco, and we went out to the *patio*, where Jean joined us.

'Bottoms up,' said Nigel, and the four of us clinked glasses.

'I wish I had a girlfriend,' said Nigel. 'But I'm never allowed out on my own.'

'Why not?' said Michael.

'I always get drunk!' said Nigel. 'I love getting drunk. But sometimes I can't find my way home.'

Jean asked Nigel to leave the two of us in peace, and they went inside.

Michael sat on the sunlounger and pulled me towards him.

'Why don't you go to King's instead of Edinburgh?' he said. 'It's just around the corner. And I'm going to be in London. And we need to be together.'

'I told you it's my second choice,' I said.

'But Edinburgh's so far away,' he said, kissing my neck – he had a bit of a thing for my neck. 'It won't be good for our relationship.'

I had an urge to swat his kisses like flies.

'If it's meant to be, it will work,' I said, thinking that, although people said this a lot, it really was a load of crap.

Back in Chelsea, wonderfully, I started sleeping again, and, even better, I went on sleeping as my A levels began and my mother came home.

'I got better for you!' she said, like when she came to collect me from Bridget's seven years earlier. 'I did it!'

I stared at her, and she looked like a stranger.

Nigel led us both to the *patio*, and my mother said, 'Jeanie!'

She really did.

Jean reached out her two hands and held my mother's two hands. I stared at them, thinking that I'd never held her hands like that, and had never wanted to.

My mother got up the next morning and got dressed, and we all four ate breakfast together, smiling at each other. The smiles carried on through the exams and the celebration parties and then I was leaving school, and off to Mirabello Bay, shuddering with anxiety at the thought of being Orsoned again.

The sun shone and the Orsons' cook made delicious dinners, and we drank champagne and went for rides in their speedboat, but Billy kept escaping alone in his kayak.

'Sometimes,' he said to me, 'I think I might get in this kayak and keep going and never come back.'

'Please don't do that,' I said. 'I'd really miss you.'

'You wouldn't,' he said. 'We never see each other.'

'We see each other all the time.'

'Because you're Michael's girlfriend,' he said. 'You never see *me*.'

'The thing is . . .' I stammered. 'I'm just not sure how . . .'

'I know,' said Billy. 'I've tried to see it from your point of view, climb inside your skin. You know, like in *To Kill a Mockingbird*. You don't need to explain.'

I hugged him, and it felt like I was hugging nothing.

As he got in his kayak, I knew that I hadn't tried to climb inside his skin and walk around in it, like Harper Lee said.

And nor had I tried to climb into Bridget's.

I watched Billy floating across the bay, and I felt fear, like smoke rising on the horizon.

When we got back to England, I was desperate to be alone.

Michael phoned to say that Billy had disappeared, and could I come over?

I didn't want to.

But I went.

I didn't stay the night.

Michael was cross.

Billy didn't come back.

A week passed.

I came and went.

I could only think of Billy.

But Michael wanted to talk about our relationship.

How it would work if I went to Edinburgh.

When Billy finally walked through the door of Fairmont House, we were all eating supper.

We stopped.

'Ah, the prodigal son!' said Mr Orson.

Christine said, 'How dare you do this to me?'

Billy said nothing.

Christine told him he was a total waste of space and would never amount to anything in the world, not unless he turned himself around.

Billy swivelled in a circle on one leg, 360 degrees.

Which wasn't wise, and he probably regretted it later.

It might have been funny if I hadn't felt so afraid.

Christine didn't offer him any supper.

I found it hard to eat.

Billy went to his bedroom.

Michael and I went for a walk.

When we got back, I whispered secretly through Billy's door.

But he didn't answer.

Michael said, 'How dare Billy put my mother through this!'

I said I was going back to Chelsea for a few days.

When the results came out in August, I'd got all As, which meant I'd got into Edinburgh.

'Edinburgh?' said my mother. 'You mean in Scotland?'

She took to her bed, pulled the drapey curtains and refused to move.

Michael appeared at the door, looking shocked.

'Something awful has happened,' he said.

I grabbed his hand.

'Billy got C, D, D,' he said. 'Mum's distraught.'

'It's OK,' I said. 'A levels aren't everything. Look at Richard Branson.'

'Anyway?' he said, looking at me.

'Anyway what?' I said to Michael.

'What did you get?'

'Who cares?' I said.

'Did you get all As?' he said.

I looked away.

'You did, didn't you?' said Michael.

'Please don't say anything to Billy,' I said.

'Please stay in London with me,' he said, and he put his arms around me, and they reminded me of those kissing gates, where you get trapped for a moment, before being let out.

'I'm sorry, Michael,' I said to his handsome fragile face. 'I'm going to Edinburgh.'

Let me out, I thought, but he still had his arms around me.

Michael looked utterly defeated by Edinburgh, but not as defeated as he would look the next day, when the gardener found Billy at the back of the garage, hanging from a rope underneath the stuffed stag's head, which his mother wouldn't have in the house.

I sat staring through the window at the golden-rain tree, hearing Michael's gaspy sobs at the other end of the phone, and Jean came in, went out, came in, went out.

Yellow petals blew in the breeze.

I tasted Maltesers in my mouth.

I saw Billy strutting like Freddy Mercury with the tree branch between his legs.

On the other end of the phone, Michael was crying, and Michael never cried, and the golden-rain tree was crying, its petals falling slowly to the pavement, and Billy was dead, Billy who wanted to kayak over the horizon to see if it was any better over there, beyond the expectations.

It couldn't possibly be true.

I should never have gone out with Michael.

I should have been Billy's friend.

Wake me up before you go-go.

I could still remember the dance moves.

But he didn't wake me up before he went.

I should have told Michael what Billy had said to me in Mirabello Bay.

I shouldn't have stayed at Fairmont House when Billy had to board.

I put down the phone.

I stared out of the window.

Jean came in.

'I don't think your mother can survive you going to Edinburgh,' she said.

Will everyone leave me alone and let me go to Edinburgh, I thought.

I am going to Edinburgh.

Nothing will stop me going to Edinburgh.

Billy has died and I can't go to Edinburgh.

The tears fountained up from my gut.

I CAN'T GO!

I CAN'T GO!

I'll have to stay.

Here.

I'll have to stay.

With Michael.

Nobody leaves a grieving brother.

And anyway, it was partly my fault, and maybe I could have stopped him if only I'd tried.

I exploded into a strange paroxysm of grief, as if everything I'd ever been sad about in my whole life was bursting through my eyes, out of my veins, through my skin.

Nigel crept into my father's old study.

'Evzy,' he said. 'I hid some Prosecco. Here you are.'

We passed the bottle back and forward, glugging it in great gulps, and Nigel held me in his chubby arms, as I sobbed and sobbed and couldn't stop, and he said, 'I felt really really sad once.'

'When was that, Nigel?' I sobbed.

'When Mum didn't let me learn to play the trumpet,' he said.

'I got over it in the end,' he said. 'Not learning the trumpet.'

Then Michael rang.

He said, 'Please please don't go to Edinburgh now, Evs.'

So that was how it was that I ended up going to King's College, London, living at home in Chelsea because my mother (via Grandpa Green who ran her finances) couldn't see the point of paying rent when we were *drowning in empty bedrooms*.

Bridget remembers writing to ask me how my A levels had gone.

I imagine I didn't answer because I was lost in my own tragedy, but she had no way of knowing that.

People don't know things unless you tell them.

This is an important point to remember.

The first thing the Orsons did when Billy died was buy beautiful new black clothes.

Black with a splash of colour.

That's what Christine Orson kept saying on the phone, staring at the garage through the kitchen window, as if Billy might come walking out of it.

'Black with a splash of colour.'

Like a parrot.

I was broken by Billy's death.

Grief exposed my heart, like when a building has its outside wall blown off, and I was vulnerable and unprotected.

I couldn't bear to be talked to, consoled, touched.

I couldn't bear to have sex.

Although Michael needed to, that's what he said, that's how he would be comforted.

I had no idea what I was supposed to do, and nobody to ask.

So I gritted my teeth and imagined myself out of my body.

'What are you wearing for the funeral?' Michael's mother kept saying. 'The dress code is black with a splash of colour.'

I felt like screaming.

Who cared – just bring Billy back, bring him back.

I had horrible thoughts, wishing other Orsons had died, and not Billy.

Then I hated myself.

A black parrot with a splash of colour, there came Christine Orson, with red lipstick, and rainbow wings, the huge silk scarf flying behind her, down the empty aisle, the slim little coffin having been dispensed with at the crematorium, the six of us holding our breath, clutching at the shiny wooden chair in front of us, as Billy went, he left us, sliding away on his back, in the oak box, holding his nose, that's what I imagined, like when he went down the slide into the swimming pool.

Billy was gone, and burning up, but there we were, two hours later, mascara re-applied, the Awesome Orsons, plus girlfriends, walking down the stone-tiled aisle, holding our pain inside our stupid, pointless shiny new clothes.

Looking at Christine's face made my heart hurt.

Because I knew she knew that she'd told him he was a *waste of space and would never amount to anything in the world.* And now the space that was Billy – every centimetre of him – had been burnt to cinders and the only thing he could amount to was ash.

I looked at Mr Orson's gold tie heading off to the right of his fat belly, and I looked at the way he was clenching his jaw to hold in his tears.

To be a man.

What the hell is a man if he can't cry for his son?

Being a man was so much of the problem here.

Mr Orson, jaw clenching, clenching, held his wife's arm, and Johnny held Antonina's, and Michael held mine.

Our presence was a tide of silence.

The church was so full that people had to stand at the back, black with a splash of colour, like spillages of pain.

Billy's friends from his boarding school were there, with their parents and the teachers and the headmaster – rows of unknown faces, black suits, pink ties, red scarves, emerald earrings.

The parents of Archie, who committed suicide in the first term, were there. Giles and Heather Morton. They were wearing badges with a photograph of Archie's face on their lapels.

Most of my year from Lewis College were there, and my year's parents, smart people in smart clothes, frozen with shock, people who hadn't necessarily loved Billy.

The whole church was crying, not only for Billy, or the Orsons, but for themselves, for the fact that soon, next week, the week after, their kids would leave for gap years and freshers' weeks, and sometimes people drowned in university rivers or in coach crashes down mountains or in night clubs taking drugs. None of us knew what was coming, and we cried for that.

Oh, abide with me, we sang together, nervously, fast falls the eventide.

Oh, abide with me, I sang.

Oh, abide with Billy.

Especially.

Please.

The holiday to Mirabello Bay was cancelled, and Christine Orson went to Home Place for the summer.

My mother kept saying, 'Poor woman!' with a look that said I'm not a poor woman any more.

Mr Orson arranged a welcome party when Christine came home, and he put a bottle of champagne with glasses on a silver tray in the hall.

And there she was, with pale patches daubed under her eyes, and a smile she'd drawn with lipstick.

'Welcome!' said Mr Orson, as if this wasn't her house.

I noticed that the chandelier was trembling.

Mr Orson said, 'I've hired the lawyer Giles Morton recommended.'

Johnny raised his glass and then lowered it, awkwardly.

'That school!' said his mother with a face that didn't move. 'It's unforgivable.'

How badly we need someone to blame, I thought.

I knew who I blamed, apart from myself.

But I couldn't say.

I mustn't say.

It wouldn't help Michael.

It wouldn't help anyone.

We started to drink our champagne, as Christine walked silently towards the staircase, and climbed the stairs, putting her right wedged foot, and then her left, carefully on each step.

'Thanks for being here,' Mr Orson said to us.

'Why was your dad talking about lawyers?' I asked Michael later.

'He's joined forces with Giles Morton, who's suing for negligence. Two powerful fathers. They're gathering evidence.'

'Evidence?'

'Apparently their safeguarding was up the creek,' he said tightly. 'Bullying. Drugs. Sexual stuff in dormitories.'

There were so many things I wanted to say, but I knew that none of them would bring Billy back, and nor would suing the school for negligence.

Billy's dried-up swimming shorts hung in the pool changing room, with the tropical fish stuck at strange stiff angles.

Christine stayed in bed, talking for hours on the phone to Heather Morton about the way they were going to *destroy that school*.

'Destroying won't help,' I said to Michael. 'Destroying will destroy.'

'When you've been through a tragedy this big, you'll have the right to comment,' he said.

I packed his comment away in the special safe, which was filling up again.

Did my life count as a tragedy, I wondered.

'I'm sorry,' said Michael. 'That was mean.'

I didn't say anything.

At the end of September, my period didn't come, but I didn't mention this to Michael, or to anyone.

Johnny and Antonina got engaged.

'We needed some good news,' said Mr Orson, tapping the fingers of his right hand, one at a time, along the pale underside of his left arm – such a vulnerable place, so much the opposite of the male forearm.

My period still didn't come.

Then one day, by the Orsons' swimming pool, two months' worth of period came at once, and Michael had to escort me inside, swaddled in bloodied towels.

'Is this normal?' he said. 'Shall I ask my mother?'

'No, please don't,' I said, bending over and clutching my stomach.

'We'll have to buy her new pool towels,' said Michael. 'There's a specific brand from Harrods she likes . . .'

Thanks for the sympathy, I thought.

The day Michael left for Cambridge, I went for a walk in Battersea Park and I found I could breathe more freely.

I remember putting my arms out and running down the slope near the bandstand, feeling the breeze in my hair, and off I flew to King's College, where I threw myself headfirst and gasping into the Hispanic Middle Ages, and where I made a few studious friends.

Despite my lack of a reply, Bridget wrote to me again from the kibbutz, and this time I wrote back and told her what had happened to Billy. I said I'd hoped to go to Edinburgh but was staying in London to support Michael. I was a tornado of pain and confusion at the time, but in the letter I sound oddly blank and unemotional. I'd shoved all my feelings down again and chosen to sound fine.

Bridget wrote back and said she was very sorry for my loss, and how loved Michael must feel that I'd changed my plans, despite wanting to go to Edinburgh so much – she hoped I was OK.

I wonder if Michael ever did feel loved by me.

I eventually replied to Bridget, saying nothing about my own feelings but banging on about the Spanish mystics, in particular the poetry of St John of the Cross, who was imprisoned in a tiny prison cell the size of a cupboard and flogged by his fellow monks.

In the dark night of the soul, bright flows the river of God, I wrote. *So perhaps there is hope in our suffering.*

You're getting way beyond me now, Bridget wrote back.

I moved on to St Teresa of Ávila, soulmate of St John, who said that our intellect was too small to understand either God or our own souls, so we should stop worrying and use our lives to love people instead.

I thought I must write to Bridget to tell her that the reason I had any chance of loving anyone else was that she'd taught me what love was.

But I never did.

I spent every spare minute reading mystical poetry or going obsessively to plays.

I met Carrie for the first time at a Spanish play in Southwark.

I remember she had a large orange feather hanging from one ear, but I'm not sure if we spoke to each other.

Remember that name.

I never stopped reading all through that first autumn term.

I wrote essays in a state of high elation.

I went to Cambridge, and Michael seemed distracted.

He'd stop talking in the middle of sentences.

I'd ask him if he was thinking about Billy.

He'd say he was thinking about nothing.

I wondered if Billy was now the same as nothing.

But I didn't say that.

'Why isn't it harder to kill yourself?' I said.

'I guess I could kill you,' said Michael, laughing. 'With this tie.'

'Don't say that,' I said.

I tried to put his words in the safe.

'But you know what I mean,' he said, blushing.

'Sometimes I dream of Billy,' I said. 'He's wearing his tropical fish shorts and he's walking in that way he had, with his skinny legs bowed out.'

'Why the hell did he do it?' said Michael.

There were so many things I could have said, but I didn't say any of them.

That night, neither of us could sleep.

Michael said could I forget that comment about killing me with his tie. He said he loved me more than anyone in the world, and he clung to me and wept until I couldn't stand it any longer.

At the beginning of my second year at King's, there was a life-changing announcement: we were going to spend the summer term at the University of Córdoba!

Thank you God thank you God thank you God – it doesn't matter who you are, you are great and wonderful and perfect.

Jean said, 'Don't tell your mother it's Córdoba. Say it's Granada.'

'But what about letters?'

'I post all the letters,' said Jean.

Grandpa Green said that he'd pay for my flights and my rent, and he raised my termly living allowance, putting a lump sum in my account for *unforeseen eventualities.*

'I don't want you getting in a tight spot,' he said.

I thanked him for his generosity.

'You need to watch out for Spanish men,' he said. 'They're only after one thing.'

Then something else amazing happened.

I was sitting, early one morning, in our cold, formal Chelsea court-yard, completely immersed in the construction of the great mosque in medieval Córdoba, when Jean brought me a letter.

I'd have recognised that writing anywhere.

Barnaby Blume!

Barnaby Blue!

'I'm going to be passing through London,' he wrote. 'How about dinner?'

Thank you God thank you God thank you God – etcetera.

I was on the top bunk in Lyme Regis looking down at his long luscious eyelashes.

You're being ridiculous, I said to myself.

'Come to Cambridge on Thursday,' said Michael on the phone.

'I can't come until Friday.'

'Why not?'

'I'm seeing a friend.'

'Well, cancel the friend.'

'You're the one who told me I should make friends.'

'What's she called?'

'Barbara,' I said, lying so deftly and so quickly that it scared me.

When Barnaby arrived, he was alone.

He looked just like Barnaby, except bigger and older – and he had exactly the same effect on me all these years later.

His hair was dark and wavy and a bit unkempt.

He still had the long eyelashes.

Obviously.

And the gold star.

Concentrate.

Calm down.

'Eva!' he said.

And his voice slid into my veins, and bubbled into the most private parts of me, catching me between my legs and on the surface of my skin.

Barnaby was wearing a tatty checked shirt with a slightly fraying collar, and his sleeves rolled up. His shoulders had broadened, and his forearms had widened, and were hairy in a nice way (not too much hair and not too little, and all heading in one direction) and I could see the shape of his biceps under his shirt, which was hanging over his crumpled jeans.

What did I actually like about Barnaby, I'm wondering as I write, except his forearms.

And what did Michael like about me – was it the shallow sliver of my personality which I chose to show him, or was it more my plum-breasts and caramel legs?

Because if it was, I can't judge him, can I?

Barnaby held out those forearms, and I sort of collapsed into them, but forwards not backwards, unlike the trust game.

It was like hugging a bear.

A really nice bear who liked you.

It was really really lovely hugging Barnaby Blue.

Even when I was doing it, I knew it was a bit too lovely.

Neither of us knew what to do with our faces, which we twisted away from each other, as we hugged.

We stood back.

I thought that if Michael could see me being hugged by Barnaby, perhaps he actually would murder me with his tie.

Barnaby looked at me and I looked at him.

And he said, 'So good to see you.'

'I brought the locket!' I said, taking it out of my jacket pocket.

'Well, look at that,' he said. 'Anyone in it yet?'

I shook my head, and put it back in my pocket, feeling absurd.

'I've asked a friend to come and join us,' he said.

'Great,' I said, feeling that this was not great.

'She's always late,' he said.

She she she – the word rang like a car alarm.

'Well, let's sit down,' I said. 'I hope you like it here. I thought tapas, you know, Andalusia. Your father's family tree!'

'You remembered,' he said. 'We've found out much more since then. And, well, so much to tell you. But this place looks great.'

'How's Bridget?' I said. 'I mean, we sometimes write to each other. But . . .'

'Lovely as ever,' he said.

'We grew apart,' I said. 'I just can't believe that happened.'

The enormity of it fell on me as Barnaby leapt to his feet.

But look, the *she* was here, and the *she* was wearing blue dungarees and DM boots, and dangly earrings, and she had long dark hair and big bosoms and a beautiful shiny face, and she definitely had a Blue Mother look about her – the same sparkly ease.

'This is Naomi,' he said.

'Naomi!' I said a bit too loudly.

'So good to meet you,' she said.

We ordered tapas.

'So, Naomi, tell me about you,' I said, feeling a bit scared of that sparkly ease.

'I'm a potter,' she said. 'I've just found a way to make this incredible fade . . .'

She pulled out some photos of gorgeous pots, fading turquoise and aquamarine, from her messy bag.

'She's selling loads of them,' said Barnaby.

'Finally,' she said. 'After not selling anything.'

'And I'm doing a bit of sculpture,' she said.

'Women with holes in their bodies,' said Barnaby.

'I haven't got too far with them . . .' she said.

'Because you're always off,' said Barnaby.

'Off?' I said.

'I can't resist an adventure,' she said. 'I have a Masters in Anthropology.'

'Brilliant,' I said, feeling enormously un-brilliant.

'And you, Barnaby?'

'Everyone calls me Barny,' he said.

'Sorry,' I said.

'I'm just doing my Masters, and then I've got funding for a PhD next year.'

'Brilliant.'

Can you stop saying brilliant, I said to myself.

'And you?' he said.

'Oh, I'm doing a degree in Hispanic Studies,' I said, gabbling slightly. 'I've got totally wrapped up in Medieval Spain, you know, Córdoba, the era of tolerance, the *Convivencia*, because it turns out that's actually where I was born. You know, my story! And where I'll be going. For the summer term!'

'No way!' he said. 'That's such a coincidence!'

'You remember your dad saying we had something in common. When we got back from Lyme Regis. When he heard from the family tree people,' and I was gabbling again. 'And I wasn't sure then, weirdly, whether I was born in Jerez or Alvera or Córdoba but—'

'I don't remember that,' said Barnaby.

I blushed. (Why did I blush? Because I knew that, unlike him, I remembered every word he'd ever said to me.)

'D and I got totally wrapped up in our Sephardi ancestors,' said Barnaby. 'So when I was thinking about my PhD, it had to be Córdoba . . .'

'I'm just reading about the building of the great mosque,' I said.

'Well you must have heard of Medina Azahara,' said Barnaby, eyes alight.

'I have!' I said, eyes also alight.

'Well that's what my PhD's about,' he said.

You can probably guess what I said.

'Brilliant.'

I finally wrote to Bridget, but I didn't tell her she'd taught me how to love.

I asked her what she thought of Naomi.

I was like a child counting down to Christmas.

I was going home.

To the place where I was born.

To the answers to my questions.

To almost-guaranteed certainty and happiness.

Before I went, I had a laparoscopy.

This is when a surgeon passes a thin tube through a cut in your skin to see if they can find any patches of endometriosis tissue. He did find patches of endometriosis tissue, lots of them, so he had to cut them all away.

After the surgery, he called me in for a meeting to discuss the fact that my chances of getting pregnant in the future were very slim. Very slim indeed. He asked me if I wanted counselling, and I said, whether I did or I didn't, I was off to Córdoba in the south of Spain, and did he know that this was the last Moorish kingdom in the whole of Europe?

He looked very serious and said that at some point I might need to consider a hysterectomy – which would involve the removal of my womb.

I thought of Naomi's clay women with a hole in their middle, and I stared at his bald head, and I mainly thought, *I'm going to Córdoba*.

He said that coping with endometriosis was difficult both physically and emotionally and I should contact a support group such as Endometriosis UK.

I gritted my teeth and stared at his bald head again.

He asked me if I had a partner. I said yes. He said I should talk about it with him.

I didn't.

I didn't talk to one single person about it.

Every time I thought about my endometriosis, I flapped it away and said to myself, I bet the surgeon wishes he wasn't bald, we all have our problems, and *I'm going to Córdoba.*

Obviously, this approach was never going to work long-term.

But it did for now.

I was packing for Spain.

In the front pocket of my huge rucksack, I put my Quest Books, my five photocopies of *the photo,* my Spanish-English dictionary, *The Rainbow Rained Us* and *Peter Pan.*

On the day I left, my mother took to her bed.

Jean said, 'Don't worry about her. We'll pull her through.'

I nodded.

'Lap it up!' said Jean. 'This is your moment!'

When she said lap it up, I tried not to think about the laparoscopy. Or the surgeon's bald head.

I smiled, and I thought that yes yes yes, it was my moment.

Then I thought that, if there was anyone I would tell about my endometriosis, it would be lovely kind Jean.

'You've probably noticed that something has changed in your mother,' said Jean, and she opened her mouth, then closed it.

'It's Nigel,' I said. 'He's making our house into a home – I can't explain it.'

There was just a little tremor of emotion in Jean's eyes.

'You'd better get going,' she said, and she reached out and clutched my hand, then let it go. 'You'll miss the plane.'

I walked down the steps and set off, with my backpack on my back.

She yelled at the top of her voice, and I had never ever heard the top of Jean's voice, 'Have fun in *Granada*!'

I turned around.

She winked at me.

Jean winked at me.

How can I describe arriving in Córdoba for the first time?

I left my backpack in my room in Hostal Jardín – a little hotel with tiled floors and walls, and an inner courtyard over-run with ferns – which was occupied for the term by King's students.

My room-mate, Carrie Felps, hadn't yet arrived. I was pretty sure she was the Carrie with the feather in her ear.

As I walked out into the late spring afternoon, I took a deep breath – I was coming home. I hoped I was coming home. To the place where I'd find my birth and my mother, and work out who I was. To the place where certainty and happiness lay waiting for me. Of course they did.

Córdoba was hot, its churches were cool, its palm trees sprouted fronds like fountains. I sat on a bench and watched a felt-hatted rider sitting, straight-backed, astride the dappled back of a horse, which, every few minutes, reared up on its hind legs. My skin tingled with the joy of being here.

I walked through the maze of flower-hung streets which I'd studied a thousand times, folding over the map in my Chelsea bedroom, and I circled back on myself, cool in the shadow, emerging into intense sunlight, and back into alleys of stone.

The city was sweet with the intoxication of orange blossom, as I'd read it would be, and I breathed it in like an addict. My father lurked around every corner, dark-skinned, black-bearded, such that I nearly touched strange men on the arm.

Turning into squares, I glimpsed huge crosses made of roses or carnations in top-to-toe red, or petalled white and blue for the festival of *Cruces*, which I'd read about (obviously).

Around a towering red-rose cross, in a small square, an old man drank fino sherry, and a granny danced flamenco with her grown-up son. A group of teenage girls twirled and stamped. A young woman arrived with a baby in a fabric sling.

She stopped in front of me so that I could see the baby's minuscule fingers holding her thumb.

And that's when it hit me.

As she started to dance, I felt the tiny hand that I would never hold, the perfect little fingers that would never curl around my thumb, the joy from which I'd be forever barred, and I was buried by the rubble of my loss, and for a moment, I was St John in his prison cell, climbing the strut of the cross towards the light, and the cross was made of roses, and the people danced, and it was no good thinking of the surgeon's bald head because I was, finally, crucified by the surgeon's curse.

Being barren was nothing like being bald.

I would never dance with my child.

I walked, no, I stomped, desolate, along the banks of the River Guadalquivir, fighting back the tears, and *bright flows the river of God*, I remembered from St John, and the river was a strange comfort, and at least I'm feeling pain, I said to myself, when I'd become so good at feeling nothing much at all.

Guadalquivir, I repeated, Guadalquivir, Guadalquivir, until I could hear the Arabic *al-wadi al-kabir* – great river – running through its current, running through time, and joggers ran where Romans once marched, and Jews once prayed, and Christians praised, and Arabs walked, robed and turbaned in the hot afternoons, perhaps Abd al-Rahman himself, newly arrived in the spring of 756.

And then.

There it was!

The Mezquita.

Nothing – nothing – could have prepared me for the size and scale of the old mosque, set high up, so that you couldn't avert your eyes, no, however long you lived here, you cricked your neck upwards when passing its ancient walls, glorious stone collages in ochre and gold and rust.

Our course began with an evening lecture.

I got back to my room, and Carrie still hadn't arrived.

I felt a little spiral of hope.

That we might become friends.

Bridget had never replied to say whether or not she liked Naomi.

I felt frightened that my flat, inadequate letters had killed our relationship.

I desperately wanted to talk to her – but was that selfish too?

Was it always about me and my needs?

Is that the danger of love, that it faces in, not out?

I knew that if I could talk to her, I'd tell her everything, about my endometriosis, and the tiny shadow-hand I'd never hold, and the Roman bridge over the ancient river, and the colossal mosque, and I'd also ask about the kibbutz and I'd also listen properly and mind about the things she minded about, but she didn't have a phone.

I sat and wrote her a string of similes about Córdoba, which I invited her to mark out of ten, like we did when we were young. I signed off Forever Eva, but the minute I posted the letter, I knew it was too flippant and all wrong.

I should have apologised, not written stupid similes, but sadly one thing nobody can do (and many must have wanted to) is get letters out of postboxes.

I thought of Michael.

I had absolutely no desire to phone him.

Could I only be close to one person at a time, I wondered – was that the problem?

It was Bridget and then Billy and then Michael – and one I'd lost, and one was dead, and one I didn't feel like phoning.

I was crap at love.

But I will change, I thought, Córdoba will change me, I know it will.

(And of course it did.)

The next day began with a guided tour of the city, starting at the old fortress, the Alcázar, its gardens ablaze with flowers and shimmering with arched fountains, which set me tingling again, like the river.

Our guide was wearing a black pencil skirt and enormous white trainers, and she spoke in machine-gun Spanish, barely comprehensible, pausing every few minutes to repeat the information in machine-gun English, barely comprehensible. Everything she said, I already knew.

We followed flocks of hot tourists with matching hats towards the orange-tree courtyard of the Mezquita – a broad cobbled terrace, whose walled interior was criss-crossed by orange trees and open to the sky.

There were six men, and a woman with no teeth, sitting along the back wall of the courtyard, begging.

Our guide machine-gunned: 'Abd al-Rahman built the first mosque in the eighth century.'

She pointed out the three extensions to the mosque, added in the ninth and tenth centuries, as if they were fire exits – with no wonder at all in her voice.

'When we go into the Mezquita,' she rattled in Spanish, 'you will see the ornate Catholic chancel, built by King Carlos of Castile . . .'

She raised her clipboard in the air, and the others followed her towards the mosque, or the *mosque-cathedral* as it is supposed to be called.

I skipped away.

She wasn't the person I wanted to be with when I went inside.

Also, it was too crowded.

I wanted it beautiful.

And quiet.

And mine.

I leant against the wall of the orange-tree courtyard and watched: a skinny boy ran through the courtyard with a tennis racquet and bowed legs – it was Billy, here and then gone, and I was sitting in a pool of sunlight, and God was hovering inside a thousand thousand murmured prayers, layered by different eras and religious ideas, fuelled by the same human hopes and fears.

The *saudade* longing came like an earthquake as a woman passed by, with long black hair like mine. I stared at her – she was probably in her early forties. The right age perhaps to be my mother?

It was possible.

In Córdoba, everything was possible.

An elderly nun came through the gate, walking with a stick, a tubular bag over her shoulder, out of which she took a grey chair, unfolding it and sitting down next to one of the beggars, handing him a huge *bocadillo*, crusty bread full of tortilla.

As I passed, she smiled.

Such a beautiful, arresting, honest smile that it made a lump in my throat.

'*Tan bonita*,' I said, so beautiful, nodding at the Mezquita.

'*Una vez subí en helicóptero*,' she said, I once went up in a helicopter. 'And from the sky, it looks like someone dropped a cathedral in the middle of the mosque, you know, by mistake.'

She threw back her head and laughed like a donkey.

'It's so busy,' I said. 'I think I'll wait and go in another time.'

'Come back early in the morning,' she said.

I noticed her grey dress.

'*Encantada*,' she said, nice to meet you.

The honest smile again.

'*Encantada,*' I said back.

When I got back to Hostal Jardín, I took out my photo and stared for a long time at the grey dress.

It was possible.

I set my alarm and went back to the Mezquita early the next morning.

I was holding my breath as I went in.

Hundreds of pillars fell away from me, one after another after another, into the distance. Solitary people walked in silence, in and out, in and out, as if we were all lost in a forest. And that's when the tears came. Tears for the Bridget I'd lost, and the Billy I'd lost, and the bits of me I'd lost with them, the future babies I'd lost without having them, and the mother I'd lost without knowing her.

The Mezquita is now walled in and full of shadows, but I tried to imagine it as it would have been when the sides were open to the air, and when butterflies and birds would have flown between the pillars and the pray-ers. That was before a Catholic chancel was slammed rudely in the middle, with gloomy side chapels, where the poor Virgin weeps behind bars.

When the Moors had gone, said a sign, the mosque's sacred beauty was so revered that the structure wasn't touched for three centuries, and when King Carlos V gave his permission to rip out its heart, the Christians who worshipped there opposed him.

As I came out, blinking, I saw the laughing nun again, and next to her a woman in a hijab handing out bottles of water to the homeless, both with covered heads and beautiful faces.

I caught the hijab-woman's eye.

She had dark eyes and smooth skin.

We smiled at each other, and it lifted me, the way a tiny human encounter can.

When I got back to the *hostal*, Carrie Felps had arrived.

She was wrapped in an orange towel, and multicoloured feathers were blowing about the room.

'The bag exploded,' she said. 'You're not allergic, are you?'

I shook my head and started picking up feathers.

'I think we met at that play in Southwark,' she said.

I smiled at her.

'Sorry I'm late arriving,' she said. 'I'm always late. How's it been?'

'I've just been to see the Mezquita,' I said.

'Is it as good as everyone says?'

'Except the Catholic bits,' I said. 'Which feel all wrong in there.'

'My mother's a Catholic,' she said.

She unknotted her towel and pulled on a crumpled red dress and a multicoloured silk kimono. Her long wet hair fell down her back.

'Anyhow,' she said. 'What are your first impressions of Córdoba?'

'It's beautiful,' I said. 'But I could never have imagined the Mezquita was so huge. The old part of the city is really very small. You can get to know it in a couple of hours. And also, there are nuns all over the place. You never see a nun in London.'

'Will you take me on a tour?' said Carrie.

When we passed the horse-drawn carriages, a man shouted: 'Half-price city tour!'

I ignored him.

'It's very touristy,' I said.

'Oh why not?' said Carrie.

Why not?

Wonderful Blumey why not!

Before I could argue, Carrie hopped in.

'Luis,' said the man, shaking her hand.

I climbed in too, and we set off over the cobbles, her hair drying to straw-blond in the sun.

We ended our third day, drinking too many plastic cups of fino sherry by the red-rose cross in Plaza del Potro, which is mentioned in *Don Quijote*, and we danced to tinny music under the stars on the cobbles of the ancient mule market.

Carrie was a little hummingbird, dancing about the square, feathers flying from her ears, spilling sherry on her toes. She had gold anklets layered around her ankles, with tiny dolphin and elephant charms.

She took my hand and whirled me around.

My skin prickled with Córdoba, and the more I drank, the more I danced, and the more I danced, the more it prickled.

Back at Hostal Jardín, Carrie collapsed onto the bed next to me.

'Have you read *Don Quijote*?' she said in a slightly slurred voice. 'It's supposed to be the first modern novel, but as far as I can work out, it's a pile of shit.'

She couldn't stop laughing.

She clutched her sides and laughed.

Her laughter was contagious, or perhaps it was the cheap sherry.

'It's something to do with perception,' she said.

And when she said perception, we both collapsed again, for no reason – except sherry.

'He thought they were giants, but actually they were windmills,' said Carrie, gulping for air. 'What kind of idiot thinks a windmill's a giant? Tell me what is good about that book?'

We let our laughter run out, and we were lying in silence.

'Maybe everyone makes a false narrative out of their life to some extent,' I said. 'Maybe that's what it's about.'

We were both drunk and it was our first evening together and I hated the way I was sounding so serious.

But sometimes I couldn't help it.

Being serious.

'Wow!' said Carrie.

Then, 'Wow!' again.

'Wow what?' I said.

'I think you're right. I think that's it. You're so clever, Eva Martínez-Green. I never thought of that! None of us tell it exactly how it is . . .'

'We make it how we wish it was,' I said. 'It's not just a *Don Quijote* thing.'

I thought of Christine Orson and her friends, curating their lives, shining up their children's achievements and their husbands and their marriages, narrating the lives they wished they were living.

I'd probably always shined up my relationship with Michael, even to myself.

Carrie sat up and gave me an emerald-green feather earring, which I put in my ear.

'Beautiful,' she said.

Then she paused.

'I had a close friend at school who used to read me her diary,' she said. 'And it never sounded anything like what had actually happened, but it was like she didn't realise. Or surely she wouldn't have read it to me? Because I knew it wasn't true.'

'Sometimes people think that if you say something enough times, it turns it true. My parents have this weird story that thieves stole my baby photos from our beach house. They've said it so often that perhaps they believe it. I mean – can you imagine thieves stealing anyone's *baby photos?*'

Carrie said, 'I think I'm going to be sick.'

She rushed to the bathroom.

It wasn't that nice, hearing someone being sick.

I heard the shower going on.

'I feel much better,' said Carrie. 'You were saying something weird – about *thieves* stealing your *baby photos* . . .'

'Basically,' I said, 'I have this theory that my mother isn't my mother.'

'Wow!' she said.

I thought of taking out the photo – I had the photocopies in an envelope under my bed. My head was throbbing, and I could feel all the sherry I'd drunk in the pit of my stomach. And maybe a lot of sherry was what I needed in order to show someone finally.

Carrie lay down on her bed and fell asleep.

Like Bridget had when I tried to tell her.

Why was it that I could never show anyone this photo?

When the phone rang on our bedside table, I knew it was Michael, and I knew that I didn't want to answer.

He kept phoning.

I kept not answering.

I watched Carrie sleeping.

She looked so pretty.

In the morning, I called Michael.

'I was so worried,' he said.

'I'm sorry,' I said. 'We were out late.'

'I needed to talk to you,' he said. 'I had a bad moment about Billy.'

'I'm sorry,' I said again.

'I'm finding it really hard, you being so far away,' he said.

'I'm sorry,' I said again.

'Can you stop saying I'm sorry?' he said.

I nearly said, I'm sorry.

'So what were you up to yesterday?'

'I went to see the Mezquita.'

No answer.

'It's incredibly beautiful, but they should never have put—'

He interrupted: 'Well, you can show me it all when I come out.'

I felt like saying, I don't want you to come.

I locked this thought in the UNWANTED THOUGHTS safe, which was getting rather full again.

'Two weeks to go,' he said.

'Yes,' I said.

'Are you OK?' he said.

'Yes, thank you,' I said.

Yes, thank you?

Always be suspicious if you say yes thank you to your boyfriend.

The flower crosses were disassembled and it was the festival of *Patios*.

Carrie and I trooped about the city with our *Patios* map, oohing and aahing at the flower-filled courtyards, the pots of geraniums, the tinkling fountains, the tiled walls and stone statues, the jasmine stars in cracked urns, and we stopped for wine and tapas, and wine and tapas, and on we went, and Carrie took my arm.

'I love those pink geraniums!' she said.

'I can't stand pink,' I said.

I found that I was telling her, in some detail, about *The Rainbow Rained Us*.

It just came out.

This was the effect Carrie had on me, the effect of making me talk, just as Bridget had. I couldn't stop: Pink Mother, Blue Mother, Bridget – I was gabbling.

'Are you and Bridget still close?' she said.

I couldn't bear to answer.

'We write letters,' I said.

'Tell me the colours again,' she said. 'I want to work out which my mother is.'

I repeated them.

'My mother's purple,' she said. 'Liturgical purple. Definitely. She loves rules. And doing *the right thing!*'

'What colour mother would you like to be?' I said to Carrie.

'Green or Blue,' she said.

'Me too,' I said. 'You've no idea how much I loved Bridget's family. I'd be a totally different person if it wasn't for her.'

And perhaps we were different people now from the ones we'd been then, and perhaps we could never have back what had once seemed ours forever. But even if we wouldn't mudlark on the grey beach by Battersea Bridge or mark each other's similes out of ten, we could maybe still love each other just the same.

I thought unexpectedly of the tiny fingers curled around the woman's thumb.

And, with tears in my eyes, I told Carrie about my endometriosis.

'I'm so sorry,' she said. 'That's tough, Evs.'

She hugged me, and we walked some more, and we came across a little Moroccan souk under an arch, selling pottery plates and bowls and silver teapots and brass lamps, with a rail of silk clothes at the back.

'Harem pants!' I said. 'These are what Blue Mother wore!'

'She sounds so lovely,' said Carrie. 'Come on, let's try some on!'

'*Tres por dos,*' said the man, who was wearing leather shoes with curled-up toes.

Carrie and I bought three pairs, in gleaming silk.

I wore emerald green and she wore tangerine orange back to the *hostal,* and the harem pants helped. I was back to baggy again and back to being myself.

On the table, there were letters.

Had Bridget written?

Had she marked my similes?

Could I have her back?

Carrie's letter was from her mum, checking she was going to Mass.

My first letter was from Michael.

'Michael?' said Carrie.

I told her all about Michael and the Orsons and their film-set life, but I left out Billy, and we moved onto Carrie's string of useless boyfriends, none of whom had held her attention for very long.

'He's booked his flight for Friday the thirteenth of May,' I said flatly, skimming Michael's letter.

'Unlucky for some!' said Carrie.

Hold on – the second was from *Barnaby Blue.*

D and I will be in Córdoba from Wed 11–Sun 15 May. How about meeting up one evening for tapas?

'You're blushing,' said Carrie. 'At the wrong letter.'

'No, I'm not,' I said.

'You definitely were.'

'You could combine them all,' said Carrie, staring at my face. 'On the Saturday night.'

'I think I'll see Barnaby before Michael arrives,' I said.

'Tell me about this Barnaby,' she said, winking.

I said stiffly, 'I told you about Bridget . . .'

Carrie nodded.

'Well, Barnaby's her brother – and he's an architect at Medina Azahara, where we're going tomorrow.'

Carrie smiled knowingly.

Then she said, 'Have you got that rainbow book with you?'

'Weirdly I have,' I said.

And we sat looking through *The Rainbow Rained Us.*

Carrie said, 'Michael's mother is Gold Mother. Obviously. You were never going to like her.'

'Also,' I said, 'there was another Orson son that I can't really bear to talk about. Probably the best of them all. He was called Billy . . .'

On the day I was due to meet Barnaby, I couldn't concentrate at all.

And I can always concentrate.

Everything I put on was wrong.

I wore dungarees.

Like Naomi – as you probably spotted.

I was late.

I rushed along the corridor, which ran in a square above the inner courtyard where we ate breakfast surrounded by ferns and piles of old *National Geographic* magazines.

I skipped down the stairs and out of the building, heading towards the Mezquita and up to the tapas bar where we'd arranged to meet.

Two brown nuns were walking together, arm in arm.

And there he was.

He was wearing shorts.

My eyes darted to his legs.

I felt myself blushing.

His Barnaby Blue lovely architecty weathered hairy shins.

Yes, OK, legs as well as arms as well as eyelashes.

Shallow as anything.

Kiss, kiss – xx – one cheek, the other, Spanish style.

I didn't fall into his arms and he didn't feel like a bear.

Nobody feels like a bear when you go kiss kiss, one cheek then the other.

He said he was sorry D wasn't there, he was having one of his days.

'I know all about that,' I said.

'Have you struggled with depression?'

'No!'

Too loud and too fast, just checking he knew that I was not the sort of person to struggle with depression because I was cool and adventuring in my dungarees, like Naomi who made pots of girls with holes in the middle, and don't you go thinking I have a hole in my middle, because actually . . . don't think of bald heads or tiny curling fingers.

'How do you know about depression then?'

'My mother.'

'Oh, of course. We never knew the detail of that. M never said.'

'I don't know the detail of it,' I said. 'But I still suspect she isn't my mother.'

'Isn't your mother?'

'Did Bridget never tell you?'

'It's odd, but we didn't really talk about you.'

You didn't *talk about me?*

Before I knew it, because Córdoba was melting my reserve, I was telling Barnaby Blue that years ago, before I went to live with them, I'd found a photo of a baby who looked just like me, I'd compared my own face in a magnifying mirror.

I was finally going to show another person the photo.

But first I'd describe it to him.

To warm up.

'It was definitely me in a beautiful *patio*,' I said, 'and definitely in Córdoba, which was definitely my place of birth.'

I told him that there was a statue of an angel behind me and an old wagon wheel, and that the hands holding me were old hands, probably the hands of my real mother, who was wearing a grey dress and who'd been deliberately beheaded, and what did he make of that?

'I guess the *patio* could be anywhere in Spain,' said Barnaby.

He paused.

I tried to maintain a confident facial expression.

'And the person holding you might be a relative.'

He paused again.

I felt stupid.

But I tried to look as if I didn't.

'Or of course the baby might not be you.'

The thing I'd been trying not to think since I was ten.

And said so *casually*.

'Or you may be right, of course,' he said.

Yes, I may be right.

And no, I definitely wasn't going to show him the photo now.

Not after that reaction.

Like I hadn't shown Bridget, and I hadn't shown Carrie.

Like I wouldn't dream of showing Michael.

Forget about it, I said to myself, and enjoy the evening!

You might even end up with your head in his lap and his gold star hanging over you like a sign!

Oh, lovely make-believe, perhaps we could rewind.

Perhaps Barnaby Blue could be perfect again, and Blue Mother could be alive, and Bridget could love me like she used to, all of us preserved forever in formaldehyde at the house in Lyme Regis.

'So tell me how your dad is,' I said, as his smile made its way down my legs.

'He never got over M's death,' he said.

'You don't get over death,' I said. 'You swallow it inside you. And your grief forms a layer of you. Because that's what we are, layer on layer of experience, like your dad used to explain history, do you remember?'

Gabbling again.

'I like that,' he said.

'You would do,' I said. 'You're an archaeologist!'

He laughed.

I was slightly hyper, but I couldn't help it.

'Your dad said all history is personal,' I said. 'We are walking histories. And the stuff that happened to us years ago is still inside us. And we choose how much to excavate.'

'I like that,' he said again.

Yes, yes, you do like that, I thought because I'm hell-bent on making you like me, and Michael flashed into my mind, all handsome and tidy, and Barnaby Blue's shirt flapped open at the bottom where there wasn't a button, showing the top of his boxer shorts, and a line of hair, going down down, Eva, Eva, Eva, I said to myself, stop that at once, you are going down down to a very dangerous place.

After we'd eaten our tapas and drunk too much wine, I said I would take him on my completely unique fact-packed guided tour of Córdoba.

'I'm going to set my watch,' he said. 'And this is the challenge. See how long you can talk about Córdoba without stopping.'

About seven minutes in, I got the giggles.

We walked down to the river, and we let our sides bump together, and I wanted to grab Barnaby Blue and ravish him in the little patch of grass by the river, my favourite spot, where the old holm oak grows next to the crumbling wall.

'You look lovely,' he said.

I stopped walking.

I stopped breathing.

We looked at the little bird-flecked islands in the river, the elms and tamarisks, the poplars and eucalyptus trees. A flock of egrets flew by as we headed towards the bridge.

Barnaby and I walked over the bridge to the tower.

I thought: I'll ravish you, or you ravish me, or we could ravish each other – I'm easy. And anywhere would do. Even here. On the pavement.

'Did you know that Medina Azahara was the largest city ever built from scratch in Western Europe,' he said. 'It was built from a single plan. There's nothing like it anywhere.'

I tried to concentrate.

'I'll see if I can beat seven minutes,' he said.

Barnaby kept going at some pace, and he was several minutes in before I said, 'Hold on! I don't think you got that date right. The first threat came in 1010, surely — when the palace was sacked by Islamic purists from North Africa. They didn't like the liberal ways of the Caliphate, did they? All this happy coexistence wasn't their thing . . .'

'I thought this was my special subject!' said Barnaby, laughing, taking my arm. 'But what you might not know is that, now, when only ten per cent of Medina Azahara has been uncovered, we have a new threat.'

We stopped in front of Heladería Torre, the famous ice cream shop.

You are my new threat, I thought.

'Construction companies are building illegal houses,' he said. 'The town hall in Córdoba is failing to protect the site.'

I couldn't care less, I thought.

I'm just a mess of whooshes.

Fall in love with me.

We sat at a table on the terrace and ordered a mountain of coconut and coffee and caramel ice cream, feeding each other with orange plastic spoons.

We stopped talking for a moment.

We looked at our watches.

We'd been talking for four hours.

'I need to get back to D,' he said.

'Anything else we should have covered?' I said.

Cover me.

Uncover me.

Either.

'Oh yes,' he said, 'I forgot. Naomi sends her love.'

'Thank you,' I said, feeling my mouth forming a very strangely shaped smile.

'Do you have a partner?' he said.

'Well, I have . . .'

I tried to pull myself together.

'Yes,' I said firmly. 'Michael!'

He didn't say anything.

'When I come out here for longer, Naomi will visit,' he said. 'So hopefully we can catch up again, the three of us.'

He paused.

'Or, I guess, the four of us, with Michael.'

We walked over the bridge in silence, and, when we reached the other side, I turned right along the river, and he headed over the road.

Then I ran back and said, 'I would really love to see your father.'

He said, 'I'll sort that,' and he disappeared under the Roman arch up towards the Mezquita.

The next morning, Carrie asked me how my date had gone.

I snapped at her that it wasn't a date.

She said, 'You're feeling guilty.'

I said, 'No, I'm not.'

'Did something happen with Barnaby?' she said. 'Like did you end up in bed?'

'Course we didn't end up in bed.'

Carrie stared at me, cocking her head to the right and then to the left.

'So how was your evening?'

'Good.'

'Will you tell Michael you went out with Barnaby?'

'I don't know.'

'I do know,' said Carrie. 'I know you won't.'

'I'd prefer you not to say anything either,' I said.

Carrie smiled.

There was a knock on the door.

It was the owner of the *hostal*, saying there was someone to see me in Reception.

'It'll be Barnaby declaring undying love!' said Carrie.

When I went downstairs, Mr Blue was waiting.

'Eva Martínez-Green!' he said, opening his arms.

I fell into them, and stayed there.

'I hadn't realised how much I'd missed you,' I said, and we held each other's hands.

'Are you OK?' I said.

'It depends on the day,' he said. 'And I woke up OK this morning. So I'm taking you out for breakfast.'

We started walking.

'Barnaby says it's still very hard for you.'

'I let the children down very badly,' he said. 'I couldn't recover.'

'You did your best,' I said.

'You rerun things,' he said. 'And wish you'd done it differently.'

'We all do that,' I said, and I thought of Billy Orson, getting into his orange kayak.

We ate croissants and we drank peach juice and we talked about the house in Turret Grove, and the bald lawn, and Lyme Regis, and fossils, but I couldn't make myself talk about Bridget.

We went to see the statue of Maimonides, the famous Jewish Sephardic philosopher, and we visited the tiny synagogue, which was converted into a rabies hospital when the Jews were kicked out.

When we hugged each other goodbye, he said, 'Bridget took the brunt of it. Trying to be a mother to the little ones when I was falling to pieces. It nearly undid her.'

My heart hurt.

I didn't know, and I hadn't been there for her, and I was ashamed.

'It's a pity you two lost touch,' he said.

Is that what she'd told him?

That we'd lost touch?

What sort of a person was I to lose touch with Bridget?

'We write letters,' I said, trying to defend myself. 'In fact, I only just wrote to her. I'm sure she'll reply soon.'

When I got back to Hostal Jardín, Carrie had dyed her hair rust-red.

'Where on earth have you been?' she said.

'With Mr Blue.'

'I was hoping for some romance,' she said.

'Would you like me to move into Jane and Dee's room while Michael's here?' she said.

'It feels a bit of an imposition,' I said.

'But it's better than watching you have sex.'

Oh yes, I thought, sex, I hadn't really thought about sex, well not with Michael anyway.

'Have you missed it?' she said.

'Sex?'

'Yup.'

'I don't think so.'

'Have you missed Michael?' she said.

I thought for a few seconds.

'I don't think so,' I said.

'I didn't think so,' she said.

'Have you missed me?' said Michael, holding me in his arms at Córdoba station.

His body felt much thinner and harder than Barnaby Blue's.

'Of course I've missed you,' I said, hearing my own voice ringing out too loudly.

'What *are* you wearing?' said Michael.

'They're called harem pants.'

'Do you mind not wearing them tonight?' he said.

Michael had booked dinner at La Bodega, the most expensive restaurant in the city.

I changed out of my harem pants, feeling furious.

When we arrived, we were ushered to our table by a slightly pompous waiter. The lights were too bright, and the air conditioning was too cold. Michael ordered lobster and champagne.

'To us!' he said, and we clinked our glasses together, and my teeth grated against each other.

I told Michael that Medina Azahara was the largest city ever built from scratch in Western Europe, but I didn't mention anything about Barnaby Blue.

'It's hard to imagine,' he said, 'without going there.'

'I could take you,' I said.

He nodded.

'So how's it all going?' I said.

'I've got some news,' he said. 'KPMG have accepted me, even before I get the results of the MBA.'

Oh my word, what a burst of acronyms, I thought.

'Congratulations!' I said, as if I was acting in a play. 'You must be so pleased.'

'Aren't you pleased, Evs? It's the beginning of our future.'

'Course I'm pleased,' I said, forcing some warmth into my voice. 'Let's go for a walk around the old town. We'll stop for ice cream.'

'Ice cream?' said Michael.

'Yes, ice cream,' I said, rather aggressively. 'It's what everyone does round here.'

'Everyone?'

'Well, obviously not everyone.'

Pedantic.

Controlling.

I shall wear harem pants tomorrow and for the rest of my life.

We stopped at Heladería Torre.

'Nothing for me,' said Michael.

'Well then I won't have anything,' I said, getting up, seething.

'What's the matter?' said Michael. 'Is it a crime not to want ice cream?'

I kept seething.

'Why aren't you talking?' said Michael as we walked.

'Look at that gorgeous campervan,' I said, pointing at two bearded guys getting out a set of drums.

'They're totally unreliable, those VW things,' said Michael. 'And a nightmare to drive.'

'What would you have then?' I said, with a little spurt of revulsion. 'A BMW?'

I wished, with a terrible ferocity, that he was a bearded man with drums and a campervan. There was no way I'd be driving around in the passenger seat of his BMW.

What if I didn't want *our future*? What if I wanted my own?

We walked on in silence.

By the Mezquita, a coffin was being taken out of a hearse.

'It's nearly two years since Billy died,' said Michael.

I didn't want to remember.

'You won't ever leave me, will you?' Michael said that night in bed.

I looked for words that wouldn't come.

'We're both tired,' I said. 'Let's get some sleep.'

I wanted to say that I'd let him turn me into someone else.

That it happened gradually.

That it was my fault not to stop it.

I wanted to say that without him, in Córdoba, I'd become myself again.

There was also the matter of Barnaby.

But he had a girlfriend.

And I couldn't sleep.

And nor could Michael.

'I've booked tickets for the Moorish Baths tomorrow,' he said, reaching for my hand.

'Great,' I said, my hand feeling like a dead fish.

'Good night then,' he said, letting go of my hand.

The next day, we sat in a tub of hot bubbling water, trying to think of things to say to each other.

Michael said, 'My parents have delayed their thirtieth anniversary party to the end of July so that you can come.'

'But I'm coming back in August,' I said.

'It's July the thirtieth – that's two days before.'

He rubbed the sole of his foot against my calf.

'I never said I was coming back on the *first* of August.'

Was I being unreasonable, or was he?

Sometimes you need an umpire in a relationship.

He had hard skin on the sole of his foot.

I moved my leg.

'Sometimes I think I never want to leave,' I said.

Michael emitted a long sigh.

'These jets are making me itchy,' I said, and I climbed out.

When Michael caught the train to Seville Airport, Carrie moved back into our room.

'How was it?' she said.

'OK,' I said.

'He's very handsome,' she said.

Being handsome is not enough, I thought.

I didn't manage to apply this excellent lesson to Barnaby.

Carrie and I went to see a horse show at the Royal Stables, and I thought how nice it was to have a girlfriend instead of a boyfriend. When we passed Bar Acebuche near the Alcázar, Jane and Dee, our closest room-neighbours, asked if we wanted to join them for tapas. I had lots of friends now Carrie was my friend. Soon all of Córdoba would be wearing feathers – she sold her earrings from a little board, and in some moods, she gave them away for free.

'Please stay, Evs,' said Carrie. 'It's not the same when you're not here.'

I felt the Bridget-glow: I was still surprised when people liked me.

'I'm tired,' I said. 'I didn't sleep well when Michael was here. I'll see you later.'

She squeezed my hand, and she flew onto the terrace.

I walked away.

And it was then that I saw my father.

He was holding the hands of two small girls with brown hair and red ribbons.

I was sure it was him.

My heart was racing.

I couldn't decide whether to run towards him or away from him.

Towards him, towards him, I couldn't stop myself.

I followed him along the street, staring at the shape of his back and trying to catch the citrus smell of him.

I'd forgotten the way he splayed his feet slightly outwards, like a penguin.

The little girls' hands were clutching his hands.

I knew the feel of those hands.

The warmth and safety of them.

The treachery of them.

I darted down a side street to get ahead of him.

There he was, his beard now grey.

'Papá,' I said, and it felt so odd to say it.

He stopped dead.

'Papá,' said the two little girls, turning their heads towards him.

For a split second, his expression became dislodged.

Then he rearranged his face into a confident smile, reminding himself he'd done nothing wrong, what could he do, Cherie was crazy, and at the same time, he was trying to make the little girl I'd been become a woman.

'*Qué maravilloso!*' he said, exuberantly, falsely. How marvellous.

I thought, you used to hang me upside down by my feet, don't you remember?

We used to see Peter Pan jumping onto the hands of Big Ben, don't you remember?

'Valentina, Camila,' he said, and then, in English, 'meet the Marvellous Eva.'

'So marvellous,' I said, 'that you've chosen not to see me in twelve and a half years.'

He made no response.

Then he stepped forward and kissed me – but, as you know, the Spanish kiss everyone.

The little girls stared up at me.

Then they started playing hopscotch.

Kiss, kiss, the Spanish way.

'You sent me orange trees,' I said, and I could feel my mouth trembling. 'It was the same date you left us, did you realise?'

(And only days after I lost my virginity in the back of Michael's Mini, I didn't say.)

'Oh yes,' he said. 'Of course I realised.'

Pull yourself together, I said to myself, because I could feel my face starting to collapse.

'What date was it then?' I said, allowing myself to sound angry because angry would be much better than face-collapse.

'I'm not going to be interrogated,' he said.

'Because you don't know the date you left,' I said. 'You can't remember.'

'You're very harsh,' he said, reaching out his hand to me.

'I'm very angry,' I said, not taking it.

'You were such a tender child.'

'Tender children are easily hurt.'

'What else could I do?'

'There were a million things you could have done. I'm your daughter.'

The slight flicker underneath his skin – what was it?

We squared up to each other, talking fast.

'Fathers look after daughters,' I said.

Again, the flicker.

He talked over me: 'Did you like the orange trees?'

'Where did they come from?'

'I thought you'd like them.'

'Be honest – it was very random.'

'A friend ordered too many for his house in London. So I . . .'

'How touching!' I said.

He stared around him.

'I need to be making a move,' he said.

'You bump into me after twelve and a half years, and all you want to do is get away?'

'I'm due somewhere, Eva.'

'Do you have no interest at all in me?' I said, my voice raised now. 'No curiosity about why I'm here? How I am? Who I am? No desire to catch up? I can't believe you—'

'Please,' said my father, nodding at Valentina and Camila. 'They're too young . . .'

He wanted *me* to calm down to protect them.

I felt guilty, inappropriate, stupid, which were all the things he should have felt – how could I be in the wrong here?

He was stroking his beard with his right hand, and I had no idea what he was feeling.

'I was a little girl once,' I said. 'Like they are. And you left me.'

'I'm trying to think what's best,' he said, and his tone was softer.

'Do you live here?' I asked, swallowing back tears.

'Some of the time,' he said.

'These are your daughters?'

He nodded, smiling.

'Do you have any other children?' I said, doing my best to smile back.

My smile was struggling to stay in shape.

I blinked my eyes and clenched my jaw.

'Only from my first marriage, but you know about them.'

'I don't know about them, and I don't know about any first marriage,' I said – there he went, forgetting his stories – and I felt a horrible emptiness inside me. 'Am I the only child you don't see? Out of the many you've spread around Europe?'

'Well . . .'

'I take that as a yes,' I said, thinking: am I that unlikeable?

'How's your mother?' he said.

We were both quieter now and I'd taken command of my mouth, pushed the tears back down, where I could feel them like water boiling in my belly.

'I think you probably ruined her life,' I said, again, trying to make myself acceptably calm, 'although I don't suppose she was easy.'

'She's not a well lady,' he said, and I felt the anger coming back.

'And knowing that she wasn't well, you didn't think to check up on me – or her – from time to time?'

He stuttered, and this gave me some small measure of pleasure, which turned quickly into the awful thought that he'd hardly thought about me all these years, he really didn't mind how I was, he had no particular desire to meet again.

'Did Cherie tell you?' he said.

'Tell me what?'

His face coloured.

'*¿Nos vamos?*' said the older girl. Can we go?

'*Un minuto,*' he said, looking at his watch.

A loud ringtone from his pocket made me jump.

He looked smug as he took out his large mobile phone – hardly anyone had them back then.

'Eva, I have to go,' he said, trying to force it back inside his pocket. 'Are you here for a while?'

'You just asked me if Cherie told me. Told me what?'

'Oh nothing,' he said. 'You know . . .'

'We clearly need to talk,' I said, as he took the two little girls' hands. 'I'm studying here. I leave at the end of July. Do you have a card you can give me? Or a number?'

'Or you could give me yours?' he said.

'I'm staying at Hostal Jardín,' I said.

'I know exactly where that is,' he said as he turned.

'You will come, won't you?' I called as the three of them headed off.

He turned around and put his thumb up.

But I wasn't at all sure that he would.

My father didn't come.

My mind raged with hypotheses, and I went on long walks trying to bump into him.

'At least you've got Michael,' said Carrie, watching me carefully as we sat drinking wine in Plaza de Tendillas. 'And he treats you well.'

'Michael treats me beautifully,' I said flatly, hoping it was true (and I wasn't spouting false narratives like Don Quijote and Christine Orson).

'Is that what attracted you to him?' she said, sitting forwards. 'Although you wouldn't have known that I suppose, before . . .'

I'd never thought about what attracted me to Michael.

'I guess I thought he was handsome,' I said to her. 'And he asked me out. That's basically the story.'

'But you've been together for years,' said Carrie. 'I never manage more than a few weeks. How do you do it?'

'I suppose I just hung on to him,' I said, thinking that sounded all wrong.

'Are you pleased you hung onto him?' said Carrie, looking doubtful.

'I don't know,' I said.

'I wouldn't want to be hung on to accidentally,' said Carrie. 'If I were him.'

'He's the only security I have, I guess,' I said quietly.

I paused.

'I want to show you something,' I said, taking the photo out of my bag. 'It fell out of a book in my father's study years ago.'

My hands were shaking as I handed the photo to Carrie.

'I'm absolutely sure that's me,' I said, pointing at the baby.

'The eyes are just like yours,' she said, looking at the photo and back at me.

'That has to be a *patio* in Córdoba, doesn't it?' I said.

'It's very faded, but it could be,' said Carrie, holding the photo very close to her eyes. 'And someone's cut off her head, the woman who's holding you. Deliberately. You can tell. They didn't get it straight.'

'I know. And also, Carrie, I think she might be my mother. You know, the real one.'

Carrie gasped: 'Really?'

Then she said again: 'Really?'

Then she said: 'Wow!'

Then she said, 'That grey dress looks a bit like a nun's dress.'

'Or could it just be any grey dress?' I said.

Carrie stared at the dress.

'I guess so,' she said.

I took the photo.

We paid the bill, and started walking back into the old town.

She put her arm around my shoulders, like Bridget used to when we walked home from school.

Bridget never did reply to the similes.

I tried not to think about it because, if I did, it felt like I had a slab of concrete on my chest.

I'd finally, and successfully, shown someone the photo.

Hurray!

It went well.

'Hold on!' said Carrie. 'Can I look at it again?'

She sat down on a bench.

I sat next to her, and took out the photo.

'What's that in the baby's mouth?'

'My mouth?'

'Your mouth.'

'Isn't it one of those teething things?' I said, peering at it.

'It almost looks like a cross,' said Carrie.

I grabbed the photo back.

'A grey dress and a cross?' I said.

She hugged me.

'Oh my word!' she yelped. 'Are we getting somewhere? Is she a nun?'

'It would feel a bit weird to have a nun as a mother,' I said.

'Or,' said Carrie, 'your mother could still be your mother and she had a nun who was a friend, and she's holding you . . .'

I felt my stomach contract.

'But everyone else has a photo of their mother holding them as a baby,' I said. 'Don't they, Carrie? Everyone. And also someone cut off her head for a reason.'

She nodded.

We got up.

'So why don't I?' I said. 'Why do I only appear when I'm three and a half?'

'We're going to solve this mystery,' she said. 'I'm going to help you.'

A group of young guys walked past in blue uniform.

'The Mili boys,' I said. 'They're doing their year of conscription here, apparently.'

Carrie stopped and offered the tallest one a feather.

He looked, unsurprisingly, surprised.

And, in front of my eyes, in thirty seconds flat, he was asking her out.

And she was saying yes.

When Michael opened his arms to me at the station, I wondered if he did feel a bit more like a bear than he had last time. Quite a thinnish bear.

I told him about my father, and he said, 'How many families does the man need?'

'It's weird,' I said, 'looking at those two little girls and thinking they must be my sisters.'

'I'm lucky to have a father who's a good man,' said Michael.

I cocked my head, wondering if Mr Orson was a good man.

'I'm sure he's ruthless in business,' he said, smiling. 'But he's good to my mother.'

'She told me he didn't want her to have a job,' I said, not smiling. 'I hope you know that I would want a job.'

'We don't need to talk about this now,' said Michael. 'I've come here to enjoy myself.'

He slapped my right buttock.

I jumped.

I didn't think he'd done that before.

We joined the streams of people heading off to the fair, women and girls, canary-coloured in frilled flamenco dresses and matching dotty shoes, and men in tight trousers and flat felt hats.

We saw Carrie arm in arm with the tall Mili guy with a red carnation behind her ear.

There were rows of striped *caseta* tents, and fairground rides, and there was dancing and music, and paella being cooked in great vats – and, everywhere, the buzz of celebration.

Michael wasn't an awful dancer.

In fact, for an English guy, he was quite good.

But Spanish men get born with different hips.

Michael's face was smiling at me, and I wasn't able to smile back.

I could still feel the shock of his hand on my buttock.

We drank cup after cup of *Rebujito*, a fizzy mix of sherry and Sprite.

'You can't imagine something like this in England,' Michael shouted across at me, above the music, attempting a flamenco move, which didn't come off.

More *Rebujito*, one cup after another, I couldn't stop – it was the only way.

We moved on to another *caseta*, and we were both drunk now, and, as we danced, people crashed into us, and we were dancing, and we were dancing, and then I found that I was looking into.

No, it couldn't be.

Take another look.

The eyes of.

Course it isn't.

Barnaby Blue.

I sobered up in an instant.

Barnaby Blue was dancing with Naomi.

It was definitely them.

Barnaby twirled her around, and he caught her, and he kissed her, and she was wearing a crocheted vest which showed a bright red bra underneath, with wide straps, which is what you need if you have big boobs.

'I've seen someone I know,' I said to Michael.

'Introduce me!' he said.

248

'Yes, yes,' I said. 'Of course, just wait a second. I think I need the loo.'

In the queue, I breathed, breathed, breathed.

Look at the way they were dancing.

And look at the way we were dancing.

I wee'd in a strange nervous state, holding up my skirt and crouching over the loo, thinking, I'm only with Michael because Billy died; thinking, I'm making amends to Billy; thinking, Billy never wanted me to be with Michael; thinking, I don't want to be with him either.

I took Michael by the arm and dragged him across to Barnaby Blue.

'Hey!' I said, when I never said hey.

Barnaby and Naomi stopped dancing.

'This is Michael,' I said, stiffly.

'So good to see you,' said Barnaby, embracing him like a bear, a gorgeous lovely bear – who in the world wouldn't want to be hugged by Barnaby Blue?

'And this is Naomi.'

Michael hugged her, and I could imagine her big bosoms squeezing into his chest. I wondered if men really do prefer big bosoms. I felt my own, tight, small and plummy on my chest.

'We got engaged last night,' said Barnaby.

I felt a pain in my stomach, or perhaps it was the start of my period, or maybe it was both.

He got engaged?

But he doesn't love her, said my drunk mind, he loves me.

'Congratulations,' said Michael. 'Let's see the ring.'

Don't be so predictable, I thought, who cares about the stupid ring?

I couldn't look at Barnaby.

I couldn't look at anyone.

Naomi held out her hand, laughing.

'Very modern,' said Michael. 'They're normally round or oval.'

Very modern?

I grimaced.

You sound like a prick.

You're drunk, Eva, I said to myself.

You don't use words like prick and hey.

Michael was holding Naomi's hand, staring at the ring.

Maybe people like him know about engagement rings.

Maybe it's part of his mother's intentionality training.

The ring was like a flash of emerald lightning on a thick gold band.

'I'm not really an engagementy sort of person,' said Naomi.

Michael laughed: 'What does that mean?'

'Who knows?' said Naomi. 'And there's a first time for everything. That's my theory. And I'm rowing up the Amazon to find an undiscovered tribe, so I'll probably be eaten by a crocodile anyway!'

She spun away from Michael, with the strap of her crocheted vest falling down and her big red bosom coming out.

'We need to go,' I whispered to Michael. 'I think I've started my period.'

How sexy can you get?

'Well, many congratulations,' I shouted over the music, sounding somehow rather elderly – maybe it was the *many*, next time don't bother with the *many* – just stick with the congratulations.

Barnaby Blue is engaged and I never called him Barny and now it's too too too late.

He loves me more than her, I know he does.

What's wrong with you? I said to myself.

Has my period really started, I thought, or is it pain writhing about inside my belly because what I really want. What I really really want.

Wasn't that a Spice Girls song?

What I really really want is to go home.

'What bad timing,' said Michael, as we walked home.

'Their engagement?'

'Your period.'

'For me or for you?' I said, and I was sobering up, and my words sounded sharp, and I felt utterly irritable.

'For both of us,' he said.

I went and had a shower and double-layered my sanitary towels and swallowed Nurofen.

'Mum says you must get them particularly badly. She says it's not normal. But maybe you're just super fertile. Every cloud has a silver lining!'

I thought, I'm not normal.

I thought, your bloody mother.

I thought bloody bloody bloody everything, washing the lining of my womb off my knickers – my womb which is not silver at all, not even bronze, but needs one of those Well Done stickers Bridget and I used to get on Sports Day. Because my womb is a loser, and Christine will hate me forever because I have a *very slim chance indeed.*

'Every cloud doesn't have a silver lining, Michael,' I said because I wanted to disagree with him. 'Does Billy's death have a silver lining?'

He stared at me.

'I'm sorry,' I said. 'I should never have said that.'

'I've given this a lot of thought,' said Michael slowly and carefully, 'and I've come to the conclusion that there was some weakness in Billy that the rest of us didn't have.'

'Don't ever say that to me again,' I said, and my voice was a zigzag of fury.

Michael looked shocked, but he didn't say anything.

I put on new knickers and new harem pants – I had six pairs now.

'You look like Aladdin,' said Michael, laughing.

'I *like* looking like Aladdin!' I snapped. 'And also, there was nothing weak about Billy. Everything that happened wasn't his fault. Everything that happened was—'

I stopped.

I marched out of my bedroom, down the wrought-iron steps, and I went and sat inside the orange-tree courtyard of the Mezquita with the homeless people, and my stomach cramped, and I sobbed.

The woman with the hijab and dark eyes came by and gave me a bottle of water. She touched my arm, and her palm was soft, and she smelled of roses. I asked her if she had a pen. She said she did: it was inset with little jewels, and she said I should keep it.

Dear Bridget, I wrote.

I am sorry that my letters have always been so crap.

I find it so hard to put my feelings into words. You must remember that I was never much good at feelings. But I'm a bit drunk so that might help.

I thought I was being funny sending you those similes. Also, at some deeper level, I guess I was trying to rewind the years and get us back to where we started. But you haven't replied so maybe you found it stupid, or even insulting. Or maybe you don't want to be my friend any more.

I saw your dad and he said you'd had a hard time trying to be a mother to Bessie and Bella. I'm so sorry. I know I let you down.

Also, what I've been meaning to tell you for some time was that you taught me how to love, and that I loved you completely from the moment I first saw you. Literally. It was like a chemical reaction, as your dad said. You were and still are my biggest love story.

There was also Billy, Michael's younger brother, who was my best friend at school. He was my second biggest love story, but he killed himself, as I told you. And it was kind of my fault. I'm not sure I've recovered. Sometimes I think I haven't recovered from losing your mum either. Perhaps we don't recover. Perhaps we're like these sunflowers I saw growing in a scrapyard on the train here from Seville, literally out of the bonnets of smashed-up cars. (Does that make sense? Am I sounding very drunk?)

Anyhow I'm sitting in the courtyard of the Mezquita, which is a mosque-cathedral (weird name, I know)—it's the most beautiful building I've ever seen and I wish I could show it to you. Perhaps one day you might come and visit it. I'd really love that. Only if you'd like to.

I've just had a big row with Michael, who I don't love any more and haven't for a long time, even though it probably looks to everyone else as if I do. I'm with him because I feel guilty about Billy. Even though Billy hated us being together.

Everything about him is annoying me right now: his lanky legs, the hard skin on his feet, the way he keeps using acronyms, and won't eat ice cream and doesn't like campervans and also can't dance flamenco properly. Do you think I'm being reasonable?

Also, we bumped into Barnaby and Naomi and heard they'd just got engaged.

Great news.

(Liar.)

It would be so good to hear from you.
Sorry I've been so crap.
I love you, Bridget, and I always will.

(With the I in – good)

Eva xxx

Michael and I ate breakfast tensely amongst the ferns.

He said he didn't know what he'd done to upset me.

I felt bad about that.

What he'd done to upset me was be himself – and that's not fair on anyone.

'So did you like that ring?' said Michael, trying to sound normal. 'You know, that girl last night. With the tits.'

'Don't say that,' I replied crossly.

'What?'

'The girl with the tits. It's disrespectful. How would you like it if everyone got to comment on the size of your penis?'

'You're acting really weird,' said Michael. 'I was asking if you liked the ring.'

'While commenting on the size of Naomi's breasts,' I said.

'So did you like the ring or not?' said Michael, and he took a sip of coffee.

'I haven't thought about it,' I said, looking down at the table.

'Well, think about it now!' he said, and he tried smiling at me, and I felt bad, at the same time as thinking that I had no reason to feel bad, why were women made to feel bad for saying things that were reasonable?

'The zigzags?' he said.

'I suppose round or oval could be a bit boring,' I said flatly.

He stared at me, a second or two too long.

Barnaby Blue is going to marry Naomi, I thought.

So that dream's over.

'I was thinking,' said Michael, taking another sip of coffee. 'Why don't we hire a car today and we could go and see that place, you know, the Arab palace thing . . .'

'Medina Azahara?'

'Yes, and we could take a picnic.'

Help, does that sound a bit engagementy?

Surely not.

Surely he knew we were struggling to talk to each other, to be near each other, even to like each other.

'What do you think?' said Michael, trying to smile.

'Great idea,' I said.

Because it was, in usual circumstances, a great idea.

At Medina Azahara, Michael and I took photos of each other, smiling. You always smile for photos. Even if you stop smiling afterwards. Like the second afterwards.

Michael left.

I reread my letter to Bridget and decided to send it just as it was – a bit pissed.

Carrie had gone off the Mili guy and was back on poetry, and we'd found a new place to read, a little square with a fountain, where sparrows chattered in the orange trees. I posted Bridget's letter on our way there.

But I found it hard to read, and kept stopping and starting.

Carrie put down her book.

'You're so sad, Evs,' she said.

'I'm fine,' I said.

'What is it?'

'Everything.'

'Barnaby?'

'Yes.'

'Michael?'

'Yes.'

'Your father?'

'Yes. I can't believe he didn't come.'

We both picked up our books.

Page 41, three times, and then again.

'We could start our investigations,' said Carrie. 'Now I've gone off boys again.'

'What investigations?'

'We could go around all the convents in Córdoba and see if any of them took in babies in January 1975.'

'Where would we even start?'

'At the first one.'

Carrie found a tourist map where the convents were all marked with a cross.

As she put a copy of my photo in her bag, I felt a stab of tension in my temples.

At the first convent, there was a tiny tiled hallway at the front leading to a shop selling olive oil and artefacts made of olive wood, with a nun behind a screen wearing grey.

'Would you ever take in unwanted babies?' Carrie asked her, as I picked up a chopping board, then a bowl.

The nun shook her head.

'We offer retreats,' she said, handing Carrie a leaflet under the screen. 'The next one's in August if you're interested . . .'

'But in the past would you have taken in babies?' said Carrie.

The nun shook her head again.

'Do you recognise the place in this photo?' she said, holding out the copy.

My temples throbbed.

'Not in the least,' she said curtly.

We bought some olive oil.

'I thought nuns were supposed to be nice,' said Carrie.

'I don't feel optimistic,' I said.

We opened our map and set off to the next convent.

There was a pale nun sitting behind a hole in the wall.

'Brown,' I whispered. 'That's no good.'

'They might have changed colours,' Carrie whispered back.

'I don't think they do. It's not like football players.'

The nun looked gaunt and lacking in sunlight.

This was a cloistered convent, she said sadly through the hole, and the nuns didn't take in babies, they just prayed – *all the time.*

'Wow!' said Carrie. 'And you don't get bored?'

The nun hesitated and shook her head weakly.

Carrie showed her the photocopy.

'Do you recognise this place?' she said, pointing to the wagon wheel and the angel.

'I suppose it could be any *patio* in Córdoba,' she said. 'But I've never seen that angel.'

'We think this baby is my friend,' said Carrie, smiling, winningly, like she does, and gesturing towards me.

'I can see that,' said the nun, peering tenderly at the photo and then looking back at me. 'It's the almond eyes.'

'Yes,' said Carrie. 'She's looking for her mother. Can you help?'

The nun looked thoughtful, and her eyes watered.

Then she said, 'There used to be a home for unmarried mothers, years ago. Run by nuns. It closed in the sixties or the seventies . . .'

Carrie was asking a million questions.

I was saying thank you.

'I feel a bit sick,' I said.

'Go and have a drink,' said Carrie. 'And join me in the library when you're ready.'

I sat in Plaza de Tendillas, and watched cars go round and round the bronze statue of *El Gran Capitán* on his horse.

I was suddenly terrified of finding out who my mother was and what had happened to me.

What if it wasn't a nice story?

I couldn't drink my coffee.

I stood up.

My legs were jelly.

In the library, Carrie had two librarians with her, and they were looking at a computer screen as I walked over.

'This is the friend,' she said.

'So definitely January 1975?' said one of the librarians to me.

'Definitely.'

'Oh, I'm sorry,' said the other librarian.

'It closed in 1970,' said Carrie.

As we left, I dropped the olive oil, the glass shattered and the oil splattered all over our harem pants.

'Why am I so upset about this?' I said to Carrie.

'It's called displacement,' she said. 'You're not really upset about the olive oil.'

The Orsons' party was approaching, and I started to pack because I didn't have the strength not to.

That was when I knew for sure that I couldn't leave Córdoba.

I'd have a week or so with Michael, and I'd come back.

'I'll keep on with the investigations while you're gone,' said Carrie. 'And let's hang on to the room until the end of September.'

'Michael will go mental,' I said. 'He thinks I'm leaving here for good.'

Carrie hugged me, saying, 'That would be *for bad*.'

'You're so kind to do all this for me,' I said.

'I always fancied being a detective,' said Carrie. 'And I made you silver feather earrings for the party.'

I hugged her, and I put on my backpack and headed for the station.

Michael was waiting as I came through arrivals.

He took my backpack with his long arms.

'It's so good to have you home,' he said.

Home?

'I feel like our life together can start properly now Córdoba's done,' he said. 'We can be back like we were.'

No we couldn't.

That was the thing.

And also, where we were wasn't great either.

Córdoba would never ever be done.

It was us who were done.

I knew that for sure as we got into his Mini at Gatwick Airport.

'We've been too long apart,' said Michael. 'It's affected our relationship.'

I opened my mouth.

No words came out.

'After the party,' he said, 'I'm whisking you away!'

Whisking, like eggs, and sour cream.

I am sour cream, I thought.

Barnaby Blue is getting married.

The sourest of cream.

I don't want to be whisked.

And certainly not by you.

I want to get back to Carrie.

'Michael,' I said. 'I never found the right moment to tell you this, but I think you should know.'

'You're not pregnant?' he said. 'I mean, I really want children, that is absolutely part of the vision but—'

'Part of the vision?' I said. 'What vision?'

'You know, the future.'

We have no future.

'We never talked about any *vision*.'

'You're not pregnant, are you?' said Michael again.

'I could not be more not-pregnant,' I said.

'What a relief!' he said.

'But what I'm about to tell you may not be a relief,' I said.

His ears went red. I couldn't stop looking at his red ears, with the waves of blond hair around them, and stubble forming on his cheeks, when he used to get it only on his chin and upper lip.

'Go on then,' he said.

'You know how my periods are really bad,' I said.

'I thought you'd been unfaithful,' he said, taking a deep breath.

I have, I thought, but only in my head.

'No,' I said. 'But I've got endometriosis, Michael.'

He kept driving.

'Is that bad?' he said, sounding anxious. 'Don't tell me it's some terminal disease, Evs?'

'Not exactly terminal,' I said. 'Well, not for me.'

'Well, who else would it be terminal for?' he said tautly.

For us, I thought, and that would be easier than finding words for the real reasons.

'Michael,' I said. 'I may not be able to have children.'

He stopped at a red traffic light.

'Hold on hold on hold on,' he said.

The light turned amber.

Then green.

When we pulled up in front of the pond, where the carp are not coy, my heart was racing, and there was a man erecting what I assumed would be a line of flamed torches to welcome guests to the party.

'Do you think you could take those ankle chains off?' said Michael. 'My mother thinks they're for prostitutes.'

Why do you always tell me what to wear, I thought, when all you ever wear are pale blue shirts.

I took the anklets off and put them in my full jacket pocket.

I looked up.

The garage had gone.

I couldn't stop staring at the empty space.

'I can't believe you told me now, just before the party,' said Michael.

'I kept looking for a good moment to tell you,' I said. 'But there isn't really a good moment for saying something like that.'

'But not just before my parents' big party . . .' he said.

Calm down about this party, I thought, it's so typical of rich people to get worked up about parties.

'You knocked down the garage,' I said.

'We couldn't bear looking at it,' said Michael.

'I understand,' I said.

There was just an empty space, with two spindly sapling trees, which reminded me of Billy's skinny legs.

Christine came out.

I felt my body stiffen.

Her nose had grown longer, or was that my imagination?

She tried to smile at me.

And I tried to smile at her.

The air was electrified with tension.

There were people everywhere: flower-arrangers, cooks, stylists.

'Such a shame you couldn't get here earlier,' said Michael's mother.

I couldn't breathe.

'Hugo, for pity's sake, will you stop tripping me over?' she said, as Michael's father came to kiss me.

'As you see,' he said, 'pre-match tension.'

He looked grey and tired and fat.

'Is anyone going to come and help me?' said Michael's mother, striding into the garden, her face all sharp edges.

'Is Michael all right?' she said.

'Yes, fine,' I said.

'I hope you haven't upset him,' she said.

Breathe, breathe.

'We don't need any more upsets in this house,' she said, and I saw that she had a cold sore that she'd covered in gold-tan make-up.

Michael went to the Mini to get my backpack, and I climbed the stairs.

I watched him from the landing, and he looked like a man in a pale blue shirt. I thought of my father saying that so many things start well and end badly, perhaps all things, and I stared at the empty space where the garage used to be.

'I think Mum needs us all downstairs,' Michael called.

'I'm just coming,' I said.

I rushed along the landing to Michael's bedroom and I threw myself on his double bed face down.

I don't love Michael Orson, I thought.

I couldn't stop thinking about Barnaby.

How we were supposed to be the Blue-Greens.

Naomi doesn't love him like I love him, that's what I thought, because, if she did, she wouldn't say she wasn't engagementy.

That's why I'm not engagementy with Michael Orson.

Because I don't love him.

When the tears came, they were particularly wet and snotty, and they coursed down my cheeks, and I couldn't stop them, but I had to. Because soon Michael would come up and berate me and his mother would be furious, and I urgently needed a tissue.

Michael always had a neat little pack of tissues in his pocket, and there was his jacket on the back of the door.

I got up and I reached into his pocket.

But the thing I found wasn't tissues.

The thing I found was a padded envelope.

You should never open other people's envelopes.

But I did open another person's envelope.

Inside it was a lump wrapped in a sheet of thin paper, with an elastic band around it.

I took the elastic band off, and inside the sheet of paper was a green velvet box.

And on the paper:

Reset > rectangle.
2.30 pm – 27.7.95

Inside the green velvet box sat a sapphire and diamond ring.
I turned hot.

Then cold.

I was looking at my engagement ring, which Michael had collected, re-shaped, at 2.30 pm on 27 July.

How hadn't he noticed that we didn't get on any more?

How hadn't I had the courage to get out sooner?

And how could I possibly get out now?

At his parents' thirtieth wedding anniversary party?

There were noises on the landing.

I shoved the receipt and the box into the envelope, and crammed it back into Michael's pocket.

Michael came in.

I stared at this man who wanted to marry me, but didn't know me.

'What are you doing?' he said. 'Mum's going hysterical.'

'Have you got a tissue?' I said.

He took one out of the pocket of his jeans.

Had he even noticed I'd been crying?

'I did at least think,' his mother screamed up the stairs, 'that if she only came back on the day, she might come and help.'

'I'm sorry,' I said to Michael. 'Tell me something I can do. Something quite far away from your mother, if possible.'

'Come on,' he said. 'I can feel this whole thing imploding.'

We walked downstairs.

Michael put his arm around my shoulders, and it felt strangely heavy.

'Look at the weather!' said his mother. 'It's going to rain. I just know it. If only we'd had it last weekend.'

I helped some pale teenager put raffia around white napkins.

Michael came over and said, 'Thanks, Evs. We have to remember she lost a son.'

'Yes,' I said. 'I know. Give me my next job.'

'I've got to sort a few things for Mum in the study,' he said. 'The next thing is writing names on the pebbles. Here's the guest list.'

Perfect.

What a relief.

My hands were shaking.

Michael was sitting at the computer in the study, with the window open.

I sat at the garden table nearby, and I breathed deeply, and I wrote shaky gold names on grey pebbles, with flicky loops.

I noticed that my ankle had a white stripe where my anklets had been, like a slave's ankle-shackle.

I thought, I am shackled to the Orsons.

I could hear Michael on the phone, then his mother shrieking, 'What the hell is this? Why are you looking up endometriosis?'

'Nothing, it's nothing,' he said.

'Don't tell me she has endometriosis. Don't tell me she's infertile.'

I got up, and I walked around the corner of the house and I opened the gate, which was garlanded with ivy and white roses, like you see in wedding photos, the kind of wedding photos I might have featured in, myself, chained to the arch at Fairmont House in a long lace dress, and I walked through the garage that didn't exist any more, between the skinny sapling trees and past the Koi carp and the soon-to-be-flaming torches, and crunch crunch crunch over the gravel, and I kept walking.

I caught a train, and I caught a bus, and I went and sat in Mongoose on the King's Road. I ordered a glass of wine, and then another, and then another, and probably another. I felt inside my jacket pockets. My house key wasn't there. My mother didn't know I was in London, and nor did Jean.

I ordered *calamares* and I closed my eyes and breathed deeply and imagined I was sitting in the tapas bar where I met Barnaby Blue, who was getting married, and I knew that Michael had re-shaped my round-or-oval engagement ring and turned it into a rectangle because I said round-or-oval was boring, and I started crying because that was such a sad thing.

Sometimes you can't solve the problems you've helped to create.

Everything in life happens slowly, without you noticing, and one minute you're a teenager eating toffee pancakes on the King's Road, and the next minute you find an engagement ring that's meant for you, and the time between flowed past like a river, because, maybe, I'd made the mistake of not having enough – any? – intentionality.

Maybe Michael's mother was right – but only about intentionality.

I took my anklets out of my pocket and they'd all tangled up into a big knotted mess, and how does that happen, I thought.

It's not as if they can move.

They're chains, not bloody snakes.

I'd had too much wine.

The more I untangled, the more the chains tangled, and in the end, it was too much to deal with, and on my way home, I threw the whole knotted mess in the bin.

Then I felt weirdly sad.

Because I really loved those anklets.

I walked, heavy-legged and veering left, into the square, passing the homeless man, who was fast asleep.

I turned the corner.

The study light was on.

I was swaying as I looked at beautiful Nigel through the window, watching *Tom and Jerry*.

I didn't want to scare him.

I knocked gently on the window.

Nigel opened the door.

He took me into his arms.

He didn't feel like a big Barnaby Blue bear.

He felt more like Paddington.

He laid his cheek against my cheek.

'I'm going to bed, Nigel,' I said.

'See you in the morning,' he said. 'I love you, Evzy.'

With the I.

'I love you too,' I said.

I went upstairs.

I crept onto the landing.

The light was on.

Every door was shut.

I opened my mother's door very quietly because I wanted to look at her, I don't know why.

The light from the landing crept towards the four-poster bed.

I opened the door a little wider, and peered in.

There she was.

But wait a second.

I creased my eyes.

There was also someone else.

Oh, look at that.

There was Jean and there was my mother, all wrapped up in each other, in their nighties, with the eiderdown half-slipped off.

Like a family of mice.

Isn't that what Bridget said?

They all slept together, like a family of mice, in the tent in the garden, the last but one night of the holiday, when the cancer was creeping round Blue Mother's body.

I closed the door.

Michael arrived in his Mini, still in his dinner jacket, with my rucksack, before anybody else was up. I was wearing one of my mother's many silk dressing gowns, and I hadn't slept.

'I thought it was best for everyone . . .' said Michael.

I wondered how much he'd drunk.

I'd never seen him looking so awful.

'Nothing is ever best for everyone,' I said, trying to sound calm, though not feeling it.

'I've decided to be totally honest,' said Michael, and he drew his hand down his face and stroked his slightly stubbly cheeks.

'That might actually be best for everyone,' I said.

'We were supposed to be going away,' he said, and he attempted a smile. 'But I don't think we are now, are we?'

'You booked it so—'

'I love you and I love Mum,' he said firmly, as if he'd been practising in the car, and I saw her power and his weakness.

'What does she say?' I said, and as I said *she*, I realised how much anger I felt towards her – or was it anger? I didn't know what it was. But it wasn't a nice feeling.

'She says I should end the relationship,' said Michael quietly, and he took a deep breath, and I took a deep breath, and felt the air in my lungs like freedom.

'She says you shouldn't have hidden the endometriosis from me. That marriages don't survive without children.'

'I only hid it for three months,' I said. 'Three months when I don't think we were planning to have any children?'

'I do really want children,' said Michael, with no guile, that was true, but with no empathy either.

'I understand,' I said. 'It's obviously been quite traumatic for me too . . .'

He didn't hear me.

Did he ever hear me?

'She's desperate for grandchildren,' said Michael, and how ridiculous to be expecting grandchildren, at our age, and how hurtful of him too. 'And Johnny might end up in Russia.'

How come Johnny could do what he liked?

'It's your life, Michael,' I said. 'Don't forget that.'

'But it's also hers,' he said. 'And she lost Billy.'

I nodded.

I couldn't argue with that.

Should I tell Michael that Billy had thought of getting in his kayak in Mirabello Bay and never coming back?

I didn't.

I couldn't.

'She basically says I have to choose between you and her, and I know she shouldn't be asking me to do that, and . . .'

Michael's face was twisted.

Choose, I thought.

But don't choose me.

I opened my mouth, and closed it, like a fish.

'. . . Dad says she can't lose another son.'

His voice broke up on *son*.

'What does he advise?'

It came out bitterly.

'He says there are plenty more fish in the sea.'

'That's outrageous,' I said. 'That is totally outrageous. I actually can't believe he said that.'

I closed my eyes and I imagined myself swimming in a huge shoal of young women, with long hair flowing behind us like weed.

I opened my eyes.

'I thought your dad liked me,' I said.

Michael was biting his lip.

I wondered if he was about to mention the engagement ring he'd had reset into a rectangle because circles and ovals are boring, if he was about to say that it had been shoved back in his pocket all wrong.

But he didn't say a word.

We never ever spoke about that ring.

I took a breath.

'You know, Michael, your mother's right,' I said, and freed from him, I was able to be nicer. 'I think you got a bit ahead of me anyway.'

I took his hand.

Michael started crying, really crying.

I started crying too.

I was crying, but also longing to be free.

You remember Mr Blue saying that the emotions that we imagine to be far apart are also close together?

I was full of joy that this relationship was ending.

And full of pain too.

It all ran together.

Michael took his neat little pocket pack of tissues out of his dinner jacket.

I didn't think Barnaby Blue would carry around a neat little pocket pack of tissues.

I stopped the thought in its tracks.

We both wiped our faces with the tissues.

When I looked at him, I remembered being fifteen again.

But we were grown-ups now.

I wondered if I was going to tell him about my mother and Jean all curled up like a family of mice.

I knew I wasn't.

I hadn't shown him my secret photo.

I hadn't told him about my memory palace.

I'd never truly let him into my soul – just my body.

Which was a sad and empty thought.

'Evs,' said Michael. 'Why do you think Billy killed himself?'

'There were probably a million reasons,' I said.

'Do you think Archie Morton was his boyfriend?' said Michael.

'Yes,' I said.

We hugged in perhaps the truest way we ever had, clinging to each other and crying so hard we couldn't breathe.

Then we separated.

Smiled at each other with our tear-stained faces.

And Michael left my life.

Forever.

'Welcome home!' said my mother, coming down the stairs, not mentioning my hiccuppy sobs or my raw cheeks.

I found that I was scrutinising her closely, following the revelation of the night before.

'I'm so sorry but I'll need to go straight back to Córdoba,' I said, because all I could think of was getting away. 'I hope you don't mind. But shall we all have lunch together before I leave?'

'I'll treat you,' she said, looking oddly calm. 'Jean and I have found this wonderful little Italian with a roof terrace.'

'You look so well,' I said, and a sob gasped up my throat.

Jean came downstairs in an almost fashionable shirt dress. Her hair had no grey in it, and fell in waves on her shoulders, with the unmistakable hallmark of my mother's favourite blow-dryer in Chelsea.

We ate garlic bread and tricolore salad in the sun.

'I'm encouraging Jean to branch out,' said my mother. 'I've thrown away all her home-made skirts!'

They both started laughing, which set Nigel off laughing, which set me off laughing – and then we all stopped and stared at each other.

'I imagine you realise that Michael and I have split up,' I said.

'We did wonder,' said Jean. 'Are you OK?'

'He looked like such a perfect boyfriend,' said my mother. 'But Jean reminded me that so did your father. I suppose it's not enough to be head boy.'

I nodded.

That was almost funny – had she meant it to be funny?

We laughed some more and ordered coffee.

When we got home, Michael texted me to say he was feeling utterly wretched, but he'd decided to take his mother to Venice. I nearly replied: Are you going to give her a nice rectangular sapphire and diamond ring?

Instead, I texted one word: *Arrivederci*.

I caught the evening flight back to Seville.

On the plane, I took out my secret photo, and I stared at it like I used to stare at Barnaby's xx.

Oh, Barnaby Blue – this could have been our moment, if only you hadn't been stupid enough to get engaged to Naomi.

I felt the shape of my birthmark through the thin silk of my harem pants.

Eva from Iberia, I said to myself, feeling a little surge of power.

Michael hated harem pants.

And now it didn't matter.

Because I was free.

My ankle shackles had come off and I had the white stripe to prove it.

We landed, and I got out of the airport bus at Seville station, next to a street-lit wall, covered in graffiti. I took a pen out of my pocket and I wrote HAREM PANTS 4 EVER in very small writing.

I took the train from Seville to Córdoba, and Carrie came racing down the platform to meet me. She'd dyed her hair burgundy.

'Nice hair!' I said.

'You look different too!' she said, as we walked, arm in arm.

'I feel different,' I said.

'You look kind of elated.'

'I feel kind of elated.'

'He didn't propose, did he?'

'Yes and no,' I said. 'Half.'

'How can someone half-propose?'

'They can buy the ring but not say anything.'

'Evs, I can't hold it in – your father came,' she said. 'But I want to ask you about the ring first.'

We stopped.

'The ring can wait,' I said. 'He'll probably give it to his mother!'

I felt myself shiver, actually shiver – apparently, it's adrenaline, and I seem to have so much of it that it can make my teeth chatter.

'What did my father say?'

'He's very charming,' said Carrie.

'Do you think of charming as a good thing?' I said crossly.

She cocked her head.

'Did you know that your father likes poetry?'

'He loves books,' I said. 'Stories. I don't know about poetry. He'll say anything to make you like him.'

'I told him to come back and see you,' said Carrie. 'And he definitely will. And I've got all his details. So if he doesn't, we can find him.'

'If he's given you his real number,' I said.

'I think he has,' said Carrie. 'Give him a chance.'

'I don't think he deserves one,' I said. 'Please be on my side.'

Carrie hugged me.

'Course I'm on your side,' she said, letting me go. 'But he might be able to help in the search.'

'Carrie,' I said – and it came out very fast. 'I split up with Michael.'

'I thought he half-proposed?'

'I found the engagement ring in his pocket.'

'Does he know?'

'No. And he was taking me to Venice, but now he's taking his mother!'

'His mother?'

'She told him not to marry me.'

'What's it got to do with her?' said Carrie.

'His mother's right, isn't she?' I said. 'I didn't want to marry him. You knew that.'

'You're free!' she said. 'Does it feel good?'

'I think so.'

'Let's stop for a drink!' she said.

We ordered wine.

'Evs,' she said. 'I'm thinking of not going back. Like. Ever. You know, dropping out.'

'But we've only got a year left,' I said. 'Isn't that a bit of a waste?'

Could I stay here too? Not go back to London?

'I've met someone,' said Carrie. 'He's from Ronda.'

'You're always meeting someone.'

'This one wears pink tights,' she said.

I thought for a moment.

'Don't tell me he's a bullfighter!'

She nodded.

'Don't you think it's a bit weird to murder animals for your job?' I said.

'I do,' she said. 'But he's very attractive.'

'I don't think bullfighters and vegetarians are the best match,' I said.

She laughed.

'You know, I don't want to leave Córdoba either,' I said.

And when I said it, I knew it was true.

'Let's elope!' I said, and we clinked glasses.

'With the bullfighter?' said Carrie, laughing. 'Let's have a ménage à trois!'

'Or à quatre?' I said.

'With the bull?' she said, laughing.

'Also, Carrie, today I did my first ever bit of graffiti – in Seville.'

'What did it say?'

'HAREM PANTS 4 EVER!' I said. 'But very very small.'

'Excellent!' she said.

We ordered more wine.

'There's something else,' said Carrie. 'I have a significant lead in the nun-hunt.'

A wave of hope ran through me.

'It only happened this morning.'

'Tell me everything.'

'I was at a Dominican convent just out of town, the one where they sell those little honey cakes, and there was an elderly nun.'

I listened intently.

'I showed her the photo, and she noticed the cross, you know, that you were chewing in the photo, and she said only Franciscans would wear one like that, shaped like a T.'

'Yes?'

'There was apparently a group of seven Franciscan nuns—'

'When?'

'Well, it was founded by someone called Sister María Soledad. She was born here around the turn of the century, and she wanted to look after the sick and poor in the city. A benefactor gave them a house around 1920-ish.'

'1920's no good—'

'But wait – it kept going until a couple of years ago. There were always seven of them, because seven's a holy number, or something. And they took in beggars and the homeless and—'

'Babies?'

'She wasn't sure.'

I felt my face fall.

'But listen,' said Carrie. 'Another benefactor appeared in the seventies when it was half falling down and he bought it and did it up for them. So it had another lease of life.'

'And is Sister María Soledad still alive?'

'She died last summer, but her sidekick's still alive,' said Carrie.

'She's called Sister Ana, and she's the only one left – and I have the address. Here it is.'

Carrie handed me a post-it note. Sister Ana lived in Plaza de la Paz, and there was apparently a huge oak door, and to the left, a bench, a bell to ring and a little wooden flap, where they used to offer prayer to passers-by.

'There is one problem,' said Carrie. 'Sister Ana's got dementia – and she often doesn't answer the door.'

'Ideal,' I said.

'I need to go to Ronda to see Pink Tights,' said Carrie. 'And then we'll call on Sister Ana when I get back.'

When we got back to Hostal Jardín, there was no letter from Bridget, but there was an envelope for me in Barnaby's unmistakable writing.

'I'm standing here hoping that an engagement has split up,' I said to Carrie. 'Does that make me a terrible person?'

'It's always a good thing if an engagement splits up because it's one way of stopping a divorce,' said Carrie, smiling.

'Are you being serious?' I said, too seriously.

'I am if it makes you happy!' said Carrie. 'I know how much you love Barnaby! But I'd advise a little pause in proceedings. You haven't been single since you were about nine years old. Perhaps you should try it for five minutes.'

I opened the envelope.

Barnaby and Naomi hadn't split up.

They were coming to Córdoba – was I around? Was Michael? Could we meet for dinner?

'I'll call and say I'd love to meet them both for dinner,' I said to Carrie, as we climbed the wrought-iron steps to our room.

But when I called the next day, I left out the both.

I said: 'I'd love to meet you for dinner.'

Which left me wondering whether Naomi was coming or not, since we have no distinction between the singular and plural *you* in English.

Carrie packed her kimono and flip-flops into her feathery bag and set off for Ronda with bows on the end of her burgundy plaits.

I wished she hadn't.

Our room felt too quiet.

I walked up the wrought-iron staircase, thinking that when Barnaby had to choose, he chose Naomi, and when Michael had to choose, he chose his mother. And also that Bridget didn't love me any more.

I lay on my bed, trying to convince myself that Barnaby wanted to be with me – despite the fact that he'd just got engaged to Naomi, and her bosoms were like mangoes.

Then I thought it would be better to think of something else.

I read the address on the post-it note, and I said aloud, 'Sister Ana.'

I wasn't sure I could wait until Carrie was back.

The heat was searing, so I walked close to the walls, heading for Plaza de la Paz. Yes, there was the square, with a hexagonal tiled fountain in the centre. And yes, next to a huge wooden door, there was a tiled bench-seat built into the wall, and above it, a little hinged flap and a bronze bell.

I felt as if I couldn't breathe.

I put my hands in the fountain and splashed my hot face.

The air blew at me like a hairdryer.

I stood and looked around me at the shuttered windows.

I walked up to the bell and rang it.

The sound of it clanged into the thick silence, and I stepped back, listening.

But there was nothing except the rippling echoes of the bell.

And the thickness of the heat.

The silence re-established itself.

I looked up at the windows of the surrounding buildings.

Nothing.

I opened the wooden flap.

I listened.

A chatter of birds.

I opened my mouth, but no sound came out.

I shut the flap as quietly as I could.

I hesitated by the enormous wooden door, but I couldn't find the courage to knock.

I headed back towards the river, walking fast, head down, and a horse and carriage came trotting over the cobbles – it was our friend Luis, who we met on Carrie's first day in Córdoba.

'*¡Qué calor!*' he said, wiping his face with a red handkerchief, and lamenting the lack of tourists in the heat.

Did I want a ride, he asked.

I nodded.

'*¡Súbete!*' he said, and I knew I should go back.

I asked him to drop me at Plaza de la Paz.

'Plaza de las Monjas, we call it,' he said. Square of the Nuns. 'They used to take in the down-and-outs there. Only one of them left, I think. And she's lost her marbles.'

He drew the carriage to a halt.

I headed up the narrow street to the square, almost running so I wouldn't lose my nerve, sweating in the heat.

I knocked loudly on the door, three times.

I heard footsteps.

Real ones.

The door shook.

A key was going into a keyhole.

The door shook more.

It opened.

The nun in the grey dress with the folding chair and the laugh and the honest smile – the one I saw when I first arrived, who said it looked as if a cathedral had been dropped on the mosque from the sky.

I'd seen her there several times since, taking food to the homeless.

'*¿Sí?*' she said, opening the door a few inches.

'*Sor Ana?*' I said.

She nodded.

'*Tengo una foto,*' I said. I have a photo.

I took it out.

I pointed at the photo: the grey body and the teething baby – me, because it had to be me – and the possible wooden T-shaped cross in my mouth and the statue of the angel behind.

She pointed at the angel in the photo and said, 'San Rafael.'

And I was going in.

I was going in!

I was in a kind of barn, or stables, with a beamed roof, slightly falling in.

I peered through the gaps at the bright blue sky.

When I looked ahead, I had to reach out and steady myself on an old stool, or was it a lectern, I'm not sure what it was, but it was covered in bird crap.

In front of me was an inner courtyard, rectangular, large and open to the air.

I stared, but I couldn't move.

'Well, get a move on,' she said.

But I was paralysed.

Here was my photo, come to life.

It was, it was, it was – and undoubtedly – my *memory palace*: the crumbling whitey-cream statue of the angel, the one that stood behind the faded baby that was me, in the faded hands of the beheaded person. The old wooden wagon wheel was leaning on the wall to the right, and there were the stone troughs of hydrangeas, and the pots of geraniums all over the walls.

I walked to the angel, and I laid my shaking hand on his arm.

The paint flaked off in my hand.

'I wouldn't touch San Rafael,' said Sister Ana. 'He's falling to bits.'

'The Jews say that Rafael is the angel that tends the wounds of children, don't they?' I said to her, and my voice came out with a strange trembly texture to it.

She placed her folding grey chair beside the angel and stared at him, and stared at me, her eyes dulling and her face freezing over.

'Does that mean anything to you?' I asked. 'Did you take in unwanted children?'

'Unwanted children?' she said with no expression to her voice.

I kept talking to try to warm her up.

'Don't Christians think Rafael is the angel who stirred the water at the healing pool?' I said, clasping my hands together to stop them trembling. 'You know, in the Gospel of John?'

A yellow budgerigar chirped from its cage, and Sister Ana's mouth thawed into a smile, which headed upwards, unfreezing her, until her eyes lit up again.

'You shut up!' she said to the budgerigar, laughing.

Then she turned to me.

'Isn't Rafael the fourth major angel in Islam?' I said.

'Major angels!' she said cheerfully.

This was not going to be easy.

She pointed to a door.

'Find a chair!' she said.

I went into a musty room, with little flurries of flies against the windows, and an old globe on the stone sill, a room which had perhaps once been a dining room, where now cats (yes, hot, dusty cats!) lay sprawled on newspapers on the battered old table. The battered old table? Not the shiny dark one in Jerez. I felt its surface with my hand: it was gnarled and dented and covered in crumbs. I reached into my mind for memories, and there were the bearded men around the table, breaking and turning like the repeating patterns of a kaleidoscope.

She followed me inside, picked up her globe, closed her eyes and spun it.

'Venezuela!' she said, and went out, holding the globe.

I swallowed, blowing air down my nose to dispel the musty smell in the room, and took a chair outside, sitting down with Sister Ana beside the angel.

I breathed in geranium.

The metal smell hit me.

The one that had followed me to London.

Sister Ana put the globe at her feet, and picked up the cream-coloured cat by the scruff of its neck.

'They think he's mending clocks,' she said, closing her eyes, her face soft and girlish for a moment. 'But he takes me out to the back of the shop, and he says stand there, that's it, move a little to the left, and he takes photographs. He says look how beautiful you are. He's the only person who ever said that.'

She smiled drowsily, and stroked the cat.

'Who's mending clocks?' I said. 'Who takes photos of you?'

'Lorenzo,' she said. 'He'll be here soon.'

She clenched her face as if something hurt.

'I don't like people coming here,' she said. 'Not now everyone's gone. So perhaps you should leave.'

'But I've only just come,' I said smiling.

She nodded.

'I know, darling, I know.'

She took my hand in her hand – and I remembered the soft hand I used to feel underneath my mother's brittle fingernails.

'What I really wanted to know, quite urgently, was whether you ever took in babies,' I said. 'You know, a long time ago?'

Her eyes dulled again.

'Babies?' I said, louder. 'It's important.'

'Important babies!' she said, roaring with laughter.

I took out the photo and pointed to the headless woman.

'Where's her head?' she said, rocking with laughter.

'Could that be you?' I said, though I could see she wasn't focusing. 'You know, you and me.'

'Excuse me,' she said, still laughing, 'but I need to pray for Venezuela.'

She took the globe and ushered me towards the door, which closed with a thump behind me.

I was elated: I'd found it, the actual place.

But horribly disappointed too: she was far too old to be my mother, and far too confused to say who my mother might be, even if she knew.

But she was funny and nice, and I already liked her.

That was something.

I walked through the thick summer heat, and, although I was twenty years old now, I thought of Grey Mother in *The Rainbow Rained Us* with her rickety shelves and her atlas – and her globe.

I lay on the bed staring at the photo that I'd stared at so many times before, but now of course it was different – my eyes had seen it, and it was real (as Billy and I had philosophised repeatedly at lunchbreak – oh Billy, who would you be now?)

Carrie burst in – much sooner than I'd expected.

'It's over with the bullfighter,' she said.

'What happened?'

'I went to see him in a bullfight.'

'And?'

'He said it was art. It was a bloodbath.'

'Did you say that?'

'No. I walked out.'

'Without telling him?'

'He was still murdering the bull.'

She joined me on the bed, leaning against the wall, and threading her hair into lots of thin plaits.

'I'm giving up on men!' said Carrie, allowing herself a glint of a smile. 'It's going to be the title of my first book of poems.'

'I like that.'

'And what's going on with you, Evs?'

'Carrie,' I said. 'You're not going to believe this. I found her. Sister Ana. In Plaza de la Paz.'

'You went without me?'

'I thought I should stop being so pathetic.'

'And?'

'The angel was there and the wagon wheel and everything!'

Carrie hugged me.

'She's the nun from the courtyard with the laugh,' I said. 'So she's obviously far too old to be my mother.'

'And is she the woman in the photo?'

'Well, I still don't know. She found it so funny that she didn't have a head that I couldn't get her back on track. And then she kicked me out.'

'Kicked you out?'

'Yes, but nicely. She wanted to pray for Venezuela.'

'Venezuela?'

'I've no idea. But she's funny and lovely and I like her.'

'We found the place!' said Carrie. 'I can't believe it! Let's celebrate! And then let's plan what happens next.'

What, in the end, happened next was that I went out for tapas with Barnaby Blue, who'd arrived for the start of his PhD.

I was struggling to arrange my expectations as I walked towards the restaurant, not knowing if he'd be on his own or with Naomi.

When I saw that he was on his own, I was overtaken with a strange wave of.

Something.

Courage?

Wickedness?

Freedom?

I was free.

But he wasn't.

And I should have respected that.

Barnaby held out his arms.

Oh, not those ridiculous forearms.

As we were sweeping our faces side to side, as you do – kiss, kiss – somehow, our lips must have brushed each other's, by mistake.

I didn't turn away.

He'd just got engaged.

And I kissed him.

A proper full kiss.

With tongues.

xx.

XX.

I'd love to tell the story differently.

Make it his fault.

I'm not saying he didn't want to.

But I'm still ashamed.

I guess I'd been planning this kiss half my life.

And nothing, even a fiancée, would get in my way.

We sat down on a stone bench, on cushions, leaning against the wall, and the waiter brought the menus, and we were both red in the face with shock, which we covered with urgent talking.

Barnaby was working on the middle level of Medina Azahara, he said, they were excavating the mosque and anticipating, in the coming months and years – I nodded energetically as he spoke – signs of the walls of the souk, perhaps fountains to show where the gardens had been and, he hoped, evidence of a menagerie of wild animals and exotic birds.

'Why do you think the place has grabbed you so much?' I asked, slightly formally, as if I was interviewing him, because we couldn't find the right tone, we could almost not look at each other, we could still taste each other's tongues.

'The poignancy,' he said, also formally. 'It took twenty-five years to build and was lived in for such a short time before it was destroyed. It's something about how short life is.'

'Does it make you think about your mum?' I said.

'Everything makes me think about her,' he said.

Blue Mother would be ashamed of us, I thought, and then, she'd love us to be together, and, for a few seconds, those thoughts went back and forward, like a ball in a tennis match.

'I read that the caliph built the city for his favourite wife, Azahara,' I said, and I felt myself blushing because this was no time to be saying the word *wife*. 'But she never lived there.'

'I read that too,' he said.

'It's a lovely name, Azahara,' I said. 'I wonder if it means orange blossom, like in Spanish.'

We were both quiet.

'Have you got used to being called Blue?' I said.

'It was a bit mad,' he said.

I am madly in love with you, Barnaby Blue, and we need to get married and be the Blue-Greens, that's what I thought, because I was eleven years old again, for a moment, I suppose.

He was meant to be mine, whatever the obstacles, that's the feeling I had – a feeling that should never be trusted. We can convince ourselves about absolutely anything – this is our intrinsic weakness as human beings.

'The Blue-Greens,' I said, tentatively. 'Do you remember? In the car?'

He laughed.

'Before everything went wrong,' he said.

'Blue and green were my favourite colours after that,' I said, 'or maybe before that. We read this book at school.'

To my surprise, I found that I was telling him about *The Rainbow Rained Us*.

To my greater surprise, he was leaning forward, listening.

Which probably encouraged me to keep going.

'You remember I told you about the photo?'

He nodded.

'Well, I found the courtyard with the wagon wheel and the angel.'

I took the photo out of my pocket and showed him.

He stared at the photo.

'Does it still look like this?' he said. 'With the angel and the wagon wheel?'

'Exactly the same!'

We looked into each other's eyes, and I thought, it's not just me feeling this.

I breathed in.

He breathed in too.

We were both holding our breath.

What exactly would I say if I said anything, I thought.

Perhaps he was thinking the same when the waiter appeared.

'*Postre?*' said the waiter, running through our options: flan with caramel sauce, *natillas de leche* or watermelon.

I said no thank you, I'd have a coffee – and the spell had broken.

If I hadn't broken it, he would have done.

My heart was broken by flan with caramel sauce or *natillas de leche* or watermelon.

'I'm thinking of staying out here,' I said to Barnaby, beyond the spell, putting the photo back in my pocket.

'You are? What about your degree?'

'I've asked if they can come to an arrangement with the Facultad de Letras.'

'And if they can't?'

'If they can't, bugger it,' I said.

He laughed.

He sat up.

'I'll get the bill,' he said.

'I'm treating you,' I said.

He refused.

I insisted.

'I split up with Michael,' I said.

'Oh,' he said.

'Oh, I see,' he said.

'I don't know what came over us,' he said.

'I'm sorry,' I said.

'Can we pretend it didn't happen?' he said.

'Yes,' I said.

Because, I suppose, it was too hard to say no.

He stood up.

'Let me pay,' he said.

'I'm paying,' I said.

And he left.

It was midnight and guess where I went.

I knocked on the old oak door in Plaza de la Paz.

Sister Ana answered the door.

Despite the time.

Though she often didn't know the time, come to think of it.

'I've done something I shouldn't have done,' I said. 'Completely deliberately.'

Sister Ana held me against her chest, and I enjoyed the unexpected alchemy between us – because I was always looking for alchemy. I stayed in her arms, and my mixed emotions were soothed by the smell of washing powder on her dress.

The courtyard, *my* courtyard, was lit by tealights, which flickered gorgeously in the dark.

Did she light them every evening?

For herself?

There was something poignant about this for me.

Cats rubbed their cheeks against pots, stalked up steps, lay sleeping in coils.

Sister Ana and I sat on wicker chairs close together in the candlelight – and it felt so good.

'Hold my hand,' she said. 'Hold God's hand. Make a circle.'

I held her hand with my left hand.

'Hold God's hand,' she said again.

'I'm not sure where God's hand is,' I said awkwardly.

'Oh, anywhere,' she said.

So I held God's hand (the air) with my right hand, and she held God's hand (the air) with her left.

'We make our own circles,' she said, out of nowhere, or perhaps it was somewhere, just somewhere I hadn't been.

I loved the warm comfort of her lived-in hand in mine: its crepey pads, its deep furrows.

'Did you remember the baby?' I said to Sister Ana, with a strange pain in my chest.

I took out my photo and handed it to her.

She handed it back.

'*Había un bebé?*' she asked. Was there a baby?

'I think the baby was me.'

She started to laugh.

'*Lo digo en serio,*' I said, I'm being serious.

She wagged her finger at me, winking, as she got up from her grey folding chair.

'We dance, Lorenzo and I,' she said, and she started to dance with nobody around the candlelit courtyard in her big old sandals.

She sat down on her chair.

'We aren't married, of course,' she said. 'I married Jesus.'

'Sister Ana,' I said, 'I just kissed a man who's marrying another woman.'

'Men don't think anything of kissing anyone,' she said.

'Oh, it was my fault—'

'It was a terrible time to be a girl. Do you remember?'

'I'm much younger than you are. I'm only twenty.'

'Are you now, darling?' she said. 'It won't make any difference in the end.'

Which I suppose is true.

'You don't remember a baby, do you, here in the courtyard?' I tried again.

'My mother wanted us all to have babies,' she said, and she paused. I nodded.

'Seen the stallions, have you?' she asked with a horrified face. 'Mounting those poor old mares at the stud-farm. Who would want to do that?'

Her expression made me laugh, thinking how much everyone else in the whole world wanted to *do that*, and nothing else, endlessly, repeatedly, in different arrangements and combinations, forever and ever amen.

'When I came here for the first time, I was wondering whether you were my mother,' I said tentatively.

She stared at me, her face stilled in horror, but whether she was making a connection with the mares, I doubt – she was more for disconnections.

'Now I've met you, I obviously see that you're too old,' I said, 'but you could have looked after me, I suppose, back then. Or you could have known my mother?'

She picked up the cream cat.

I took out the photo again.

'You don't think that could be you?' I said slowly and loudly, trying to keep her attention by pointing at the grey dress. 'Or perhaps one of your friends?'

'That blessed head of hers!' she said, hee-hawing with laughter.

It always took her off course.

'Do come again,' she said. 'I like you. We always have such fun together.'

'Yes, I will,' I said, getting up.

'Oh, yes you will,' she said. 'I can tell. I can always tell the ones who'll come back.'

When Carrie hadn't quite woken up the next morning, I told her about the kiss.

'Bastard!' she said blearily, assuming instantly that I was in the right.

(This is a possible disadvantage of love, its blind willingness to take the loved one's side.)

'No, Carrie,' I said. 'The bastard was me.'

'You can't kiss on your own,' she said, which is a fair point.

She took a sip of water and lay back down.

'What do you think's going to happen now?' she said, picking off her mascara.

'Probably nothing,' I said.

'This might make him see the engagement's a mistake,' said Carrie.

'What might?'

'Kissing you.'

'How good a kiss do you think it was?' I said.

'Do you feel shit?' said Carrie.

'Yes,' I said.

We lay quietly, staring at the ceiling.

'I went to see Sister Ana afterwards.'

'Not again! Without me! Now I'm jealous!' said Carrie. 'And how was she this time?'

'She made me hold her hand and *God's hand* to make a circle.'

'Where was God's hand?'

'Anywhere, she said.'

'Makes sense,' said Carrie.

'It was a bit awkward,' I said.

'God makes me awkward,' said Carrie.

'Or is it your mother that makes you awkward?' I said. 'And you've started imagining God's like her.'

'Maybe,' said Carrie. 'Poor God!'

I laughed.

'Can we go and see Sister Ana together today?' she said.

We didn't know that today would turn out to be a significant day – the day my father came.

My father leant forward to kiss me.

He was sweating, the way everyone sweats in Córdoba in August: it beads on your upper lip and runs in rivulets from your armpits.

I stepped back to not be kissed.

Carrie led us both into the ferny courtyard, where we sat down, around a glass table.

'Where shall we start?' said my father, authoritative, confident.

'Shall we start here?' I said, getting out the photo.

My father grabbed it.

'Where did you find that?'

I grabbed it back.

'It fell out of a book in your study,' I said.

'I put it somewhere that nobody could find it,' he said, pretending to look amused, 'but then I couldn't find it either!'

Carrie laughed appreciatively.

'Like squirrels,' she said.

I glared at her.

'With their nuts.'

'Anyway,' I said to my father, holding the photo tightly. 'I've found the courtyard with the angel. It's in Plaza de la Paz.'

'How did you . . .?'

'Blame her!' I said, pointing at Carrie.

'So I've been meeting with Sister Ana,' I said.

'We think she might be the person in the picture,' said Carrie.

'No,' said my father firmly. 'She isn't.'

He smiled, though this was (obviously) no time for smiling.

'I wouldn't listen to *her*,' he said. 'She's lost the plot.'

He was putting on a show of amused calm, or perhaps he felt amused and calm.

I did not.

'Who was holding me in the photo then?' I asked. 'I assume it's me.'

'She was called Sister María Soledad,' he said, clearing his throat and crossing his arms. 'She was quite a woman.'

'Did she take me in?' I said urgently.

'Did she?' said Carrie.

He nodded, arms still crossed.

'She died last summer,' said Carrie. 'That's what I was told.'

'She would have been in her nineties,' said my father.

The beheaded woman was *dead*.

'So she obviously wasn't my mother?' I said.

'Oh no no no,' said my father, wagging his finger.

'Why did you cut her head off?' I said.

'Cherie did it.'

'Because?'

'She wanted you to bond with her. She didn't want you to know there'd been anyone else.'

'But you said the woman in the photo wasn't my mother? So what was the problem with me seeing her face?'

My father hesitated, and for the first time he looked flustered.

'I came here to be honest,' he said.

'That makes a change,' I said.

'Evs,' said Carrie, glaring at me.

'So Cherie isn't my mother either, is she?' I said, looking into my father's eyes.

'Let me explain,' he began.

'Can you tell me the whole story?' I said, and my teeth had started chattering, even in the heat.

'Your mother—' my father began, now colouring slightly.

'Cherie—' I interjected.

But he was determined to stick to his speech.

'—was desperate for a baby,' he said.

I clenched my jaw to stop my teeth chattering.

All these years not knowing.

And what was I about to find out?

My father reached across the glass table to hold my hand.

I didn't take it.

'Eight years we tried for a baby,' he said.

Was I supposed to feel sorry for him?

I felt, for a moment, sorry for her instead.

'Did you love her?' I said.

He answered a different question.

'It sent her crazy, waiting every month, and the baby never coming.'

'It must have been really hard for her,' I said, while at the same time thinking that she never acted like someone who was desperate for a child.

'And with my other children in Jerez.'

'Are you ever going to tell me about these other children?'

'You know,' he said. 'From my first marriage, four of them.'

I certainly didn't know.

He couldn't remember his own stories, couldn't find his own nuts. Oh, his nuts – so much the problem, I suspected, his nuts!

'So, the other four are older than me?' I said, feeling my way. 'And you have seven children, including me?'

'Except that—' he said.

'Seven seems a bit greedy,' I said, and the humour probably didn't help anyone, least of all me.

'Let's keep the story going,' said Carrie.

'Your mother—'

'Cherie—'

'She couldn't stand it in Jerez, living so close to the other wife and children.'

'I don't blame her,' I said.

'So she was mainly at the beach house, on the coast, in Alvera,' he said. 'I planted her two hundred palm trees.'

Well, aren't you the big hero, I thought.

'Can we get to the point faster?' I said.

'Well, I was often here in Córdoba,' he said, waving his arm around, in command again. 'We have property around the city.'

Property makes people feel powerful. I know that now. I feel much safer in the world. Much bigger.

'And?' said Carrie.

'I'd seen Sister María Soledad out and about,' he said.

'And Sister Ana?' I asked, feeling we were possibly getting somewhere.

'There were seven of them,' he said, and he cleared his throat to get back to his speech. 'I'd seen Sister María Soledad out and about with a baby.'

'A baby?' I said, heart now thumping.

Had one of the nuns had sex? Broken their vows? Had me?

'Was the baby me?'

My father ignored the question.

'And this really was no place for a baby,' he said. 'The house was full of tramps and drunks. It had been left to them by some bene-factor, but the idiot had left no funds for keeping it going. So I thought I'd do them all a good turn. Buy the house and sort it out for them.'

He was the benefactor in the seventies who the Dominican nun had mentioned to Carrie.

It hit me.

What he was saying.

'You bought me!' I said. 'That's actually horrible. You bought me!'

'Don't be ridiculous,' said my father. 'I saved you.'

'You bought me.'

We leant forward and faced each other.

'They were looking for a couple to take the baby, so the baby would have a mother and a father,' he said proudly.

His trump card!

'A mother and a father?' I said. 'How ideal.'

Carrie's eyes said, less of the sarcasm.

'And the house was falling around their ears,' my father went on. 'Sister María Soledad was very grateful. She felt the baby—'

'Me.'

'You, yes, you – let me explain. She felt the baby needed a proper family life.'

'A proper family life?' I said, unable to stop my tone of incredulity – did the man have no self-awareness?

'So that's it. We got you and we spent the summer at the beach house. In the autumn, I took you both back to Jerez. But it didn't work out.'

'So what happened?'

'Cherie said she needed to get back to London to be near her parents, then she'd be able to cope with you. So we went to Chelsea. Her parents were no help at all. And I couldn't stand the rain.'

Cope with me?

'Did you actually adopt me or was it a few backhanders to your friends in high places?' I said.

He didn't answer.

Carrie said, 'I wonder if you should stop and let Eva take it all in.'

I did my best to hold myself together.

'My intentions were good,' he said, and perhaps he believed that. 'I can honestly say I thought it would work.'

He held out his hand to me again, but there was no way I was taking it.

What a cold bastard this man was.

'So you've told me you're not my father?' I said. 'Just like that?'

He shook his head, looking something: wistful, winningly tragic.

'And you don't look the slightest bit guilty?'

His expression didn't change.

'You don't want to apologise for your deceit? Or your neglect? Or your total abandonment of a child?'

Carrie took my hand.

'You don't have seven children – you have six,' I said to him, slowly. 'That's why you never gave a shit about me. My whole life was a lie.'

I drew my feet up onto my chair and hugged my knees.

My not-father wrung his hands.

'You were a crap father,' I said, my voice breaking up. 'But at least you were *my crap father.*'

'So who is Eva's mother?' said Carrie.

My not-father looked at Carrie and then at me, and his face gave nothing away, and he said nothing.

'You must know,' said Carrie. 'And the least you can do is tell Eva.'

He stammered.

'Please,' I heard myself saying.

'You mother was a student, your sort of age,' he said. 'That's what we were told.'

'A student?'

I let go of my knees and leant forward.

'She came to Córdoba to study at the Facultad, in the seventies,' he said. 'Like you. It's a rather nice symmetry . . .'

Nice symmetry? Did he actually say that?

'And she got pregnant?' said Carrie.

'She was a Muslim girl, originally from Peru, who'd come from London.'

A Muslim girl.

Wasn't I supposed to be Catholic?

Could I be both?

Like the mosque-cathedral?

Or C. S. Lewis's wife, Joy?

Or the Jewish Virgin Mary who presumably became a Christian because, if she didn't, who would?

I was burying my shock in questions, question after question, to stop me feeling.

Like I always had.

Now take it in, I said to myself.

A Muslim girl from Peru who came to London who came to Córdoba?

It was hard to imagine this girl.

And much harder to imagine that this girl.

Breathe.

Was.

My mother.

I was shaking, and I knew it showed.

'And my father?' I said. 'Who isn't you?'

'He was a priest. I don't know anything else about him.'

But priests weren't supposed to have babies.

'You never liked priests,' I said.

'It was a love affair,' said my not-father. 'Nothing . . . nothing fishy.'

The ground had lost its solidity, and it felt like I was standing on something inflatable, which might not hold, which made it much harder to speak.

'So to be clear,' I said, and my voice came out high and tremulous. 'She gave me up, the girl from Peru – my mother?'

'I think there was a lot of pressure on her from her own mother.'

Pressure buzzing at the bridge of my nose, between my eyes, drilling through my temples.

'Do you have a name for her?'

He cleared his throat.

'Sister María Soledad gave us a few details about her background. Her name and address. The birth certificate.'

'A name? You have a name?'

'A memorable name,' he said. 'Jhazmin Benalcazar.'

My mother had a storybook name.

I was someone.

'Where's that name from?'

'Her family migrated to Lima from Palestine in the 1940s, and Jhazmin ended up in London as a teenager in 1967, the summer of love!'

'How come?'

'Jhazmin's aunt was marrying an English man. So she took her sister – Jhazmin's mother – and her husband, with her. For a better life, I suppose.'

'How can I get hold of her?' I said urgently.

'*Tranquila,*' he said, with a calm-down-dear tone. 'Of course her surname may well have changed, and the address I have is from twenty years ago.'

'I can't believe you bought me!' I stared at him, still trembly, but calmer.

'I didn't buy you, Eva,' he said.

'What did you tell Sister María Soledad you would do for me?'

'That we'd look after you as if you were our own, give you the best of everything.'

Did he not see it?

'And you one hundred per cent reneged on the deal,' I said. 'She wanted me to have a father and a mother.'

'You had your mother.'

'She was very ill,' I said.

My not-father said nothing.

'You abandoned me,' I said. 'What do you think Sister María Soledad would have said about that?'

He looked, for a second, frightened.

The little boy with the blackboard of sins.

'I'll find a way to make it up to you,' he said.

'I don't know how,' I said.

'I suppose we have to look forward,' he said. 'We can't change the past.'

'How convenient,' I said.

'May I take you to dinner this evening?' he said.

'Say yes,' said Carrie.

Her eyes bored into my eyes.

'Say yes,' she said again.

I said yes.

My not-father was waiting at La Bodega, and the waiters were fussing around him, showing him a range of tables, and it came to me how well he would get on with Michael Orson.

We sat down.

Carrie had told me to be firm and frank, but if my emotions got the better of me, that was OK too, because it would help him to see the impact it had all had on me.

'The priest definitely didn't rape my mother, did he?' I said, my tone of voice firm and frank, though underneath I was fearful. 'You would tell me, wouldn't you?'

'Sister María Soledad said it was a short-lived relationship, but he'd already signed up for the priesthood. He was a young man, and the family expected it of him.'

'That's something,' I said, sitting up straight.

'You know, Sister María Soledad wasn't made for motherhood,' said my father, swilling his wine around his mouth and saying yes, it would do, to the anxious waiter. 'Not everyone is.'

'Oh, come on,' I said. 'You were solving your own problems, not worrying about the maternal qualities of nuns.'

He coloured slightly, or was that my imagination?

'So there were no thieves stealing photo albums at the beach house?' I said. 'I presume you know how ridiculous that sounded. Even to a child.'

He shrugged, like someone in the wrong.

I remembered my fake baby photo on the display board in the classroom at St Hilda's, him pretending to be me, how strange and empty it made me feel.

'You got me when I was three and a half, I assume?' I said, and my voice was quiet now. 'So that's why you didn't have any baby photos I could take to school?'

He didn't answer.

'And I imagine you'll have made a nice profit on the house too.'

'I wasn't particularly motivated by profit, Eva. I'm a wealthy man.'

Oh, don't say that, I thought, you remind me of Mr Orson.

'The house is a total mess,' I said, firm again. 'I think you should do something before it falls down on top of Sister Ana.'

'I'll do it up at some point.'

'Don't you feel any responsibility? To anyone?'

Now unable to stop my anger.

'I'll call by,' he said. 'I'm a busy man.'

'So I was here in Córdoba with Sister María Soledad and the nuns from birth to three and a half?'

Still angry.

Feeling I was right to be angry.

'That's right,' he said. 'We picked you up and headed straight to the beach house in Alvera with suitcases of clothes your . . . Cherie . . . had been stockpiling her whole life!'

The lilac dress, the lilac cardigan, the lilac shoes, the lilac ribbon.

They picked me up and took me away and dressed me up like a doll.

'Cherie felt you didn't take to her. You preferred me. You seemed sullen.'

She wanted a doll, not a child.

'I was probably traumatised. You'd just kidnapped me.'

My not-father winced.

But it was true.

'Did you ever love her?' I asked him, as I'd asked earlier.

'In the beginning,' he said. 'But eight years trying for children nearly destroyed her. I honestly thought she'd be happy in London. I thought I could come and go.'

'Perhaps you should try staying put somewhere,' I said. 'Being moored. Like the Darlings. Do you remember?'

'I'd rather be Peter Pan,' he said.

We smiled at each other because Peter Pan was our secret, no one else's – we didn't have much, but we had Peter Pan.

'That's perhaps my problem,' he said.

So he at least admitted he had a problem.

We ate quietly, looking at the table.

'What would help make it up to you?' he said, softer now.

'I've no idea,' I said.

'Eva,' he said, slapping his hand on the table. 'That's it! You can have the house. That's how I'll make it up to you. I'll get the house repaired. And then when Sister Batty dies, it's all yours. How about that?'

Money had yet again bought him solutions for his bad choices. But also, wow.

'I'm not really in the mood for being thankful to you,' I said, 'but thank you anyway. And don't call her Sister Batty. You might get dementia too.'

'Not me,' he said. 'I'm strong as an ox.'

'Everyone gets old. Even you.'

A tiny tremble of fear in the skin of his face.

Because nobody is Peter Pan.

He gave me an envelope.

'Everything I know is in here,' he said. 'Let's see where you get to.'

'Thank you,' I said. 'And thank you for dinner. And thank you for the house. And can we meet there this week to talk about the repairs? I want it to be safe for Sister Ana.'

Too many thank yous?

Had he bought my forgiveness with the house?

Should I have said no?

'I'll speak to my men,' he said in that grandiose voice of his, the one I like least.

My men! How some men love to say *my men.*

'This week,' I said again.

'You're very bossy these days,' said my not-father.

'Why is it men don't get called bossy?' I said.

He smiled in a way that looked like I was growing on him again.

'Carrie, Carrie, Carrie!' I yelled as I went into our room.

'I'm just in the loo!'

'He's giving me the house!' I shouted through the bathroom door.

'What house?' she shouted back.

'Sister Ana's house!'

'The whole house?' said Carrie, coming out of the loo. 'Isn't it massive? Do you think we could go and live there?'

'It's falling down,' I said. 'But he's going to get it repaired. It's rammed full of crap.'

'We could make a start on the clearing,' said Carrie. 'And Sister Ana might like some company.'

'Are we really staying in Córdoba, Carrie?'

'We really are!' she said.

'You don't think he'll go back on his word, do you?'

'Definitely not!' said Carrie. 'He's feeling guilty!'

'Isn't this incredible?' I said. 'Or incredibly weird?'

'Do you think you'll ever forgive him?' said Carrie.

'What *is* forgiveness?' I said. 'I've been trying to work it out, and I honestly don't know.'

'Well, forgiveness is just—' said Carrie, and she stopped.

She crumpled her brow.

'You're right,' she said. 'Now I'm trying to describe it, I can't. Is it a feeling, do you think, or a thing you say? Or maybe it's something you do?'

'But what exactly do you do?'

'I'm not sure.'

'I suppose forgiveness might be a great big house in Córdoba,' I said. 'Or at least that might be the start of it.'

'No house would be big enough to make amends,' said Carrie.

'You're right,' I said, and it hit me then.

The size of his betrayal.

We hugged each other, and I didn't say anything for a long time, until I said, 'If I take the house, will he think everything's instantly OK? When it isn't. Will he feel exonerated somehow? Back in the right?'

'He might,' said Carrie. 'But if you don't take it, what do you gain?'

'Is gaining bad?'

'Perhaps it's time for a bit of gain at his expense?' said Carrie.

'But is it greedy? Or immoral?'

'If it is, let's be greedy and immoral,' said Carrie.

'If you're sure,' I said. 'And please could you be sure? I'd rather blame you instead of me.'

'I'm just thinking,' said Carrie. 'What happened is probably lots of people's fault, isn't it? Not just his? Like your real mother and father's. As well.'

I certainly wasn't prepared to blame my real mother. No, I couldn't write her off before we'd even got started, after all these years dreaming of her. And as for my priest-father, I didn't know what to think about him. No, I'd chosen my villains, and would not be diverted.

'I don't blame the others,' I said. 'No one else bought me.'

'It was the nuns who gave you away,' said Carrie. 'Sister María Soledad has to take some of the blame.'

I didn't want to blame the nuns either.

I'd totally fallen for Sister Ana.

Her heady lightness.

Her freedom from the constraints of reality.

But here was my reality, which before I'd found it, had felt as huge and open as the sea.

But now I saw that reality is what's left behind when the other possibilities fall away.

'Anyhow,' I said, to stop Carrie in the tracks of her blame-game, 'I must write to *my mother!*'

Reality had shrunk to the size of the sheet of paper I tore out of my writing pad.

'What shall I call her?' I said.

'Maybe Jhazmin at the start?' said Carrie.

'Or I could go straight in with Mum,' I said.

'I'm not sure,' she said, handing me a glass of wine. 'I'd go slowly.'

'You know I've never called anyone Mum?' I said to Carrie, taking a sip of wine. 'And that's not a nice feeling.'

I put the glass down and quietly took the mother-daughter articles out of the back of my old Quest Book – and I thought, the quest is over. And then I thought the opposite – perhaps it's beginning.

'A girl's mother is her North Star,' I read to Carrie. 'I used to read these things and think they were beautiful. And dream of this perfect mother who was somewhere waiting for me. But now they sound a bit . . .'

'The line between beautiful and cringerama can be very thin,' said Carrie.

'What do you think she'll be like?' I said.

'I have no idea,' said Carrie. 'And I don't want you to over-expect. I feel a bit scared for you now we've actually found her.'

'How can I over-expect?' I said. 'I've been waiting for this moment my whole life.'

'Real mothers can be highly disappointing,' said Carrie, looking at me. 'Take it from me. And you do realise she might have other children. A husband—'

'You're being very negative,' I said.

318

'I'm being realistic,' said Carrie, looking anxious. 'I want to protect you. We don't know how she'll react to your letter, whether she'll be pleased or not. Please don't set yourself up to be hurt.'

I looked down at my mother–daughter articles and refused to meet her eye.

'Would you like to be left alone?' said Carrie. 'I'll go and sit downstairs.'

I said that perhaps I would.

I had a horrible dark feeling inside me.

I wrote about fifty-seven versions of my letter, feeling tight and taut and unhappy when this was supposed to be the happiest day of my life.

Dear Jhazmin . . .

I kept it short and to the point.

No beauty.

No cringerama.

I endlessly checked the post table.

Nothing.

I busied myself.

I phoned King's to see if they could liaise with the Facultad de Letras in Córdoba, so that Carrie and I could do our final year here. Then Carrie decided she wouldn't bother.

Nothing on the post table.

The University of London agreed to let me study in Córdoba, but warned that this would rob me of the Hons bit of my BA Hons. I thought briefly of Christine Orson – how traumatised she would be on my behalf.

Nothing on the post table.

Carrie got a job in the dance shop where they sold flamenco dresses and dotty shoes. She started on her poetry book called *I'm Giving Up On Men* and made earrings out of peseta coins.

My not-father phoned and gave us the earliest date his men could come and look at the house, which wasn't this week but next, could we please tell Sister Ana? Carrie and I tried ringing on her bell, smashing on the door, ringing on the bell again, but she didn't answer.

I spoke to a neighbour, who gave me a key.

We let ourselves in, nervously.

Sister Ana was lying next to the wagon wheel, not moving.

I rushed over and touched her arm.

'It's Eva,' I said.

'*No puedo levantarme*,' she said. She couldn't get up.

She'd been watering the geraniums on the steps and she'd slipped.

We called an ambulance.

We fed the budgerigars.

Sister Ana lay flat on her back, looking at the sky.

'Sister Sky,' she said. 'Brother Sun. You knew that?'

We shook our heads.

'God pours his love into visible forms,' she said, with that heavenly look she sometimes got. '*El sol, el cielo, la luna, las estrellas* – sun, sky, moon, stars – some people call it the Big Bang. But I call it Christ.'

As the ambulance man lowered the ramp, she said to him, 'You call it the Big Bang. I call it Christ.'

'Do you, love?' he said, wheeling her up the ramp.

'I do, love,' she said back.

It made us laugh.

How we loved her already.

It turned out that she'd broken her left leg; other than that, it was cuts and bruises. If we were willing to stay with her, they'd let her home in a hospital wheelchair.

Carrie and I moved in.

'Let's take some photos of the whole place,' said Carrie. 'Like a before and after.'

The walls at the back were bulging outwards, and the flat roof terrace needed mending – there were plants snaking through the gaps in the red tiles and all the washing lines had collapsed.

'We're going to clear everything up,' I said to Sister Ana. 'Get rid of the rubbish. Make you a lovely bedroom.'

'I don't want you to,' she said.

'There are mice on every floor.'

'I like mice.'

'We think it would be better without mice.'

'I have plenty of cats.'

'While that's true . . .'

'It hurts me that the cats kill the mice,' she said. '*Pero así son los gatos.*' That's just cats being cats.

She sighed.

Then she looked around as if she'd lost something.

'Being human,' she said. 'What is it?'

We hesitated.

'Is Lorenzo coming?' she said, reaching into the air.

'He won't be long,' said Carrie.

'You know that Lorenzo isn't a *real man*,' said Sister Ana.

'We get real by being loved,' said Carrie. 'There's a children's book about that. With rabbits. I love it.'

'I love Lorenzo,' said Sister Ana.

'Then he's a real man,' said Carrie. 'You made him real.'

'Is that how we make God real?' I said.

'No, that's how God makes us real,' said Sister Ana.

My not-father was wrong to say she talked rubbish.

'How did Jesus walk through walls after he died?' I asked her, because it's something I'd always wondered, knowing that he also had a body and ate fish.

'He was more substantial than the stone,' she said. 'But less rigid.'

And so was she.

It's hard to explain.

But it's what I look for in a person.

We washed her sheets, and we hung them on the line.

Sister Ana pulled one off and draped it over her head like a bridal veil.

'I married Jesus,' she said. 'He's the only man a woman can rely on.'

We smiled.

'Men!' she said. 'You've got to watch them! Once your tits start sagging, they're gone!'

She was laughing again.

'*Son todos cabrones,*' she said. They're all bastards. This was one of her favourite lines, and it always amused her to say it.

'Did you expect nuns to swear?' said Carrie.

'Everyone thinks religion's about not swearing,' I said. 'But I think God's probably bigger than that.'

'These things don't bother Jesus,' said Sister Ana. 'Saggy tits.'

She closed her eyes.

'Do you think I'll ever get married?' said Carrie. 'My relationships never last.'

'We're only twenty, Carrie,' I said. 'I wouldn't get too desperate yet.'

'How about you?' she said.

'I would only ever want to marry Barnaby, and he's taken.'

Sister Ana opened her eyes.

'Let's sing a hymn,' she said.

'Does she think we're nuns?' I whispered.

'We practically *are* nuns these days!' said Carrie.

We were awkward and didn't know the words. But here we are, in a frame on the white stone windowsill of my bedroom: Sister Ana has her arm around me, the angel is watching, our eyes are laughing and our mouths are wide open, singing hymns.

Carrie and I were soon belting out 'Mine Eyes Have Seen the Glory' and 'He's Got the Whole World in His Hands' and Sister Ana clapped her hands and spun her globe. Carrie and I felt ridiculous at the start, but we came to love it, losing our boundaries, storming through the wall, our three voices merging, as if, for a few moments, we were one, glory glory hallelujah!

We had a phone line installed, and I called Cherie and came clean about everything: Córdoba, my not-father, the house. Because Carrie said it was right to. And I agreed.

'Did he tell you he never married me?' she said. 'By the time the divorce law was passed in Spain in 1981, he'd changed his mind.'

'I'm really sorry,' I said. 'I didn't know that.'

'That's why there were no wedding photos,' she said.

'I'm sorry,' I said again.

'The man is a total bastard,' she said. 'So I wouldn't side with him if I were you.'

'I know what he's like,' I said. 'And I'm not siding with anyone.'

'You're not siding with anyone?' she spluttered. 'You stay in Córdoba and let him buy you with houses. And you're not siding with anyone!'

I hated her saying that.

In case it was true.

'You should have said no to him,' she said. 'No one ever says no to him.'

I wanted to say sorry but I couldn't get the word out.

Perhaps because she still hadn't said sorry to me.

'I did everything I could for you,' she said.

Which wasn't true.

'But you never liked me.'

Which possibly was true.

'Even when you were little.'

Could she take a tiny bit of the blame, I wondered.

'And also you lied to me,' she said. 'You said you were going to Granada.'

'You lied to me too,' I said quietly. 'My whole life.'

'I'm so sorry, Eva,' said Jean, coming onto the phone. 'That was my fault. The bit about Granada.'

Our conversation was over, and only Jean had said sorry.

My not-father appeared with men in boiler suits, who went off to inspect the upper floors.

I felt greedy and unprincipled and utterly entranced by my house.

'Can you tell us about Lorenzo?' I asked him.

'He ran the clock shop, and he was a photographer. And also the only gay in Córdoba!'

He waved his arm about limply.

'Can you stop that?' I said.

'Tell me Lorenzo is all right,' said Sister Ana, stroking the piebald feather she'd chosen from Carrie's board, which hung with her T-shaped cross on the leather strap around her neck.

'Lorenzo is fine,' I said.

'He never comes,' she said, looking broken. 'I think I've lost him.'

The men came down from the upper floors, saying they could start the repairs next month.

Carrie and I began to work our way through the piles of rubbish.

Every day, I checked the post table at Hostal Jardín.

Every day, there was no letter.

Neither from Bridget.

Nor from Jhazmin Benalcazar.

I started my course at the Facultad de Letras.

'I'm like a living embodiment of the *Convivencia*,' I said to Carrie. 'My mother's a Muslim, my father's a Catholic priest and—'

'The man you want to marry is Jewish?' said Carrie. 'Get over it, Evs. He's taken.'

'You said that. I was going to say that my favourite family in the world is Jewish.'

'I was thinking that I really want to meet Bridget. And we should invite her over once we've got everything sorted. And Mr Blue maybe too. And let's *not* invite Barnaby!'

'Bridget hasn't written for a while,' I said, trying to sound casual. 'I wrote to her in May when the *feria* was on.'

'Well, perhaps you should write again.'

'Even though she hasn't replied?'

'She might be busy,' said Carrie.

'I've actually written twice,' I said. 'But nothing from her.'

'She was practically your sister – you don't need to wait for a reply, do you?' said Carrie, looking at me as if I was mad.

'Also, I've still heard nothing from Jhazmin.'

'Give her time,' said Carrie. 'The letter probably came as a shock.'

And talking of shocks, I'd bumped into Barnaby Blue in Plaza de la Corredera, the big old square where, once the *Convivencia* was over, heretic-converts were burnt to death in the Inquisition.

'How's Naomi?' I said awkwardly.

'She's in Brazil,' he said, 'doing research into an uncontacted tribe. She's totally caught up in it all. Wants to be the first to contact them.'

'Sounds exciting,' I said. 'Or unethical. One of the two.'

I shouldn't have said that.

Barnaby shifted from foot to foot.

'How's it all going?' he said.

'I've found my real mother. I'm just waiting for her first letter.'

'You're joking?' said Barnaby, and his voice sounded like Barnaby again. 'That's incredible. I'm so happy for you.'

He opened his arms to me.

And before he could change his mind, I fell into them.

It was still lovely.

He remembered that hugging me was a bad idea, and he stepped back.

'I really hope she's how you want her to be,' he said seriously.

'So do I,' I smiled. 'I'm sure she will be.'

'I wonder what colour she'll be,' he said, which touched me.

'Shall we meet up again?' I said. 'I've missed you.'

I shouldn't have said that, and I knew this as I said it.

But doesn't everyone sometimes want to do the wrong thing?

Even St John of the Cross and St Teresa of Ávila?

'Yes, maybe,' said Barnaby. 'Maybe we could have a drink some time.'

But he didn't say he'd missed me too.

'I've moved,' I said. 'Have you got something I can write my new address on?'

'My arm?' he said.

Oh, not his arm.

I wrote my address on his gorgeous Barnaby Blue forearm.

'Come and see my new house,' I said.

'Thank you,' he said. 'See you soon. Maybe.'

'Also,' I said. 'Is Bridget OK?'

'I haven't heard from her for a while,' he said.

I walked back to Hostal Jardín, thinking that the first thing I would do was write to Bridget.

Carrie was standing outside, unable to contain herself.

She started fumbling in her bag and pulled out a pale pink envelope.

'Don't worry about the colour,' said Carrie. 'It's probably all she could lay her hands on.'

I held the envelope in my hands.

I sniffed it – it smelled of envelope, nothing else.

Please don't make her pink, I thought, not another pink mother, I couldn't take it.

'Do you want to be alone?' said Carrie.

'You can come with me, but no talking,' I said.

'Maybe it's better I don't come then,' she said. 'I never really mastered the not talking!'

I walked slowly through the ferns and up the wrought-iron staircase.
I opened the door.
I took the pillows from Carrie's bed and put them on mine.
I lit some tealights, like Sister Ana.
It might be a very long letter, I thought.

Dear Eva,
This is Jhazmin Lane, your mother.

Lane?
I nearly cried.
What happened to *Benalcazar*?
You don't get magical princesses called Mrs Lane.
People called Mrs Lane have children, you can just tell.
She'd left a biggish gap after the first line, and I put my hand over
the writing beneath.

This is Jhazmin Lane, your mother.

I read it again and again, trying to make it magical.
Perhaps the next sentence would be.

I still live at the same address, in the house we moved to when I was
twelve.

Or maybe not.

So your letter reached me.
As you see.
I have often wondered if this day would ever happen.

Breathe.
Pause.

What I would feel and what I would do.

Pause.

And now it has happened.

Pause.
Breathe.
I covered the page, imagining what she might say next – the magic
was definitely coming.
I looked up.
I looked down.

And I don't know what I should feel or what I should do.

Disappointing.

I never forgot you.

Of course you didn't, I thought, because that would be inhuman.
And you are my North Star.
Possibly.

But of course my life moved on.
It had to.
I have a husband and a son.
We live with my father.
Perhaps we should start by writing letters to each other.
What do you think?
Yours

Jhazmin

Writing letters?

Not Mum or Mother or Mummy.

Just Jhazmin.

Yours?

That's how she signed off.

Not exactly warm.

Or excited.

Or urgent.

Yours?

Mine?

Was she mine?

Not really.

She was theirs: her father's, her husband's, her son's.

But we would write letters.

That was it.

Carrie burst in.

'So?'

'You can read it. She's got a husband and a son. And she signed off Jhazmin.'

I handed the letter to her and I lay on the bed staring at the ceiling, remembering that when Peter Pan flew back to his mother, the window was barred and there was another little boy sleeping in his bed.

We lay on our beds saying nothing.

'Are you OK?' said Carrie, lying very flat on her bed because I'd stolen all her pillows.

'No,' I said.

My Jhazmin-mother had failed me.

Like my not-mother had failed me.

Like my not-father had failed me.

Like the whole project of family had failed me.

Carrie got up, and she climbed next to me on my bed.

'This is really hard, Evs,' she said.

Maybe Carrie could be family.

'I don't know what I can say that will help,' she said.

'Just stay lying here next to me please,' I said.

'When I'm really down, I find dyeing my hair helps,' she said.

'I don't think that will work for me,' I said.

'We're all different,' said Carrie.

'I love you, Evs,' said Carrie.

'That does help a bit,' I said.

'Did you write to Bridget?' she said.

'Not yet,' I said. 'But I will.'

Maybe Bridget could be family again, if only she'd reply to my letters.

I wrote to Bridget again.

She apologised for her lack of reply.

She said please could I always write to her when I was drunk.

She said Bessie was having a really crap time – but she'd write properly when she was feeling better.

I tried not to dwell on the brevity of her letter.

'Poor Bessie,' I said aloud, when I was actually thinking poor me, Bridget doesn't love me any more.

I wrote back, fast as anything, saying that she and Bessie and Bella would be very welcome here in Córdoba, and that I was longing to see her. I didn't show the faintest glimmer of how sad I was feeling. Same old story.

My Jhazmin-mother used her letters to rehearse the detail of her days, focusing on the weather and her job at a Hispanic restaurant in Tooting, and favouring commas.

'I got up, awful rainy day, I went to work . . .'

'So cold today, Deborah was ill, I had to work a double shift . . .'

'Finally a bit of sun, I sat on a bench in my break . . .'

'I finally find a mother,' I said to Carrie. 'And she's so *boring*!'

Carrie laughed, but I felt a horrible mix of orphaned and mean.

Bridget didn't write again.

I tried not to think about her.

My Jhazmin-mother took to sending me recipes, and I didn't have the heart to tell her I hated cooking. I passed them onto Carrie, who tried them out.

'I'm starting to love cooking,' said Carrie. 'Tell Jhazmin.'

I told her.

She made no comment.

She never asked questions about my life.

But I asked about hers.

Nothing too threatening.

Questions about her family's flight from persecution in Lebanon (before her time, she wasn't sure), life in Lima (busy, full of friends, she left when she was twelve), Machu Picchu (she'd never been).

I bought an old yellow van, and Carrie and I filled it with rubbish, day after day, as we cleared the old house.

Carrie stuck stickers of butterflies and ladybirds onto the van doors.

We went on clearing.

We came to several towers of boxes, all marked Lorenzo.

The first five boxes were full of clocks.

'Choose one for your room,' we said to Sister Ana.

She picked the gold one with winged eagles on top.

'Put the clocks everywhere!' said Sister Ana. 'All over the walls!'

'Shall we wind them up?' I said.

She shook her head.

The clocks hung with their hands pointing to different times, as if we'd all been released from time like she had.

We came across boxes of photos, all of Sister Ana, sitting in different parts of the city, sometimes holding a red rose – each with a date on the back, and an L for Lorenzo.

There were only two photos of skinny Lorenzo.

I kept hoping to find a photo of myself in the boxes.

But I didn't.

I kept hoping to find a photo of Sister María Soledad with me as a baby.

But I didn't.

I asked my Jhazmin-mother if she had a baby photo of me.

She didn't.

Or a photo of herself.

She never sent one.

Or ideally a photo of me and her together with her arms around me, kissing the top of my head. Like someone loved. The sort of photo I'd wanted to take to school for Miss Feast to put on the display board.

No photo arrived.

I cleaned and scrubbed my way through my horrible disappointment.

My lack of mystery.

My lack of magic.

When Carrie and I went out to buy a ladder, we bumped into Barnaby Blue at the hardware store.

'Why didn't you come and see me?' I said, wondering how awful I was looking. 'I wrote my address on your arm.'

'It rubbed off,' he said.

'You didn't think to write it down before it rubbed off?' I said.

'Why don't you come and see the house?' said Carrie.

Barnaby walked a foot away from me.

'This is where you're living, right?' he said as we opened the huge door.

'Not just where we're living,' I said. 'This is my home!'

Lovely word.

I'd never felt it fully before.

We walked into the courtyard where Sister Ana was letting the yellow budgerigars out for their daily fly.

'Sister Ana,' I said. 'This is Barnaby.'

Barnaby took her hand, ducking to miss a bird.

'*Encantado*,' he said. Pleased to meet you.

'*Bastante guapo*,' she said. Quite handsome.

I laughed.

Barnaby laughed.

Carrie disappeared.

Sister Ana sat down, spun the globe, stopped it with her eyes closed, opened her eyes and said delightedly, 'Burkina Faso,' before kneeling on the stone floor.

'She prays constantly,' I said. 'For the whole world.'

'Should we be quiet?' said Barnaby.

'No, she's very loud once she gets going,' I said.

'You actually own this house?' said Barnaby, over Sister Ana's prayers. 'It's beautiful. It must be, what, two hundred years old?'

'So?' I said, looking steadily into his eyes.

'So what?' he said, as if he honestly didn't know.

'You know exactly what,' I said.

He still tried to look as if he didn't.

'We kissed each other,' I said. 'And then we never talked about it. What was it?'

'What do you mean what was it?' he said.

'What was that kiss, Barnaby?' I said, feeling vulnerable.

Surely you know what a kiss is, Wendy said to Peter Pan.

'I think it might have been the kiss we didn't have on Charmouth Beach,' he said, in what was quite a tender voice.

I softened, and then I didn't.

I saw what he was doing.

He was making it something inconsequential, childish.

'It felt like the *beginning* of something.'

He shook his head.

'It was definitely the *end* of something,' he said. 'Closure.'

'You don't end things with tongues.'

'Was it really tongues? I don't think so,' said Barnaby, and his face was contorted, and I suppose we all have the ability to deceive ourselves, see giants where there are windmills.

'Now that is total bollocks,' I said.

'No tongues or bollocks involved,' he said, and he attempted a laugh.

'I wonder what Naomi would say about our kiss,' I said triumphantly. 'If I told her.'

I hadn't expected to say that.

'You're acting like a bastard,' I said, and then in Spanish: '*Un cabrón.*'

'*Son todos cabrones,*' said Sister Ana, pausing her prayers for a moment.

'I didn't think you were a bastard,' I said.

'I didn't either,' said Barnaby. 'And I honestly didn't mean to be. But I love Naomi. And I know that's not supposed to be possible. Feeling things for two people.'

'I hate hearing you say that.'

Sister Ana was rising to a crescendo, and Barnaby stood very still, staring at me.

'I hate feeling things for two people,' he said.

'Don't try and make me feel sorry for you!' I said coldly.

'I'm trying to be truthful,' said Barnaby, wringing his hands. 'And you were with Michael.'

'I hate you being truthful,' I said.

'I'm sorry,' he said.

'I think you should go,' I said.

He started to walk towards the door.

I stayed where I was.

'*Son todos cabrones,*' said Sister Ana again.

This really isn't true.

Carrie went to the craft shop to buy feathers, and I walked along the river and sat under the holm oak picking up acorns and putting them in my pocket. I've no idea why, but that tree always comforted me.

At the craft shop, Carrie met a man called Gabriel, who was also buying feathers.

They walked out together, and he asked her to have dinner with him.

This is the effect Carrie has on people.

Carrie came home very drunk.

'That was the best night of my life,' she said, before falling sound asleep.

She often had best nights of her life, and worst ones too – and she slept as deeply as Bridget.

In the morning, I said, 'Did you really meet this guy in the craft shop?'

She nodded, holding her head.

'Was he really buying feathers?'

She nodded, holding her head.

'Also,' said Carrie. 'He has biceps.'

'He was buying feathers and he has biceps?' I said. 'You will never ever find that combination again.'

I stand by this opinion.

'Also,' said Carrie. 'He has dark wavy hair like Jesus.'

'Also,' said Carrie. 'He may be Jesus.'

Gabriel was a primary school teacher: his pupils made birds out of feathers and collages out of anything and he found an old sofa and turned it into a pirate ship – and this is the sort of man he is.

'I think he's hyperactive,' said Carrie.

'Hyperactive is the best fault anyone can have,' I said. 'It's what you should say in interviews when you're asked what your weakness is.'

When Carrie had been dating Gabriel just over a month, he offered to paint the courtyard, so we took the flowerpots off the dirty walls and we left them in rows. When Sister Ana came outside, she fell forward, twisting her right leg and bashing the side of her face on the pots.

Once the paint was dry, we put the pots back, but she was never the same after that. Her walking days were over. We bought her the best possible wheelchair, one with knobs and levers, self-propelling, even over cobbles and up slopes – Gabriel called it her Porsche.

She zoomed about the house too fast, over thresholds, round corners, straight into the bathroom, where she overran and practically joined me in the shower.

We both laughed.

She reached out her hand.

She ran it over the birthmark on my thigh.

Her mouth looked for words, but didn't find any.

I turned off the shower.

Tears were streaming down her face.

But still no words came.

She traced the land mass of Iberia on my thigh, naming cities as she went, in perfect order: Barcelona, Valencia, Alicante.

'*Mi pequeña España,*' she said. My little Spain.

I felt the realest I'd ever felt – Eva from Iberia.

She knew me, she remembered me, from the beginning.

It felt so good.

The best ever.

338

She turned her wheelchair and left at speed, and the moment was gone for her, and un-remembered ever after.

But I had it.

I had it!

I treasured it in my heart, still do.

Sister Ana was as excited as a teenager who'd passed her driving test, and she started slipping away at night with supplies for the homeless hanging off the armrests of the wheelchair.

We'd wake and find her bed empty, and we'd rush about trying to find her.

She'd be donkey-laughing with the beggars in the orange-tree courtyard.

Or whispering at the old olive tree, next to the city walls.

She got a cold, which turned into a chest infection.

While Gabriel, Carrie and I painted the whole house bright white again, like it was in the old photographs, she watched us from her wheelchair. Then she was better, and once again propelling herself out of the door in the dark and the damp with bags of bread rolls.

Barnaby's wedding invitation arrived on the same day as a letter from my Jhazmin-mother, and on the same day as Sister Ana came down with another horrible cold.

'There's no way I'm going,' I said to Carrie.

The phone rang.

As the voice said the *E* of my name, I knew.

I knew before the *va*, I swear I did.

'Bridget!' I yelled.

Her actual voice!

I was crying.

'Where are you? I thought there were no phones in the kibbutz?'

'I left!' she said. 'In the end, I hated it. Communal living is better as an idea than a thing.'

'And how's Bessie?'

'Bessie was always fine,' said Bridget. 'It was me who was feeling shit and I couldn't admit it to you. It's been an on-off thing. And I'm feeling so much better right now.'

'I'm so sorry,' I said. 'I can't imagine you ever feeling shit. I always think of you as happy. Happy all the time.'

'That was before M died,' said Bridget. 'And when you've been a happy person, it's so hard to be unhappy. But you didn't see us afterwards. We all lost it in Israel.'

'Oh, Bridge,' I said. 'I'm so sorry. Will you come to Spain? My friend Carrie is dying to meet you.'

'Perhaps after the wedding?' said Bridget. 'I can't wait to see you at the wedding!'

Oh, not the wedding.

'Actually see you in the flesh!'

'I'm not sure if I'm going,' I said.

'Of course you must!' said Bridget. 'You totally have to! If you're not going, I'm not going. And I *am* going!'

I laughed.

'Don't forget you're an honorary Blue!' she said.

'The thing is . . .' I began. 'The thing is . . .'

There was no way I could, or should, tell her.

About me and Barnaby.

'So is that a yes?' said Bridget.

Oh crap, I thought.

'I suppose . . .'

'Fantastic!'

Carrie came shopping with me, and we found an emerald-green dress, with frilled cuffs, which flared out at the bottom, and Carrie made me peacock feather earrings, and bought me twelve silver bangles like Blue Mother's.

I suggested to my Jhazmin-mother that I could go to Tooting and meet her after the wedding, but she wrote back and said she wasn't prepared to take the risk, what if anyone saw me? I threw the letter in the bin.

Sister Ana was wheezing, but she refused to see the doctor. She said she was fine, and could I stop fussing and go with her to the olive tree?

'Did you know the olive tree is two thousand years old?' she said. 'Think what it's seen.'

'It saw the Muslims and Jews and Christians all chatting together by the city walls in the *Convivencia*,' I said, as she trundled beside me in her wheelchair.

'I first heard God talk to me from the olive tree,' she said once we got there. 'I was a child. And God was very talkative.'

I smiled.

'God seems a bit speechless these days,' she said.

'Perhaps he regrets what he made,' I said. 'When he looks down. I assume he's up. I never know where he is.'

'Oh, you haven't lost him, have you?' she said. 'I'm always losing things. I think I've lost Lorenzo.'

I took her right hand.

'Free will,' she said. 'Risky risky risky.'

She groped at the air with her left hand.

'Will someone pull up my socks?' she said.

'You're only wearing one sock, Sister Ana,' I said, pulling it up.

'You can't force love,' she said.

'That's true,' I said.

'I truly love you,' I said to her. 'I hope you know that.'

'I wish someone would pull up my other sock,' she said.

'That, Sister Ana,' I said, 'is one of your hardest ever requests.'

I set off for London, reluctant to leave Sister Ana (even with Carrie and Gabriel), and even more (much more) reluctant to go to Barnaby's wedding.

As I walked towards the pub in cold misty Baker Street, I felt a growing terror about seeing Bridget. I couldn't imagine a version of her that wasn't happy.

And then there she was, resplendent in a turquoise and fuchsia dress with a silver fur stole, and when she took me into her arms, she felt as soft and gorgeous as she'd always felt, and she smelled of freesias and champagne and pears. We clung to each other and danced down the street.

Then Bridget said, 'This'll be playing havoc with our wedding outfits!'

Then she said, 'I can't believe I just said *wedding outfits*! Who says wedding outfits?'

'You!' I said.

And we were crying laughing, like when we were eleven.

Oh, the joy of it – time had rewound.

And she was the happy Bridget that I remembered.

'You are happy,' I said. 'I was so worried you'd be different.'

'It's seeing you,' she said. 'And maybe a little bit the pills, but today isn't a day to talk about pills.'

'Are you sure?'

'I'd rather drink champagne,' she said, ordering a bottle. 'Though I shouldn't have too much.'

We glugged champagne.

She said, 'I'm sorry I'm still so fat.'

'You're beautiful, I always told you that.'

'I'll never get a boyfriend, Eva! I still haven't. It's tragic!'

'Rubbish. Beauty is in the eye of the beholder.'

'If you find me a beholder, I'll be eternally grateful,' she said.

'He'd be the luckiest man,' I said.

'What do you think of Naomi?' said Bridget.

'She's great,' I said very fast.

We glugged more champagne.

'I think Barny was looking for M, don't you?'

'Probably.'

'I hope it'll work. Are you still with Michael?'

'No . . .'

'You met someone else?'

'I did,' I said, blushing. 'But it turned out he was engaged.'

'I'm sorry,' said Bridget. 'But I'm sure they're queuing round the block for you.'

'Not exactly,' I said.

'Look at the time!' said Bridget.

She grabbed the bottle, and we ran to Marylebone Town Hall spilling champagne on our toes. When I saw Barnaby, standing alone and not-yet-married at the front, I thought that I could rush towards him, like in a Richard Curtis film, and he would perhaps say, This is the biggest mistake of my life, and he would turn and walk away with me, and we would hail a taxi to Heathrow Airport and get on a flight to, I don't know, Zanzibar – because it has two zs in its name. I caught Barnaby's eye, and he looked away.

Should I go over to him? Did I dare?

There was Mr Blue, whose body had been eaten by grief, and whose face looked like a large walnut.

Naomi appeared, on her father's arm. I couldn't bear to look at her, but I held my head high and smiled. As Barnaby Blue promised to love her forever, my bangles fell down my arm with a big clink.

At the reception, I never left Bridget's side.

Naomi came over.

'Congratulations!' I said, grabbing one of her sleeves, over-affectionately. 'Is that antique lace?'

As if I cared.

She squeezed my hand.

'I love the way you gave all your mothers colours,' she said.

Let go of my hand, I thought.

'Barny told me,' she said.

I wish he hadn't, I thought, it's private.

Naomi didn't let go of my hand, and I really didn't need to see that great big zigzaggy engagement ring and the gold wedding band up close.

'And I thought what colour mother would I like to be,' said Naomi.

Bridget said, 'What colour did you think?'

'Red,' said Naomi. 'Wild and full of passion. I'm going to be one of those mothers who takes their baby travelling around the world to far-flung places. In a sling. With none of the paraphernalia. Just my boobs.'

Oh, not your boobs, I thought.

They get everywhere.

At the airport, I wrote Jhazmin a letter, trying a different tack – easy questions such as her favourite food and her favourite colour, like Bridget and I used to ask each other in those paper whirlybirds we made incessantly in Class 4.

When I got back to Córdoba with Bridget, Sister Ana was lying in bed, with a croupy cough.

I was shocked by how tiny she looked.

'Are my flowers still alive?' she whispered, coughing into her handkerchief.

'Your flowers are looking more beautiful than ever,' I said.

'Can I go and see them?' she whispered, and speaking made her start coughing again.

'You can go out there tomorrow,' I said. 'It's dark now.'

I sat holding her hand.

She made circles with her forefinger around my palm.

'Round and round,' she said. 'Round and round.'

I liked the feeling of it, and I wondered if she'd done this when I was a baby, and I chose to think she had.

'We're in the circle,' she whispered. 'With Sister María Soledad.' She smiled.

'What is the circle, Sister Ana?' I said.

'Round and round,' she said in a fading voice. 'Love love love.'

I sat up with her through the night, putting flannels on her forehead, watching her shrink before my eyes.

She did go out to the *patio* the next day. She went out on a trolley, being pushed by the ambulance driver, a slim man, with strikingly thin arms, like Lorenzo, like Billy.

'Could you pause here?' I said to him.

'Open your eyes,' I said.

'My flowers,' she whispered.

I knew that she would never see her flowers again, not in this life.

'Lorenzo!' she whispered to the ambulance driver. 'Will you let my birds out?'

Carrie, Bridget and I opened the cages, and the yellow birds flew in circles around the courtyard. Sister Ana lifted her thin right arm, and one of the birds swooped over her, grazing her forefinger with its wing.

It was a fragment of a second.

I took her hand.

I could see the imprint of swept feather on her finger.

I didn't try to explain it.

Because not everything needs an explanation, she'd taught me that.

She was softening into death.

And this isn't an explainable thing.

'Bridget, I'm so sorry not to be with you today,' I said, holding myself together. 'But I have to go to the hospital.'

'That's totally what you should do, Eva,' said Bridget.

'She'll be safe with me,' said Carrie, taking Bridget's arm.

It felt so good, looking at them together – spindly Carrie, with her wispy plaits, blond again, and her too-big kimono, arm in arm with beautiful Bridget, her pale porcelain face, her dark hair, falling in waves around her shoulders, her lovely balanced body, curving in and out like a Greek vase, bare feet flat on the stone floor.

It is, surprisingly, possible to feel deep joy inside deep sadness – like Mr Blue said, they all run together.

The budgerigars flew back into their cages.

I climbed into the ambulance with Sister Ana's bag and her globe.

'Do you have my clock?' she whispered.

I took it out.

'Wind it up!' she said.

'I thought you didn't want the clocks wound up.'

'I do.'

I wound it up.

'Look at the time,' she said.

It was the last thing she ever said.

'Are you the granddaughter?' said a nurse, when we arrived.

I nodded.

Because I wanted to have a family.

Just for a few moments.

As I sat holding her disappearing hand, her globe trembled back and forth with the swish of nurses' aprons.

'It's pneumonia,' the doctor told me. 'Your grandmother's very weak.'

Sister Ana was falling slowly out of this world.

The day seemed motionless, but for the tick tick tick of Lorenzo's clock.

I kissed her forehead.

'I wish you remembered it all,' I said. 'My life with you all. I wish you could have told me about it.'

She said nothing, but her eyelids trembled.

'I wish I'd known Lorenzo,' I said.

Her face was set with a tiny hopeful smile.

'I wish I'd known Sister María Soledad. And all of you. *My first family.*'

Carrie and Gabriel and Bridget brought food in Tupperware boxes for me to eat, and they kissed Sister Ana's forehead, which was turning into tracing paper.

I said that life was a very sad thing, and Carrie told me it could be happy too, but Barnaby Blue was on honeymoon with Naomi Blue, who was his *wife*, and Sister Ana, who was the closest I'd ever got to the beginning of me, was nearing her end.

And I couldn't bear the thought of the world without her in it.

I trusted God had someone precious lined up for her on the other side of death, the way there's always a mother waiting on the other side of birth.

I hoped it would be Lorenzo.

With a red rose.

Sister Ana's funeral was at the Mezquita.

As we came out wiping our eyes, on 5 January, the wise kings came into the city on camels, bearing gifts, and the children laughed and leapt and caught sweets.

I saw a young man with a sling, and inside was a tiny baby in a pink hat. When I asked how old she was, I started crying again.

'*Tres días,*' he said.

Three days since Sister Ana died, and three days from death to resurrection – she'd have metamorphosed, grown wings. Maybe. Who knows?

So many threes.

Though threes aren't always popular, Carrie, Bridget and I were turning out to be one of the best.

Three in one, one in three, the priest said at the funeral, a circle of love.

God can't be one, he said, because God is love and love doesn't work on its own.

Like Mr Blume said.

Love has to be *between*.

We walked past the *Belén* – the little stable scene, set up for Christmas, the clay Jesus under the Moorish arch, with his clay mother and his clay not-father, Joseph.

Three kings carrying gold, frankincense and myrrh.

Myrrh to embalm him.

Next to the manger.

Because death always stands over life.

The homeless men came to our party. And a few nuns. And the woman with no teeth. And the kind woman with the hijab and soft hands who'd given me her jewelled pen. And my not-father, whose hair was thinning, and who looked not-strong-as-an-ox. We ate *roscones de reyes*, the special ringed Epiphany cakes, decorated with dried fruit, and the cats snaked around people's legs begging for crumbs. Then everyone left. And it was too quiet.

I wandered around our beloved house, my beloved house – my not-father had transferred it into my name, but it would always belong to Sister Ana and the nuns. I ran my hand along the old white walls, and saw her shadow around corners.

'It's weird to think of me here as a baby being bottle-fed by down-and-outs,' I said to Carrie and Bridget.

'It's beautiful, your story,' said Carrie. 'The way you've ended up where you started. Like a circle.'

'I still can't believe that in all those boxes I never found a baby photo of me with Sister María Soledad. I so wanted to see her face.'

Bridget took my hand.

'At least you found your real blood mother,' she said.

'But all she does is write me boring letters about Tooting,' I said. 'With too many commas and no full stops!'

'I like commas,' said Carrie. 'The way they race along. Full stops feel a bit final.'

'What's your favourite punctuation mark, Eva?' said Bridget.

'Obviously the question mark,' I said.

'I always loved the way you asked so many questions,' said Bridget.

Gabriel was clearing up – we could hear him clinking and crashing in the kitchen.

'The *Angel* Gabriel!' said Bridget, laughing. 'And it's exclamation marks for me!'

'They always seem as if they're trying too hard,' said Carrie.

'But they're so jolly!' said Bridget. 'Though really far too thin for a girl like me! Too easy to lose down the bottom of the bed!'

Carrie laughed.

'There's something else I'd like to *lose* down the bottom of the bed,' said Bridget.

More clinking came from the kitchen.

'Don't ever leave Gabriel, Carrie!' said Bridget.

'I don't think I will,' she said. 'And I never thought I was the sort of person who'd say that.'

'I think everyone has the potential to be that sort of person,' I said. 'Don't you?'

'Another question mark,' said Carrie, smiling, and she went to join him in the kitchen.

Bridget and I sat on the sofa close together.

'Perhaps I don't need a man,' said Bridget. 'Now I've got you again. Forever Eva.'

'It's like that summer,' I said, looking at our interlinked white and brown fingers. 'Sitting waiting for your mum to come and say good night.'

We gathered Sister Ana's books, her blankets, the worn mat where she used to pray, her folding chair, her three grey dresses, her two grey cardigans, her old black shoulder bag, her few pots and pans.

There it was, in three rubbish bags: a life.

I folded her wimple and put it in my drawer.

I kept the globe and put it on my windowsill next to the photo of us singing hymns.

I picked up her bible.

In the front cover, it said *Sor Ana* in black ink.

It had a brown leather cover, and the spine was cracking.

I let it fall open, and there was the white back of a photo.

Could it be?

A baby photo of me and Sister María Soledad?

It said *Gracias*.

I turned it over.

It was thin-armed Lorenzo.

With Sister Ana.

At the *Batalla de las Flores*.

Flower-covered carriages processed down the street, and people threw white carnations.

Thank you for what?

I'd never know.

Lives stop with frayed ends.

Dirty washing still in the laundry basket.

I threw her dirty washing, the last vestiges of her livingness, away.

When I should have been writing an essay, I started to read her bible, beginning with the Gospel of John, where the angel, who might be Rafael, stirred the waters in the pool of Bethesda, where the sick and frail gathered.

Bridget and Carrie came in.

I put the bible into Sister Ana's oak box.

'Bridget, I'm sorry I've been so miserable,' I said. 'It hasn't been much of a holiday for you.'

'Death is miserable-making,' said Bridget.

'I've got a plan,' said Carrie. 'And it's all booked.'

'All booked?'

'And paid for.'

'Where are we going?'

'You'll see when we arrive. Pack for three nights. And beach.'

On our way out of the door, I saw that a letter had arrived from Jhazmin.

'Oh no!' I said to Bridget and Carrie. 'More commas from Tooting.'

I put it in my pocket, thinking that she would probably rain Deborah and double shifts on me forever.

It was hard to feel she loved me in any meaningful sense.

But love wasn't only found in blood-mothers, that's what I'd realised.

Love wasn't only found in romance with men, though I wouldn't have been averse to some romance with men. By which I mean, obviously, *man*. Unlike Barnaby, I was opposed to the plural.

No, love was here in the yellow van, as we drove south, with Carrie map-reading, as love had been in the courtyard with Sister Ana and the angel, and at the top of the hill with Blue Mother and the picnic.

Once we reached the coast road, I saw the signpost to Alvera – so strange to see the name in real life. We climbed up a winding road, craggy hills to left and right, paused to gasp at the sea below, at the birds of prey hanging on the air currents.

I tried not to think of the cancer bird waiting to pounce.

We parked outside Hostal Playa, and were shown to our room by Luisa and Elvira, two cousins from Seville. It had three single beds with iron bedheads, and three glass jam jars full of wild flowers.

When we went for a walk through the hamlet of white cubed houses, we took the path along the back of the beach. And there it was – it had to be – the beach house, with its blue gate and its rows of two hundred palms swaying against the purple dusk sky, planted by my not-father for my not-mother, before I arrived in their life and made everything worse.

Cherie loomed into view in my mind: a desperate young woman who'd kind of stolen me, thinking she would love me and I would love her, but finding that we didn't quite, that you couldn't force it. Free will risky risky risky, isn't that what Sister Ana said by the olive tree?

'I feel really odd,' I said. 'Imagining myself arriving here, such a tiny thing, with two strangers. I wonder what was going on in that little mind of mine.'

The dogs went crazy behind the wall.

Bridget started to make a barbecue on the beach.

She always knew how to do things like that.

Carrie had brought champagne.

Bridget opened it.

The cork flew off and landed in the sand.

Carrie ran after it.

She took a penknife out of her craft bag and made a space to put in a five-peseta coin.

She handed it to me.

'To you, Eva!' she said. 'For coming through!'

We clinked glasses.

'To the holy trinity of us three!' I said.

'To the beach house!' said Bridget. 'And skinny-dipping later!'

'Definitely!' said Carrie.

'To Alvera!' I said. 'I can't believe I never dared come before.'

'So many exclamation marks!' said Bridget. 'Heaven!'

'To Sister María Soledad!'

'I really can't drink to her,' said Carrie. 'I can't forgive her for selling you.'

'I still think she loved me,' I said. 'And I still hope we find her face some time.'

'How can you forgive *her* so easily?' said Carrie. 'And not the others?'

'Maybe because she doesn't have a face,' I said.

'Let's drink to all the faces we'd love to see again!' said Bridget. 'Especially M!'

'And Billy!' I said. 'He had the loveliest face.'

'And Sister Ana!' said Carrie. 'She was so irreverent.'

'And also so reverent,' I said.

'I love a contradiction,' said Carrie.

'Let's drink to contradictions,' I said.

'And let's drink to your real mother!' said Bridget. 'Though she doesn't have a face yet either . . .'

'My life is full of headless women,' I said.

'Is finding her better than not finding her?' said Carrie, looking worried.

'I guess so,' I said. 'Notwithstanding the commas.'

We clinked our glasses again.

Bridget opened another bottle.

Carrie said, 'You never opened your letter.'

I took it out of my pocket, saying in a monotonous voice: I got up, I went to work, it was raining, love from Jhazmin.

But when I opened the envelope, I could see that this was not like her normal letters.

No, this was a long letter – with paragraphs.

Something had changed.

Maybe I'd asked the right questions.

'Make yourselves comfortable!' I said.

'*Dear Eva,*' I read, the words a bit champagne-slurry.

You asked me what my favourite food was.

It's funny, but the way I remember things is by food.

My childhood is ceviche made with prawns and chilli and herbs, with a twist of lemon juice. We used to buy it from stalls on the street in Lima, and Papas a la Huancaina, *eggs and cheese and spices, creamy as anything.*

And then Córdoba is sugary ensaimadas *for breakfast, and pastry* pasteles *for lunch, and doughnuts oozing custard at that lovely bakery on Calle Cervantes, your father loved my home-made tortilla, and Sister María Soledad used to feed the homeless with tortilla.*

Córdoba makes me think of tiny budgerigars on balconies, the sun in the sky, and your father and I driving out in his campervan to the countryside in May 1974, to the sunflower fields, did you know that there are 45,000 hectares of sunflowers in Córdoba, they bloom in May.

The day your father left, he arrived at my little flat with thirty-one sunflowers, for each of the days we'd had together, then he left for the priesthood.

Sunflowers stand tall through the hottest days of summer, and they turn their heads to the sun, their Spanish name is girasol, *turn-to-the-sun.*

'Stand tall, Jhazmin,' he said, and he left.

Later, I found out that sunflowers come from Peru, the American Indians cultivated them and the Incas worshipped them, and they were symbols of holiness and fertility.

So when I got home to London without you, I planted sunflowers in our garden in Tooting, and they grew to be ten foot tall.

'Stand tall,' I say to the sunflowers every morning, although perhaps I'm saying it to you, Eva.

So, this is a very long way to say that my favourite colour is
YELLOW.
Love,

Jhazmin x

I paused.
Finally, a kiss.
Stand tall – have I stood tall?
'That was actually beautiful,' said Carrie.
We clinked glasses again.
'My father had a campervan!' I said. 'I love people who love
campervans. Michael hated them.'
I imagined my real father and my real mother driving out among
the sunflower fields, and my real mother looking at the sunflowers in
her damp little Tooting garden every morning for the last twenty
years and thinking of me.
'Maybe you were conceived in a sunflower field,' said Carrie. 'In a
campervan – a VW split-screen, a light blue and cream one!'
'Let's drink to that!' said Bridget.
'I've really got a proper past,' I said. 'Like your dad said, Bridge.
A history! A real family tree!'
'To your yellow mother!' said Bridget.
We clinked glasses again.
'I never really loved the colour yellow,' I said.
'But you bought a yellow van?' said Bridget.
'It was very cheap,' said Carrie.
'Wasn't there a yellow mother in that book you were obsessed by
at St Hilda's?' said Bridget.
'You're right, Bridge. You actually remembered something!' I said.
'This girl has a photographic memory,' said Bridget.
'I didn't do very well in the mothers department,' I said. 'But let's
raise our glasses to girlfriends. Where I aced it!'

'What was Yellow Mother like?' said Carrie.

'She wore a dress that looked like a yellow nylon nightie, and she had a slightly tense look about her,' I said. *'Yellow Mother is pretty and happy and full of energy. She goes about being busy, tending her lemon orchard and looking after her bees.* I always thought she sounded a bit annoying.'

'Lemons and bees – could be sinister,' said Carrie, sounding a bit slurry.

'Buttercups?' said Bridget.

'Are we just saying any yellow things?' said Carrie.

'Swimming hats,' said Bridget.

'Lemon sherbets,' I said. 'You remember how they made your tongue hurt?'

'Spanish postboxes,' said Bridget.

'Bath ducks,' said Carrie.

Bridget squeezed my hand.

The magnitude of bath ducks was possibly not explainable to Carrie – some things really aren't.

'Have we had too much to drink?' said Bridget.

'Tie a yellow ribbon round the old oak tree?' said Carrie. 'That's a beautiful song.'

I can still see us sitting together on the huge great beach in Alvera, which sweeps round in an arch, with grass at the back where wild ponies graze.

Our arms were around each other and we were singing: tie a yellow ribbon round the old oak tree. And I was imagining that my mother – Jhazmin Benalcazar – might eventually come home to Córdoba singing that it had been twenty long years and did I still want her?

And did I still want her?

You always want your mother.

Whatever she's like.

Over breakfast, Bridget asked us whether we ever felt broody.

'For babies?' said Carrie, looking at me meaningfully.

'Well, what else would you be broody for?' said Bridget.

'Cats?' I said, hiding as usual.

I told Bridget about my endometriosis.

'You don't have to be a mother to have a good life,' said Carrie. 'Look at Sister Ana.'

Bridget said she was so sorry and why hadn't I said, and I said, because I'm crap at saying except when I'm drunk, and she said do you want to talk about it, and I said not that much.

'Except – if you two have babies and I don't, I'm scared of feeling left behind,' I said. 'Like when I actually prayed to God for pubic hair because you got ahead of me.'

'Do remember you're talking to the Virgin Mary here,' said Bridget.

Luisa came over to clear the table, and we got talking, and she told us that she and Elvira had been on holiday when they saw the hotel for sale and thought why not?

'That's what your dad used to say,' I said to Bridget.

'Did he?' said Bridget.

'You know what,' I said. 'Once I've finished my degree, I could turn the house into a hotel.'

'You could,' said Bridget. 'You actually could.'

And there was this little glint inside me, like the sun coming out.

'You could give tours and lectures,' said Carrie. 'You'd be brilliant at it!'

'And we could call it Historical Holidays,' I said.

'And I could help you run it,' said Carrie.

'And I could be your first guest,' said Bridget.

And I said, 'Why not?'

Back in Córdoba, I took Bridget to the station, and hugged her goodbye.

It was so sad coming home without her.

I picked up my notes on the Spanish picaresque novel, but couldn't find the energy to write my essay.

I stared out of the window of my bedroom over the courtyard, imagining guests eating dinner by the stone walls, beneath rows of geranium pots, with tealights flickering, perhaps a flamenco guitarist sitting over there in the corner and San Rafael keeping watch.

I aced my not-Hons degree, put away my files and phoned my not-father to tell him about my tentative hotel plans.

'Make it exactly how you want it, Eva, and I'll cover the cost,' he said, showing either that all of us are better than our worst behaviour, or that you can buy love, or both, maybe.

'We're going to call it La Convivencia,' I told him.

Carrie and I met with an architect called Susana, and we started dreaming, and she started drawing.

First, a flat for me and Carrie (and often Gabriel), with white-washed walls and turquoise doors and a spiral staircase to the flat roof, where we toasted San Rafael at sunset as he stood angelic guard over the city on top of the bell tower which was once a minaret.

On the first floor, eight bedrooms with ceramic-tiled floors and shuttered arched windows. Eight more on the top floor. We hung one of Lorenzo's clocks on every bedroom wall, put coloured Moroccan rugs on the floors and imported lamps from Tangiers which spread patterned light over the white ceilings.

We made a dining room in the huge cavernous room on the left, and let it spill into the courtyard, with tables arranged around San Rafael, and blue-and-white porcelain fountains, overhung with cascades of flowers, and a covered section, with low leather pouffes and couches, brass tables, shelves of books, and lanterns with coloured glass.

In every corner, on every wall, terracotta pots, bursting with hydrangea and jasmine and bougainvillaea and geraniums.

The big room on the right we kept for lectures and exhibitions and concerts, decorating it with a wooden cross, geometric Islamic tiles and engraved Jewish Sephardic poetry.

We were ready to open, so Carrie left her job at the dance shop to help me. As a leaving present, the owner gave her a pair of purple flamenco shoes with yellow dots, which she might have been struggling to sell.

We hung the wrought-iron sign over the door – *La Convivencia* – and we embedded a ceramic plaque into the external wall, September 1997, and we asked the homeless people from the orange-tree court-yard to come and drink champagne with us, as Sister Ana would have wanted. Carrie flamencoed around the stone courtyard in her garish shoes, tap tap tap, serving them drinks and tapas.

Bridget arrived with a suitcase for the weekend because she abso-lutely had to be my first guest. We visited Medina Azahara and walked in the hills with my butterfly guide, ticking off species.

'Why did we grow apart?' I said. 'Was it because my letters were terrible and you had no phone at the kibbutz? Or was it something else?'

'Was it true that those three letters of mine never arrived?' said Bridget. 'And did you really move out of the Chelsea house? Or was that an excuse so you didn't have to deal with me.'

'Deal with you?'

'And my depression.'

'I can't believe you thought I lied,' I said.

'It's just you sounded so weird in that letter, like you were hiding something.'

'Maybe I didn't want to admit how unhappy I was with Michael.'

'Unhappy?' said Bridget. 'I thought you were madly in love.'

'I was very young,' I said. 'I had no idea how to have a proper relationship.'

'In those letters you didn't get, I told you everything,' said Bridget. 'How bad it was with D. His depression, the whole thing. That's why we all moved to the kibbutz. He couldn't handle living with us. So I left with the little ones. But I was really a child myself.'

'I'm so sorry,' I said. 'Why didn't you say?'

'I did say. In those letters.'

'Why didn't you say again?'

'Because I didn't think you'd be interested. And I felt like a failure. And you were halfway on your way to being some kind of posh wife. I didn't think you wanted me once you had Michael,' said Bridget.

'I always wanted you,' I said, taking her arm.

'You sounded so together,' she said. 'And so grown-up.'

'I so wasn't together,' I said. 'I was scared and miserable and I had insomnia and panic attacks and had to move back home. I think I just latched onto Michael because there wasn't anybody else and he was handsome and he asked. But that sounds mean.'

'Isn't that what most people do?' said Bridget, laughing.

'I'm not sure,' I said.

'I wish I'd known,' said Bridget.

'I wish I'd known,' I said. 'I'm really sorry, Bridge. How bad were you?'

'Really bad,' she said. 'But I still wouldn't see a doctor, you remember, I never would. Not after visiting M. The trauma of it.'

'What? You still won't?'

'I can't make myself,' said Bridget. 'It's a phobia of doctors. It's got a name. And everything.'

'Which is?'

'Iatrophobia.'

'You should maybe see someone about that, Bridge,' I said.

And we burst out laughing, like eleven-year-olds in the playground, and then we stopped.

'I talked to a doctor by phone in the end and I got myself some pills.'

We hugged.

'I'm so much better now,' she said. 'I don't think it's just the pills.'

'I'm so so sorry,' I said. 'For being completely shit.'

We sat holding each other's hands.

'Why don't you stay here?' I said. 'I'll look after you, and we'll be happy again. Like we were before. You can get a job.'

'I can't speak Spanish!' said Bridget.

'It's very easy,' I said.

'Because you're Spanish,' she said. 'I was always bottom in French, don't you remember?'

'You've actually remembered something,' I said.

Bridget went back to London, joined a beginners' Spanish course and started mudlarking again by Battersea Bridge.

I employed a serious-looking manager by the name of Adriana, who wore mannish suits and lace-up shoes. If you left anything on her desk, it would disappear into the shredder in seconds.

'Only touch things once,' she said.

'Even lovers?' said Carrie.

Adriana didn't smile. She flicked happily through her to-do lists and her spreadsheets, dreaming up systems and processes, tick tick shred shred, flushed with the thrill of her own capability. Carrie went on a Moorish cookery course, and threw herself into becoming the hotel cook. I gave tours of the city and historical lectures with slides, and sat about answering the guests' questions on Córdoba, in a swooning joy – the joy of being an expert.

A joy not often talked about, the joy of expertise.

I recommend it.

Finding your thing.

Your place in the scheme of things.

Carrie cooked and cooked and cooked, tossing herbs into frying pans and singing, and she also ordered boxes of souvenirs which she put in baskets along the reception desk: Mezquita magnets, geranium-painted thimbles, Córdoba pens, silver earrings, palm tree pendants and post-cards. Then Gabriel started a children's history programme, and he set up special holiday weeks and school discounts and fancy dress.

Carrie and Gabriel were a proper grown-up couple now, with couple-friends, and it was time for them to move out and rent a flat over the river. Although I was happy for them, it felt sad having nobody to say goodnight to.

I wrote and told my Jhazmin-mother my news, and I asked for the second time if we could meet.

She didn't answer.

Time passed, in a haze of guests arriving and guests leaving.

She still didn't answer.

Barnaby arrived to give a lecture on Medina Azahara at the newly opened Research Centre. I watched him from my window over the courtyard, trying to argue myself out of my desire, telling myself it was a pathetic childhood crush, and I'd turned him into something he wasn't, and he was married, and what was the matter with me, I was a grown-up now, and it was only a kiss.

I must sort myself out, I said sternly, but I was still a river flooding its banks.

I went downstairs to greet him.

'How's Naomi?' I forced myself to ask.

'She's doing well,' he said.

'Good,' I said. 'I hope the talk goes well.'

'Thank you,' he said.

He stayed two days.

I stayed away from him.

When he left, he said it was a shame he hadn't seen more of me, oh yes, what a shame, I agreed, but he said he'd be back to give another lecture, and he'd definitely stay at La Convivencia.

Oh lovely, I said, treading water, yes do stay, if the place isn't ten feet underwater, you'd be most welcome to stay.

'Your taxi's here,' said efficient Adriana to Barnaby, tick tick shred.

And he was gone.

What a relief.

Mop the floors.

'There's a letter for you, Eva,' said Adriana.

Dear Eva,
I can't meet you.
No one knows you exist.
It would be too much of a risk.
Please know I think of you, wrote Jhazmin.

What was the point of this mother, who was only prepared to think of me but never see me?

I spent Christmas with Carrie and Gabriel.

I wrote to Jhazmin in the new year, asking her to tell me a bit more about her husband and son, who she rarely mentioned. She didn't reply.

Guests arrived and guests departed.

And guests arrived and guests departed.

The hotel was full that spring for the festival of *Cruces* and *Patios* and the May *feria* where we partied day and night and never slept.

Summer was hotter and harder to fill.

In the autumn, two years after we'd opened, every room was taken, and all my lectures and tours were over-subscribed.

The success of La Convivencia was such a joy to me.

Success is almost as good as love, I find, but not quite.

The greatest joy of all was when Bridget moved to Córdoba to help me in November of 1999. I gave her Carrie's old room in my flat and felt the ginger delirium of our childhood friendship. She was off the pills – hurray! – and feeling well and hopeful, so I felt well and hopeful too. The way we catch each other's feelings, that's the joy and the agony of love.

For now it was a joy.

The agony came later.

I wondered if I'd ever tell Bridget about Barnaby.

I didn't think so – she'd be too conflicted.

'Listen to me!' said Bridget. '*Me llamo Bridget y tengo veinticinco años y vivo en Córdoba.*'

'Completely fluent!' I said. 'I can't believe you're twenty-five!'

'And I still haven't *done it*!' wailed Bridget.

'Wait until my millennium party!' I said.

My not-father came to the millennium party.

He wasn't Peter Pan, and he couldn't grow old peacefully.

He'd dyed his hair tar-black and doused it in oil to hold it in place across his scalp.

Bridget looked beautiful in a silver silk dress.

Gabriel had – with some intention – invited a friend called Gerónimo, a giant of a man, loud-voiced and laughing, wearing black-rimmed glasses with a big, majestic nose and a bigger and more majestic smile. Imposing, if not exactly handsome.

Bridget and Gerónimo were standing on opposite sides of the angel when it first came to me that Gabriel was right, this really might work.

You know how some people look right physically together.

These two did.

I smiled to myself as Gabriel introduced them, as they laughed, as they sat down and talked and talked and talked. I lost sight of them, and suddenly it was the end of the 19s, and aeroplanes didn't fall out of the sky and computers didn't crash, and on the other side of midnight, after we'd eaten our twelve grapes the Spanish way, after we'd popped champagne, there they were, kissing, in front of my eyes.

Bridget had invited the twin brothers and the twin sisters.

Boaz still looked like a mole.

Barnaby arrived without Naomi, who was making a TV programme about her latest expedition.

I avoided him, as planned.

I walked around talking over-animatedly to everyone else, knowing exactly – exactly – where he was. Hoping he knew where I was. Hoping he was dying of desire. Hoping he'd noticed how much I didn't need him. How happy and laughy and desirable and desired I was.

I danced with the whole world, even my not-father and Boaz, to make Barnaby jealous – I hoped he was watching.

But I didn't dance with Barnaby.

When everyone had left, Barnaby stayed, sitting in a corner, smoking.

'Come and sit down,' he said.

Pathetic, but I did.

'This is our baby,' he said, holding out a blurry black and white photo. 'I wanted you to know before anyone.'

I remember the knife-wound I felt in my heart.

The betrayal.

Betrayal?

That a married couple were going to have a baby.

I found it disconcerting.

'It's a girl,' said Barnaby.

'Lovely,' I said, not getting the tone right – was there a right tone?

'We're going to call her Azahara,' said Barnaby.

'The caliph's favourite wife,' I said, and now I had a headache coming on in my temples. 'You stole my name. What if I want to call my daughter Azahara?'

'I thought you said—' said Barnaby.

'Nothing is certain,' I said crossly. 'All they have are statistics.'

I defy the statistics, I thought, don't nick my name, and don't show me photos of your embryo – it's not appropriate. Who wants to see photos of anyone's embryo? Is nothing private these days?

'It's a bit weird to call her the name I suggested,' I said. 'In the circumstances.'

'I hadn't really thought of it like that,' said Barnaby, looking almost apologetic.

I got up.

Bridget came through the oak door with Gerónimo, and they went and sat in a dark corner.

I went to bed without saying goodnight to Barnaby.

I avoided him in the morning.

Or he avoided me.

It's all a question of perception.

'Gerónimo's invited me to New York!' said Bridget.

I hugged her.

'It's such a great name!' I said. 'Don't people say it before they jump off bridges?'

'I'm going to jump,' said Bridget. 'I've decided.'

'You look nice together,' I said.

'I think he might be rich,' said Bridget. 'But I don't like him for that. I like him because I like him. He's funny. And I don't feel big next to him.'

Carrie and I waved her off – first stop, Granada.

I whispered, 'Jeronimo!'

She'd be doing it within hours.

Whoosh whoosh whoosh!

Exclamation marks all round for Bridget.

When I went inside, there was a letter from Jhazmin, answering the question I'd asked a year before.

'My husband was a regular at the Spanish restaurant. That's how I met him, we got married and moved in with my parents, and pretty quickly we had our son, Liam. He's nineteen and a Chelsea-supporter, like his dad.'

Commas commas commas.

And still not magic at all.

In the slightest.

Bridget and Gerónimo came back.

Bridget was bursting out of herself.

'Do you like Gerónimo?' said Bridget.

'He's lovely,' I said.

I did like him, but I found it hard to get to know him.

I often find this with jolly people, whose jolliness, though apparently welcoming, can keep you out.

'He gets on with everyone,' she said.

I went on bad dates with his friends.

A lot of bad dates.

Let's not major on the bad dates.

Life stories are allowed to be selective.

Bridget whirled about the world with Gerónimo as he did important deals, something to do with cooking oil – I've always had a loose hold on jobs.

I called Cherie in Chelsea, but Jean said she hadn't persuaded her to talk to me – she still felt betrayed.

I felt bad.

And sad.

But I couldn't make myself regret taking the house.

In a burst of courage, I wrote a letter to Jhazmin asking, directly, whether she would ever let me go to Tooting and meet her in the flesh.

She didn't mention it in her letters, all through the year, and then in the spring of 2001, out of the blue, she wrote this:

We come on holiday to Gibraltar every September, and we always cross into Spain for one day, and the men all go to the bullfight in La Línea, and I catch a bus to a village called El Manantial, which has a harbour and some restaurants, and I go to a little boutique there, and I let myself think of your father, just for one day each year, I look in the mirror and ask him which dress he likes. Enough of that! I could meet you there. Café del Mar.

'Please wear yellow!' I replied. 'So I recognise you.'

I drove through fields of dead sunflowers towards the coast road, heading left towards Gibraltar, turning off when I saw the sign to El Manantial, which means a spring where water spouts.

There was a miserable strip of grey sand, with pedaloes on it and rows of sun umbrellas. I took my seat at a plastic table with a red plastic ketchup bottle on it and ordered a coffee.

Buses kept arriving at the far side of the promenade.

I tried to look comfortable.

I ordered a second coffee.

There was a small sticky patch of something on the table: jam, or tomato ketchup.

I scratched at it with my fingernail.

Women walked along the promenade.

A woman in a yellow scarf – I smiled.

Yellow flip-flops – I smiled again.

A pale yellow sundress.

My real actual mother?

Shaking hands.

I stood up.

Shaking legs.

The sundress had daisies on it, with heads made of tiny yellow beads.

She started crying.

She had the same eyes as me, or I had the same eyes as her, dark and shaped like almonds. I liked her eyes, which must mean I liked my own eyes – these are extraordinary revelations when you've never had a real mother. I looked down and saw that she had dark hairs on her big toes. I had those too. I plucked them out with tweezers in the mornings.

'What should I call you?' I said.

She didn't answer.

She wiped her eyes.

'I thought it would never happen,' she said. 'I never forgot you. And I can prove that.'

'You don't need to prove anything,' I said.

We didn't hug.

We stood, staring at each other, this stranger-mother and I, and I couldn't work out what I felt.

'Every year on the thirty-first of January I bought you a card and a present. I've got them in a case back in Tooting. In the attic.'

She knows the date of my birthday.

Of course she knows the date of your birthday.

She was there.

You came out of this woman's body.

It looks too small, I thought.

'I'll buy you a cake,' she said. 'They do a lovely almond cake. And do you want tea?'

I nodded, though I've never liked almond cake.

We sat down, and I felt a strange darkness inside me.

There was no magic.

There was slightly greasy almond cake, which I found I couldn't eat: it turned into little balls, like the ones they put inside bean bags, and the balls rolled around on my tongue, sticking to the inside of my cheeks and my gums. My thighs sweated against the plastic chair, and the tea wasn't very nice, and nor was the cake.

'Perhaps we should try a hug,' I said, blushing furiously. 'I mean, if that's OK.'

'It's not something we really do in our family,' she said quietly, looking away.

'How funny!' I said, feeling it was the least funny thing I'd ever heard. 'Nor do we in mine!'

'Except you are my family, I suppose,' she said, looking down.

Look up, I thought, please look up, because we don't feel like family.

'Yes, I meant my other family who adopted me,' I said. 'We don't really hug either.'

'The nuns?'

'No, the couple who got me from the nuns. Did you know about them?'

She shook her head.

'I'll explain,' I said, trying to sound cheerful. 'I had a very fragile mother and a very absent father.'

As I said it, I started feeling cross with her, which I hadn't expected at all.

'You didn't live with the nuns?' she said. 'With Sister María Soledad?'

It wasn't going right.

I leapt to my feet.

'Shall we give the hug a try?' I said. 'It might help.'

She got up.

I'd pictured myself falling into her arms, but she fell into mine.

I'd been looking for a mother to lean on, but she was leaning on me.

And, what's more, she was much smaller than me.

I felt big with her in my arms.

Which I didn't like.

Maybe my father was tall.

The hug came to an end quickly, and we sat back down.

A girl with black plaits rode along the walkway on a bike.

'I used to stare at brown girls with black hair,' she said. 'And now I don't need to.'

'Isn't it strange how we both went to Córdoba?' I said. 'The way we were both drawn to the same city?'

'But there again,' she said, 'you would have known you were born there, wouldn't you?'

'I guess so.'

'And you like Córdoba, do you?' she said, unmagically.

'Oh, like isn't the word for it.'

'I felt the same.'

Of course you did, I thought, because you and I are mother and daughter, and we have almond eyes and hairy toes, and we could be written about in a Sunday magazine – but I'm not yet totally sure you're my North Star.

She ordered more tea.

'At school, I was always top of the class in Spanish,' she said. 'I bet you were too.'

'Did you like being top of the class?'

'I loved it.'

'Me too.'

Me too me too me too!

What a relief: we were a little bit the same!

She'd taken a year abroad in Córdoba, as part of her Spanish degree, working in a school, just up from Plaza de Tendillas, in the modern part of town.

'I know exactly where you mean,' I beamed.

'It took a while to get my confidence up in Córdoba,' she said. 'But I started to make friends, and then it was *Cruces* – and that's where I met your father.'

My father?

I have a father – a real one.

'I've got a photo of him.'

Yes, he was a tall man, I knew it.

He was standing in front of a cross made of red roses – I was sure it was Plaza del Potro, the Don Quijote square. He was wearing a blue polo-shirt, with the collar standing up and beige Chino trousers. I thought he'd look like a priest, rather than somebody who shopped in Gap. I squinted at this stranger with his black hair and big hands.

'His friends were dancing in the square. And he wasn't,' she said.

'And what happened?'

'He said why wasn't I dancing, and I said I was too shy. He said would I like to go somewhere else. I said yes. And he took my hand. I'd never held a man's hand.'

I smiled at her.

'Was it love at first sight?' I said. 'Was it like a chemical reaction?'

Like Blue Mother and Mr Blue!

Like Bridget and me!

'Definitely.'

It was!

Oh, what a relief, it was!

A love story!

'But he told me he was going off to be a priest. It was a family tradition. For the youngest brother. His mother expected it. He only had a month left. A month seems a long time when you've only known someone an hour.'

I nodded, but I couldn't find any words to say.

'What happened?'

'You happened.'

'Were you in love?' I said.

'Very deeply.'

Very deeply.

I was made in love.

I had a branch.

'Did you stay in touch?'

'The night before he left, he came with the thirty-one sunflowers, I think I told you. And we ran through the thirty-one days, one by one – I'd kept a diary of our time together, the things we'd talked about, the food I'd cooked him. He obviously never knew he had a daughter, we had a daughter.'

He brought her thirty-one sunflowers – I loved him for that. I felt hot and my mouth was dry and I was horribly thirsty for her, for him, for my story, and it really pained me that my father didn't know I existed.

But I was a *daughter*.

Finally.

A real one!

With a real blood mother and father.

'I stood on the roof terrace of my little flat in the Judería,' she said, 'and I watched him go down the street, except I was crying so much I couldn't see him. He got smaller and smaller, that's what I remember. I held up my thumb and my forefinger, and measured him as he shrunk, smaller, smaller, smaller, until he was the size of a fly.'

She stopped.

It felt too sad.

I thought, he should have stayed, and then I could have had parents – the world could have done without one more priest.

My father might have been substantial – I hoped so – but he was too rigid.

'Then my thumb and my forefinger met,' she said, bringing her own thumb and forefinger together. 'He was nothing. That's what we agreed. That when he left, we wouldn't exist to each other. But then there was you.'

'Why didn't you run away together?' I said.

'He'd committed to being a priest,' she said. 'He'd promised his mother.'

'Surely this wasn't about his mother?' I said, thinking for a moment of Christine Orson – what is it about mothers? 'It was about you two, or maybe us three.'

I felt shaky as I said it.

'He was clear from the beginning that I couldn't have him,' she said, perhaps a bit defensive.

'I love someone I can't have,' I said.

'I'm so sorry,' she said. 'It's a terrible thing, isn't it?'

'It is,' I said.

And that's when something changed, I suppose – we started to connect, a tiny bit.

'Why can't you have him?' she asked.

'He's married.'

'Oh, I see.'

'We haven't had an affair or anything,' I said. 'But we've kissed. Maybe that is an affair. I'm not sure what the definition is.'

I was gabbling.

'What's he called?'

'Barnaby Blue,' I said. 'Funny name but there's an explanation . . .'

'Like that Rabbi. Lionel Blue. You know, the one on *Thought for the Day* on Radio 4?' she said, and she was gabbling too, we were both gabbling, we were a little bit the same, and I liked that.

We looked at each other.

'I often hope your father turned out a bit like that Lionel Blue. He always seemed so kind. Although he's gay of course.'

'I had a friend who was gay,' I said. 'He killed himself. He was eighteen.'

'I'm so sorry,' she said. 'What happened?'

'It's too awful to talk about,' I said. 'So maybe we'll leave it for another time. We should get back to your story. I think I might be about to arrive on the scene, and I can't wait to meet myself!'

'Well,' she said, biting her lip. 'This was my first kiss. With your father. But things didn't stop there . . .'

'I worked that out!' I said. 'By existing!'

She didn't laugh.

'I told my mother I was pregnant,' she said, 'and she told me to stay where I was, and she'd come over. She said I mustn't tell my father – it'd kill him.'

'How did she take it?'

'She'd been having an affair with an Englishman, so she seemed pleased that we were in it together.'

'In what?'

'Sin, I suppose,' she said. 'Safety in numbers.'

'Are you religious?'

'I don't know,' she said. 'Does it matter, do you think?'

'To me or to God?'

'Either. Both.'

'I don't think so,' I said. 'Were you close to your mother?'

'We were then. She said I had my whole life in front of me. I was too young to be tied down. She stayed until the birth.'

I have a birth.

'She covered my eyes and she handed you over to Sister María Soledad. She said it was better not to hold you. Not to look. Not to see your face.'

I felt my eyes smart.

She'd never know how bad it felt to have no baby photo to put on Miss Feast's display board. My mother never held me, never kissed my scalp. She handed me over without looking at my face – how would you do that to your own child?

'I was very young and very scared,' she said. 'The birth wasn't easy.'

I found a smile from somewhere, which I arranged onto my mouth, like those plastic lips you can buy in joke shops.

'My mother went back to Papi in the end,' she said. 'She did her duty. But I never felt she was at all kind to my father after that. She was there on sufferance.'

I kept my plastic smile tight on my lips.

'My mother blamed him for what *she'd* done wrong, and she was always cross with him. I didn't trust her with him. So I guess that's why I stayed. I got the job in the restaurant and lived with them. Eventually she left again.'

'And you fell in love again?' I said.

She shook her head.

'I wonder if you only fall in love once,' she said.

Oh dear, I thought.

'I'd done my falling in love,' she said. 'With your father.'

I so hoped you didn't only fall in love once.

But I was pleased that my parents had a love story.

At the start, anyway.

So many love stories don't have happy endings.

So many things begin well and end badly – that's what my not-father said, and I'd written it down. But not all things, in my opinion, whatever he thought.

Other things that begin badly, like my life, might end well, in a big flourish of loveliness to make up for the crap start.

'Have you been happy?' I said, trying to like her again. 'In your life?'

'Not really,' she said. 'But I had those thirty-one days.'

Thirty-one days of happiness, and that was it.

I wondered how many days of happiness Cherie had had in her life.

I hoped it wasn't fewer than thirty-one.

And what about Christine Orson – how many had she had?

And did she have any happy days at all now that Billy was gone?

Can we be happy when the people we love die?

Did happiness fall down from the sky on Blue Mother, or did she make it, herself?

Like Sister Ana?

How do we make happiness?

Is it by loving other people?

Is that how it works?

I'd found my real mother, and yet I still didn't feel happy like I'd imagined mothered people felt.

We went for a walk along the back of the beach, and we couldn't find anything to say to each other.

There was rubbish stuck between rocks: sweet packets and ice cream wrappers.

We reached a big wire fence and that was the end of the path.

We walked back, and headed for the bus stop, where we sat on a bench in the burning sun.

'I've suddenly realised,' I said. 'I've stopped you going to buy your yearly dress for my father.'

My father! How weird and marvellous to say it.

'This is more important,' she said, looking down.

'I wanted to ask you what Sister María Soledad was like,' I said, also looking down.

'Very strong,' she said.

'What did her face look like?' I said. 'I have a photo of her, but with no head.'

It sounded ridiculous, but she didn't smile.

She said: 'It's hard to describe faces.'

'Could you try?' I said.

'She had grey eyes,' she said.

'Anything else?'

'She said that we all need desires that are bigger than our own happiness. She found happiness by living for the people no one else wanted.'

'I suppose I was a person no one else wanted, and that's why she wanted me,' I said. 'Until she didn't.'

'Don't say that,' she said.

'I'm sorry,' I said.

'I've tried to do my best for them all: Papi, Chris and Liam. But my heart has never been totally in it. My heart's always been somewhere else.'

Neither of us spoke.

I didn't dare ask her where exactly her heart had been.

'Chris wants us to move out to Gibraltar when Papi dies,' she said.

'Fantastic,' I said. 'You'll be much nearer me!'

She smiled shyly at me.

'I was so nervous about meeting you,' she said. 'But it's been nice. Now I've just got to keep it a secret.'

Just nice?

'For now,' I said. 'But maybe one day—'

'Chris and Liam want to buy a bar,' she interjected. 'Make it into a football pub.'

'Great,' I said, thinking that *football pub* was one of the least promising of phrases. But not for everyone, wouldn't Rabbi Lionel Blue say, because he's unjudgmental?

'It's not really my thing,' she said blankly. 'But I can do the cooking. And at least the weather's nice.'

Nice.

'What's Gibraltar like?' I said.

'Nothing special,' she said. 'But it's the closest I can get to your father.'

She smiled.

'It's so odd to talk about him,' she said. 'He was a wonderful man.'

'I'd love to meet him one day,' I said.

'I don't expect either of us will ever see him again.'

'Don't say that,' I said.

The bus arrived.

'Well, it's so good to meet you,' I said. 'And we must do this again. I'm so happy to come to Tooting.'

We stared at each other, trying to work out how to say goodbye.

'Love you,' I said, leaving out the I, like I used to with Michael.

The words hung around my mouth, like flies.

'Oh,' she said. 'Oh.'

It was a relief to get into my yellow van.

I definitely shouldn't have said *love you* at the end.

I couldn't believe she hadn't looked at my face when I was born.

I couldn't believe she hadn't said sorry for that.

Had it gone OK or not?

I couldn't work it out.

At least she'd bought me birthday presents and kept them in a case in the attic.

That was something.

Even if she didn't love me.

That's what I told Bridget, sitting under the holm oak amongst the acorns.

'This was only the start,' said Bridget. 'It will take time to get to know each other.'

'I guess you're right,' I said, and we headed back to La Convivencia, where a school party was arriving from Madrid for one of Gabriel's themed history weeks.

When I'd finished my evening lecture, there were children in the courtyard, all wearing purple caps, spinning hula hoops – round and round – like Bridget and I used to on the bald lawn in Turret Grove.

Carrie was cooking in the kitchen, singing along loudly to the radio.

I told her about Jhazmin.

'Are you happy, Evs?' she said, and her face looked shiny and radiant.

'Maybe,' I said. 'But also not really.'

Then Flight 11 crashed into the north tower of the World Trade Centre.

Carrie turned up the radio.

The second plane crashed into the south tower.

The third plane crashed into the US military headquarters in Washington DC.

The fourth crashed into a field.

Bridget rushed into the kitchen to say that Gerónimo was fine, he'd phoned her from New York, and I felt bad that I hadn't even thought of him once.

We sat glued to the television, watching people dive headfirst into the pavement.

The teachers spoke in low voices to their purple pupils.

The purple pupils' parents called and said they loved them.

Bridget, Carrie and I sat up late, wanting to be together.

'This doesn't seem that important now,' said Bridget. 'But Gerónimo's told me he doesn't want children. Like, ever.'

'How do you feel?' I said.

'Confused,' she said.

'He'll probably change his mind,' said Carrie.

'Do you think people change their mind at thirty-five?' said Bridget. 'He says it's a deal-breaker.'

'Do you love him?' said Carrie.

'I think so,' said Bridget.

'Enough?' I said.

Bridget said, 'Maybe.'

We smiled.

But her *maybe* wasn't really a smiling matter.

'This is the wrong time to say it,' said Carrie. 'For both of you. But I just can't keep it in! Perhaps it would be better—'

'Of course you have to tell us,' I said.

'Gabriel proposed to me,' she said, her face lit with joy. 'And I said yes.'

I caught Bridget's face flinching.

'I wish it wasn't today,' said Carrie. 'It feels like the wrong day to be happy.'

'Gabriel is my favourite man in the world,' I said.

I should have said my equal favourite man in the world, but I don't think we can love our friends' partners equally.

'Wouldn't it be amazing,' said Carrie, 'if there could be one day when everyone in the whole world was happy at the same time? I would love that so much.'

'Or sad at the same time?' said Bridget. 'All those people have died. And not everyone is sad about it.'

A letter arrived from Jhazmin saying that Papi had died of a sudden heart attack soon after their return from holiday; that they really were moving out to Gibraltar; that Chris and Liam were off on a boys' fishing trip, and she wondered if this would be a good moment for me to come and visit her in Tooting – she was struggling without her father.

Reeling from so much news, I wrote back and said I'd come on my birthday, and then immediately regretted it.

It was strange to be back in London.

It was freezing.

And I was twenty-seven.

So old.

So cold.

I walked from Tooting Bec tube, pulling my scarf over my nose, down the High Road, past the halal butchers and the fabric shops, past stalls of fresh fruit in Tupperware bowls, and up the path of a small terraced house with an overgrown lawn and net curtains and a *Sold* sign nailed to the fence.

Jhazmin opened the door wearing black trousers and a cream jumper and bobbly beige wool slippers. She looked pale and strained.

She gestured towards the sign and said, 'We're moving next month.'

The house smelled shut.

'This was my father's chair,' she said, taking me into a very brown small sitting room. 'And all his books. I can't bring myself to throw them away.'

On the low coffee table was a tray with a teapot in a tea cosy, and two cups and saucers, and a loaf-shaped cake, with one candle in it, which had been sliced.

'Almond cake?'

'Thank you.'

I ate the slice of almond cake, gagging.

In front of the coffee table was a garish pink suitcase with a heart in the middle.

'This is yours,' she said, pointing at it. 'With all your birthday presents in it, from back when you were one. To twenty-one. And this is for today. Happy birthday!'

I opened up a pale watercolour painting of the Mezquita in a gold frame.

'Thank you,' I said, trying to look pleased.

'I bought it when I was there,' she said. 'Do you like it?'

I strained my voice to say, 'I love it.'

But I didn't love it.

And this felt bigger than the painting.

I stared at the framed photographs of her father, of balding Chris, of Liam in too-short school trousers, and then I looked through the glass doors at the rockery and the pond and baskets hanging from metal brackets, with trails of dead flowers.

'Look at your lovely garden!' I said, for something to say, because it really wasn't lovely.

She stood up and opened the sliding glass doors, letting in the chill damp air.

In the corner of the garden, there was a clump of dried-up sunflowers, bent over, faces to the ground. I hoped she might mention them.

'My father liked birds,' she said. 'We haven't got round to filling up the bird nuts since he died.'

A spindly bird table stood, empty.

'I'm finding it so hard without him.'

'I'm sorry,' I said.

'He was your grandfather,' she said in a slightly undecipherable tone of voice.

'You could have asked me to meet him, and I'd have come like a shot,' I said.

'Have you ever thought what it's been like for me?' she said. 'Trying to keep you secret.'

I felt a horrible burst of anger.

'Have you ever thought what it's been like for me?' I said. 'Not having a mother. Being parented, or actually not parented, by a totally unsuitable couple. Nobody ever telling me the truth.'

We stared at each other.

Then we got in her car, in silence, and we drove down Tooting High Road, so that she could point out Restaurante Hispánico, where she worked, and the mosque where her father had worshipped, and we went back to her house for lunch.

'*Una comida cordobesa,*' she said in Spanish, and we sat at her kitchen table, quietly eating delicious *salmorejo* soup, followed by *pastel cordobés,* those flaky pastry pies full of sweet pumpkin.

'This is what I make at the restaurant. Your father loved my cooking.'

'It's amazing, all of it,' I said.

'Would you ever try and find him?' I said.

'I promised I wouldn't,' she said. 'I promised not to get in the way of his vocation.'

'What about *your* vocation?' I said.

'Oh, I'm not sure I had one.'

'I think everyone has one,' I said. 'Something that's just right for them. For me, it's running the hotel.'

'I'm sorry I can't let you stay longer,' she said. 'But I don't want the neighbours seeing you. And the longer you're here . . .'

'I understand,' I said.

'Take the suitcase,' she said. 'Happy birthday!'

'I saw the sunflowers,' I said on the doorstep. 'You know, you said in your letter . . .'

But she was already closing the door on me.

I got off the bus, dragging the awful pink suitcase and feeling a terrible ache of disappointment inside me for what my real mother wasn't, and maybe could never be.

I took a deep breath, and walked towards the square.

I rang on the door, heart palpitating.

Nigel answered.

We hugged.

'Where are Cherie and Jean?'

'Out for the day,' he said. 'They've started leaving me on my own.'

I left the case in the hall and sat and watched *Tom and Jerry*.

Nigel asked if we could go out for pancakes.

The place had hardly changed since my first date with Michael.

When we got back, Cherie and Jean still weren't home.

I walked around the house, and saw myself everywhere: walking along the hall in my olive-green uniform, talking to the flowers through the shut glass doors, up in the wicker furniture room letting Michael take my clothes off – I didn't want to think about that.

I went up to the roof terrace and stared at the view, then back downstairs to the hall, where the pink suitcase stood glaring at me.

I opened the case, and there were the presents, each with an enve-lope, numbered from one to twenty-one. I put them in a line and stared at them. The wrapping paper changed each year, matching itself to my new age, and this moved me, the thought of Jhazmin, in the card shop, or W H Smith, I didn't know if there was one on Tooting High Road. I pictured her, biting on her lower lip, as she does, trying to choose. I thought of all the people rushing past her, seeing only a woman choosing wrapping paper.

'Nigel!' I called. 'Do you want to come and open some presents?'

Nigel opened a rattle; a squeezy octopus with textured tentacles; a Sooty puppet that he put on his hand; three different dolls; a princess dress; a snow globe; stationery sets; gel pens; a muffler and a scarf and a beret; bangles; different styles of earrings; winter gloves with fur cuffs; a gold necklace with a heart pendant; a sign which told me to follow my dreams, my life on fast-forward, year by year.

The phone rang.

Nigel answered.

'Evzy came,' he said.

I took the phone and told Jean I was sorry but I had to leave for the airport.

'Why didn't you say you were coming?' she said.

I stuttered.

'I didn't think Cherie would want to see me,' I said.

'Were you here to see your birth mother?' she said.

'Yes.'

'Cherie will really struggle with that,' she said.

'I'm sorry, Jean,' I said, 'but none of this was my idea. I was a zygote.'

I left the pink case and the presents under my bed, and I put the unopened cards in my rucksack.

On the plane, I opened my pile of birthday cards, each with the age on the front, all saying *To My Daughter* in gold foil.

Signed *with love from Jhazmin.*

In June, Gabriel and Carrie got married.

Carrie had sewn several layers of white feathers to her dress.

Gabriel carried her over the threshold of La Convivencia, and she looked like a tiny swan nesting in his arms. She was three months pregnant, and occasionally had to disappear to throw up, but this was one of those weddings where you know you're in the presence of true love.

You can't stop staring at it.

You look away and you look back to check it's real.

And it is.

I had the feeling that this marriage was something that was beginning well and would end even better.

Their wedding reception was held in the candlelit courtyard, overlooked by the Angel Rafael, and they left for honeymoon on Gabriel's motorbike.

When I went to bed that night, my heart felt swollen with joy.

When they came home, Carrie swelled with baby.

By August, the baby had broken through Carrie's stomach muscles, and by September, she started holding her lower back and sighing a lot, so I told her to stop working and employed a temporary cook called María.

Bridget loved to put her hand over Carrie's belly to feel the little kicks and punches of cherub-limbs, and when I watched her, I knew that she was someone who should have babies.

Jhazmin, now living in Gibraltar, wrote to tell me she'd bought a mobile phone, so we could text each other.

Sunny day! she would text.

Another lovely sunny day!

Beautiful again!

Exclamation marks these days, rather than commas – Bridget's favourite.

Barnaby kept coming, three times a year, to deliver his lectures at the Research Centre. One night we stayed up late drinking coffee and – I'm not sure how it happened – we kissed again.

I told no one about that kiss.

It was more shameful and depressing than the first.

A text arrived from Jhazmin.

'I can't stand it here!'

'What's wrong?'

'Everything!'

'The bar is terrible!'

'All I do is cook!'

'Chris and Liam spend all day drinking!'

Bridget came around to say that Gerónimo had taken her to Granada for the weekend and they'd climbed into the hills, and the peaks of the Sierra had a dusting of snow on them, and he'd proposed, and she'd said yes, and she was moving into his flat. Straight away.

Straight away?

My spare bedroom would be empty again.

I forced my mouth into the biggest smile I could manage.

'I was wondering if we could hold another reception in the courtyard,' she said.

'Of course,' I said, hugging her and trying to sound as happy as I'd sounded for Carrie.

Carrie barged in with her big baby belly to hug her too.

'Did you talk to Gerónimo about babies?' she said.

'He hasn't changed his mind,' said Bridget, staring at her diamond ring.

Should we have said something then?

We didn't want to spoil the moment.

Adriana called loudly from Reception: 'Eva, someone's here for you!'

And who do you think it was?

It was a woman, not a man.

I'd wondered if it would be my priest-father with sunflowers – I don't know why.

I'd started staring at priests' faces.

No, she had a pink suitcase on wheels, to match mine – except huge.

There she was, my Jhazmin-mother, staring around her at the courtyard, at the angel and the wagon wheel leaning against the wall, and I immediately felt, what was it, burdened by her arrival.

'The last time I was here,' she said, looking at me, and then gesturing towards Carrie. 'I was the same size as you.'

'You were pregnant with me? That's a weird thought,' I said.

'You look so like each other,' said Carrie.

I guess we do.

'That bitter smell of geraniums!' she said.

I felt as if I should try hugging her, but I didn't.

'This is my mother,' I said to Carrie and to Bridget.

My mother, my actual mother, though I definitely didn't call her Mum.

'Bridget's just got engaged!' I said.

'And I've just run away from my husband,' said Jhazmin, and she had a strange air of euphoria about her, as if she'd escaped from prison.

'Congratulations all round!' said Carrie, waddling over with champagne glasses.

Jhazmin pointed at the awful pink suitcase: 'This is all I have in the world.'

It really was.

Her father had left all his money to Chris – man to man, it was what he was used to.

'I can't believe I've done it. I got away.'

We clinked glasses.

'I'm exhausted,' she said.

'Have my room!' said Bridget.

I dragged the huge pink suitcase up the stone steps.

Jhazmin collapsed onto Bridget's bed, and Bridget threw her things into an enormous suitcase and left.

I had a strong coffee, and then felt faintly sick.

The next morning, Jhazmin didn't get up.

She lay pathetically in bed, like Pink Mother, and I felt out of sorts, put upon and guilty.

'I can't believe this is happening to me,' I said to Carrie. 'Again.'

'You need to get up,' I said, impatiently, opening the shutters, around eleven o'clock.

'I think it's being back here,' she said. 'And feeling the pain again. Or maybe it's because I've been looking after people my whole life. Holding it together. Holding everyone together. And I've stopped. And I'm exhausted.'

I didn't feel sympathetic – is that terrible?

She finally came downstairs at noon and sat sipping peppermint tea in the courtyard, reading the English newspapers and *¡Hola!* magazine, before having a siesta as a break from doing nothing. This became her pattern.

I, on the other hand, got up extra early, slamming cupboard doors to wake her up, and headed down to greet María, the temporary cook, who wore thick black tights and white plastic clogs, and who resented cooking eggs for breakfast because, she said, this was Spain.

Meanwhile, Carrie gave birth to Ignacio, and he lay in his pram in the courtyard being admired, like perhaps I had.

One morning, María the cook didn't turn up at her allotted time of six o'clock, nor did she answer her phone when I called.

Six thirty, six forty-five.

I wondered if I could manage breakfast, though I was a truly awful cook.

I phoned María again.

She didn't answer.

I left a loud angry message on her answerphone.

Jhazmin appeared on the stairs.

It was seven o'clock, and she was dressed.

'I heard you on the phone,' she said. 'I'll do breakfast.'

I nearly collapsed.

She pulled her hair into a bun, put on an apron and headed for the kitchen.

I watched, spellbound, as she made her special mix of olive oil and tomato with paprika and bay leaves and oregano, and served it with *jamón serrano* on toasted sourdough bread. I watched as she made *churros* from wheat flour dough and served them with rich hot chocolate. She squeezed oranges and made fresh fruit smoothies. She fried and poached and boiled and scrambled.

It gave me goose pimples watching her, how good she was – the joy of expertise! – and I think this was when I began to like her a bit more.

The guests went crazy with delight, which must have helped.

But it was also that she started to be interested in me.

Having hardly spoken, she now asked me questions.

About my childhood.

About Cherie.

And my not-father.

My schooldays.

My struggles.

My relationship with Michael.

How I ended up in Córdoba.

She talked about her relationship with Chris, the multiple ways she didn't love him, the terrible way he drank.

The terrible way her son, Liam, drank.

How Liam could never hold down a job.

She tried to make contact with Liam, but Liam wouldn't answer.

'He was such a lovely baby,' she said, and I tried not to mind.

'His father will be poisoning his mind,' she said.

Liam still didn't answer.

There were endless phone calls and texts and letters.

'When you think what I gave him,' she said. 'My whole life.'

I tried not to mind again.

'It's so hard being a mother,' she said.

I told her about my endometriosis.

'It's so hard not being a mother,' she said.

(These two statements are both true, I think.)

She said she was so sorry, and she patted my upper arm.

It was what she could manage.

Gabriel helped her find a lawyer to fight for her father's money, but the lawyer said it would be complicated.

At Christmas, I drove her to Alvera, leaving Carrie and Gabriel and Bridget and Adriana in charge, and we stayed at Hostal Playa. We went for walks on the beach and looked at the two hundred palm trees over the stone wall.

Back in Córdoba, she read books about the history of Spain.

She came to my lectures and sat in the front row, taking notes.

It touched me.

Liam still didn't answer, and the lawyer had no news.

We drove to a nearby village called Cazorla to have lunch.

There were crinkly scarves hanging from a tall wooden ladder against the wall of a little shop, arranged in rainbow order: reds giving way to oranges and corals and golds.

'I've always loved those scarves,' she said.

'Me too,' I said, my heart racing, remembering Blue Mother's electric blue one, twisted around the banisters.

'Eva,' she said.

And she stopped.

'I've been wondering.'

We went on grabbing at the scarves, nervously.

'Would you ever think of calling me something else?' she said. 'Not Jhazmin?'

We were both crinkling and uncrinkling the scarves, and I was also panicking because I knew what was coming.

'I was thinking . . .' she said. 'I don't know . . . Would you ever consider calling me Mum?'

It felt like a marriage proposal that had come too early.

'I think it will come,' I said. 'Eventually. But I'm not sure I'm ready. I'm sorry.'

I was biting my lip, and my chest hurt.

'The thing is,' I said. 'If it helps. I've never managed to call anyone that.'

'Let me buy you a scarf,' she said, and maybe it was a way to talk over the awkwardness, but it still felt kind. 'Which colour would you like?'

'That emerald-green one, if it's OK,' I said.

Bridget bounced Ignacio on her knee as we planned her wedding, and Carrie and I worried about the baby she wasn't allowed to have.

Naomi was about to begin a canoe journey up the Amazon, and wasn't coming.

I tried not to look pleased.

It was still so strange not telling Bridget what I felt about Barnaby.

Barnaby lost contact with Naomi, and had to fly out to Brazil with Azahara, meaning he'd probably miss the wedding.

Bridget was sad.

So was I, but I still didn't tell her.

I went to the station to pick up Mr Blue, and he took both my hands in his.

'Well, Eva Martínez-Green,' he said. 'What a pleasure to be here.'

Martínez-Green, I thought, do I really want to be called Martínez-Green any more?

Why hadn't I thought of this before?

Benalcazar would be more glamorous.

I could have a name-changing party.

With dancing.

And speeches.

And a long white dress.

And presents!

And no husband.

I introduced Mr Blue to Jhazmin.

It was strange seeing them together.

She disappeared into the kitchen, and Mr Blue and I sat on wood-and-wicker chairs, next to San Rafael.

'We're inside M's painting,' said Mr Blue. 'She got it just right. Except the walls were green – for longing. Did you get what you longed for?'

'Yes,' I said. 'Look at this place. How utterly beautiful it is.'

Mr Blue stared into my eyes, and he said again, 'No, but did you get what you really longed for?'

'No,' I said.

'I didn't think so,' he said.

'You said that the energy between us is so powerful it can turn our life around,' I said. 'But you also said that it's powerful enough to destroy us.'

'I remember,' he said. 'It's seventeen years since M died, and I suppose I did let it destroy me. Bridget must have told you what a useless dad I turned into without her. I got stuck.'

'So did my mother,' I said.

'Is she what you'd hoped for?' said Mr Blue. 'Your mother?'

'Who knows what I was hoping for?' I said.

'But you get on with her?'

'At the beginning, it was pretty disappointing. But since she took on the cooking here, she's come to life a bit and we've had a common purpose, and . . .'

'You've come to love her?' he said.

I looked at Mr Blue's walnut face.

I felt my green crinkly scarf.

'I've never thought this before,' I said. 'And I'm not sure when or how it happened. But yes, I do love her now.'

'Sometimes these things happen when we're not looking, like falling asleep on the sleeper train and waking up in another country in the morning,' said Mr Blue.

'She's had a sad life,' I said. 'She fell madly in love with my father, but they only had thirty-one days together.'

'I had seventeen years,' said Mr Blue. 'Over six thousand days of love. But no matter how many days you have, it's never enough. Life is never enough for us. That's the great tragedy of being human.'

The next evening, Mr Blue took Bridget and Gerónimo out for a special dinner at La Bodega (so perhaps it wasn't such a terrible place).

I sat next to San Rafael, and I told Jhazmin the story of my life with the Blumes. I told her about the fossil-hunting and the metal-detecting and the picnics. I told her about the liver pâté sandwiches and the flapjacks and the meringues and the brownies and the pots of white chocolate mousse. But I left out the moment Blue Mother put her arms around us and we looked out to the feather-yachts at sea because I thought it might be hurtful.

The next night, I saw her chatting to Mr Blue by the angel.

'I was just saying that you've brought me back to life,' she said to me.

'Have I?'

I still felt bad about not calling her Mum.

'It's the way we're doing this together, as mother and daughter. We're running a hotel. An actual hotel. Together!'

Oh my word, I thought, bring on the *Sunday Times*, we could be interviewed on the spot!

'Perhaps Bridget's wedding will cheer Mr Blue up,' she said as we blew out the candles in the courtyard.

I think it really did – he waltzed with Jhazmin round the courtyard, and I was mesmerised.

Bridget and Gerónimo were dancing amongst the flowers, when I heard the bell.

I went to the door.

It was Barnaby.

With Azahara.

Who was now eight.

A small version of Naomi – dark-haired, pale-skinned and exuberant. Bridget was shrieking with joy as Barnaby hugged first her, and then Gerónimo.

'I found Naomi in the end,' he said. 'It was some problem with the satellite, or something.'

Barnaby took Bridget onto the dancefloor, and I watched them.

Gerónimo danced with little Azahara, spinning her round and round.

'Come on, Eva!' said Barnaby when the song ended.

I'd had a lot of champagne.

A lot of champagne.

I felt Barnaby's arms around me, pulling me closer, and the small of my back was hot under his palms, and he held me tighter and tighter, hard against him, and the courtyard was flooded with my desire, it was lapping at our feet, and I closed my eyes, and then, in a flash, Carrie danced me off the courtyard and up the steps into my flat, and she said, 'If anything happens with you and Barnaby tonight, you will have hijacked and ruined Bridget's wedding. Do you hear me?'

'I bet they all wish he'd married me,' I said to Carrie. 'Bridget and Mr Blue and all of them.'

'Are you drunk?' said Carrie.

'No more than you are,' I said.

'Don't do something you'll regret,' said Carrie, as we went down-stairs. 'And not in front of his daughter.'

Gerónimo and Bridget left in Luis's horse and carriage, and they were off to New York, where he had a business meeting.

A business meeting on honeymoon?

'Just one,' said Bridget, blushing.

The guests left, and I poured myself a glass of wine and sat in the mess and the silence, waiting for Barnaby to join me.

Barnaby never joined me.

He left the next morning with Azahara without saying goodbye.

I felt sick and stupid.

I filled in the paperwork to change my name to Benalcazar.

Gerónimo and Bridget returned from honeymoon.

'Was Barnaby the man you fell in love with?' said Bridget. 'The one who was engaged?'

I blushed.

'Why didn't you tell me?' she said.

'I couldn't,' I said.

'I saw you two dancing,' said Bridget. 'And the penny dropped. Are you having an affair?'

'Certainly not,' I said.

Bridget raised one eyebrow.

I laughed.

I stuttered.

'He won't leave her,' said Bridget.

'He may,' I said. 'There are things you don't know.'

'We can all see the marriage is a mess,' said Bridget. 'But he's totally in awe of her.'

'I've always hated it when you disagree with me,' I said.

'And she's the mother of his children.'

'Children?'

'She's pregnant again.'

Naomi is pregnant.

'There are plenty more fish in the sea,' said Bridget.

'I hate that expression,' I said. 'And there are no fish like Barnaby.'

'I compromised,' said Bridget. 'I've had to give up the idea of children. Sometimes we have to compromise, Eva. You're too fussy.'

'It's good to be fussy,' I said.

'How were the honeymoon whooshes?' I said.

'Pretty good!' she said.

Mr Blue phoned to ask if he could come over to La Convivencia at Hanukkah, around 10 December.

Jean phoned to say, hurray, Cherie had finally softened, and they would both love to visit for Christmas, and they thought they would fly before the school holidays and all the hullabaloo, say, around 10 December.

I felt shocked: it was eight years since I'd seen her.

It also came to me that I'd introduced Jhazmin as *my mother* to everyone I knew in Córdoba, yet I assumed that Cherie still saw herself as my mother too. I'd never thought she'd come.

'Well, it all worked out OK in *Mamma Mia*, you know, with the three dads,' said Carrie.

'Please don't mention the new surname,' I said to everyone.

The plane from Gatwick was delayed, and Mr Blue arrived first, in the rain.

It was evening by the time I drove up to the station, shaking with nerves. Nigel had the Sooty puppet sticking out of his cagoule pocket and was leaning a long rectangular parcel against himself. Cherie was wearing a floral raincoat which I imagined she'd bought from the Boden catalogue.

'I brought your painting,' said Nigel. 'I knew you'd want it.'

'It's been an absolute nuisance,' said Cherie as we brushed cheeks, nervously.

'Welcome to La Convivencia!' I said as we went through the oak door, where everyone was waiting awkwardly in the courtyard, and I introduced Jhazmin (getting that over with first, feeling trembly), and swiftly on to Mr Blue, and Bridget and Gerónimo, and Gerónimo's sister, who lives in Arcos de la Frontera, and Carrie and Gabriel and little Ignacio.

Mr Blue said, 'You know the meaning of *convivencia*? It means happy coexistence, which is probably what we should aim for! Despite the potential complications all round!'

Cherie pulled down her hood and started to un-pop the poppers of her raincoat.

'I feel as if I recognise you,' she said.

'Bridget's father,' he said.

I swept Cherie and Jean upstairs, and Nigel followed with Sooty.

'I gave the two of you a twin room,' I said. 'But do say if you'd rather have singles. And Nigel, you've got your own room.'

They didn't answer.

'That little Jhazmin woman?' said Cherie, unpeeling her floral raincoat and handing it to me. 'Is she who I think she is?'

'I think she is,' I said, hanging up her raincoat.

'The one who gave you to the nuns?' she said, collapsing onto one of the beds. 'The desperate little Muslim girl from Tooting?'

'When her father died,' I started, trying to get the right tone, 'he left her nothing. Not a penny. So she had to come here. Her marriage had gone wrong.'

'She won't be celebrating Christmas,' said Cherie. 'They don't believe in it.'

'And nor does Mr Blue,' I said. 'Though everyone likes presents and eating.'

'I've always thought it was very odd the way they changed their name,' said Cherie. 'But each to his own.'

Now this was a new Cherie – *each to his own*.

'What does she do here anyway?' she said. 'Jhazmin?'

'She's the cook!'

Genius master stroke – it spoke not of love but of employment.

It kept Cherie in the top spot.

'Ah, I see!' she said.

'Ideal!' said Jean, smiling.

'I'm sure you're going to love her food,' I said.

'Well!' said Jean, letting out a deep breath.

'Well what?' said Cherie.

'Aren't these mattresses comfortable?' said Jean, lying back on the second bed.

'Your father should never have told you about her!' said Cherie. 'To think where you grew up. The education you've had. The best of everything.'

'We both know he's a law unto himself,' I said, trying, again, to win her over. 'I'm so sorry that he treated you badly. I see that clearly as an adult.'

Another genius stroke, I thought, and also true.

'You've done these rooms beautifully,' said Jean.

'They have quite different ideas about taste in Tooting,' said Cherie. 'Have you found that?'

She closed her eyes, and then she opened them.

'This place is magical,' she said.

Wow! Was that a compliment? From Cherie?

Jean was really rubbing off on her.

I felt flushed.

'Bridget's father has become rather distinguished-looking,' said Cherie.

It was going to be all right.

I hung Blue Mother's painting on the wall of my bedroom with a gold spotlight on it. Every night, before going to sleep, I turned all the lights off and stared at it from my bed. It gave me strength.

It still does.

I need strength now.

More than ever.

Nigel popped open bottles and entertained Ignacio with Sooty shows.

Happy Christmas!

Happy Hanukah!

¡Feliz Navidad!

¡Feliz Año!

On 6 January, I arranged plates of tapas on tables around San Rafael.

In the kitchen, Jean was helping Jhazmin prepare lunch. She caught my eye and nodded out of the window towards Cherie, resplendent in a long silk dress, throwing back her head to laugh at something Mr Blue had said. I smiled.

Gerónimo was staring at Nigel.

In fact, Gerónimo was always staring at Nigel.

Gerónimo didn't look jolly when he stared at Nigel.

I didn't like it when people didn't like Nigel.

Jean started to serve the soup.

'You look sad,' whispered Carrie.

'I've had enough of being on my own,' I said, thinking that I couldn't keep this in any longer, even if I liked to appear fine. 'I couldn't have better friends, but I guess we all want our own romance. If that doesn't sound too pathetic.'

Carrie took my hand.

'Also,' I said. 'Is Gerónimo a bastard? I've been wondering.'

'No,' said Carrie. 'Bridget married him knowing he didn't want children.'

'Yes, but he looks at Nigel weirdly,' I said.

We sat down at the long table to have Christmas lunch: baked *dorada* fish with lemon and herbs, followed by flan and apple tart.

Cherie tapped her glass with her teaspoon.

'To the chef!' she said, raising her glass to Jhazmin.

Jean whispered in my ear, 'You thought it would never happen.'

I whispered back, 'Is she drunk?'

Dishes of Christmas nougat and almond cookies called *polvorones*; *Orujo* liqueurs and Baileys and Limoncello; coffee with lemon olive oil cake.

Nigel was asleep in the corner with the ginger cat on his lap.

Sooty had fallen off his hand and was lying limply over the geraniums as if he'd been shot.

The day before my twenty-ninth birthday, Naomi gave birth to a little girl called Esther.

She'd wanted another daughter, Bridget said.

Barnaby had hoped for a son.

Bridget was staring at me.

'I'm sorry,' she said. 'This must be so hard for you.'

'I'm sorry too,' I said. 'Everyone's having babies, and I know you'd like one.'

'You'd like one too,' she said.

'I'm not sure life ever works out exactly as we hope,' I said. 'And even if I was Mrs Fertile, there's rather an absence of sperm in my life.'

'I know you'd do anything to have a husband,' she said.

'Well, not anything,' I said. 'And not any husband.'

'Please give up on Barnaby,' said Bridget. 'I feel so bad about it all. Like he's got it so wrong. Even if he is my brother.'

'I know, I know,' I said. 'I've got to move on.'

'I can't move on, Eva,' said Bridget, and her face looked very pale. 'I can't seem to give up the idea of babies. And Gerónimo will never change his mind. About anything!'

'Oh, Bridge!' I said. 'Why is life so complicated?'

I hugged her, and I could feel her heart against mine.

We let each other go.

'It's like my maternal urges are going crazy,' she said. 'And I know I shouldn't be saying this to you. Because of your thing, you know, I can never remember what it's called . . .'

'Endometriosis,' I said.

'Yes, and at least I've got a husband.'

'Having a husband doesn't mean everything's perfect.'

Bridget reached up her hand and squeezed mine.

'That's true,' she said. 'It isn't perfect, Eva. Did you realise?'

I squeezed her hand and said I was sorry, and that no marriage was perfect, as far as I knew.

'Except Carrie and Gabriel's,' she said.

'Maybe.'

I went to the card shop.

I stared at pale pink cards.

I wrote nothingy words to Barnaby and Naomi, scribbled their address on the envelope and propped it against the mirror in my bedroom.

That night, I couldn't sleep.

I tried closing my eyes and counting, but when I got to a hundred, they sprung open.

I crept down the steps, grabbed some bread rolls from the kitchen and I unlocked the big oak door. This is what Sister Ana used to do – prowl around the city at night feeding the poor. I knew I needed a desire that was bigger than my own happiness. Like Sister María Soledad said to Jhazmin.

I took the bread rolls into the orange-tree courtyard to see if that would make me feel good about myself, but all the homeless people were asleep. I awkwardly put a bread roll next to each of them, on a tissue, wondering if Sister Ana would have woken them up. I didn't like to. As I walked away, I wondered if the rolls would attract rats, but I couldn't exactly take them away – it would look like I was stealing from the homeless. If anyone was watching. Which they probably weren't. I scuttled out through the gate, thinking that I wasn't a total natural at bigger desires.

I walked to the postbox and dropped in the card to Barnaby and Naomi. Then I stopped off at the Puerta del Puente and stared at San Rafael, teetering at the top of the pillar. Was he really the angel who stirred the water at the healing pool of Bethesda which I'd read about in Sister Ana's bible?

I wondered what the healing pool of Bethesda had looked like, if it existed.

Bethesda, that was a lovely word.

The rain got heavier, so I walked home, still feeling wide awake. I changed out of my wet clothes and sat down at Adriana's computer, and I looked up Pool of Bethesda.

The Pool of Bethesda is in the Muslim Quarter of Jerusalem, on the path of the Beth Zeta valley, it said. *In the Christian bible, in the fifth chapter of John, such a pool is described, surrounded by five covered porticoes. Until the late nineteenth century, there was no evidence outside John's Gospel for its existence at Bethesda, and most scholars dismissed the hypothesis of a pool with five sides. But when the site was excavated, it revealed a rectangular pool with two basins separated by a wall – a five-sided pool, each side with a portico. Exactly as it had been described.*

How wonderful!

Time for more research.

In the absence of romance and the failure of altruism, there was nothing I liked better than some research.

In March 2004, the Cercanías train system in Madrid was bombed and nearly two hundred people were killed – the deadliest terrorist attack ever carried out in Spain.

First José María Aznar's government said that it was ETA, then that it was al-Qaeda, and then Aznar lost the election because everyone thought he'd caused the tragedy by taking the country into the Iraq War.

A vigil was held in the courtyard of the Mezquita to remember the *Convivencia*, when the three religions of the Book had lived happily together for 250 years.

We lit candles and prayed for peace.

April came, and the flowered crosses were raised around the city.

Carrie gave birth to a little girl who she called Lily, after her grandmother – a sister for Ignacio. She lay pale and exhausted, with flat hair and boobs dribbling milk.

'Look how beautiful you are,' Gabriel said to Carrie.

I thought how nice it would be to have someone to say that to me – especially if I was looking as awful as she was. There is an awful-beautiful, though, the way people look in the morning when they wake up, sometimes better than beautiful-beautiful, which can be lipsticky and unreal.

Bridget sat by Carrie's bed holding Baby Lily in her arms.

'She's making my boobs ache!' she said, laughing.

'That's not funny,' said Carrie. 'Are your boobs actually aching, Bridget?'

'Everything's aching,' she said.

It wasn't long after that Bridget called to say she needed to talk to me, alone, about *something important.*

'We'll go walking,' I said.

Jhazmin said she'd make us a picnic.

We drove out beyond the city, and we parked in my normal place beside the gate.

'When are you going to tell me the something important?' I said as we walked in the sunshine.

'Not yet,' she said. 'You tell me things.'

I told her about my research into the healing pool at Bethesda in the Book of John, where the sick used to sit, where the angel – probably our angel Rafael – used to stir the waters. I told her that everyone thought the pool wasn't real. But architects had uncovered it, and it was exactly as the bible described it.

'I love that,' I said. 'The thought that angels and healing pools might be true.'

'It's a beautiful word, *Bethesda,*' said Bridget, as we climbed.

'Does this remind you of anything?' said Bridget.

'That day,' I said. 'The picnic on the hill.'

She smiled.

'Happy memories,' she said. 'Life seemed so simple then.'

'Not to me,' I said.

'She was such a special lady,' I said.

'You never stop needing a mother,' said Bridget. 'And I could do with her today.'

'Are you going to tell me yet?' I said.

'I will when we find the picnic spot,' said Bridget.

'Look at that butterfly! It's a Lorquin's Blue sunbathing on a rock!'

'Quite the expert!' said Bridget.

'Inspired by your gorgeous father,' I said.

I laid out a rug, and we both sat down.

'Let's get started,' said Bridget. 'I love your mother's food.'

I still wasn't used to having a real mother.

I pulled out the first box, and in it were, I hesitated, and tasted one – liver pâté sandwiches. Jhazmin never ever made liver pâté sandwiches.

'Did you tell her to make these?' said Bridget.

I shook my head.

The next box was full of home-made meringues, sticky in the centre like Blue Mother's.

I rushed to open the next.

I couldn't believe it.

Flapjacks.

The next.

Brownies.

'*Have as many as you like!*' I said to Bridget.

'My gorgeous mother!' she said.

And I thought: my gorgeous mother! My own actual one! How lovely of her.

'It feels such a long time ago, that picnic,' said Bridget. 'Like another lifetime. But this is just what I need today. Comfort.'

I held her hand.

'Gerónimo's left me,' she said.

'I wondered . . .' I said.

'But that's not all,' she said. 'I stopped taking the pill but I didn't tell him.'

I waited.

'I'm five months pregnant,' she said.

'Five months?'

'It's harder to tell when you're fat,' said Bridget. 'I thought when it actually happened, he'd change his mind.'

'He didn't?'

She shook her head.

I put my arm around her.

I don't want to say any more.

They loved each other in the beginning, even if it didn't end well.

'Congratulations,' I said.

Bridget was crying.

'So it's over, no discussion?' I said.

She nodded.

In the last refrigerated bag, there were two tiny glass jars of white chocolate mousse.

Jhazmin had remembered!

Which is what real mothers do.

Even mothers who you might think are disappointing at first.

I thought then that one day I'd be able to call her Mum, and when it happened, I would want to – I nearly did already.

I held up my white chocolate mousse, and Bridget clinked hers against mine, and I said, 'To your beautiful baby! You're going to be the best mother in the world!'

'Do you want to join in?' said Bridget. 'As I don't have a husband any more.'

'Join in?'

'We always planned to share everything *our whole lives*,' said Bridget. 'Do you remember?'

I took her hand.

'I'm the one who remembers everything,' I said.

We were little girls wrapped in bath-towels.

'I feel scared doing it alone,' said Bridget. 'And also I'm so tired all the time these days. Will you do it with me?'

'Course I will,' I said.

'I feel so bad that you might not have a baby,' said Bridget.

'It's not your fault,' I said.

'You can choose the baby's name,' said Bridget. 'But only if I like it!'

We both laughed.

'How about Bethesda if it's a girl?' I said.

'The healing pool!' she said. 'I love it!'

So there we are, Beth!

It's a strange name, but I hope you like it.

'What colour do you want to be?' said Bridget.

'I think I'll be green,' I said.

'That's the baby moving. Put your hand here.'

I held my hand over Bridget's belly.

And I felt a fist maybe and then some toes.

Your fist and *your* toes, Beth.

'Baby, this is Green Mother,' said Bridget to her belly. 'She was barefoot in the grass, wasn't she?'

I nodded: 'And there was a little waterfall running over the rocks.'

Bridget took my hand.

'What colour mother are you going to be?' I said.

'Can we have Blue again?' said Bridget.

'Blue is totally the best,' I said. 'Yes, mark 2, and just as gorgeous!'

Blue Mother number 2 – I can't really bear to say it.

Bridget gave birth at our flat at La Convivencia because she wouldn't go to the hospital, no, not for one appointment, and certainly not for the birth – her phobia was such a big and traumatic thing, the mark of her terrible grief.

But enough of grief.

Here was joy.

I saw you come out, Beth, on 5 September 2004.

You had one hand on your cheek.

Making an entrance into the world.

You had dark hair, plenty of it.

A little snub nose.

Blue eyes like your mother.

Your mother held you first.

I held you next.

Then Grandpa Blue.

He was crying.

We were all crying.

Because you were little and perfect and beautiful.

There we were, making a circle – you can have any number in a circle, and you can add people as you go along, odd numbers or even numbers, anyone can fit in, at any point.

Bethesda – you were here and real.

Bethesda, the pool where the angel, Rafael, stirred the waters and made people well.

You made your mother the wellest she'd ever been.

She should never have agreed not to have babies.

She was a born mother.

Just like your grandmother, Blue Mother.

Your beautiful grandmother with the heaven-breasts and the scalp tingles and the kindest heart. How it pains me that you never knew her.

'I'd like to have seven!' your mother said the day after.

The day after giving birth!

Your mother and I gazed at you.

As if you were a masterpiece.

'Mothers *are* artists!' said your mother. 'Do you remember M's note with the tampons?'

My scalp tingled.

'We should write our life story for Beth,' I said to your mother. 'So she can understand the difficult bits.'

'Like you didn't?' said Bridget.

I nodded.

'I think you'll be better at this than me,' said your mother. 'I'm maths and you're English. And you're the one with the photographic memory and the diaries.'

'You can be the editor,' I said.

And we began.

Jhazmin moved to an upstairs room to vacate the flat for the three of us, our new little family – yes, I finally had a family: you – Beth – and your mother and me. On free evenings, when you were in bed, I wrote, and she tried to edit, but mainly fell asleep, telling me motherhood made her tired and achy. I felt worried.

'I can try to pay for a doctor to come and see you here in your room,' I said.

'I'm fine,' she said. 'I've just had a baby. It's normal to feel like this.'

But I really didn't think it was normal.

Carrie had never seemed this exhausted after having a baby.

Our world shrank and time merged into a blur of feeding and washing small cotton vests and not having proper conversations, though eventually we started going for walks and drinks and tapas, and I returned to lecturing.

'I thought you should know things aren't too good with Barnaby and Naomi,' said your mother. 'She's been having an affair in Brazil.'

'I'm sorry,' I said, although I don't think I was.

'Are they getting divorced?' I said.

'She's looking for a more open marriage or something,' she said. 'It all sounds weird. Be careful, won't you?'

I remember feeling a bit neutral, as if the spell had broken.

Perhaps you broke it, Beth, by being even lovelier than he was.

Or perhaps you'd grown me up.

Or perhaps I was exhausted, which is a great cure for lust.

Or perhaps my head was too full.

Barnaby came for Christmas.

So did Grandpa Blue, and Cherie and Jean and Nigel.

Your mother had bad backache, that's what I remember, and spent a lot of time in bed, but wouldn't talk about it, not to me, not to Grandpa Blue, not to anyone.

I want you to know that I tried, Beth.

Maybe I didn't try hard enough.

Barnaby was flirtatious.

Barnaby with his newly open marriage.

Isn't that an oxymoron?

If you want the *open*, don't bother about the *marriage*.

Barnaby and I sat up late.

'I think the time has come,' he said, and he reached to take my hand, but I didn't let him.

'The time for what?'

'Our time,' he said, looking into my eyes, with those dark eyes, with those long eyelashes, with that gold star around his neck.

'Meaning?' I said, not coldly, but not smiling.

'The affair we've been waiting for our whole lives,' he said.

But his smile was not enough any more – the waters had finally dried up.

'I'm not looking for an affair, Barnaby,' I said. 'And I'm reclaiming my heart from you. I need to give it to someone else.'

'Don't you think it's meant to be?' he said, sounding a bit desperate.

'People say that a lot,' I said. 'But I think it might be a load of crap.'

He looked startled, and then sad.

'Naomi's been having an affair,' he said. 'It turns out you can be in love with more than one person at once. You remember me saying?'

'So you thought you'd use me for revenge?' I said, and I was pleased that I sounded calm. 'And stay with her?'

'I didn't say that, Eva,' he said. 'I was saying I was in love with you.'

'At best, you were saying you were in love with more than one person,' I said. 'Which slightly takes away the magic.'

'You sound bitter,' he said.

'I think I am, Barnaby. Or if not bitter, embarrassed. I waited far too long for you.'

'But I never promised you anything. I was always truthful.'

'You indulged me with kisses,' I said.

'A kiss is nothing.'

'I totally disagree.'

'I think about you all the time,' said Barnaby. 'I always have. Come on, Eva, we know we both want to. We always have.'

'I know I don't,' I said. 'Thank you for the offer. But it's too late. It was always too late once you'd met Naomi. I'm sorry I didn't have more courage.'

'Who is it you're giving your heart to?' he said nervously. 'Am I allowed to know his name?'

'No,' I said. 'I'm afraid not.'

(It was you, Beth. It was you!)

'What terrible timing,' said Barnaby.

When Jhazmin held you, Beth, I could tell she was remembering Liam.

It hurt me that she'd never known me as a baby, but Sister Ana had traced the outline of my birthmark, and I would forever be her *pequeña España*, and that helped.

Jhazmin longed for Liam to write, but when he wrote, he blamed her that their pub in Gibraltar had failed.

'They needed a woman's touch,' she said to me, as if it was a compliment.

'A woman's touch?' I spluttered. 'You don't believe that crap?'

'I feel like I let them down,' she said.

Then the next day: 'They treated me like a servant my whole life.'

I wanted to point out her inconsistencies.

'Just listen to her,' said Bridget. 'That's all she wants.'

Naomi arrived with Azahara and Esther to see the procession of the wise kings, but Bridget didn't feel like coming out, which ruined it for me. I was properly worried about her now. I knew something was wrong.

Naomi was actually very nice.

Perhaps she always had been.

Perhaps it's all a question of perception.

Giants and windmills.

Nigel loved jumping for sweets, and so did I.

We bumped into Gerónimo's sister, who was visiting friends.

We hugged each other and didn't mention that her brother had left Bridget when she was five months pregnant.

She looked into the pram.

I said, 'This is Bethesda.'

Tears welled up in her eyes when she looked at you, Beth.

'My niece,' she said, taking your tiny hand.

As the wise kings left, she said, 'We had twin brothers, Gerónimo and I.'

She gestured towards Nigel.

'Born not right,' she said. 'You know. In the head. Like Nigel. My parents sent them away as babies. It destroyed the whole family.'

Nigel was perfectly right in the head, I wanted to say, but she'd hurried away.

So, Beth, your father had his reasons.

His reasons were those twin brothers.

It wasn't you he didn't want – it was a hypothesis.

He made himself jolly to cover up his pain.

We all find different ways to cover up our pain.

Most of them don't work.

I'm so sorry you haven't met your father yet.

But nor have I met mine.

We're in it together, and we won't sweep it under the rug.

Because pain is better not covered up, but channelled into something else.

Perhaps that's what motivates me to write.

Perhaps that's what motivates Jhazmin to cook, endlessly refilling our industrial fridges and freezers, forever walking around the courtyard with her trays of love and regret.

'I love it here,' said Cherie. 'I always dreaded Christmas.'

'We love having you,' said Jhazmin.

I'm not making this up.

'I always wanted to be part of something bigger and noisier,' said Jhazmin. 'Our house in Tooting was so quiet and tense.'

'I did too,' said Cherie. 'All only children do.'

That's true – that's why I loved the Blumes.

All our Christmas guests left in mid-January.

And you were four months old, and growing into yourself, Beth.

We closed the hotel for a month: Carrie and Jhazmin experimented with new recipes; Gabriel painted the walls; Ignacio staggered around the courtyard; I sanded down Rafael and painted him; and your mother watched.

'I don't think I'm well,' she said finally. 'I tried so hard to convince myself it was the pregnancy. But I've been feeling weird for a long time.'

I paid for a doctor.

I couldn't believe how terrified she was.

Laughing happy Bridget.

I held her hand, but it didn't help.

Nothing helped because she'd left it too long and the breast cancer had already spread.

I don't want to major on this, Beth.

Life stories, as I said, are allowed to be selective.

I ran the hotel with Jhazmin, with Carrie and Gabriel, and Adriana, and extra staff in the busy months. And I mothered you with your mother. I had to give her drugs to get her to hospital, and we came away with more drugs as we left. It was a cocktail of drugs by mouth at the beginning, and possibly surgery, but then not.

'But it's not hopeless,' said Carmen García, the strong warrior oncologist. 'Many people live long productive lives with metastatic breast cancer. You can still live life to the full.'

Well, kind of.

The hotel grew, and you grew.

I'd found a desire bigger than my own happiness.

You.

You weren't a good sleeper in the beginning.

And I wasn't that good with the endless crying and the endless waking.

But I did my best.

You had colic.

You teethed loudly, thrashing about in your cot.

In the in-between times, the up weeks, your mother had this amazing ability to not sleep and still be reasonable. I never had that. And whether this was biology – you were her egg – or nature, my nature, I don't know.

What I do know is that I loved you from the start.

I wasn't so good at the practical stuff.

I'll be honest.

Your mother, regardless of how she was feeling, still mashed food, packed your sunhat, washed your hair, remembered the soft bit behind your ears, which she dabbed with cotton wool and olive oil.

I, on the other hand, preferred to show you butterflies and flowers and birds and the shades of colours.

I took you to the peace festival in March 2005 – you pointed at the white doves as they were released over the river.

You always wanted to fly.

Perhaps you'll be a pilot.

I'd love that, Beth.

But I'm taking that right back.

Because it might turn into an expectation.

And expectations are too heavy for us.

As Billy showed.

By being crushed by them.

Be anything.

Find your thing.

I started to read you books.

Anything I could get my hands on.

In Spanish and English.

I read you *Peter Pan* endlessly, doing my not-father's funny voices.

I walked you around Córdoba in your buggy and stopped to let you feel the texture of the old bricks and the bark of the olive tree.

I told you stories about Sister Ana.

I read you *The Rainbow Rained Us.*

'Sister Ana was just like Grey Mother,' I told you. 'She even had a globe she liked to spin when she prayed for the world.'

I knelt down every day and I asked Sister Ana to send help from heaven if she could, to make your mother better. I wished so much she was here to still and steady me. Like Blue Mother had. They were probably the realest of my mothers in the end.

We sang 'He's Got the Whole World in His Hands' and 'Mine Eyes Have Seen the Glory' as we walked along the river.

You started crawling just before *Cruces*.

You were walking by your first birthday and eating geraniums and pulling over pots.

By the next March, the peace festival had grown, and we held an exhibition of Lorenzo's old photographs at La Convivencia – how Sister Ana would have loved to see the people crowding in to admire his work. A thin man with a beard held hands with a fat man with a moustache. And that was fine with everyone because time does sometimes make people kinder.

Your mother made it to concerts and plays and food festivals and Arabic poetry recitals and peace processions along the river, and some days we nearly forgot about the horrible bird of prey that had been after us ever since we were in Class 1 with Miss Dixon.

You were one and a half, walking, holding my hand, dancing (kind of).

I talked to you, and I longed for you to talk back.

Eventually, you did.

Mamá to your mother.

Ebba to me.

Cat naughty.

Butter-fy.

Wanium.

(Geranium)

Patio.

Ángel.

We skipped through the pillars in the Mezquita.

We watched butterflies swooping through the fountains of the Alcázar.

You turned two, and we held a birthday party in the courtyard on

5 September 2006 with a butterfly theme. We all wore wings. It was a good day.

Jhazmin waited and waited for letters from lawyers and letters from Liam, which didn't come.

On sad days, she took to wild experimenting in the kitchen, and didn't speak to us.

But hope would rise again, and she would skip and spin hoops with you, Beth.

'I never did this with Liam,' she said. 'He was a bit of a loner.'

You wanted your mother to skip and spin hoops with you, Beth, but it was hard for her, and hard for you.

You were heading for two and a half, and the peace festival had started attracting people from all around the world.

We had a huge inter-faith service in the orange-tree courtyard, and I stared into the faces of the rows of priests to see if one of them was hiding a sunflower in the folds of his robe.

Not yet.

It was the first day of *Cruces* – 1st May 2007 – when they said that
the treatment had stopped working, and your mother had to start
intravenous chemotherapy.

The three of us held hands and walked out of the hospital, and
everything looked completely different from when we walked in.

We didn't say much to each other in the van.

As I parked, I said, 'Do you still want to go tonight?'

Your mother said she did.

And on that first night of *Cruces*, 1 May 2007, the colours of the
flowered crosses were somehow a deeper red and much more beautiful,
the rose petals softer, the fino sherry on our tongues richer and the
stars brighter than we remembered them.

'I was thinking,' I said, looking at the sky, 'that if stars only came
out once every thirty years, we'd be totally mesmerised by them, and
we'd stay up all night lying on our backs looking at them. Don't you
think?'

'But because they're here forever we take them for granted?' she
said.

She had a tear running slowly down her cheek – just one big tear.

She held my hand and she said, 'Forever Eva.'

You looked up at us, Beth.

And the tinny music struck up.

And you started to dance.
Wiggling your hips.
Strutting your sandalled feet.
Hands in the air.
Glittery wings on.
Like a butterfly.

We got a letter from the Oncology Department with details of chemotherapy appointments.

We sat in the courtyard reading it, and I could feel your mother's fear.

We never nailed that iatrophobia, and that made it so much worse.

We looked up at the sky.

I remember that flocks of starlings were twisting across the sky like great wrung sheets.

Dpto Onc, it said at the bottom, in red.

Carrie was playing Ignacio's favourite songs from *The Lion King*, *Beauty and the Beast* and *The Wonderful Wizard of Oz*.

'The Wonderful *Wizard of Onc*!' said your mother.

'Exclamation mark!' I said.

'Now is the moment of the exclamation mark!' said your mother. 'Now is the moment to be as jolly as we can! And full of hope!'

I went for a walk – the crosses from the festival had been dismantled, and the city bins were full of browning flowers.

I'd have to get her to the hospital every three weeks from now on.

There was no way round it, and it felt so cruel.

'We're off to see the Wizard! The Wonderful Wizard of Onc!' we sang in the car, hollering out the song in case the Wizard was deaf.

And you joined in, Beth, shouting out the song, with no clue what we were on about.

What were we on about?

We were calling out to God in the manger, between the pillars, in the current of the river, in the mosque-cathedral, in the tiny synagogue, in the olive tree, in the orange-tree courtyard, in the stars, in the hands of San Rafael, in the healing waters of the pool of Bethesda.

We were reading the science and the data too, begging it to bend to our hopes.

The five-year survival rate for Stage 4 breast cancer is 22 per cent, I read.

I counted 1, 2, 3, 4 all the way to 22, and I said to myself, 22 is a lot of people.

I definitely did not say to myself, 78 is a lot more people than 22 because what would be the point of that?

We have faith, we said to each other, as our hopes refracted and danced through sunbeams, as the hospital air conditioning units strained against the summer heat, which hit us as we crossed the car park, holding hands, the three of us, with you in the middle. You liked us to swing you up so that your feet left the ground.

Oh, if only we could all leave the ground and fly away.

All our lovely easy rhythms seemed to stop.

Time was punctuated by appointments, and getting your poor mother in the car.

And waiting for results.

Week after week.

Month after month.

'It's not all bad!' your mother said. 'I don't have to wax my bikini line!'

I laughed because I thought that was what she wanted from me.

But inside I wasn't laughing.

I said, 'Let's go to Alvera!'

Because Alvera always made us happy.

But when we got to Alvera, she was still bald and scared.

We jumped in the waves, though.

We ate a picnic.

We talked about Lyme Regis and chocolate brownies and gold ammonites.

We got home and there were envelopes.

I remembered coming home to envelopes from Lyme Regis, back when I didn't tremble as I opened them, when envelopes weren't the enemy.

I remembered the way Blue Mother lay down and held her chest.

I went and sat on the low couch in the courtyard under the sky.

I sat fighting off my hypotheses, like demons in the desert, and you crawled onto my lap, Beth, and you felt the skin of my arms, and you clinked my bangles back and forward.

And you were me.

And I was you.

A girl just back from the beach.

And I remembered the things Blue Mother did that felt so good to me as a child, and I put my hand into your hair and did those little tingly-scalp-rubs she used to do.

I hoped you felt like silk blowing in the breeze.

Even if I didn't any more.

I remembered Blue Mother saying, 'We're going to stay big and hopeful.'

And I thought, *We're going to stay big and hopeful, Beth.*

'We're going to be big people,' I said to you, bending my arm at the elbow to make muscles.

'Big people,' you mimicked back at me.

I piled up your mother's hospital paperwork on my desk, highlighted and stapled.

I would dominate the cancer bird with staples and paper clips and post-it notes.

I would clip its wings.

We would get on with running the hotel.

Thank God for the hotel.

The lovely guests.

News from outside.

Purpose.

We went back and forth from the hospital, singing, singing, crying sometimes, mainly laughing.

More letters arrived from *Dpto Onc.*

Letters full of words we never used to need.

Words like metastasise, which means to spread.

Before it was a word we used for butter.

But now it wasn't.

I spread *Nocilla* onto warm bread for you, Beth – you liked the white chocolate more than the dark.

Gabriel spun hoops with you in the courtyard.

'You remember you taught me how to play?' I said to your mother.

'Hoops first, then elastics,' she said.

'On your bald lawn,' I said. 'You changed my whole life, Bridget Blue.'

She paused.

'I hated M's bald head, and now I've got one.'

'You will always be beautiful to me,' I said.

'I love the way you've always said that,' she said. 'Even when I look awful.'

I said, 'Awful can be beautiful.'

You danced flamenco, Beth.

You fed the runt kittens with a bottle.

You matched your Superman suit with the butterfly wings; a bullfighter cloak with a pilot cap; fairy wings and wellington boots.

'The sacrament of the present moment,' said your mother. 'You remember that weird nun who came to school. With buck teeth.'

I laughed.

She'd started remembering.

'The one I loved. Until you didn't,' I said. 'I was under your spell from the beginning!'

I noticed how much we were talking about the past.

I said to myself, of course we are, we're writing our life story.

'You remember the way Mr Altman tiptoed about in his velvet shoes at St Hilda's?' said your mother.

'Nobody else knows all this,' I said.

'Except Sophia and Laura Stephenson and awful Annabel!' she laughed. 'Who will all have married millionaires and be living in Fulham!'

Such lovely power in a shared history, and partly we don't want people to die because we want to keep our own stories alive. But your mother would beat the odds, I knew she would, she was a winner, we were survivors, like the geraniums, as long as we knew how to love, I knew we'd stay alive!

We will survive oh-oh!

Hairbrushes for microphones and badminton racquets for guitars.

We sang Gloria Gaynor loudly together, and it felt like it might help.

I said, 'I wonder what would have happened to me if I hadn't met you.'

'And me,' she said. 'What would I have done if I hadn't met you?'

I propped her up with cushions.

I tied her turban.

I painted her nails turquoise.

Grandpa Blue didn't tell Bridget she was invincible.

Like he'd told his wife.

Grandpa Blue has given up too early, I thought.

This time it will be different.

You started collecting dead insects, Beth.

You kept a dead cockroach in a matchbox.

You lined dead flies up along the windowsill.

It unnerved me.

I remembered how adults never spoke about death when I was a child.

I wondered if it would be helpful to do so.

To try to make it normal, easy-breezy.

'Poor flies,' I said, anxiously.

'Poor flies!' you said, laughing and sweeping them off the windowsill with your hand.

So where would one go from there?

I couldn't work it out.

And what if I started crying in the middle?

Or what if it scared you?

Beth doesn't want to talk about it, I told myself, I will take my lead from her.

Did your mother want to talk about it, I wondered, or did she want to go on following the yellow-brick road?

Every time I thought of bringing it up with her, I couldn't.

So I gave myself a *deadline*.

An actual deadline, that is, a date before which to talk about being dead.

'If you ever want to talk . . .' I said.

'What about?' said your mother.

'It begins with d,' I said, feeling my teeth starting to tremble inside my mouth.

'Dessert?' she said, laughing.

And I laughed too.

Laughed hysterically with relief.

That she didn't want to talk about death.

'The Golden Opulence Sundae costs around a thousand dollars,' your mother said. 'And when I get better, we will go to Serendipity 3 in New York and order one each.'

'Yes we will!' I said, laughing too hard.

I pictured us flying on a private jet drinking champagne and then stuffing our faces with Golden Opulence Sundaes, with cream all over our face.

Hurray, let's talk about whipped cream instead of death!

This is how adults deal with death.

I had a vivid memory of the toffee sundaes they served at Smugglers Restaurant in Lyme Regis, with squeezy cream and sprinkly bits on top.

And I remembered Bridget saying *I wish it was then.*

And I wished wished wished that it was any time but now.

Time, please will you bend, I prayed.

Autumn came, and you turned three, and we went to Priego de Córdoba for the quince festival, and we made quince jam and quince paste and stored it in jars for the whole year, but I noticed we didn't talk about the whole year any more.

Your mother was finding it harder to walk to the Mezquita, or to the river to see the holm oak.

'You go!' she said. 'Take Beth!'

You liked to run everywhere, like a puppy, Beth.

You liked to count the orange trees in the courtyard, putting stickers on the bark as you went. I watched you stickering the orange trees, skipping over the cobbles and I knew that you were my bigger desire.

I'd give my life for you, I thought, as you walked between the pillars.

And having that thought felt like the deepest happiness.

I wondered if that was a morbid route to happiness, or the only one there was.

I knew for certain then that, although I'd always wanted a bloodline, you could love a child just as well without one.

A bloodline could be a bloodcircle too.

You and your mother had curved your line around to fit me in.

December came with stables and shepherds, and you cut out paper shapes and put them on the Christmas tree, and you took to wearing angel wings and a gold star sticker in the centre of your forehead.

We watched two brown nuns put the clay Jesus into position with his clay mother and his clay not-father under the arch.

I might have been a not-mother but I didn't feel like it.

You helped the nuns scatter the straw about on the stable floor.

A priest walked by.

I smiled at him.

I always smile at priests these days.

Just in case.

One day he'll come to La Convivencia with sunflowers, and I will fall into his arms and love him forever.

I do believe that, Beth.

Perhaps your father will come too.

Jeronimo!

Just like that!

In the last appointment before Christmas, the Wizard of Onc wasn't wizardy – her voice was softer and she held your mother's hand. She said the disease was progressing significantly, and I thought that until that moment, *progressing* had been a good word. She said it was time to take a break.

I think we all knew what taking a break meant.

When we got back, you ran in circles around the courtyard, trying to fly, Beth. Then you sat down and burst into tears because you couldn't. Something was stopping you, holding you back, keeping you down. Your mother gathered you up and held you against her bosoms. And I thought of Blue Mother. And I couldn't hold back the tears. And nor could your mother. And soon all three of us were crying. Because taking a break didn't mean what it used to mean. It used to mean a little holiday, or a drink, or an ice cream, or a walk by the river. No, nothing meant what it used to mean. It doesn't when life starts turning into death. I don't want to say any more. At the time we didn't say much at all. We cried and we hugged.

'This will do us good,' I said.

'It will,' said your mother. 'I've had enough of being brave.'

You started running in circles again with your gold angel wings splayed out.

You ran and you ran, and you shouted, 'I can fly!'

You were in Neverland, Beth, where we so wanted to go. We could hear the sound of the surf but we could no longer land.

We clapped.

'Hurray!' we said.

'Reality is so constricting,' I said to your mother.

'Yes,' she said. 'I'm slightly over it now!'

'Sister Ana was always slightly over it,' I said. 'Was that why we loved being with her?'

'It probably was,' she said.

'It was a bit like being in Neverland where the normal rules don't apply,' I said.

'Can we live there now?' she said. 'Where impossible things are possible. Where facts don't matter.'

'Definitely,' I said.

'Can we not go to the hospital?' said your mother. 'I hate it.'

And because facts didn't matter, I was able to say, 'Course we don't need to go to the hospital. We'll stay here together.'

'Excellent,' said your mother. 'Let's open some champagne! Because we have absolutely nothing to celebrate!'

'Perfect,' I said.

'And can we light the tealights like Sister Ana used to?'

'Yes,' I said.

'Beth,' I said. 'You must be careful with the candle flames.'

'It's OK,' said your mother. 'Flames don't burn here. Not any more.'

'Oh, what a relief,' I said. 'But Beth, don't touch them anyway.'

We sat and drank champagne and the tealights flickered.

We clinked our glasses and said, 'Happy Christmas!'

The wise kings came into town throwing sweets, and the new year came.

We couldn't stop it.

Your favourite cat, Clavel, gave birth to kittens.

You chose the white one with a black pirate patch over her eye, Beth.

You called her Smee like the pirate in *Peter Pan*, except you couldn't say it.

We had a kitten called Mee.

Happy New Year!

Of course it would be, now we were living in a world where the Wizard would make a miracle-spell which would fall from the sky and sprinkle the courtyard with eternity.

I hope the peace festival will happen forever.

It seems to honour everything that is good about Córdoba's history.

All of our history.

Being human.

The peace festival makes a circle big enough for anyone – anyone – to join in.

Where once they burnt heretics in Plaza de la Corredera, now we light candles and dance.

For the festival in March 2008, I'd arranged to hold a concert at La Convivencia where Grandpa Blue's *Quartet for the End of Time* would be played in the courtyard. Back in reality, where we sometimes had to go, I offered to cancel it or relocate it to keep things quiet for your mother, but she absolutely wouldn't hear of this, and wanted it to go ahead.

The four musicians would stay at La Convivencia.

The piano came before they did.

I remember their arrival.

Tall David, the pianist, with his long fingers.

Long-bearded Abed with his huge cello in its wheeled case.

Bald Seth carrying his clarinet and a suit bag.

Yosef's violin strapped across his back.

Mostly I remember Yosef.

I was reading you *Peter Pan* in the shaded corner, on the Moroccan couch.

I read: '*Surely you know what a kiss is?*'

And Yosef said: '*I shall know when you give it to me.*'

'You know it?' I said.

'My favourite book!' he said.

'Mine too,' I smiled.

'The acorn and the thimble!' he said.

'Exactly!' I said.

Adriana took the musicians to their rooms, and Carrie and Jhazmin clattered comfortingly in the kitchen. I loved watching them cooking together. Liam had sent her a birthday card saying *Happy Birthday from Liam*. It had given her hope. Perhaps too much hope.

You joined Ignacio and Lily at the table for lunch, Beth, but I wasn't hungry.

The musicians were rehearsing in the lecture room, and I liked listening to them.

I remembered poor Grandpa Blue playing *Quartet for the End of Time* over and over in his study in Turret Grove, as he felt his happiness slipping away from him.

Peter Pan was Yosef's favourite book, and kisses could be acorns and kisses could be thimbles, and the starlings in the sky above the courtyard were turning into a hot-air balloon, and rising, rising.

All of this comforted me.

I was still praying for a miracle.

I still didn't know exactly how to pray.

So I said, like Sister Ana, 'Round and round. Love love love.'

I wheeled your mother into the packed candlelit courtyard for the concert.

She was very weak.

She closed her eyes.

I made circles on her palm.

The moment was the biggest place you could imagine, far far bigger than the time we lay on our backs on the grass with Sister Ruth at St Hilda's.

The present was all there was and would ever be, that's what I felt, and that's what we must feel whenever we can.

The quartet started to play.

Yosef stood with his violin, his feet flat on the ground, fully balanced – the way I loved, the way the Blumes stood in that photo at the edge of the sea – and he seemed ready for anything life might throw at him.

He seemed.

Substantial.

He looked at me, and I smiled at him, and he smiled at me. He closed his eyes, and the four of them started to play *Quartet for the End of Time*.

In the hot evening, the music, which had once rung out in the chill of Stalag VIII-A, made a ring around La Convivencia, a ring around

Córdoba, spreading concentrically, wider, wider, wider, until it circled the whole earth, at least that's how it felt that night.

I closed my eyes.

Blue Mother was there inside the music, clinking her bangles as she danced.

Sister Ana waltzed in her big old sandals with Lorenzo.

And Billy Orson moonwalked backwards.

There is a door in the wall, Beth, your mother was wrong.

The door sometimes opens!

But you can't plan when.

And it's not us who open it.

I went on making circles on your mother's palm.

Then, when the music stopped, I opened my eyes, but your mother didn't.

We sat together, holding hands: brown fingers, white fingers, interlinked, like on our first day in Entrance Class at St Hilda's.

The guests left.

And the chairs were cleared away.

Your mother still didn't open her eyes.

'It was like I was deep-sea diving,' she whispered to me, her voice tiny now, fading. 'It was wonderful. Like great shining coral reefs.'

I smiled into her beautiful radiant face.

She opened her eyes.

'Look after Bethesda, won't you?' she said.

We were holding hands.

'Will you miss me?' she said.

We were eleven, and we were standing in her garden, and she was going to Israel.

I couldn't speak.

The musicians crossed the courtyard to go to bed.

I stood up.

I said the music had been out of this world.

'Actually,' I said.

Tall David, the pianist, scratched his chin, said it had been a pleasure.

Long-bearded Abed and bald Seth smiled.

I said that the music had taken Bridget somewhere she'd never been.

Yosef, the violinist, walked over to your mother in her wheelchair.

I watched him as he took her hand, and held it.

'There were colours I'd never seen before,' she said. 'And I finally saw my mother. I've missed her so much.'

'Thank you,' he said. 'I won't forget that.'

She smiled.

Then Yosef came over to me.

Brown fingers, brown fingers – he held my hand.

I loved the feeling of it.

He raised my hand to his lips, and he kissed the back of it.

Surely you know what a kiss is?

Maybe I didn't.

I shall know when you give it to me.

And now I did.

'This must be so hard for you,' he said.

As the musicians walked away, I felt overwhelmed.

Not with one feeling but with every feeling I'd ever had, all of them running together, as if the rainbow had collapsed and its colours were seeping into each other.

I heard myself saying Bridget Bridget Bridget over and over again, and I was crying, and she and I were seeping together, all the versions of ourselves – little girls, teenagers, adults, mothers – all that we'd meant to each other, all that we'd made each other.

Carrie and Gabriel came into the courtyard with you, Beth.

You were wearing pyjamas and a tiara, and playing that screechy plastic violin, and your eyes were flushed with the thrill of staying up very late.

'Can we do spinning?' you said to Carrie, and she took the yellow hoop and you threw down the violin and crawled in, and the hoop was spinning around the two of you, and you were laughing as it spun round and round, round and round.

'Watch Mummy! Watch!' you shouted.

Your mother smiled.

And the moon was whole, above the courtyard.

When the musicians checked out the next afternoon, I asked if they'd like to come back the next year and do it all again.

'We'd love to,' said Yosef. 'I'd love to.'

'Great!' I said.

'Confirmed,' said Yosef. 'In the diary!'

Yosef smiled at me, and I smiled at him.

He reached into his pocket.

'I found this down by the river!' he said, smiling. 'Far too early for acorns. But there you are.'

A tiny green acorn, out of season.

'The holm oak!' I said. 'My favourite tree.'

I hesitated.

'I wish there was something I could give you,' I said.

I caught sight of Carrie's little china thimbles, painted with red geraniums, on the reception desk.

And I thought, 'Why not?'

Go on, *why not?*

Be Blumey.

I gave him a thimble.

He smiled.

He said, 'See you next year!'

The others gathered their things.

'If not before,' he said. 'I think it will be before, don't you?'

The musicians left, as it started to rain.

I walked into the centre of the courtyard and I stood next to San Rafael and I held out my arms and tipped back my head and felt the raindrops on my skin and on my tongue.

I went to your mother's room.

Jhazmin was sitting on a chair to the right of Bridget's bed.

I sat on the left.

Your mother, my beautiful Bridget, smiled at me and closed her eyes, and I thought of the way the curtains close at the end of a play, and you hope that they'll open again, and the actors will still be standing there, and you'll go on clapping, and the curtains will go on opening, and you hope they will never leave, and it will never end.

Your mother took Jhazmin's hand and my hand – and Jhazmin and I took each other's, so that we were making a circle with our hands.

You were in the circle too, Beth, though you were playing with Mee next to the angel.

There was room for Mee in the circle too.

And other kittens.

As many as we needed.

I suspected that we were going to need a lot of kittens in the days ahead.

I looked at you and I saw myself.

You were three and a half, the same age I was when my father drove to Córdoba and took me away from my life.

Your mother opened her eyes, and she squeezed my hand as if she was trying to tell me something.

Perhaps she was telling me what I was thinking.

That Yosef was the sort of person, even maybe the actual person, who I could imagine adding to our circle.

Some time.

No rush.

But only if it was OK with you, Beth.

That's what I thought.
I'd given you my heart.
And you'd given me mine.
If we were to go adding to the circle, we would both have to agree.
That, I knew, from now on, was the deal.

Twenty-two per cent of people live for at least five years after diagnosis with Stage 4 breast cancer, that's what I knew.

So I'd sat your mother on a nice living sofa with twenty-one survivors.

Safe as anything.

The champagne was on ice for the last chapter.

And here we are, and here it is.

We're in it, together, you and I.

Whatever *it* is.

Whatever happens next, Beth, we will survive.

We will even flourish.

Like the geraniums.

I pushed through.

Like you will.

And I found the mother I was looking for.

And she was me.

Green Mother.

Here I am.

I'll take you to the waterfalls in the Sierra Morena where they grow cork trees, and we'll walk barefoot in the grass together, like in *The Rainbow Rained Us*.

We'll stand together under the gush of falling water and feel alive.

And.

Meanwhile.

I'll be the best mother I can be for you, Beth.

Blood isn't everything, it turns out.

I'll give everything I have to loving you.

She died so peacefully.

With all of us gathered around.

The shutters open.

San Rafael gold in the dusk.

Dearest Beth

You've turned into the most beautiful Blumey nearly-sixteen.

Did I ever tell you that?

I still sometimes keep the things I feel inside, but I'm getting so much better at letting them out.

You've taught me that, Beth.

You've carried on what your mother started.

London already feels like a dream, doesn't it?

Fireworks over the Thames.

Lunch with Cherie and Jean in their favourite little Italian.

Mudlarking on the beach near Battersea Bridge.

Finding rocket shells in the mulchy sand.

Writing your mother's name with our feet.

B-R-I-D-G-E-T.

Drawing her kisses from the wall to the water.

Watching the tide come in and carry them downriver.

Finding the plastic duck, faded and washed up and winking at us.

Here it is, yellow and sparkling – Yosef cleaned it up for you.

And here's our story, Beth, typed and bound, ready for you to read – nothing left out (except my bad dates).

It's been waiting for you in Sister Ana's wooden box for twelve years.

The time feels like now.

XX

PS

Don't think your Uncle Barnaby's a bad man.

We were both looking for something we couldn't have again.

The past.

Acknowledgements

First, in a book called *All My Mothers*, I want to acknowledge the impact that my own mother, Jennifer Simmonds, had on my life. She was, in my view, the perfect mother – radiantly joyful, deeply loving, full of fun. She inspired me to write about motherhood. Her presence shaped me, and so does her absence.

All My Mothers is a novel about mothers, but also a novel about friendship, and I want to acknowledge, with gratitude, the many friendships which have deepened and brightened my life. Eva's relationship with Bridget and Carrie is inspired by a cornucopia of wonderful friends. My deepest love and thanks to the Pinner girls (one non-Pinner member) with whom I grew up; friends from my much-loved school, and from heady university days in London and Córdoba; those who helped me grow babies; those who helped me grow myself; those who worked alongside me in the deep bond of demanding jobs; those who generously shared my past and share my present. As Eva discovers, friends dance miraculously into our lives, and also out, separated by geography and impossible schedules and work and parenting and general hopelessness (I'm sorry) but they sometimes dance back in too. That's been my experience of late. Thank you. You're all part of this story.

Then there's the other big presence in my life – a place, not a person. My love affair with Spain began as a child in Denia, collecting beetles and snails on the sandy path to the beach, and exploded into life when I studied at the *Facultad de Filosofía y Letras* in Córdoba, the most soul-stirring place I've ever lived. It was a joy to set much of the story there.

Eva calls her hotel *La Convivencia*, the word *convivencia* conveying a sense of happy co-existence for which the city is famed. The publication of my first novel, *The Other Half of Augusta Hope*, created a new and happy co-existence – the incomparable team that made it happen. And now they've done it again. My huge thanks to my wonderful agent, Susan Armstrong, my first reader, always brilliant, always there with the *mot juste*, the right answer and the unstinting support. Likewise to my trusted and esteemed editor, Carla Josephson, who sheds her special brand of light and love on my words. To Andrew Davis, who's created a cover of such evocative beauty that the air around the book smells of orange blossom. To Ann Bissell, publicist extraordinaire, a woman of untold energy, talent and *joie de vivre*; to Katy Blott, Izzy Coburn and Sarah Munro, who find unimaginably ingenious ways to put the book into the hands of readers, without whom it cannot live.

From the deeply happy co-existence of childhood – Mum, Dad, Richard – to the deeply happy co-existence of adulthood – Mark, Nina, Charlie (and now Holly too), I owe you all everything.

Postscript

I arrived in Córdoba when I was twenty, like Eva did, driving through the scrappy suburbs and entering the city between palm-lined parks, my heart thumping.

I remember opening the door to my black-barred flat, just up from Plaza de Tendillas.

There were cockroaches living under the fridge.

My friend Drusilla and I swapped from single bed to sofa-bed, one week on, one week off, because the flat didn't have enough bedrooms.

The residents thought we were prostitutes.

I remember a sand-coloured church close by, the church of San Miguel, built after the reconquest of the city. It was the end of 800 years of interplay between three religions and three cultures, the extent and duration of which is still hotly debated in academic circles.

What, however, most agree is that for at least 250 of those years, there was an enlightened and unlikely harmony in the city, which is known as the *Convivencia*.

And for 100 years, Abd al-Rahman III of Córdoba was the legitimate caliph of the whole Islamic world, and Córdoba was the largest and most prosperous city in all of Europe. Art and architecture and literature and science bloomed, perhaps creating the foundations for the Renaissance and Enlightenment of Europe.

And there I was, standing on layers of history, in a tiny back street, where leathery old men hissed at me like snakes, '*Sssss, sssss, Rubia!*' (*Rubia* meaning blondie – and blonder I would become, helped by sunshine and lemons.) These were unenlightened days and blonde girls, presumed English or Swedish, were known to be *easy*. But let's leave the hisses behind. You stopped hearing them after a while.

It was time for my first walk into the Judería (the old Jewish and Moorish quarter), the path that Carrie and Eva took after the revelation of *the photo*, and down I went with frilly girls from the flamenco school, happily losing myself in a maze of white buildings hugger mugger on narrow cobbled streets.

The houses taunted me with their black wrought iron gates – *verjas* – through which I caught slivers of shady flower-hung terraces, not quite visible.

Above, women in aprons hung their sheets out on roof terraces (because roof terraces weren't yet fashionable), wearing straw hats designed to keep out the sun.

Everything was designed to keep out the sun and dissipate the heat: the white paint; the heavy wooden shutters; the narrow sloping streets, houses inclining inwards; the hand-held fans which old ladies unfolded with a flourish from their handbags.

We, on the other hand, sought out the sun, heading to our friends' roof terrace, crawling under the hung sheets and there, hidden from prying eyes, taking all our clothes off and dousing ourselves in olive oil, before we knew that the sun was dangerous.

Then we were back to lectures in the old university building, through the tree-lined streets, past shops selling painted tiles and bullfighting postcards and silver rings.

I can see the huge old wooden door to the *Facultad de Letras*, and beyond it a shady quadrangle, always cool on the hottest days. I can see my Spanish cardboard folders with elasticated bands at the top right-hand corner, scattered on the street when I fainted in the heat on the way to lectures because I'd forgotten to have breakfast and it was forty degrees already, not yet ten o'clock.

The sun was the brightest yellow; the geranium petals were vivid red; the sky and the river dazzled blue; and gold shone from the portal of the mihrab, made with 1600 kilograms of glistening mosaic cubes.

The city's colours shimmered into my mind as I wrote *All My Mothers.*

Spring unfolded like a love affair, a whirl of green and orange and white, fragrant with blossom and Spanish cologne (like Eva's not-father wore), the citrus smell blowing through the streets and still today reaching me in dreams, and in the arrivals lounge at Seville airport, where one day I will go again. I will, I will.

And through the streets we skipped, love-struck with life, to cellar-bars, and out for tapas, and to dance bad flamenco.

And through the streets came nuns in pairs, arm in arm, waiting in the recesses of my mind to become Sister María Soledad and Sister Ana, in grey veils and big sandals.

And through the streets came pale priests, whose trousers stuck out beneath their long black robes, perhaps Eva's father. One day. One day he'll come. I just know it.

And through the streets came the Mili boys because Spain still required a year of national service from her sons (not daughters) – I remember them, climbing over their barrack walls after lights-out.

Young, olive-skinned, blue-uniformed, black-booted.

In the novel, they asked Carrie out.

They took Drusilla and me to the Seville *feria.*

As I write, their names miraculously come back to me across the years.

Paco (the funny one) and Miguel (the sidekick), both full of life and delight, a wonderful retort to the city's hissers.

I hear Paco on the train, telling us over and over, '*Sevilla es una maravilla.*'

Seville is, by the way, a marvel, but my heart was lost to Córdoba. Because you love a place the more you know it.

Paco and Miguel were young and they were laughing, and we were young and we were laughing, and I drank too much sherry, and I accidentally went to the men's toilets, but I didn't notice.

And there was Eva drinking too much at the Córdoba *feria*. But I didn't let her go to the men's toilets in the end because she'd spotted Barnaby dancing with Naomi, and she was falling out of love with Michael and getting a terrible stomach ache, and I thought she had enough on her plate for one evening.

And talking of plates: Spanish omelette, *tortilla*, soft with fried onions and potato; *bocadillos* stuffed with *jamón serrano*; huge tomatoes, good enough to eat alone with salt and olive oil; and *gazpacho*, ice cold soup; and plates of fried fish – *pescaíto frito* – in the centre of the table to be shared, before sharing was imaginable in England where we kept our plates to ourselves.

All washed down with a glass of sherry.

I was twenty years old, and doomed to like sherry. And everyone would laugh at me forever in England where nobody knows that it's delicious, that it's *fino*, and *manzanilla*, and *amontillado*, and *palo cortado*, and *oloroso*.

It's stored in barrels under the streets of Córdoba, where you can visit it and be cool, and we were learning to jump from shadow to shadow, to stop and chat only in the shelter of trees.

I sat for a whole afternoon under a tree, as Eva did when she first arrived, watching a rider beneath a palm, on a dapple-grey horse, fine-tuning his dressage on the spot, and I didn't move because it was siesta time and you were supposed to be lazy, and the shops were closed until six o'clock, and there was nothing to do but stare and sweat.

The old Royal Stables (where Eva and Carrie went to a horse show) stand behind the Alcázar, which was built on the site of the residence of Abd al-Rahman I, the seat of power of Moorish Al-Andalus, ruined as the caliphate collapsed and rebuilt as a palace for the Christian monarchs, Ferdinand and Isabella, architects of the Inquisition – a slap in the face to the ideals of the *Convivencia*.

The gardens, added later, are filled with cypress, orange and lemon trees, and flower-lined pools with fountains which wet your legs if you can get near enough without being shooed away by guards.

By the ninth century, it is said that the city was known as *the meadow of murmuring waters.*

Along the river, eleven water-wheels turned – only one, the Albolafia, remaining, and now restored.

My second-favourite Spanish poet, Antonio Machado, wrote a poem called *La Noria,* in which the sound of the water-wheel's circling sorrow is divinely sweetened by music of the *water dreaming.*

I thought of that when I passed by.

Life's sweet sorrow.

The water dreaming.

I loved the thought of water dreaming.

I dreamt of being a writer.

Near the water wheel, the water had dreamt little islands, leafy with tamarisk and poplar and eucalyptus, stalked by bittern, egret and heron.

Eva saw these on her love-struck walk with Barnaby.

I too was in love.

With neither Paco nor Miguel, but with Spain – the taste of it, the smell of it, the sound of it, the feel of it on my skin as I walked along the banks of the River Guadalquivir.

Here I place the fictional holm-oak, shedding its acorns out of season, little symbols of the beginnings of love between Eva and Yosef, which grows into a tree out of our sight.

Perhaps they're walking now through the city, visiting the tiny synagogue and remembering Bridget and Blue Mother, chancing upon the remains of the tenth-century Moorish hammam – there were once hundreds of these public baths throughout the city, where men bathed in the morning, and women in the afternoon, a towel hung outside to denote the change of gender!

Michael took Eva to the reconstructed hammam, the fake one, near Plaza del Potro. It was not their happiest moment, and their love was not to be reconstructed.

Plaza del Potro is a favourite little square of mine, housing the flamenco museum – Posada del Potro – whose courtyard partially inspired the courtyard of Eva's home and hotel, La Convivencia, in *All My Mothers*. When I last visited, there was an old wooden cart wheel leaning against the wall.

Plenty of pots dripping flowers.

No angel.

I put San Rafael in the courtyard of La Convivencia.

Because he's everywhere in the city, guarding us carefully from the Roman bridge which leads to the *other side of the river*, where we were advised not to go when I was studying there.

No, it was *dangerous*, we were told.

Peligroso.

It belonged to the *gitanos*.

There they danced flamenco – the sort that wasn't for tourists.

We looked across and it was dark and alluring.

'People get stabbed,' we were told. 'Stay this side.'

This scene, the *gitano* community flamenco-dancing among rubbish bins and old sofas, finds its way into my first novel, *The Other Half of Augusta Hope*.

So of course, having been told not to go, we all went, and told tales of it, exaggerating, all bravado and nonsense and too much wine – and nobody got stabbed.

Now it's full of modern hotels with roof terraces, which got fashionable when they worked out that the tourists wanted sunburn, not shadows.

But don't book a room there – go back over the bridge and under the Roman arch to the cool ferny courtyards of simple old *hostales* like the fictional Hostal Jardín, where you are close to the centre of things.

And I think we're ready now for the centre.

I've been skirting around the edges, putting off telling you the biggest thing of all.

Because I save my best Christmas present until last.

Because I enjoy leaving love letters on the doormat and not opening them, when there used to be love letters.

I think this might be a love letter.

To Córdoba.

To the Mezquita.

I know I can't do it justice.

Because it's indescribable.

Because it's my favourite building in the world.

Because no matter where you go, it's always there, the central character of the city, its head raised above the other buildings, against the sky, the way to get your bearings, tell other people where you are.

Oh, the Mezquita.

Which wasn't done up when I was there the way it is today.

Which hadn't yet appeared on international travel itineraries the way it has today.

Which wasn't crowded the way it is today.

Crowded now but mercifully not roped and corralled like the Alhambra in Granada where you are no longer allowed to stand alone and stroke the marble lions as I did back then, as I did on my honeymoon – no, you are herded in groups behind ropes.

Like you still aren't at the Mezquita.

There it stood.

And there it stands.

Guarding the magic of its story, holding its silent witness.

So let's go back in time.

First there stood a monastery dedicated to Saint Vincent in the sixth century.

Then a Visigothic church.

Then Abd al-Rahman I reached an agreement with the Visigoths, buying part of the church, so that the Muslims and Christians could worship side by side.

But they didn't have enough space so the Visigoths sold him the whole lot, and the first mosque came into being.

Are you ready?

Close your eyes tight.

Now open them.

My first time and I was awe-struck.

The pillars, the pillars, the pillars, the pillars.

A stone forest of columns, where people appeared and disappeared, like ghosts of all the city's pasts, or all its futures, come to visit.

In the original mosque, each aisle is separated by walls leaning on columns held by arches making endless mirrored arcades, the upper parts semi-circular, the lower, horseshoe-shaped, echoing the shape of date palms, brick and stone alternating in mesmerising red and white stripes. This isn't just a Moorish design, but inspired by arched Roman aqueducts and Visigothic horseshoe arches, with old pieces of the original church of San Vicente recycled and remodelled into a glorious piecemeal patchwork, itself a symbol of a place that grew organically, layer upon layer, extended by Abd al-Rahman II, Al-Hakam II and Al-Mansur.

And these are the layers on which Eva found herself reflecting as she caught sight of the ghost of her dear friend Billy who ran through the orange tree courtyard in the body of a young boy with a tennis racquet.

And here's the orange tree courtyard through which you enter the Mezquita, where there are four water spouts at the fountain, where we drank, thirstily, because we were sweltering and those were the carefree days when we didn't worry about germs, and when (hard to believe now) we didn't walk around carrying water bottles. Perhaps that's why I fainted in the street on the way to class!

The courtyard is a wonderful brouhaha of coming and going, the lines of shade and lines of sun intimations of our own mortality and immortality, of death and life, the stones holding the history of two millennia of stories of people and religions and cultures.

That's what I sensed as I walked the city's streets, young and hopeful, inclining forwards towards my own dreams, but also backwards towards the dreams of medieval people who were perhaps not so very different from me, as I sat with my book of poetry (in the city of poets, Seneca born there in 4 BC and Lucan, in 39 AD), my glass of *sangría* and slice of *tortilla* resting on an old black barrel beneath the olive tree by the city walls, the tree another silent witness to the city's past, and reconfigured as a place where God appeared to Sister Ana in *All My Mothers*.

Córdoba has regrown into an easy-going peaceful city, a minor provincial capital these days – a shadow of what it once was at the height of its medieval greatness, which didn't last, because things don't last.

By 1031, Al-Andalus had divided into *taifas*, fragmented mini-states, and there followed the decisive Christian victory at Las Navas de Toledo in 1212, and one by one the southern cities fell – Córdoba in 1236, Seville in 1248 and finally Granada in 1492.

A few years later, the cathedral was plonked at the centre of the Mezquita, a cathedral that could be beautiful somewhere else, but seems to trespass on the divine symmetry of the original stone forest.

The bishop who thought up the idea was opposed by the citizens, who were supported by the Town Council. With Church and Town Council in dispute, the Emperor, Charles I, was called to adjudicate.

Build, said Charles I, which meant *destroy* the centre of the mosque.

When he saw the finished cathedral, he famously said: 'You have built what you or others might have built anywhere, but you have destroyed something that was unique in the world.'

The Mezquita, much changed, still stands, unique in the world, now walled in where once all nineteen naves were open to the orange tree courtyard, allowing Eva to picture birds and butterflies darting between the pillars, like prayers on the air, prayers which echo across the centuries from the minaret of the Mezquita, the bell tower built by Abd al-Rahaman III in 957, remodelled and reinforced over the years, and topped by the angel, San Rafael.

And there is San Rafael again, by Puerta del Puente, precariously atop a very tall thin column, in a *plaza* where locals gather, where Eva stopped on her night-time mission to the homeless, and where, if memory serves me right, I had my first experience of the festival of *Cruces*.

First we saw a cluster of people, and more arriving. On moving closer, a towering cross appeared, about three metres high, made of roses and beside it, a makeshift drinks bar. People started to dance, and we joined in.

We left, and we came upon gathering after gathering, each little scene similar: a tall cross packed with flowers – red, white, sometimes blue and yellow – the same wooden drinks bar, the same dancing, the same tinny music.

You can get a *Cruces* map but we didn't know that, and anyway, it's preferable not to.

It's always far better to stumble upon.

And Córdoba is the greatest city for stumbling upon.

Put your map in your pocket and wander.

The festival of *Cruces* begins with the Battle of the Flowers (a petal riot as Eva sees in Sister Ana's photo) and the crosses are in position from the end of April to the beginning of May. I've been back many times. I go to enjoy the simple spontaneity of the thing, the anything-goes and anyone-comes.

In fact, this is a competition with forty neighbourhood associations vying for the prize for the best-decorated cross, the preparations taking place secretly for months beforehand. It's all statuary and candles and tapas and guitar and *sevillana* dances and live music and flounced dresses and beating hearts and beating feet and twisting hips, loud until midnight, quieter until 2, turned down a touch to respect the neighbours, who seem all to be there, whether they're eight or eighty-eight.

Once this festival is over, it's time for *Patios*, another competitive festival where those glimpsed slivers I'd seen behind bars on my first foray into the old quarter are opened up in a great glory of trailing floribunda, the white walls packed – packed – with shimmering flowers, which hang from railings and under lamps, encircling pools and wells, burgeoning from stone pots beneath the chatter of birds, and oh the fragrance of it, and oh the beauty of it – I was blown away and I'm still blown away.

And we haven't even got to the May *feria* where nobody sleeps day and night for a week and the city swells with tens of thousands of visitors for flamenco and fireworks and fair rides.

So the year is structured, one festival at a time, and this, I noticed from the beginning, gave a communal feel to life in the city. The streets were nearly always full, and packed for the daily *paseo*, a leisurely evening stroll, with drinks and tapas and greeting the neighbours.

When later, as a teacher, I arranged an exchange between my own students and a school in Andalusia, as we bussed the Spanish students in from Gatwick Airport on a rainy English evening, they kept asking, 'Where is everyone?' and, 'Is this town uninhabited?'

'No,' I said, 'Everyone's inside their houses.'

But in Córdoba, we were never inside our houses, unless we were asleep, which we mainly weren't.

Because we knew our time there was finite – and there was so much to do and love and drink and think and find and find out.

My favourite Spanish poet and playwright, Federico García Lorca, himself a son of Andalusia, catches life in images so true they hurt – and it was he who spoke of a thousand butterfly skeletons sleeping inside walls.

I think they're still sleeping inside the hot stone walls of Córdoba, waiting to resurrect with a thousand untold secrets.

And I will keep going back.

To see if I can catch them.

Joanna Glen, April 2021